JOURNEY

To All Those Unnamed and Unknown

OTHER TITLES BY GARY V. BRILL

DRIVING IN BUDAPEST
"One of the Best Books of the Year" KIRKUS REVIEWS
Available on Amazon and BN.com

DESCENT
Available Spring 2021

Please visit www.gvbwrites.com for reviews and much more news!

JOURNEY

The Story of an American family

By
Gary V. Brill

PART 1

THE BANNER

The light from the small front window of Jones' Tavern cast a warm and inviting glow on to the street. A light snow was falling silently, wrapping everything in a cold blanket. The glow was especially inviting to James, who was watching from the shadows, waiting for a good moment to cross the street and enter that familiar safe haven. He stole another look around the corner of the crate he was concealing himself behind and quickly pulled his head back, his heart racing.

Constable O'Malley and another man James did not recognize were approaching from the direction of the town, poking around in the shadows on the other side of the street. James leaned back against the crate, trying to control his breathing and remain silent. Suddenly, a figure broke from the alleyway across from him and started to run down the street. O'Malley and the other man were after him like a shot, calling for the fleeing man to halt.

Another constable stepped into the street while the fugitive was looking over his shoulder. When he turned, this officer struck him in the chest, knocking him to the ground. The fugitive looked up to see a large figure looking down at him, a cocked flintlock pistol in his hand.

"You know your type is not allowed on our streets after dark, so why are you out alone then?"

The fugitive was gasping for breath. "I am a…. I am a free man. You have no right to assault me this way."

"You may very well be a free man, boyo, we'll see about that later, but you are a black man and no blacks are allowed out at this time of night under penalty. You should know that by now."

O'Malley and the other officer came up to the fugitive, still lying on the ground, gasping. "What have we here, Mister Murphy?" he asked the man standing over the prostrate figure.

Murphy spat to the side. "Another damn black who thinks he is above the law, Mister O'Malley, just another 'free man' who thinks the laws don't apply to him."

"I am a free man," the man on the ground said, trying to get to his feet. "I own a farm outside of the town, just east of here".

"Well, boyo, you may be a free man on your farm, and you may be a free man when the sun is up, but at night you're just another damn nigger on our streets and that's against the law. Now let's go down to the jail and figure out what's what, shall we."

The three policemen led the unfortunate man off, back towards the town and away from James' hiding place. He waited until they turned the corner, then stood and walked quickly towards the tavern, his feet crunching on the newly fallen snow. He did not run, even though he wanted to badly. He did not want to draw any further attention to himself. As it was, he caught a quick glance from two men walking by who saw him. He was afraid they might raise an alarm, but they just looked away and kept walking.

He opened the heavy door to the tavern and stepped into the light. Several of the other patrons looked towards him as they heard the door open. A few of the drinkers nodded to him, but he thought he heard some of the other men in the room muttering about him being there. He looked around the smoky room and saw Daniel at a table talking to another man. "James. James, join us."

James crossed the room, not meeting the eyes of several of the drinkers who obviously did not care for his presence there. He joined Daniel and the other man at their table where he was handed a foamy mug. "James, I want you to meet my cousin

2

Matthew. Matthew, this is my very good friend James. He owns the stables at the end of the street. It's the one down near the river I showed you."

Matthew shook hands with him and nodded. James could definitely see a family resemblance up close. Both men had the same unruly shock of ginger hair, the same blue eyes that were always smiling. "What brings you to this seat of democracy, Matthew? Just visiting or considering a move?"

"Came to see my very favorite first cousin, James. Haven't heard from him in a while and thought maybe I better pay him a visit and see how he fares."

"Did I mention that I was his only first cousin, by the way?" Daniel said. "I may have left that part out."

Matthew was looking over James' shoulder, and his smile suddenly seemed odd. Then he noticed Daniel had the same look.

James turned and saw three roughly dressed men standing in the center of the small room, the larger one swaying slightly. "What's he doing in here?" the swaying man asked. "It ain't allowed for no niggers to be out after dark and you all know it."

"Sir, if you look around you will certainly notice that this gentleman is not outside, but he is indeed inside, enjoying the warm conviviality of friends and drink, much as you yourself are doing."

The larger of the three men took a half step forward. "Pretty words, friend, but it don't change the fact that my brothers and me don't drink with no niggers." James stood at his approach.

Daniel smiled then and motioned grandly towards the door which had just opened for another patron. "Well then, my kind sir, please feel free to leave this fine establishment at your leisure. My friends and I choose to stay and enjoy the pleasant warmth of the place."

"You don't understand, mister. I want this…" He reached out to grab James by the collar, but James stepped aside, took the man's arm and twisted it behind his back, driving him forward into one of the wooden columns. He landed on the floor in a heap.

The man looked up in shock, his two companions advancing.

"Why you stinking nigger son of a bitch. You can't attack no white man like that. You'll pay plenty for this." He spit out some blood from his split lip and looked up. "And right now is as good a time as any."

As he scrambled to his feet the other two men advanced further and were closing on James. Daniel and Matthew intercepted them and suggested they move back out of the smaller area and into the main room.

"Sorry, gentlemen, this is not your fight. If your brother here wants to match himself against our friend, well that's his decision." Daniel glanced at the larger man who was dusting himself off, and at James, who was preparing to defend himself. "And I would wager that was not a very wise decision for him to make."

The owner of the tavern appeared suddenly. "Now James, please let the man go on his way. I'm sure he meant no harm, did you sir? You don't want to see my place get broken up again, do you?"

James looked at the owner. "I'm sorry Mister Jones. The last thing I want to do is harm your furnishings or disturb your patrons." He looked back just in time to sidestep a lunge and swing from the larger man, who then turned back to him. James dealt him a very quick right jab to the nose, followed by another. The larger man sank to his knees covering his face, blood spurting from between his fingers. His two companions tried to push their way into the room, but now several of the other patrons were helping to restrain them.

"What kind of people are you?" one of them bellowed to the people in the room, looking around. "What kind of people would allow a stinking nigger to assault a white man like this and get away with it?"

An older gentleman threw a coin loudly on the bar. Everyone in the room suddenly turned towards the sound. "I'll tell you what kind of people we are, stranger, since you have been kind enough to inquire. We are the kind of people who stick by our friends, and this man is a friend to many in here." He took a final sip from his glass and placed it gently on the bar. "We are also the kind of people who don't use words like that, especially in polite society such as this," he said as he bowed to the room. There was a smattering of appreciative sounds. "If you use that word in my presence again, sir, I will take this horse crop to that thing you call a face." He turned to the room. "Goodnight all. It has once more been a pleasure to share a fine evening with you." He bowed once more at the door and was gone.

The two men who were being restrained went to help their brother to his feet. "You ain't heard the last of this business. None of you," one of the brothers said to the room at large. "Where we come from, this black bastard would be swinging from a tree by now, and I aim to see that happens."

The mood in the room suddenly became very quiet. Daniel stepped forward and handed the loser of the fight his hat. "This is a nice warm place to meet friends and enjoy a drink or two. You have just threatened a man many of us consider our friend with bodily harm. It would be best for all if you left. Now."

The younger of the three men was pulling on his brother's elbow. "We should go, Sam, we don't want no more trouble," he urged quietly.

The larger man shrugged off his smaller companion. "I don't need nobody's help." He dusted himself off and adjusted his hat, looking slowly around the room. "I have heard about people like you. Won't stand with your own kind. Well, we'll see about that."

The three left and the mood relaxed noticeably. Matthew shook James by the hand. "Very nice work there, James. Such restraint. I had the feeling you could have killed him if you wanted. Where did you learn to fight like that"?

"My father taught my brother and me to fight like gentlemen," James said. "Broughton's Rules of Boxing and all that. We thought it was stupid at the time."

"That's not all, cousin Matthew. Young James here is serving in our militia company. He is not only a very fair shot with that rifle of his, but he is also teaching some of the men his style of fighting. You should come to our next encampment. You might learn a thing or two."

"I don't doubt it. How often does your militia meet?"

Daniel led the others back to the table. "More than we used to with this damn war now spreading southward. You've heard about the setbacks in Canada?"

Matthew nodded. "Yes, but Perry beat the stuffing out of the British on Lake Champlain don't forget."

Daniel took a long pull on his mug. "That's all well and good, but the rumors are starting to fly that the British want to, or need to, move south, to move against places like Baltimore or Philadelphia if they ever want to win this foolish war."

"What about Washington, what about the nation's capital? Don't you think they would move on you here?"

James gave a short laugh. "Why would they waste time and men on this place? There is very little trade here by comparison. There is no reason to think that attacking this little sleepy town would make any military sense. No, Baltimore will be their target mark my words."

Matthew leaned in a little closer. He was a stranger here and did not know where the sympathies of the others in the room lay. There were pockets of virulent protest both for and against the war everywhere. "There is news about American soldiers burning York during the Lake Erie campaign. The British newspapers are full of stories of looting and worse by our troops."

"I can't believe our men would do those things. I have heard the stories as well, but I can't put much stock in them," James said.

"Similar stories from the fighting at Port Dover turned out to be true, don't forget. Some of the troops apparently forgot themselves and destroyed private property there as well. I'm afraid we've managed to anger the British lion more than is wise," Matthew said. "And gentlemen, if I wanted to teach this young upstart America a lesson, I would burn it's capital to the ground, let them know they are but a mosquito to that imperial British lion."

James remained skeptical. "I don't see why they would do that.

It makes no military sense to come here. It would be a waste of time, of men and material. No, they will make for Baltimore before they would come here."

Daniel picked up his drink from the table. "Gentlemen, here is to the redcoats just going home and leaving us be."

Just as they clinked glasses, the door swung open. Constable O'Malley and his two officers stepped in off the street, looking around the room. The three men who had been in earlier also stepped in, snow swirling in the doorway.

The larger one, whose shirt front was bloody, pointed to the table where James, Daniel and Matthew were sitting. "There he is constable. That's the nigger that assaulted me." He started advancing towards them. "Why you son of a bitch. Now we'll see your black ass in jail."

O'Malley was shaking his head. "I might have known it was you again, James. I might have known. Don't you ever get tired of breaking people's noses?"

James wisely stood up again to address the constable. "Just defending myself, Mister O'Malley, sir. Just like any man would do."

"Well now, James, you aren't just any man now are you? You know we have laws about blacks being on the street after dark. Come along with me now so we can sort this all out."

Daniel looked up from the table. "Sort what out, Mister O'Malley? My friend here just told you he was defending himself." He gestured around the room. "We have more than a few reputable witnesses to that affect."

"I'm sure you do, Daniel Lawrence, I'm sure you do. But we're going to take this man in for questioning and for being on the street contrary to the laws of this city."

Daniel looked around the room, seemingly puzzled. "Your three new friends here made that very same mistake, Mister O'Malley. I think if you take a moment and look around at your surroundings, you will see right away that we are not out on the street. Indeed, we are indoors, having a drink and enjoying a very lively political discussion. You are most welcome to join us if you choose sir."

The man with the bloody shirt erupted. "God damn nigger son of a bitch. You're coming outside right now."

O'Malley put his hand on the man's shoulder, something he clearly considered distasteful. "That's enough of that kind of thing mister. Quite enough. James, come along now."

James set his half empty mug down on the table. "Gentlemen, I take my leave of you now."

Daniel stood and faced the deputy. "My cousin Matthew will accompany you to the jail, constable, just to make sure our friend is safe in your custody."

"The hell he will, Daniel. James, let's go."

Daniel was reaching for his hat. "Yes, constable, my cousin," and he looked around the room and saw several others getting to their feet, "and it looks like some others, will join you on your stroll this fine evening. I, meanwhile, will go and wake Judge Adams and bring him along as well."

"Now why would you bother that fine old gentleman over a trifling matter like this, Daniel?"

"Well, the judge was sitting right over there," Daniel said, pointing to the chair where the judge had been sitting earlier, his coin still on the bar, "and he certainly saw the whole incident. James did not assault this gentleman. On the contrary, this man and his brothers were disorderly and making threats to harm our friend. He merely defended himself. I'm sure the judge would be very happy to verify that account. You remember how happy he was to deal with you the last time."

O'Malley hesitated, stroking his chin. "The judge saw what happened then, did he now? Well, maybe it's best not to disturb him this evening after all." He turned to James' accuser. "Why did you tell me this man assaulted you?"

"That man is a liar. A dirty stinking lying...."

"That's enough now. I know most of these men, and if they say the black man was defending himself from you, then I have to believe them. Now, let's get out of this tavern and go back to my office. We need to go and have a talk about making false accusations."

The man turned as he was leaving the room. "You ain't seen the last of me, nigger, no siree."

The door closed behind them as they left. There was a moment or two when no one moved or made a sound. Everyone was just looking at the door. Then, as if at a signal, the room returned to normal, men sitting and resuming their conversations and card games. A few looked over at James and nodded, then went back to what they were doing.

The trio went back to their table near the bar. "Well now. That was certainly interesting, cousin Daniel. Does that sort of thing happen here very often?"

Daniel started to reply, but James cut him off. "More often than it should, Matthew. More often than it should." He took a long pull from his mug and motioned for another. "You see, there are two types of 'free men' here in this fine cradle of democracy. There are men who are free twenty four hours of every day, and some who are only free in the sunshine."

"I've heard about the Black Codes, James. It's shameful it is. Most where I come from do not consider them to be legal or proper. They are not what America is supposed to stand for and that's the fact of it."

"Yes, well, the fact of it is that if I am ever caught out after dark there will be hell to pay. I do believe Mister O'Malley there would see to that."

They drank in silence for a moment, each reflecting on what had just transpired. Daniel set his mug down with a thump. "So, cousin, you feel that the next move the British will make is to attack our little village here?"

"I don't pretend to speak with any military authority since I have not been with the Maryland militia for long, but I just think that is what I would do. Think of it this way. If they really wanted to humble us, to teach us not to fool with their superior power here or anywhere else in the world, I think it is a very logical move. Anyway, they cannot let Port Dover and Troy go unavenged now, can they?"

"He makes a good point there, don't you think, James? What he doesn't know is that there are several thousand militia and regular troops stationed in the District to defend against just such a move."

James nodded. "Why don't you come out to our next encampment, Matthew? You could see for yourself some of the preparations for the defense we are working towards."

Matthew started to reply, but this time Daniel cut him off. "Time for us to retire, cousin. We have a very busy day ahead, and it starts very early. James, we'll meet you at your stables in the morning then."

The proprietor Jones came out from behind the bar. "I suspect you'll be needing the spare room again, James. It's all ready for you," he said, handing James a key.

"Well then, good evening to all," Daniel said to the room at large. "I must say that this fine establishment seems to attract a very elegant class of people."

There were a few chuckles in response, a few muttered "good evenings yourself" and the two cousins were gone. James went to the bar. "Mister Jones, sir. I'd like to apologize for what happened here tonight. It certainly is not my wish to disturb your establishment or your patrons."

Jones looked at him kindly. "I know the trouble is not of your making, son. These Black Codes are an abomination against God and man. Some day we will be able to walk together after dark, James. You and I. It will happen, you'll see."

"I hope so, Mister Jones, but I can't see it happening very soon." He picked up his coat from the table and started for the spare room he used from time to time when it was not safe on the streets of Washington for him to be out. He turned back towards the ruddy faced proprietor. "I just want to…" His voice trailed off and he gave a little shrug.

"I know, son, I know. Good night to you."

The next day dawned bright and clear, the sun shining brightly off the fresh new snow from the previous night. James was walking down the street from the tavern back to his stables. It was safe to do that now, he was thinking. Safe now, but last night he could have landed in jail, or worse, for doing something as simple and as innocent as walking down the street to his home and his business. "All men are created equal my ass," he muttered to himself.

But even these thoughts could not take away from the simple pleasure of being alive on such a glorious morning. He greeted several of his neighbors, stopping for a short chat with old Mister. Jenkins, owner and proprietor of the small general store across from his stables. There was still no tea available, Jenkins informed him. "The British blockade has seen to that I'm afraid, James. Unless I can get a bit that's sometimes being smuggled down from Canada, I don't think I'll have any to offer for some time to come."

As he passed the last house on the street, he noticed the gentleman who had his law office there, and was also an officer in his militia unit, on the front step. He was in the process of moving his home and office closer to town, and James had been hired a week ago to move some furniture and books for him. "Good morning, Lieutenant Key, sir."

The man looked up from a paper in his hand and into the blazing blue sky. "Why, good morning James. And how are you on this very beautiful morning?"

"I'm very well, sir, thank you. I'm off to see that my horses are as well," he said, tipping his hat.

"I will see you in the next encampment, then? I do believe that the men are looking forward to another boxing demonstration."

"Yes sir. You can count on that." He gave a short laugh. "Unfortunately, I had a chance to brush up on my technique some last night."

The other man looked thoughtful for a moment. He knew there was only one reason why James would have engaged in any fisticuffs. "I'm very sorry to hear that, James, I truly am." He paused for a moment and smiled. "How's the unfortunate other fellow?"

"Last I saw of him he was angry and very unhappy."

The lawyer turned towards his door. "I don't wonder James. I don't wonder." He gave a wave as he disappeared indoors.

James continued on to his stables. As he pulled the large double doors open, several of the horses started stomping and blowing big clouds of steaming breath. "Good morning, ladies. I trust we all passed a quiet evening." He went first to the horses he was boarding for others, giving them a pat down their manes and offering soothing words. After their needs were seen to, James went to the last stall in the back. It was occupied by his beloved Annie, a very large chestnut mare who was obviously glad to see him.

He took her huge head in his hands. "I'm sorry, Annie. I know how you hate to be kept waiting." He pulled an apple from his pocket and offered it. "Compliments of Mister Jenkins, my sweet girl."

She took the apple gratefully, then followed him out to the front of the stables with the other horses. James led them all to the big doors he had come in through and out into the paddock. "There you go, ladies, and you sir," he said, standing to attention and saluting the lone male horse in his charge. "Enjoy this beautiful day that the good lord has seen fit to provide for us."

The horses meandered out into the sunshine, finding bits of hay and oats in troughs against the fence. James went back into the stables to do those things that have to be done to keep the place operating. He used a rope and pulley to pile up several dozen bales of hay he had recently purchased. He fixed one or two of the stall fences that had broken or fallen slats. He was about finished mucking out the stalls when a motion at the front doors caught his eye.

"May I be of some service?" James called. He listened for a moment, then laid his shovel down. He was about to walk out to the front when he had a thought and picked the shovel back up, hefting it in his hand. "Is anyone there?" he called again.

He walked quietly to the front, keeping his back to the wall and listening closely. The horses were suddenly moving in the paddock and whinnying. James walked to the door, and his heart missed a beat.

The three men from the previous night's trouble at Jones' tavern were outside of the fence, looking over the horses. The big one, Sam, looked across the paddock. James noticed he had changed his shirt from last night.

"Well now, lookee here, brothers. It's that uppity nigger from last night, the one who ambushed me. You work here, do you boy?"

"You could say that".

"I'm sorry. What did you say, boy? Answer my question, damn it. You work here or not?"

James was leaning on his shovel, watching the three closely. "Is there something I can do for you…. gentlemen?"

"Yer damn straight there is, boy. You can go get yer master and tell him we would like to buy us a horse or two."

"We don't have any horses for sale at the moment….. sir," James said. "These are all being boarded and are not for sale."

The men were slowly moving to their left, towards the outside gate to the paddock. "You mean to tell me you have all these horses here, and you won't sell me even one?"

"I'm afraid their owners would be very upset with me if I sold any of them," James said. He was moving slowly to his left also, trying to keep the wall of the main building close behind him.

"Well now, what about that big ol' chestnut there? Why, I'd give you twenty dollar for that fine animal right here and now. Yes sir, I surely would."

"That's a very generous offer, but as I said, her owner would be highly upset if I sold her at any price." The youngest of the brothers was moving slightly away from the others, trying to get behind James.

James turned, hefting the shovel in his hand. "If there is nothing else I can help you with then…"

"Looks like you ain't got any friends to help you out this time, do you nigger? Now we'll just see if we can't teach you some manners."

The younger brother made his move. James figured he was the least of a threat. He struck him across the face with the flat of the shovel with both hands on the handle. When he turned to the other two, he was ready to use it again.

He arched his eyebrows, looking at them. "Who's next, then?"

The two rushed at him, cursing. James stepped aside, swung the shovel hard and hit one of them square on the back of the head, the shovel ringing metallically. That brother also went down in a heap.

Sam turned on him and reached into his coat. "Let's see how you handle this boy," and pulled a pistol out, cocking the hammer. James took a step back, glancing from side to side. "Ain't nobody gonna help you now, boy," he said, smiling.

"You know, Samuel, you do seem to have a way of always mis-judging a given situation."

Sam looked toward the gate. Matthew was aiming a very large rifle at his head, Daniel was just smiling. "It's just like last night. You weren't able to judge if you were inside or outside. Then, you seriously misjudged the people in the room." He nodded towards his cousin. "I beg of you not to misjudge this particular situation, Samuel. My cousin there is a most excellent rifleman, aren't you, cousin Matthew?"

"That's what people say, cousin Daniel."

Sam lowered his pistol as Daniel approached, then put it back in his coat. He bent down to help one of his brothers up.

"I'll make you a deal, Samuel, and I think you will find it both a good and fair one," Daniel said, smiling.

"What's that? What kind of deal?"

"If you take these flea bitten brethren of yours and leave my friends premises, I won't have my cousin here shoot you. Now, is that not fair?" Daniel was close enough now so that Sam could see his smile was as cold as the river ice.

Sam looked at James. "I ain't done with you yet, nigger…"

Daniel punched him in the mouth as hard as he could, stagger-ing the man. "I thought we made it clear last night that we don't much like that word around here. Gentlemen, the gate is over there. Use it."

The three men left, Sam mopping his bleeding lip, his brothers muttering threats to the world in general. Sam turned to face James when he was outside the gate. This time he was smart enough not to say anything. He just stood staring for a moment, then pointed at James who just turned his back on him and walked away, shaking his head.

"Well, Daniel, that was a little more action that I thought this day might bring. Are you ready for the task at hand?"

"We are indeed. The furniture is in storage, and the other property is ready for transport. Since we have many a mile to go today, I suggest we put this ugly business behind us and proceed."

"Here, here," Matthew added.

The three went into the stables and pulled the wagon James used for transport jobs into the center of the paddock. They then hitched up two horses, one of them Annie, and after securing the premises drove away together.

After picking up the client's furniture at a nearby warehouse they made their way to his residence to load the other belongings for the man's move out of the town. By the time everything was loaded the sun was climbing the sky. The job was a small one but hiring out with his wagon and team to move furniture and any other goods that needed transport enabled James to keep his business afloat in the slower winter months.

Their destination lay a few miles north and east of Washington. The roads were good and the day was glorious, though a little chilly. The three men sat on the bench seat, not saying anything for the first mile or so, just watching the world go by.

James was handling the team with ease, with a slight smile on his face. "Thanks for arriving when you two did this morning," he said quietly.

'That was a bit of ugliness, wasn't it? It's a shame on a day such as this to have to deal with people such as those," Daniel said. "Do you know those gentlemen? Have you had any dealings with them before last night?"

James gave a cruel laugh in response. "No, Daniel. No, I have not had the pleasure of their acquaintance before our meeting at Jones', but I have met plenty of others like them. Quite a number, actually."

They rode on in silence for a few moments, Daniel looking down at the ground, lost in thought. "I can't imagine what that must be like, James. I can't imagine people treating you the way those three did just because of the amount of pigmentation in your skin."

"Yes, well, I can tell you it came as quite a shock to me when it first happened. You know I grew up on a farm in Pennsylvania. One of our closest neighbors was another black family. My brother and I hardly ever came into contact with white people when we were children."

"What about at school or at church? Surely there must have been times where you associated with whites."

"Not at first. My mother and father taught us to read and write, and mother held bible study every single Sunday morning after early chores." He shook his head and smiled at the memory. "She could put the fire in her words when she read that bible. She was completely transformed whenever she read verse."

"Yes, I know what you mean. The only time I ever heard my mother raise her voice at all was when she would read from the bible to her children. She almost became a different person," Daniel said. "It was something to see."

"I came to believe they kept us at home to protect us, to shield us from the racial hatred that seems to be everywhere in this country, not just down here in the south. They were both born free, but like all black men and women they knew that they would always be something less in the eyes of others."

"Is that why your father taught you to fight like that?" Matthew asked.

James was silent for a moment. "He always told my brother and me that it would probably come in handy someday. We didn't understand then, but I certainly do now."

"Where is your brother, then? Is he still on the farm?" Matthew asked before Daniel could stop him. He already knew the story and also knew how upsetting it could be for James to tell it again.

"No, Matthew, he isn't back on the farm…. at least not our family's farm. He was kidnapped by slavers and taken south. I heard he was sold to a family in North Carolina, but I have no way of knowing if that's true or even if he is still alive or not." He negotiated a small gulley in the road, then turned to Matthew, a single tear running from his left eye, his voice even. "I couldn't protect him, Matthew. He was my little brother, and I was not there for him."

Matthew didn't know what to say. He had heard about such things happening, but it had always seemed to be far removed from his life. "I'm sorry, James," he said quietly. "I didn't know….."

James was thoughtful. "First Jonathan was kidnapped and then Mother died shortly after, probably from a broken heart. I thought my Father would just curl up and die. He hasn't worked his land in years now. He moves like a man in his sleep."

"Do you get the chance to see him often?" Matthew asked.

"It has been a while now, I'm sorry to say. It used to be easy to arrange extended leave from the militia until recently. Now, with the fear the British may soon move south at any time, it's almost impossible."

"Surely they could make an exception for a family emergency?"

"Perhaps. We'll see. Lieutenant Key is acting on my behalf with the adjutant. I'm hoping he will have some good news for me at the encampment next week."

They had been ascending a gentle rise for some time now, and as they reached the crest the little valley ahead opened up to them. Off to the east side was a tidy house, smoke curling from the chimney. They stopped for a moment to let the horses get a rest.

"Now that's a beautiful scene, gentlemen."

"Yes, cousin Matthew, it's almost enough to convince a man to marry and settle down somewhere nice and peaceful."

"Why cousin Daniel, I didn't realize you were turning into an old man already."

"I said almost cousin, almost."

The three shared a laugh and more ribbing as they descended toward their client's new home. The man had seen them coming and was waving from the front porch.

The following weeks brought with them slightly warmer weather. The late snow and freeze of the pervious weeks had been a bit of a surprise, but was now becoming a distant memory as the wild-flowers started to make their annual appearance, the trees slowly starting to fill in.

Many of the militiamen were milling about in the chill air, some bending over campfires staying warm, others getting their equipment in order. James always enjoyed these encampments, but now the fear of a southward move by the British had everyone on edge. He noticed that everyone had been preparing for their training more seriously than other encampments and that there was less horseplay and more determination.

The camp was alive with motion on this first day, everyone setting up tents, finding comrades and getting ready for the days ahead. Even though he knew the officers were busy at their jobs as well, he was anxious to know about his request for extended leave and made his way towards the camp's headquarters area.

As he approached, he could see Lieutenant Key standing outside his tent in intense conversation with Major Peter. He waited a short distance away and could not hear what was being said, but it was apparent that the major was in a very agitated state.

After he had delivered his message the major left, Lieutenant Key saluting smartly. After a moment, the officer noticed James waiting.

"Yes Private. Did you wish to see me?"

James stepped forward and saluted. "Yes sir, Lieutenant Key, sir. I realize you're very busy, but I was hoping if you had a moment you could let me know the status of my leave application."

The Lieutenant's shoulders sagged just a bit. "I'm sorry, James.

Please, let's sit a moment. I have something to tell you and it is not good news, I'm afraid. Not good news for any of us."

They moved to the trunk of a fallen tree and both sat. James watched the Lieutenant as he idly drew lines in the dirt with a stick, waiting for him to begin. James liked this officer as did all the others in their unit, the Columbian Light Artillery. He knew that as a lawyer, the Lieutenant had represented many free blacks with legal problems and had spoken out against the kidnapping slavers like the ones who took his brother. He also knew that the man owned about a dozen slaves, and although he had a reputation for fairness and good treatment, it was still a dichotomy that James could not resolve in his mind.

"I'm sure you have heard the rumors of the British moving south from Canada. I'm afraid they are not just rumors. I have just been informed that the British have regained Fort Erie and Fort George and feel they now have the upper hand in Canada. That will allow them to free troops up for redeployment, and the feeling is they are in the process of doing just that."

"Is there any information as to their likely destination?"

Key laughed. "Oh, there is a lot of information in that regard to be sure. Unfortunately, it is all wild speculation at this point. It's no secret that they cannot win this cursed war without attacking and winning in the south. They must attack Philadelphia or Baltimore... or perhaps even Washington itself. General Winder believes that Washington will be the target, but Secretary Armstrong is just as sure it will be Baltimore."

"What do you feel, Lieutenant?"

Key stood and James followed suit. "I am only a lowly part time Lieutenant, so my opinion is worth as much as a plate of cold beans. I am very sorry to say, though, that because of this situation no extended leaves will be available anytime soon. I'm very sorry, James. I know how concerned you are about your father. Hopefully, it won't be much longer."

James braced and saluted. "Thank you for asking anyway, sir."

"There will be a lecture from the Commanding Officer tomorrow

evening about the situation we are currently facing. In the meantime, try not to pay too much attention to the rumors going around
the camp. Tomorrow we will all know the facts of the matter."

James slowly walked back to his tent. He was not surprised that
his leave had been denied. He knew and liked his officers and they
he, so he knew he was not being singled out. But he also considered what Lieutenant Key had just passed on to him. What if the
British do move against Baltimore or Washington? He had done
his share of training it was true, but he had never faced combat
and wondered how he would fare, or how the militia as a whole
might behave in a battle with seasoned and veteran British soldiers. He did not relish the prospect at all.

The next morning, the first full day of the encampment, began
with a bugler blowing reveille. The men began to muster into their
proper place in their respective units, many still rubbing the sleep
from their eyes. James looked over his fellow militiamen with a
critical eye. He enjoyed these men, knew many as friends. He had
helped several when they needed help with transport or boarding for their animals. They were a good group of men, eager and
proud, but he knew in his heart they would be no match for the
British regulars if it came to that.

The training was more rigorous than the last encampment.
The officers seemed much more strict in their orders and their
reprimands for poor performance. It is not easy to keep amateur
soldiers in a line, much less have them maneuver by formation, or
to turn when it might be necessary to face an enemy's threat from
another direction. The Columbian Light Artillery moved through
their paces as well or better than most units, but maneuvering
gun carriages and a small unit of supporting infantry usually goes
much more smoothly than having an entire company or battalion of infantry alone trying to move together as one, or to turn
as a single unit to face the enemy with their weapons massed. A
unit that could not do these things, could not maneuver to bring
massed firepower on the enemy, would be slaughtered. The British
were justifiably proud of being able to fire three rounds a minute

and being able to bring that power to bear when and where it was needed. Militia were usually capable of only two rounds a minute at best, and their lack of coordination in movement lessened their effectiveness even more.

The morning echoed with the officer's orders and shouts to keep together, the clanking of gear as several hundred men did their best to follow orders. The artillery did not move as much as the infantry or cavalry units, so James and his unit were able to watch while others stumbled through their paces, officers becoming more frustrated.

The men were given a meal break at noon, and as they sat to eat the rumors started to fly just as they have done in every military camp since time began. James had the impression that not everyone shared his unease, and that some still thought the war was far away and had nothing to do with them.

He and Daniel sat together on a low hillside, resting and eating. "Well, that could have gone a little better, I think," Daniel said between mouthfuls.

They had actually performed fairly well for being out of practice. "We didn't do badly, but we will all have to do much better, all of us, if we hope to be able to face the British anytime soon."

"Why do you think it may be soon?"

James looked around conspiratorially. "When I spoke with Lieutenant Key this morning, he told me that the British are already moving troops down from Canada. Everyone knows they have already been raiding towns on the Chesapeake for over two years now. They have had our ships bottled up there and in New York and Philadelphia for quite some time."

"And you think their next move will be against us here?"

James was thoughtful. "It has to be either here or Baltimore.... or both perhaps."

"As I recall not long ago, you scoffed at the idea of the British coming to town. A waste of men and material, you said."

"I'm not so sure anymore. The British are a prideful people, and we have angered them. Not only by daring to declare war against their mighty Empire in the first place, but also by fighting against them with some success."

"There is also the matter of Port Dover and York. They have been vowing vengeance ever since," Daniel added.

"Yes, I'm afraid so. It seems that cousin Matthew may have been right in his assessment. We have tweaked the lion, and now the lion must strike back. It must."

Any further discussion would have to wait as they were all being called into formation again, a red faced sergeant walking amongst them. "All right, gentlemen, if you don't mind we'll do it again," he said with a pleasant smile. "Now get back in line, you lazy, mis-begotten imitations of soldiers. Move!" He was shouting now as loudly as he could. "And the next man who fails to differentiate between his left hand and right hand again will be a very sorry lad, that I can promise you. Attention in the line!"

The men spent the rest of the afternoon maneuvering around the field or trying to as best they could. James and Daniel made note of the senior officers on a small hill south of the grounds watching them closely, making comments to their aides who were writing them all down in notebooks.

The Columbian Light Artillery was looking very smart as far as James could tell. At least their officers were not threatening hell and damnation on them as some of the others were. Maneuvering a half dozen gun carriages and their crews was far easier than try-ing to get a rifle regiment with up to two hundred men to march in order, reposition in order and fire on order. There was a unit of Militia Cavalry from Alexandria on the field with them who seemed to be moving about the field with relative ease. They also added a bit of color to the other militias drab makeshift uniforms.

When the order to fall out came as the sun was sinking, the exhausted troops went to their areas and collapsed. The smell of the cookfires was especially appealing as the afternoon meal had been scant and rushed. Word had gone around that their commanding officer, Major General Smith, would be addressing them after the eve-ning meal and the speculation and rumors had started immediately.

James and Daniel tried to relax as they ate, but the tension was palpable. "Well, James, what do you suppose Old Smith is going to tell us this fine evening?"

"My hope is that he will be able to tell us something that is worth knowing and not just more speculation."

"I'm sure he will, if indeed he knows anything worth knowing."

James laughed at that. "That is a very good point, my friend. News is slow to travel, but rumors fly like hawks."

Several lieutenants and sergeants were filtering among the men, calling them to the lecture at the near end of the grounds. There was a bit of a natural amphitheatre where a small hill made a curved area of grass. As they arrived, James and Daniel saw the area was filling fast. They took a place near the front as they were very anxious to hear what their general had to say.

They could see the senior officers who had been observing from the hillside gathered with their aides and the commander. They were obviously having a lively discussion but they could not hear anything being said. After a few more minutes, they proceeded to the head of the group.

The commander stepped forward as the men settled in, straining to hear. "First of all, I would like to thank each of you for answering the muster call." He looked over the assembled group, an unhappy look on his face. "Apparently not everyone could find their way, even in these critical and desperate times."

A murmur went through the crowd at his description of the times. He held a hand aloft, asking for quiet. "I want to tell you men what we know, as well as what we think may happen in the next months ahead." He paused, looking over the now silent group.

"There have been several recent developments in our little scrap with Great Britain. After our arms scored many successes in Canada against the English, the tide has now turned in their favor. It has not turned enough to give them a final victory, indeed it has convinced the enemy that the only way to achieve victory over the United States is to bring the war south again, to assail our commercial centers at New York, Philadelphia and Baltimore."

The murmuring started again with several soldiers within earshot wondering if the capital would be a target now. Again the commander raised a hand and the group went quiet. "There is also news from Europe that Napoleon has surrendered in Flanders, and the war with France is over. This will release another four to five thousand battle hardened and seasoned troops to join the fight here. It is my belief, and the belief of many others in command, that they will be coming to the eastern seaboard, possibly to the Chesapeake area as soon as they can be brought."

Instead of a murmur, a deathly silence ensued after that announcement. "I don't need to tell you men what that means. We can expect to face them within three or four months at my estimation. The only question, my good lads, is not when but where. We have a lot of work to do if we hope to be able to defend our towns and our homes against invasion. They are veterans, but we will be fighting on our home grounds. They will be thousands of miles from their own hearths and homes and will only have the supplies they bring with no hope of more. We will have far more men in the field than they, and far more cannon."

He paused now and looked over the eager faces of the men assembled before him. He had great affection for these men, both the few regulars and the many militiamen. He knew something they did not, however. He knew war. "As I mentioned," he continued, "these troops are veterans of some of the fiercest fighting imaginable. They move smartly on the battlefield. They follow orders exactly and fight with valor. We are many more in number but lacking in experience. Listen to your officers, gentlemen, listen well. They are teaching you not only how to fight, but how to survive. Order and discipline must be the rule for us as it is for them."

Again he looked out over the silent crowd. "Learn your lessons well, men, learn them well. God willing, we will prevail on the battlefield when our time comes."

The men stood as one at his closing remarks. A soldier near the middle shouted, "Huzzah for General Smith!" and the cheer spread quickly through the ranks. "Huzzah, huzzah, huzzah!"

The commander left and made his way back to the officer's area with several of the more senior officers following. Several captains and a major stayed behind, the major preparing to address the men.

"Gentlemen, the general is exactly right. There will be a fight, and it is coming soon. As soldiers we do not need to know where, so I would advise you to concentrate very hard on the how." He stopped and looked at the papers in his hand.

He looked up at last. "After watching the maneuvers today, it is safe to say that we all have a lot of work to do to get ready for our visitors. Quite a lot. If you wish to emerge not only victorious but alive, I would urge you in the strongest possible way to learn these movements and learn them well. Our country's life and your own lives will depend on it, of that you may be sure."

By the last day of the training there was a general feeling that the men could move through their paces. The lines of infantry looked smarter, the wheeling lines no longer fell apart every time, the number of rounds loaded and fired on command was rapidly improving. More importantly, the men were beginning to think of themselves as soldiers with a sacred mission to defend their homes and families from the invaders.

James always offered a boxing demonstration on the last night of the encampments, and he was pleased to see a few dozen gathered by the ring area when he arrived. "Come on now, James. We might have a match for you this time," one of the onlookers cried out.

James smiled at him. "Is he as big as the last one, Jeremiah?"

"Bigger, James, much bigger," the man laughed.

"All right, before we start any bouts, who remembers the proper stance? Who remembers how to hold their fists ready?"

The young man who had called out stepped forward. "So, Jeremiah, would you care to show the others how it's done?"

The young man moved to the center of the area that was defined by lines drawn in the dirt and assumed what he thought was the proper posture. "Like this?"

James cast a critical eye. "Not bad, Jeremiah, not bad at all. But your feet are a little too far apart and your left is a little low. Try this…'" he said as he adjusted the youth's body. "That's much better. How does it feel?"

"Like I could slay a dragon," Jeremiah said.

James tossed him a pair of thick gloves. "Well, now is your chance to try." James said as he pulled on a pair of gloves himself. "But remember, we are friends and this is a lesson. No slaying is allowed."

Their gloves on, the men started to circle, each looking for a chance to land the first blow. James faked a move to his right and Jeremiah took the bait. James moved inside and landed what would have been two very punishing blows if he had not pulled them some.

Jeremiah staggered back, wiping sweat from his eyes. "I did not see that coming at all." They circled again for a bit, Jeremiah trying his best to get James to fall for the same trick with no result. After a few minutes, James called a halt.

"I have told all of you before, don't watch your opponent's head or eyes. They are liars. Watch his shoulders, especially the leading shoulder, and the hips. A man cannot make a move without his shoulders or hips leading. It's easy to bob your head and fool someone. Don't let that someone be you."

There were comments coming from the group with questions about stance and movement, some disparaging of the entire method. "Well, James, your Broughton Rules method seems to work with little fellows like Jeremiah here," one of the older men called out to some chuckling from the crowd. "How does it work against a more, dare I say, experienced fighter?"

James saw a very large man approaching the area, then step inside. His face was impassive, almost blank. He stretched his arms and shoulders, twisting his thick frame to loosen up. "Good evening," he said quietly.

"Good evening to you, sir. Have you been to one of these demonstrations before, may I ask?"

"Nope." Nothing else was forthcoming.

James hesitated. "All right, then, let me explain the rules." He eyed his new opponent up and down and let out a quiet, slow whistle. "You're a big one, aren't you? Everyone back home this big?"

"Nope. I'm the smallest."

James rolled his eyes. "I was afraid you might say that," again drawing laughs from the men. "As I was saying, let me explain the rules. This is merely a friendly exhibition, with the emphasis on friendly. There will only be one round, and if possible, no bleeding."

The catcalls started coming as the two men pulled on the gloves and then started to circle each other. The larger man seemed to be intent on getting a wrestling hold on James. If he did, James knew, he would be finished. Suddenly he lunged at James with his arms wide. James easily stepped aside and landed a blow on the man's right cheek as he went by. Stunned, the man turned and James landed a left right combination to his midsection.

James was impressed with how strong this man was. It almost hurt his hands to punch him in the gut. He had staggered him a bit, but the man showed no sign of going down at all. He took another step towards James and swung a clumsy right haymaker that was easily avoided. When they again faced each other, James landed two quick jabs to the man's face very lightly, then jumped back.

He raised both gloved hands in the air to much cheering and jeering. "Time, gentlemen. I hope I have proved my point yet again. This kind gentleman here is twice my size. If he ever did get a hold of me, if he could fight in his style, I would be finished." The men settled down a bit. "I used his size against him, to make him fight in my style. I am faster, but he is much stronger."

One of the lieutenants stepped out of the shadows. A few of the men murmured "Good evening, sir" as he moved to where James and his opponent stood. "That was very interesting,

Private Woodman, very interesting indeed. I have heard of this method before but have never seen it demonstrated. You have made me a believer." He then turned to the men crowding around. "Do any of you see a parallel here, a parallel to our present circumstance?"

The men looked around at each other, then at the ground. This particular Lieutenant had a habit of asking open ended questions like this. Finally, a voice answered, "No, sir."

"It's quite simple, really, when you stop to think. This man here," he said, motioning to the opponent, "I'm sorry, soldier, what is your name?"

"I'm Corporal Cowan, sir, from the First Regiment, District Militia.."

"Yes, well. Our Corporal Cowan here represents our enemy, Great Britain. He is stronger and has much more muscle to flex as it were." He then turned to James. "Our Private Woodman here represents the United States. He is younger and faster, he is well prepared and he has a unique style of fighting."

"When we meet the British, and make no mistake we will meet them soon, we must not allow the fight to go on their terms. We must somehow force them to fight on our terms, in our time, on ground of our choosing. If we can all work to do that, to make it happen, we can whip them, boys, I am sure of it!"

James and Daniel walked the last mile or two back to the stables after hitching a ride on a friend's wagon from the encampment. The talk on the ride back had been all about the training and about what the officers had shared with them about the current situation. The general consensus was that Britain would be foolish to attack any militia unit that they belonged to.

After jumping down off the wagon, the two friends started up the long slow hill that leads into Georgetown from the northwest. Just in the last week the trees had begun their spring renewal in earnest, wildflowers growing along the side of the road and a definite change in the air itself.

"Spring is a wonderful time to be alive, don't you think?" Daniel said.

James took a second to respond and seemed preoccupied. He looked around at their surroundings. He could hear birds calling in the forest, the water in Rock Creek splashing on its descent to the Potomac. "That it is," he said finally.

"Are you still back at camp, then?"

"I suppose I am." He looked around again. "It's hard to believe that all this could be a battlefield before too much longer, that so much death and destruction can be visited on this beautiful home of ours."

"Oh, I don't know James. I think the men are well prepared. You saw them yourself. The improvement was very noticeable, I think."

They were moving up the road at a leisurely pace. The morning was warm and the road grew a little steeper as they went. "Yes, I agree. There was a lot of improvement, but there was a lot of room for it. However, there is nothing more important than experience, I should think. I've never been in war, never fought other men like that." He walked a few more paces and stopped. "I just don't know if I'll have the courage to stand and not run for my life."

Daniel laughed at that. "You will have nothing to worry about on that score, my friend, as I will be standing right next to you, and if you run, I'll shoot you. How about that?"

"Just the encouragement I need." James just shook his head and started up the road again. "We'll make a fine pair when the time comes, one of us always watching the other."

The talk turned to the job at hand. Daniel needed James and his wagon to finish a job he had started the previous week. They would need to hitch the team, drive across town to the docks near the Navy Yard to get the needed materials and then take them over to Alexandria. It would be a long day.

The view from the top of the rise looked across most of the

buildings in the northwest part of the sleepy town, with the docks on the river clearly in view. It always brought a smile to James, but something was wrong with the picture today. He could see his stables, and the paddock, which should have been full of horses at this time of day, was empty. Daniel noticed as well.

"Where's Luke? That boy is supposed to have watered them by now and led them outside."

Daniel was looking over the scene. "I don't see anything moving around there."

They picked up the pace as they started down the hill into town, a sense of unease growing in James. When they were nearing the corner nearest the stables, Mister Jenkins motioned to them. They crossed the street, trying to conceal themselves and having no idea why.

"What is it, Mister Jenkins? Is something wrong? Have you seen Luke about today?" James was getting more worried as he watched the old shopkeeper's face.

"I don't know if it's anything at all, James." He hesitated before he went on. "I saw three very rough men go into the stables there just after Luke arrived. I heard some commotion, some loud voices and such you know, then some more commotion and then nothing. I haven't heard anything since. Nothing at all. And the horses aren't in the paddock."

"Did you see those three men again after that?"

"No, that's the funny thing. It's been as silent as the grave over there. No coming or going. No noise. Nothing."

James lowered his knapsack to the ground and gripped his rifle. He had used the last of his powder at the camp, but nobody he pointed it at would know that. Daniel had the same thought, he could see.

"What do you propose, James?"

"I propose to go over to my property and see what the situation is. Do you care to join me?"

"Wouldn't miss it for the world." Daniel gave him an unpleasant smile. "Not for the world."

There was a small window on this side of the stables that looked over the street. It provided some light into James' living quarters but was very thick glass. He wasn't worried about anyone seeing them through it. They moved under the window and listened.

There was definitely some muffled movement in the room. It was very soft and they could not determine what it was. They moved quietly along the wall towards the paddock. From there they should be able to get a look into the interior of the barn.

James worked his way down the paddock fence, keeping as low as possible as he went. Daniel stayed at the corner where the fence met the wall of the building, his empty rifle at the ready. Just as James was getting ready to move again, the large door into the paddock opened a crack and a face peered out. Apparently satisfied, the man went back inside and closed the door.

James' heart sank. The face belonged to the smaller of Samuel's brothers, the one he had decked with the flat of the shovel at their last meeting. He looked over to see if Daniel had seen the man as well. Daniel was nodding and motioning towards the door.

James thought for a minute, then started making his way back to Daniel's position. "It's those three troublemakers from the night at the tavern."

"I saw him, all right," Daniel said. "What now? We could go for the city police."

"I'm afraid Mister O'Malley might have other priorities than coming to my assistance. No, I have to go in there and have this out. I want to be finished with this business once and for all."

"All right. You go in and see what they want. Then, I'll come in after a few minutes and we'll see if we can't get the best of them one more time. Can I get in through the door in the side?"

"No. It's blocked by all the hay bales I bought last month. Damn."

"All right. If this door is the only one in, then this door it is. Just try and keep their backs to the door and their eyes on you."

James nodded agreement, then made his way along the wall of the stables to the door. He stopped with his ear against the wood.

After a moment, he shrugged at Daniel and started to pull the door open. As soon as the door was open a crack, a muzzle was pushed through the opening. James lowered his rifle to the ground and raised his hands in the air. Daniel could see him as he did this, and saw him step inside to an unheard order, then the door quickly closed again.

"Damn," Daniel muttered under his breath. There were three of them at least, and he had no weapon other than a rifle with no powder. He weighed his options and knew he had only one.

He waited a few minutes, listening hard, then moved slowly towards the door. He stopped there and listened again. This time he could hear Samuel's voice booming inside.

"Well lookee here, brothers. It's that damn uppity nigger again, and now we know why he's so damn uppity, don't we boys."

The two brothers looked at each other, then back at Samuel. "Why's that, Samuel?"

"Why, boys, this here ain't no slave. This here is a free man, and a free man who actually owns his own business. Can you imagine that? A damn black man having his own business. If that just don't beat all." Samuel had his hat off and was brushing dust off his trousers with it. "Yes sir, if that don't just beat all."

Samuel then turned to James. "But you ain't a free man at all, are you nigger? I'll bet you are just another damn runaway, aren't you boy? Who'd you run away from, tell me that boy."

James was calm. "I am a free born man just as you are. I was born on my father's farm in Pennsylvania."

"Here that, boys. He's a free man… just like us." He swept his arm around the stables to include the brothers. "Now ain't that nice?"

"What is it you want here, Samuel?"

"Hear that, boys? He called me by name and wants to know my business here." The two brothers laughed nervously. They often couldn't follow what their older sibling was saying. "Now, mister free man, where are your friends today?" he asked, looking around mockingly. "I don't see hide nor hair of anyone coming to your rescue this time." He looked over at the younger brother. "Jed, you get over there beside the door just in case one of his friends does decide to drop in for a visit. We've got work to do and I don't want any interruptions."

"What work do you have to do here in my stables?"

"Funny you should ask that, it truly is, so I'll tell you. I asked around about you, nigger. It sure was a surprise when I heard that you own these here stables, that you weren't someone's slave working here. Yes sir, that was a surprise all right."

Samuel seemed to have lost his train of thought for a second. James moved towards the rear of the room a few feet, trying to keep all eyes on him and away from the door.

"So, as I was saying," Samuel went on. "I figured, hell, we can grab up that damn black bastard and sell him back across the river. I figured we'd get a mighty good price for you, too. Then, when we got here this morning, we found another damn nigger here in your place. Imagine that. We'll get two for the cost of catching us one."

"What do you mean. What have you done with Luke?"

"If you mean that little colored boy who was here this morning, he's trussed up like a Christmas goose back there in that bedroom. He's come to no harm… so far."

James knew that Luke was an escaped slave from Virginia. He had found him hiding under the small dock at the back of the stables used for deliveries a few months ago. It had not been easy to coax the boy out but seeing a black man with his hand out to help him finally worked. Luke was a strong boy and did not mind hard work. He had very little to say to anyone, and James knew nothing about where he lived now. He just did what he was asked and only wanted to be left alone. James had seen the scars on the boy's back and knew he had secrets he wasn't yet ready to share.

"If you've harmed that boy…."

Samuel acted offended. "I already told you that no harm has come to him as yet. He's in the back, resting is all."

Just at that moment Daniel stepped into the stables through

the large doors, his rifle leveled at Samuel. "Good morning again, gentlemen. To what do we owe the pleasure of this visit?"

James had not been facing the door, and Daniel's voice surprised him. He started to call out, but the brother Jed stepped out of the shadow next to the door. Daniel felt a sharp blow to the back of his head, then a sensation of falling. James tried to go to his aid but was held back by Samuel's firm grip.

"I was wondering when he was going to join us." Samuel said. "Don't you worry none about him, boy. You got your own troubles now." He pushed James away. "Now let's go on back there and get that other nigger up and get about our business."

Samuel shoved him towards the small room at the back of the stables where James lived. It was a small room with a bed, a table and chairs and some eating and cooking utensils. Samuel pulled his flintlock pistol from his waist and pulled the hammer back.

"Open it," he said to James, motioning with the pistol. "Let's get that other one and be on our way."

James opened the door slowly. Luke was lying on the bed, his back to the door. He seemed to be breathing normally. "Luke, are you all right? It's me, James."

"Get out of my way, damn you," Samuel said as he pulled James away from the bed. He reached a hand down and grabbed Luke's shoulder. "Get up, you lazy damn nigger. We have a long day ahead of us…"

Luke didn't respond at first and Samuel leaned over him a bit and shook him harder. Luke turned on the bed suddenly and thrust a knife that James used to make meals deep into Samuel's midsection. He then rolled away from him and backed away towards the door.

Samuel staggered backwards, a look of shock on his face. "You've killed me, damn your soul." He had one hand on the blade protruding from his belly. He started to raise the pistol at Luke, but it discharged towards the floor. He staggered towards James, then fell over the small table, the cutlery and dishes crashing to the floor.

The other two brothers heard and came running into the room. "What have you done?" Jed shrieked. "What have you done?" He turned to James, a look of sheer terror and hatred on his face. "You are going to die for this, you damn black bastard."

Jed lunged at him, but James easily avoided his rush. When he turned again, James met him with two quick jabs to the center of his face. He brushed them off, then lunged again. This time, James got his leg out in front of him and tripped him as he went by. Luke was trying to get to the door.

"Hold it right there, dammit." The third brother, whose name James did not know, was standing in the doorway, another cocked flintlock pistol in hand. "Get up off the damn floor, Jed."

Jed staggered to his feet. "They killed Samuel. Look at him on the floor. They've murdered our brother."

Jed turned on James, absolute fury written all over his face. "And now I'm going to kill you."

There was nowhere for James to step aside this time. He took Jed's rush full on and used his momentum to throw him to the floor, falling on top of him. The other brother kept the muzzle of his pistol aimed squarely at Luke. "Now we'll see if that fancy fighting is going to do this nigger any good."

The two were rolling around in the cramped room, each trying to get the advantage by getting on top of the other. Jed had James down, his hands closing around his throat. James started to feel dizzy and weak, the light growing fainter. He reached up and put his thumbs into Jed's eyes and pushed with all his remaining strength.

Jed screamed and took his hands off James' throat and covered his eyes. The other brother let out a curse and started to step forward to help. James was puzzled by how he then actually flew across the table and landed in a heap in the corner, dropping his pistol. He looked at the open door and saw Daniel standing there, a grin on his face. "Am I interrupting something?" he asked.

James scooped up the dropped pistol as he stood. Jed was wailing on the floor. "My eyes, damn you, my eyes. You blinded me you damn nigger. I'm blind."

Luke was trying to slip out the door as quietly as possible. His experience taught him that he did not want to be here when people in the neighborhood came to investigate the gunshot. "It's going to be all right, Luke. You haven't done anything wrong."

"Mister James, sir, the truth of the matter is I am a runaway and that there dead man is white. This here ain't no place for me to be at the moment." He started for the door again, but Daniel blocked the door.

"No, he's right, Daniel. Let him go. He's right. O'Malley would not even give him a chance to speak or offer any sort of explanation." He turned to Luke. "Where are you going to go?"

"I be around, Mister James. I be around, don't you worry none about me." He looked down at the floor. There was a dead white man and two more badly injured. "This ain't no place for me."

The other brother was trying to stand in the corner. "I'll get the law on you bastards. You'll pay for this."

"Will, is that you?" Jed cried out. "Will, they blinded me, they put out my eyes!"

There was another knife on a counter along the wall next to Will. He grabbed it and started towards James. James raised the pistol and aimed for Will's face. "Just put the knife down, Will, just stop and put it down." His voice was very calm. "No reason for you to die today."

Will looked down. His older brother was lying dead on the floor, his little brother moaning and clutching his face. "Go to hell," he said as he came at James.

James fired the pistol, striking Will in the face. He fell over backwards to the ground and did not move. "What have you done? Will, are you there? Will?" Jed was screaming from the floor.

Daniel went over and looked at Will, then turned to Jed who was moaning and crying softly. "We should get a doctor for this one. The other two don't need anything."

"Oh, what have you done? What have you done?" Jed kept moaning over and over.

"Guess we ought to get O'Malley over as well," James said. He looked over at Luke, who was staring at him wide eyed. "Go on, Luke. Go. No need for you to be here."

Luke didn't need to be told twice. He nodded to James and Daniel and disappeared out the door. In another minute, the small room was starting to fill up with curious neighbors who had heard the shots. James and Daniel were trying to keep everything as it was, trying to get everyone out into the main part of the stables.

After a few minutes spent trying to tell everyone what had happened, constable O'Malley's booming voice filled the room. "And what, pray tell, is happening here, Daniel Lawrence? Could you please tell me that?"

"Well, constable, there was a bit of a set to here as you may have heard." They could just make out Jed's soft moans from the bedroom. "There are two dead men back there I'm afraid, and one who is badly injured and needs attention."

"The devil you say," O'Malley said, looking around at the space. Even in a place as messy as a stables it could be seen that there had been some kind of struggle. "And just who are these men, then?"

James started to speak, but O'Malley cut him off. "I'm not talking to you, James. I was asking Daniel Lawrence here a question." He turned back to Daniel. "I'm waiting."

"You remember a few weeks back, constable, there was a bit of a fuss at Jones' tavern on an evening. Well, I think maybe they came back because James here hurt their feelings."

"As I recall, he hurt more than their feelings. Is the big one dead?"

"Completely."

"And just how did that come to pass, may I be so bold as to ask?" O'Malley had his hat off and was brushing at his sleeve.

Daniel glanced at James. "I'm afraid that you'll have to ask James about that part. You see, I was somewhat incapacitated at that time." Daniel was rubbing the back of his head as he spoke. "I didn't see much for a bit."

O'Malley was growing exasperated. "James, what happened then?"

James told him about coming back from militia training and finding the three men in his place waiting to ambush him. He explained how he had been taken and that Daniel was supposed to burst in and surprise them.

"And did you surprise them, Daniel?"

"Well, actually, it was the other way around," he said a little sheepishly. He was not proud of being taken like that. "I made my dramatic entrance right on cue, as it were, and the next thing I know I'm taking a little nap on the floor there," he said, pointing to a spot near the large doors.

There were still a dozen or so curious neighbors standing around, watching and listening. O'Malley turned to them. "Did anyone here see or hear anything? Anything at all?"

Old Jenkins stepped forward. "I knew something was wrong when I came to open my store this morning. There were no horses in the front paddock. There are always horses in the paddock. Every day. No, I knew there was something wrong right then."

"Did you see anyone here then?" O'Malley asked. James was afraid the old man would mention Luke.

"I saw three very rough looking men. They were just waiting around. I didn't like the look of them at all. No sir."

"If you were at the militia camp all week, James, who takes the horses in and out and feeds them?"

James hesitated for a second. "I usually just hire one of the older boys from the neighborhood who wants to earn a little money. Just any one of the boys," he said, his eyes fixed on Mister Jenkins.

Jenkins started to say something, but Daniel cut him off. "That's right. Mister Jenkins there met us out front and warned us about these three. Said they were inside the building or we might have just walked in."

"Yes sir, I met them at the corner and warned them. I said I didn't like their looks at all." The old man looked around the room. "Where's Luke? He could tell you about all this. He must have seen them."

"And who is this Luke fellow?" O'Malley asked. "Why isn't he here?"

James was glaring at Mister Jenkins, who finally seemed to understand. "He was gone when we got here constable," Daniel said. "Those men must have scared him off. He probably just ran as soon as he had a chance."

"Is this Luke a nigger?"

James answered him very slowly and calmly. "He is black if that's what you mean, Mister O'Malley. I don't allow people in my home and business to use that word."

"All right James, all right. I just figured if he was a nig.... a black, then he had good reason to run from these men."

They could hear a wagon pulling up outside, then two men entered the stables. O'Malley jerked a thumb over his shoulder. "There's two dead and one injured back there. Take the injured man for now. I want a look at that room back there." The men shuffled off, one carrying a stretcher under his arm.

"What did you mean, Mister O'Malley? Who are these men?" James asked.

"Well, we'll get to that in just a bit, boyo. Right now I want to see the room and hear the rest of this story. Then, we'll all settle in for a nice long chat." He looked around at the room. "You can all go on about your business now. It's all over here." He walked towards the back room, James and Daniel following.

The men with the stretcher passed them as they got to the door. Jed was very still, his hands still covering his face. O'Malley stood in the door and surveyed the scene. The dead men lay where they fell, the floor littered with broken furniture and dishes.

He let out a slow whistle. "This must have been one hell of a fight, boyo, one hell of a fight. Want to tell me what happened here?"

James was thinking fast. "The big one there, Samuel, was trying to kidnap me. He accused me of being a runaway and said he was going to sell me south. Well, he took his eyes off me for a second and I grabbed the knife there. When he came at me, I shoved it in as far as it would go."

O'Malley was looking at James' hands and clothes. "Not much blood for a stabbing, especially if he was up close like that. So, go on. What happened then?"

"That's where I come in," Daniel said. "I had awoken from my short nap and heard a commotion back here. As I approached, I could see the other brother, Will I think his name was, holding that flintlock and threatening to kill my friend here."

"And what did you do?"

"I struck him in the back of the head with that shovel," he said, motioning to the floor. "He went sprawling and dropped his weapon. When he stood, he picked up a knife and charged at James, who then shot him dead with his own gun. He did try to warn the poor fellow, though, but he obviously was not a good listener."

Constable O'Malley took a few steps around the room, stroking his chin and lost in thought. He looked down at Samuel and where he lay. "So then, after you stabbed this man, what happened?"

"He staggered around a bit," James said, trying to think. "He cursed me a bit and tried to raise his gun to me but it went off and he fell there."

"Just the two of you were in here?"

"Yes, sir. Just us. When Samuel fell it made quite a commotion, and the brother Jed came running in to see what had happened. Then Daniel arrived and you know the rest."

"Oh, I don't know about that, gentlemen. I do know I heard what you have told me happened, but I don't know how much I really know about the events of this morning."

The men with the stretcher were back. "All right, boys, you can have these two, God rest them." To James and Daniel he said," Now let's us go back to my nice cozy office and continue this conversation. What do you say?" he said, motioning towards the door.

They shrugged and started for the door. "Do you mind if I let the horses out for a bit, give them a little feed?"

"No, you go right ahead. I'll just poke around in here a bit more."

"Take a seat, gentlemen, take a seat," O'Malley said, motioning to some chairs against the wall. "Now, let's just go over this eventful morning once more," he said after they were settled.

"I don't know if there is much we can add to what we already told you, constable," Daniel said. "We came back from our encampment and saw the horses were not out in the paddock when we crested the hill on Rock Creek Road. You know the place. You can see all of this part of town from there."

"I know the place, Daniel. Go on."

"Well, anyway, we hurried down the hill to see what the problem was, and Mister Jenkins met us and gave us warning."

The constable's face was impassive as he took this all in. "I'm still curious to know who has been keeping watch on the stables for you, James, while you were in camp. Who else was there this morning?"

"Like I said, Mister O'Malley, sir, it's just some boys from the neighborhood. It's not always the same one. I'm not even sure which one was supposed to be there this morning."

"Let me refresh your memory then. Jenkins mentioned a lad named Luke, I believe."

James looked thoughtful for a moment, stalling. "Well, it's like I said. There are three or four boys who like to pick up a little money doing chores around, not just for me but some of the others in the neighborhood. I let the boys work it out amongst themselves. As long as the work gets done, I don't care who does it."

"So, then, if I go ask around the neighborhood, maybe someone else might know who this Luke boy is?"

James tried to shrug it off and wanted to change the subject badly. "I wouldn't know, really. I suppose so. But who were those men, constable? You implied there was some threat to me or any black person from them."

O'Malley looked James hard in the face. He knew he was try-ing to change the subject away from Luke's identity. He sat back in his chair, knowing he wasn't going to get any more from these two about that, at least not for now. "They were indeed a threat. They are, or were, slavers, James. Didn't you suspect something like that?"

"No, sir. Why should I?"

"I heard that they stopped by the stables the day after our little party at Jones' tavern that night. Is that true?" He was looking back and forth at the two of them.

"It is indeed," Daniel said.

"Do you care to tell me about that, James?"

"Not much to tell, really. They came around saying they were looking for some horses to buy. I told them I didn't have any, that all the horses at the stables were being boarded and were not mine to sell."

"Is that all?"

Both Daniel and James shuffled in their seats. "Well, no. Not exactly." The constable was waiting for someone to go on. "They tried to settle the score from the previous evening."

"And how did they do that?"

"Two of the brothers came at me in the paddock."

The constable smiled. "That doesn't sound like good odds.... for them, anyway."

James nodded. "I agree. They should have all rushed me together. As it was, I had no trouble putting the first two on the ground and then Samuel pulled that pistol of his from under his coat and raised it."

"That's when I made my entrance," Daniel broke in. "My cousin Matthew and I were coming down to the stables that morn-ing to help James move some furniture and household goods for a mutual client. Well, as we came up to the paddock, there was James with Samuel's pistol in his face and his brothers on the ground. My cousin and I convinced Samuel it would be the better part of valor for him and his to move on."

"Hmm… I see. And where is cousin Matthew these days, may I ask? Did he see any part of this business today?"

"No sir. Matthew went back home up near Baltimore the day after we helped James with the move. His militia company was scheduled to encamp for training in a few days."

"The militias all seem to be very busy recently, and that's a fact. We've all heard the rumors about the British coming back soon," O'Malley said. He looked very thoughtful for a moment. "Are you sure you didn't know about these brothers and their business?"

"No sir. How could I have known anything about them?"

"Well, James, I heard that they were asking a lot of questions about you around the town. I thought maybe you heard about that as well. Maybe started asking some questions of your own."

"No, sir. I didn't hear anything like that, and I didn't ask anyone about them. I wouldn't think anyone around here would know them."

The constable shuffled through some things on his desk. "Yes, I found that these three make a living kidnapping nig… blacks and selling them back across the river. They were plying their devilish trade a little north of us, but the authorities there ran them off."

"I take it then that you don't approve of their business," Daniel said.

O'Malley looked back and forth between them again. He leaned forward with his folded arms on the desk. "I know what you both think of me, that I am sometimes a bully, or that I treat some people unfairly. But let me tell you something. I hate the slavers as much as any man. I cannot understand why any man thinks he has some God given right to own another man. It is a sin and an abomination to think that way. There will come a day, and not too far off, when this country will have to choose to stand for what we say we stand for or admit that we are hypocrites. There will be a lot of blood spilled then, much more than has been already."

James was looking at the man with a new curiosity. "Why constable, are you telling me that you are a secret abolitionist?"

"Blacks are not the only people to have suffered persecution in this land of the free, boyo. My father fought in the Revolution with the New York infantry. He risked his life, his home, everything, just like the others. He shared the same danger and the hardships as the rest, but after the war ended he went back to just being another dirty Irishman. Decent folks did not want his kind around them."

"It's true," Daniel said. "My father faced the same stupid bigotry. It's not as bad as it was, but I'd be willing to bet that you still are not treated equally. I know I'm not. People look down on me just because of where my father was born."

"My father was a foot soldier in the Fourth Connecticut Regiment," James said. "If you know your history, then you know about them. He saw plenty of fighting and suffering as well. When the war was over, he went out west and bought a farm for him and his wife. He only wanted peace in his life after all the violence he had seen and he knew that no man could mistreat him on his own property. He rarely ventured far after that."

"If you hate this bigotry so much Mister O'Malley, why do you enforce the fugitive laws?"

"Did you not see the sign on the door when we came in? It says Chief Constable. I am paid to enforce the laws of the city. I am not paid to pick and choose which laws to enforce, nor am I paid to make new laws. That is for people who know much more than I do. When this evil of slavery comes to an end, then there will be no law to enforce."

"You don't like blacks much, do you?" James asked, looking him in the eye.

"I have no animosity towards coloreds like some on this force. I can't reach in to a man's heart and make him feel one way or another. We two races are just too far apart to be able to live together in peace forever. I'm sorry that your people were ever brought to this land. I think it would be better for both of our people if that had never happened."

"But it did happen. Some say it is still happening right now even though it's been against the law for a few years. We can't go back in time and make the world right again."

"Aye, that's the truth. I suppose that my views will eventually die out, I don't know. Your neighbor lawyer Key is thinking of trying to establish an organization to repatriate blacks to Africa. Did you know that?"

"I'm not African," James said, bristling. "I am an American. I was born in this country. My father risked his black neck fighting to make it a free country. I don't belong in Africa any more than you do, Constable O'Malley."

"James, I know you. I know you are an honest and hardworking man. You don't make trouble for people, aside from the occasional broken nose, and you have many friends in our little community here. I don't know if we could ever be friends at all, really, but you do have my respect for the man you are." He laughed then. "Who knows, maybe the Irish and the blacks will run this country some day."

James nodded. "Are we done here? I'd like to get back to my business and my horses now."

"Well, I suppose for the moment we are, but there is something about this whole business that doesn't quite ring true for me. These men start a fight with you, not once but twice. Then the third encounter ends in the death of two white men and the serious injury of another." He shook his head. "There will be a lot of questions being asked around, and I just hope it is all just as you said. I truly do. The world is a better place with those men not in it, God help me for saying that."

"I don't know what else we can tell you," Daniel said. "It's all there."

"Well, we'll find out soon enough I suppose. But James, I should think it would be a very good idea that you consult with the lawyer Key about this matter. He has taken on cases to help blacks before the law in the past, and I'm certain he would help you as well."

Daniel started to say help with what, but James interrupted. "I will do that, constable. Mister Key is in our militia unit as well as a neighbor. Thank you for the advice."

As the two men rose to leave, Chief Constable O'Malley offered one more observation. "It's a sometimes wicked world we live in, James, but it is the only world we have for the time being and it is not of my making. If somehow it was up to me, it would be a far better world than it is, believe me." He stood and offered James his hand. "I'm sorry if I ever offended you. It was not my intention. I do sometimes speak without thinking, at least that's what my good wife often tells me."

James took his hand and nodded. "Thank you Mister O'Malley," He turned to Daniel. "Shall we go? We still have a job to do today."

It took several days until James was able to meet with Key at his office. Key had his family home well north of Georgetown, near Frederick Town in Maryland. He was also frequently out of town on business and could be gone for a week or more at a time.

When he got to the lawyer's new office, he saw a number of workmen doing some construction on the back, maybe adding a room or two to the modest house. When he was shown inside his observation was confirmed. The house was in disarray as workmen and others moved in and out, some of them unpacking small crates of household goods.

"Hello, James. Please do come in." Key stood as he entered the office, which was an oasis of calm amid the uproar of the rest of the house. "Please sit down and tell me how I can be of assistance to you."

James sat and told the whole story from the first encounter until the killing of the two slavers in his stables. Key listened intently, occasionally taking notes as James went along. When he had finished telling the story, Key sat back in his chair and looked at James very directly.

"Well, I must admit I have not had to handle a problem like this before. I have taken on murder cases, but not one like this."

"Is it murder to defend yourself from being kidnapped and sold into slavery?" His voice was tight.

"No, James, it is not. I should have chosen my words more carefully. I apologize. You have every right to defend your home and business and especially yourself. It's just that I'm afraid some will raise the issue of a black man killing not one but two whites, and since there had been confrontations before, I imagine some will have their own theories about what happened."

"Do I need to worry about what other people think, Lieutenant? Aren't the facts more important than someone's theory?"

"Well, first, I will not be a Lieutenant much longer, James. I have been asked to take on other more administrative duties for President Madison's new Military District of Washington. I will still be serving, but not on the field I'm afraid, and yes, in a more perfect world the facts would indeed be more important. As I am sure you are very much aware, this is not a perfect world. Feelings on both sides of the slavery issue run deep and warm, as do the feelings about this cursed war."

James certainly knew that for a fact. The pro war riots in Baltimore two years ago that resulted in the murders of General Lingan and others, and the brutal beating of Light Horse Harry Lee, a true American hero who did not deserve such a fate, had touched a raw nerve in the country and especially here in Washington. He had seen violent arguments on the street and even in quiet meeting places like Jones' tavern over both of those issues.

"What do you suggest I do from here, Lieut... I'm sorry, Mister Key?"

"The question is what do we do from here, James. I know you and know you are a good man. I also know that you would never have done any of this if you did not feel a very serious threat from these men, a very real and personal threat. I'll be more than glad to help you with this matter, so you let me think on this for a few days and let me speak with Constable O'Malley as well."

James was greatly relieved but a little hesitant. "I am not a rich man, Mister Key. I'm just getting by with my stables..."

"You let me worry about that, James. I have always felt that I have a calling from the Lord to help others when it is in my power to do so, especially those without a voice in our society."

"That's very kind of you, sir. I know you have helped a good many black folks with legal problems before. I know some of those folks well, and they speak highly of you and are truly grateful."

They were walking towards the front door, dodging workmen as they went. "As I said, James, I'm just doing the Lord's work. It's my duty."

"I would feel better if there was something I could do for you, Mister Key. There must be some service or something I can do to repay you."

"You don't have to.." Key stopped and looked around at the chaos around him. "Actually, James, there is a very large favor you could do for me if you're able."

"Just name it, sir. It would be my pleasure. Anything at all." James was animated at the prospect of being able to repay a kindness like this.

"Lets step outside. As you can see, we are in the process of enlarging this place and moving house into town. I miss my wife and children very much when I'm away from the family and want them here with me more. It's been very hard on all of us to be separated with me in the city and them up at Terra Rubra."

"Do you need me to help you move? You know that I have a very good wagon and team. I could bring quite a load down for you. Just tell me when."

"Thank you, James. That would be a very useful service to me and my family. Mister Swenson was moving us, but his wagon broke an axle and a wheel as well, so he will be out of commission for a bit. If you could fill in, it would be a very great help."

"Then it would be my pleasure..." James stopped as the front door opened. A young black woman stepped out on to the porch with a small box. She was slightly built, with her hair worn short. She looked James straight in the eyes and gave a shy smile.

"I'm very sorry, Mister Key sir. I don't want to bother you, but Jeffery wants me to ask you about this box."

"That's quite all right, Abigail, quite all right." He looked into the top of the small box. "Tell Jeffery that these can go in my office on the desk and I'll take care of them."

"Yassir, I'll tell him that." She turned to leave.

"James, have you met Abigail? She is a house servant on the estate. Abigail, this is James. He'll be helping with the move in the next few days."

The girl gave a very slight curtsey, her eyes down on the porch. "How do, Mister James," she said quietly.

"How do you do, Miss Abigail," James said. "It's nice to meet you."

Abigail muttered a quiet "Likewise," and disappeared back through the front door.

"Can you come around soon, James? There are one or two small items here that will be going back to Terra Rubra and a good size load to bring back from there."

"Is tomorrow morning soon enough? I don't have any other clients for my wagon or me this week. I can be here at 6."

As they shook hands on the steps, Key said, "I may need most of that week if possible. It's some 60 miles from here to the estate, so it will mean two days up and two back I'm afraid."

"That's fine sir, truly. I am at your service."

"That's very generous of you, but could you please make it 8 o'clock instead if you don't mind, and I thank you. Until the morning then."

James was up early the next morning. It was a crisp, clear morning with a blustery breeze from the southwest hinting at warmer weather to come. The wagon was already in the paddock and ready except for a team.

"It's a beautiful day for a ride in the country, don't you think Annie?" He brought the big chestnut and another horse out and hitched them up. He went back into the stable and put a spare shirt and a book he was reading in a sack and put them under the wagon's seat, then went to open the paddock gate. Luke was across the street, watching him. James beckoned him over.

"Are you going away Mister James?" the boy asked.

"Yes, Luke. I'm moving some things for Mister Key. I'll be gone a few days at most."

"Do you want me to look over the horses for you again?"

James led the boy back across the street. "I think it would be best for you to not be seen around here for a while. The constable suspects that you or someone was here when the trouble happened. He may come by or be in the neighborhood asking questions about you."

James could see the fear in the lad's eyes. "I ain't in no trouble, am I Mister James? I didn't do nothing wrong 'cept protect myself."

"I know you didn't Luke, I know. I didn't tell O'Malley anything about you, but he knows someone was here since I was at the camp for the better part of a week. He asked me who and I just told him that some boys around here took turns watching the place. I said I didn't know which one was here that morning."

"I dunno, Mister James, sir. I'm thinking it might be best if I went away from here, maybe go up north somewheres."

James had a sudden thought. "I have an idea, Luke. Why don't you go on up on the Rock Creek road to the top of the grade there. You know the place I mean? Good. I have to go to the. Key house and load up, then I'll be up that road after that, and you can ride with me. You could be a big help, too, and it would get you away from here for a few days."

Luke thought it over. "All right, Mister James. That might be a good idea right about now."

"Will anybody miss you if you're gone for a few days?"

The boy looked down at the dirt in the road. "No suh, ain't no one gonna miss Luke, at least nobody who don't already."

James knocked on the door at precisely eight and was met by a large black man who did not appear to be a workman. "Good morning, Mister James. Mister Key is expecting you," he said in a very deep baritone. He stood aside and motioned him in.

The lawyer was in his office, unpacking more boxes. There

were still several unopened crates on the floor. "Ah, good morning, James. Come in, come in. As you can see, I still have a lot to do here to get settled. You are doing me a great service today, a great service indeed."

James was slightly embarrassed at that. "I'm very happy to be of any help I can, Mister Key. I was raised to always repay favors, especially one such as you honor me with."

"Nonsense, James. I explained that I consider it my duty to God." Motioning towards the hallway he said, "Now, let's see what Jeffery has packed for your trip this morning."

There were several small wooden crates and a chest in the hallway, along with a stack of books that had not been boxed yet. "It doesn't look like much, but I would prefer to have these things back at Terra Rubra. Silly of me really," Key said. "I should have been more careful about what came down, I suppose."

James set about loading his cargo aboard and securing it so it wouldn't shift on the rutted roads outside of the town. A few more small boxes were added to the collection, and he was almost finished by nine.

As he was lifting the last box aboard Key came out on to the porch, smiling. "Well, that's fine James, just fine. When you're finished come into the office. I need to show you where I want you and your passenger to stay tonight."

"Passenger, Mister Key? What passenger is that?"

"Why, Abigail, of course. Didn't I mention her before? No? I'm sorry, but my wife asked me to send her back to Terra Rubra as soon as I could. Abigail practically runs the house for her. My poor wife can barely keep up with all the children and the household duties, too, so I must send her back with you." He hesitated for a moment. "You don't mind, do you James? I should think you might like a little company on such a trip."

James tied the last box down in it's place. "No, sir, I don't mind if she doesn't. Just took me by surprise is all."

"Well, come inside when you finish then, and you can be on your way."

When he came into the office Abigail was there waiting. She had a small valise as well as a large basket with her. "There you are James. Come in. Abigail has packed a nice meal for the two of you for the trip up and some extra water as well. It's already starting to warm up considerably."

James nodded to the young woman, who was watching him silently. "Good morning, Miss Abigail. I trust you are well."

"Morning, Mister James. I'm very well, thank you," she said quietly.

"Now let me show you on this map, James. You can see Terra Rubra is here. I'm sure Abigail will be able to show you the way when you get in the vicinity. It's not hard to find and the roads are very good most of the way. Now, this farm here," he said, pointing to a spot just beyond Montgomery Courthouse, "this is where my family always stays when we are traveling back and forth. They provide good quarters and meals and are used to seeing us there from time to time. I'm sure they will remember Abigail so you will have no trouble saying you are in my employ."

James looked over at the girl, then back at Key and cleared his throat. "Well, Mister Key, I hope so. I hope they won't be taken aback by two negroes asking for accommodations."

Key could see that he was a little uneasy. "Don't worry, James. Mister Thompson is a crusty old cuss, but his wife is a good God fearing woman. As a matter of fact, she is of the same church as I. We frequently read the bible together in the evening when we stay with them. She is a generous and decent person who is always kind to all of God's children."

James nodded slightly and looked towards Abigail again. "I hope you're right, sir. I have not always found church people to be so kind."

"I understand, James. Truly. You will have no trouble there, I can assure you of that. I have also written a letter explaining to anyone who may ask who you both are and that you are in my employ and not to be detained." He handed him the letter and extended his hand. "I thank you again, James. You are doing me a great service. Abigail I will see you back home soon."

They pulled away from the house in silence and turned north at the street. There were several blocks of houses to pass before they passed the stables on the way to Rock Creek Road. James finally broke the silence. "That's my place there," he said pointing. "That is both my business and my home now."

She looked at him curiously. "What do you mean your place? Does your master live there, too?"

Of course she would not know anything about him but his name. "I am not a slave, girl. I was born a free man in Pennsylvania, the same as my father."

She still had that curious gaze as she looked him over. "Never met a free born black man before. Knowed some been set free, but never one born free."

"How can that be? Washington has hundreds of free born men. You must have met some at sometime."

"Well, if I did I didn't know it. Besides, I usually stay at Terra Rubra. Only been to the city once or twice myself."

They drove on a while longer without speaking. There was clearly something on his mind. "Does Mister Key own you, girl?"

"Yassuh, he does. For almost all my life."

"I don't want you to call me sir anymore, you hear? My name is James. Just James."

"Well, I will call you James if you don't call me girl. Hows about that? I ain't hardly a girl I'll have you know. I'm twenty two years old now, and my right name is Abigail."

James laughed out loud. "All right, Abigail," he said, touching the brim of his hat, "you have yourself a deal."

She smiled and looked around at the countryside. They were starting up the first long grade out of town and the horses were taking it easily. "It's a lovely day, isn't it, James."

"It is that Abigail, it is that." He looked up the road and saw a figure standing off to the side of the road and cleared his throat. "I have a bit of a surprise. That boy up ahead is going to ride along with us if you don't mind."

She looked at him curiously again. She was not used to being asked her opinion about anything, much less permission. She could see that the figure by the road was a young boy around thirteen or fourteen. "Who is he?" she asked.

"Well, for now let's just say he's a friend of mine. He's going to help me with the cargo and such. He won't be any bother I promise."

"That there boy is a runaway, isn't he?"

They were pulling up to Luke and coming to a stop. "Does it matter?"

"Not to me it doesn't, but it just might do to some folks along the way."

James was already thinking that might be the case. The letter from Key explained the two of them, but not three. There was no way that James was going to leave the boy behind in Georgetown after all that had happened. "Well," he said, "let's just hope the subject doesn't come up."

Luke came over to meet the wagon as they drew up. He was very surprised to see Abigail, and he took off his cap and waited.

"Luke, this is Abigail. She's a house servant for the Key family and I'm taking her back to her home. Abigail, this is Luke."

"Mornin' Miss Abigail, ma'am," the boy said quietly. He was so used to thinking of himself as at the bottom of any pecking order that he called her ma'am.

"Mornin' Luke. It's a beautiful day for a ride in the country, don't you think?" She smiled down at him and he felt much better.

"Yes'm it is," he said as he climbed up on the seat. He smiled at her. "I hope I ain't bein' a bother to y'all."

They drove on for three hours or so, making small talk or just admiring the blossoming of spring in the countryside. James pulled the wagon off the road in a shady spot near a small creek. "I don't know about you two, but I'm getting to be hungry. Luke, hand me down that blanket and the big basket, please."

Abigail smiled to herself at that. Please was not a word she heard very often, even with a family as kind to her as the Keys. She was beginning to really see James for the first time. As they ate, she also took a good look at the boy. He spoke very quietly when he spoke at all and was very deferential to them both.

She also saw that he had the hands of a much older person and knew that he was very familiar with hard work, probably on a plantation. She didn't ask and he didn't say.

Luke stood up after they finished eating their lunch. "Is it all right if I go down to the creek a minute, Mister James? I'd like to wash up a bit."

They watched the boy walk off. He limped a little but otherwise radiated a very real strength. "Who is that boy, James? I mean, who is he to you?"

James thought for a moment. Who was he indeed. He was still watching the boy as he said, "He's a child who needs my help."

"He's not blood?"

Now he turned to face Abigail and shook his head slightly. "No, he's not blood. I did have a younger brother once. He was kidnapped by slavers and sold south." He was thoughtful a moment. "Maybe I want to help this boy because I couldn't help my brother, or maybe it's because…" His voice trailed off and he turned back to watch Luke. "He's a good boy, strong and reliable. I trust him to watch my business whenever I am out of town."

"Do you know where's he's from at all?"

"He doesn't say much, and I don't want to pry. He'll tell me when he's ready to, I'm sure." He stood and offered her his hand and they started to gather up their things. "I know he did not come from a good place, though. His back and legs are covered with scars." He shook his head at the memory of seeing them. "What kind of animal would beat a boy like that?"

They drove on as before for several hours, both Luke and Abigail nodding off from time to time in the warm sunshine. James was filled with an unfamiliar sense of contentment in the company of these two fellow travelers, sometimes softly humming an old song his mother had taught him years ago.

As they approached the little hamlet of Montgomery Courthouse it was getting on towards dusk. They passed through the town virtually unnoticed except for a few curious looks, from both black and white. They did not stop in the town and took the road that lead to the northwest, James breathing a sigh of relief when they were well clear.

"Are you sure you'll know the Thompson farm when we get near?" he asked Abigail.

"I'm sure, James. It's just a little piece further on up this road." She then asked the question they had all three been wondering. "What are we going to do with Luke?"

James stopped the wagon. "I don't think it would be wise for him to sleep in these woods tonight. If someone should find him there he would be taken for a runaway for sure." He handed Luke the reins and climbed in the back of the wagon. "Look, I can clear a space here on the floor between these crates. With the cover up no one will see him." He gave Luke a hard look. "You'll have to be very still, boy, not make a sound. You understand?"

"I understand, Mister James. Won't nobody know Luke is sleepin' in there."

James started to shift the cargo around. "That's good, because if anyone does find you, it will be very hard to explain." He stopped and looked at the girl. "Are you in agreement, Abigail?"

She returned his look, and once again was perplexed that anyone would ask her opinion on anything. "It's fine by me, James… thank you for asking."

They rolled in to the gate at the Thompson farm as darkness was spreading across the nearby hills. The clouds were broken, and a full moon shone through from time to time, casting shadows across the path. With the sunset the air was becoming chilly.

James set the brake and jumped down from the seat. He approached the door with his hat in his hand and knocked gently. He heard movement inside, and when the door opened he was facing an older white woman who did not seem the least surprised to see him. She held the lantern up so she could see him better.

"Do you need some shelter this evening, young man?"

"Miss Margaret, it's me Abigail," the girl called from the wagon. She climbed down and came up on the porch.

"My word, it is indeed Abigail. How are you, my dear? Is Mister Key with you tonight?"

"No ma'am, not tonight. Mister Key has hired James here to fetch me and some belongings back to Terra Rubra. He said we should stay here tonight if that's all right."

James just stood there with his hat in his hand. The woman looked him up and down, not unkindly. "Of course, my dear, of course. Have you had your supper."

"No, ma'am….."

A loud voice came from the interior of the house. "Who's there, Margaret. Who are you talking to out there?"

The woman suddenly seemed a little nervous. "Why, it's Abigail from Terra Rubra dear. She and her driver were told to stop here for the night by Mister Key."

A large man appeared behind the woman. His face was hard as he looked the two of them over, then he turned back inside. "Well, she knows where they belong," he said over his shoulder. "Give her some blankets and a lantern."

"I'm sorry, James, I should have told you. Mister Thompson doesn't allow black folks in his house" Abigail said softly.

The woman Margaret looked pained. "I am sorry, dear, but you know how he is. I still pray he will change his mulish ways, but Lord knows I'm not having much luck." She disappeared inside and returned with a pile of blankets and gave them to James. "Might be a little chilly tonight, but you should be warm enough with these."

"Thank you, ma'am, and don't worry. I'm plenty used to sleeping in a barn."

"You go on ahead and I'll bring you some supper. I'll just be a few minutes."

"Yes, ma'am." He started to turn away and stopped. "Miss Abigail here has told me what a wonderful cook you are, Miss Margaret, and I sure am hungry. Would it be rude to ask for just a little bit extra? We've had a fairly long day on the road."

She beamed at him. "Not at all, not at all. I love to cook for a hungry working man. Now you go on. I'll be along."

James led the wagon over to the paddock and unhitched the team. After leading the horses inside and seeing to their needs, he came back to the wagon.

"I'll be bringing you a blanket and some food later on, Luke," he whispered. "Now just lay quiet."

When he came into the barn, Abigail had made up the beds in two separate stalls near the back of the barn. The lantern light cast a golden glow, and he was taken by how she looked kneeling and straightening the blankets. "You take this one here, James. I'll be over there." She pulled a thick blanket from her stall. "I saved the warmest one for Luke."

The hinges on the big door groaned as they opened and Mrs. Thompson stepped in, struggling with a large tray. James sprang to her side and took the load, setting the tray on a stump against the wall. The aroma was wonderful and James said so.

"Oh, it's just some stew and fresh bread. Baked it this afternoon." She looked around the barn. "Well you two look situated."

"Yes'm. We'll be just fine. I hope we haven't been any bother to you tonight."

"No bother at all. James is it? No bother at all." She smiled sweetly at them both. "There should be enough food there for three hungry people." She turned and walked towards the door. "I'll wish you good night and may God keep you in his sight."

After she had gone, James was nervous. "What do you suppose she meant by that? How could she know there are three of us?"

"We don't have any reason to fear from her, James," Abigail said as she ladled stew into a bowl for him. She broke off a piece of bread and handed him both. "I have never known anything but kindness from her." She looked down at the tray as she was filling another bowl of stew and stopped. "Look here," she said quietly.

James came over and looked down at the tray. There were three spoons on it.

James was up just before dawn. He didn't see any light coming from the house, so he slipped into the paddock and led the team out and hitched them up. He gave a soft rap on the side of the wagon away from the house and got a soft rap in reply. A hand appeared from under the tarpaulin with a bowl and spoon, followed shortly by the blanket.

James folded the blanket quickly and went to the rear of the barn and entered through the small door there. He gave Abigail the blanket and utensils and went to the large door facing the house. A light was showing from the kitchen in the front now, and he could see a figure moving around inside.

Abigail came up behind him carrying the tray. "I'll take this on up to the house and say our goodbyes."

James nodded and went back to the paddock to bring the wagon around front. He went around the wagon, checking the security of the tarpaulin and inspecting the wheels and axles.

Mrs. Thompson and Abigail were approaching as he finished. "Thank you very kindly for everything, Miss Margaret. Abigail was certainly right about your cooking."

"I hope all of you were comfortable," she said, looking at the wagon and back to James. She took another step forward and looked up at him. "It is my duty, and my pleasure, to help any travelers that God sees fit to bring to my door, James. Now, I'm sure you're anxious to be on your way, so I won't keep you any longer. I wish you all Godspeed, and I'll say a prayer for your safe journey."

James pulled the wagon over after they had gone a mile or so and crossed over a hill. He kept looking back over his shoulder in case anyone was coming after them. Abigail kept telling him there was nothing to fear from this white woman, but he believed in being cautious just he same.

He reached back over the seat and undid one line securing the tarpaulin. Luke looked up at them, blinking in the sudden daylight. He sat up and looked around. "All right if I come up now, Mister James?"

"It's fine now, Luke. Don't worry. We're far away from town and we have the road to ourselves at the moment." He climbed down and offered his hand to Abigail, who joined him in the road. "There's a little stream over yonder. Why don't you go stretch your legs some and wash up, then we'll be on our way."

They continued northwest through the day, never stopping in a town no matter how small. They stopped for a lunch break in an open area where they could see anyone approaching and had the bread and dried meat that the farmer's wife had kindly provided them.

"We should be there in another hour or two, I think," Abigail said as the sun was sliding off to the west. She had no idea of distance, only the travel time.

"Are there any more towns or such the rest of the way?" James asked her.

"No, just some farms and a few houses, mostly scattered about. We shouldn't see anyone, and if we do it will probably be a neighbor coming or going to the market like the one in Taney Town."

They crested one of the low rolling hills and crossed another small creek. James could see larger hills or maybe small mountains out to the west. He wanted to relax and try to enjoy the rest of the trip, but the closer they got to Terra Rubra the more anxious he was becoming.

The road curved gently due north soon after crossing the stream and James could not see very far ahead. When the road straightened again, he was surprised to see three men on horseback coming slowly from the other direction. They stopped when they saw the wagon coming their way.

James kept the same pace. "Do you know these men?" he asked quietly.

"I do know the one in the middle," she replied, her voice nervous. "I ain't never seen those other two." She looked at him, her eyes wide. "That one I know…. he's a slave catcher."

It was too late to run and too late to try and hide Luke in the wagon. "We'll just go on and be about our business. Let me do the talking and stay calm."

"Hold up there, nigger. Just stop right there," the man known to Abigail said. "Who are you and what's your business here? Whose wagon did you steal?" He was grinning at them, his voice menacing.

"We's on our way up to Mister Key's place, Terra Rubra. Why, I didn't steal no wagon. This here wagon belongs to Mister Key, and so do this load," James drawled, affecting a speech pattern he had heard many times in his life.

"Don't I know you, girl? You from around these parts?"

"Yassuh, I seen you before. My name is Abigail. I be a house servant at Terra Rubra for Miss Polly."

One of the other men walked his horse over to the side of the wagon and pulled back the tarpaulin. "Just some boxes and some small furniture here, Cap'n, house stuff looks like."

James knew better than to offer anything else until spoken to. He looked at the ground most of the time but glanced up at the men to try and see what they were thinking. The big chestnut mare wanted to get moving again and stomped her front feet, shaking her head.

James gave a tug on the reins. "Hold on there, Annie girl, hold on. We'll be on our way shortly." He looked at the man that was addressed as Captain. "Sorry about that, Cap'n, but ol' Annie there gets to going, she don't want to stop," he said, trying to smile.

"And just who might you be, boy? You a runaway?"

"Oh, no sir. I live near the city, near Washington. I just drives for Mister Key and some of the other white folks from time to time is all. Like I said, Mister Key done hired us to deliver this load to his place and bring back another."

"You got any proof of that? I can't be takin' the word of no nigger,"

"Yes sir, Cap'n, I surely do." James reached under the seat and pulled out a small bag. He fished around for a moment then handed him the letter from Key.

The man looked disappointed and grunted under his breath. He took the letter, unfolded it and looked it over closely. He then looked at Luke. "Anything in this letter about that boy?"

James realized then that the man could not read. "Oh, yes sir, Cap'n, sure should be. This here is my nephew Luke. Mister Key done hired him as well, you know to help with the loadin' and the drivin'."

The three men walked off a few paces and talked about the situation, one of the men looking back at Luke, then they came back and handed James the letter.

"I think maybe we better take you all down to Frederick Town and see about this. It don't feel right to me," the captain said.

"Now Cap'n," Abigail spoke up. "Y'all know me, you seen me around with the Key family and we are here doin' work for them right now. They are expecting us this afternoon and will be mighty unhappy if we don't show up. Course, if you want to have a dispute with lawyer Key, that's your own business."

James met the man's stare for just a moment, then looked away. It wouldn't do to try and stare down a white man, especially this far from home. The three rode a few steps off again and talked. The only thing James could hear was when the youngest one said, "Hell, if there ain't no reward, what do we want with a wagon full of niggers? Let's just keep searching."

The men came back, and this time did not block their path. "Go on and git, then. You best be at Terra Rubra by dark, you hear? We don't like niggers moving about after dark 'round here. It makes it hard to see 'em." He had that malevolent grin on again, the others laughing at his joke.

James put the letter back under the seat. "Yes sir, Cap'n. We'll keep on goin'. No doubt we'll be there by dark. Thank you, Cap'n."

James slapped the reins on the horses backsides, and they started to move off slowly. "Come on, Annie girl, time to get back to work. That's it, that's a girl." He gave them one more gentle slap. "Do not look back," James hissed under his breath.

When they had gone another mile, James stopped the wagon and climbed down. He pretended to check one of the wheels, all the time sneaking looks back the way they had come. There was no sign of the slave hunters. He came back and patted Annie on her rump, looking up at the two of them.

"You two are about as pale as I've ever seen a black person look," he said, chuckling. "Girl, I mean, Abigail," he said, bowing slightly, "where'd you learn to bluff like that?"

Luke looked like he might vomit. His hands were shaking and his voice thin. "I thought we was goners, Mister James, I truly did." He took a deep breath and let it out slowly.

Abigail laughed nervously. "I don't know what came over me. I ain't never spoke to no white man like that." She looked down at James, smiling. "And where'd you ever learn to talk like a slave, anyway?"

The taste of it was still bitter on his tongue. He shook his head and said, "Sometimes it's better to let white folks think the worst, that you aren't educated at all. Did you see that dumb son of a bitch? He couldn't even read the letter…" His voice trailed off as he realized that neither of them could read either. "I'm sorry. I didn't mean to offend. It's just that most of the white folks I know can read, that's all."

"It's again' the law to teach a slave to read or write where I come from," Luke said quietly. "Even the bible."

James climbed back up and sighed deeply. "I know, Luke, I know. I'll just have to find a way…"

The sun was just sliding down in the west and the day warm when they pulled the wagon into the lane leading to the house. It was a choice piece of land, James could see, with gently rolling hills and a good sized stream at the bottom. There were several small houses back off the lane with the main house at the top. It wasn't as elegant as James had envisioned on the ride up. It was actually very spartan but had a large porch that wrapped around two sides, with views off to the south and west. There were several small children in the yard, and they came running up when they spotted the wagon.

"Abigail! It's Abigail, it's Abigail," a little girl shouted to the others. James had to stop the wagon for fear of running one of them over. "Did you bring us something from the city, Abigail?"

"I certainly did, children. I brought you hugs and kisses from your Papa." She reached under the seat and brought out a small, bright box, "And some of this, too."

The children were very excited. They knew the box held some hard candy from Mister Jenkins' store that their father had purchased for them. He always sent the same kind. "Oh, please, please, can we have some now, Abigail?" a little tow headed boy cried out.

Abigail affected a stern look. "Now children, you know you have to ask your Momma and she will say you have to wait 'til after dinner."

The oldest child, a girl with tight rings in her hair, went running off towards the house shouting, "Mama, Mama, Abigail's home. Come see."

A moment later a slender woman came out on the porch, shielding her eyes from the sun getting ready to set in the west. When she saw Abigail she smiled.

"Praise the Lord, it is Abigail." She came to the wagon and embraced her warmly. "I have missed you so. These children have been keeping me busy, and that new house girl in no replacement for you. She's just a child herself."

The children were all clustering around Abigail, obviously very glad to see her. Abigail seemed very happy to be with them as well, James noticed. He also noticed she had a very sweet and gentle smile.

"It's very nice to be home again, Miss Polly." She bent and lifted the littlest one up. "Have you been wearing your Momma out, Edward?" she laughed.

James and Luke were climbing down from the wagon. "I don't know if you remember me, Miss Polly," James said. "My stables are near your old place in Georgetown. I serve with your husband in the militia."

"Of course I do, James. Of course I do. Who is this?" she asked, motioning towards Luke. "Is he here to help out?"

James nudged him forward. Although the woman was looking at him very kindly he still was worried and frightened. His contacts with other whites had not often gone well. He took off his hat, looking at the ground. "Yes'm. Mister James brought me along to help him. My name's Luke." He did not look up.

"Well, welcome to Terra Rubra to you both." She walked over to the wagon and looked over the side. "My goodness. Did we not just have these things sent to town? What was my husband thinking?"

Abigail explained the situation to her mistress, about how the work on the house was going and that her husband had decided he would rather have these things back here. The two women started to walk up to the house, all the children crowding around them.

"Well, James, why don't you men bring those things in after you rest a bit, then you can take the wagon and team down to the barn and see to them. Abigail, I have some things to show you in the kitchen."

As they were unloading their cargo, James was getting concerned with Luke. It would not be a good idea to take him back to Georgetown, and he certainly knew he could not leave him here. The only blacks at Terra Rubra were slaves. Even though some were called "house servants" they were still slaves held in bondage. No, he would have to come up with an idea and soon. They were expected to leave tomorrow for the city.

They finished unloading and took the wagon and team of horses down to the barn. It was probably the most recent building on the estate, with a large paddock surrounded by new fences. There were three other horses in the paddock as they led them in, and like horses do, they came over to see the newcomers.

James truly loved these big animals. They were so majestic, so calm. He was stroking a large shining black gelding down it's mane, speaking gently to it. "He's a beauty, don't you think?" he asked Luke.

James had never really seen Luke smile before, but he certainly was now. "Hey big fella," Luke said, patting the horse on the rump. "He surely is Mister James. This is one beautiful animal."

"Do you have much experience with horses? I mean, besides helping out at the stables?"

"Oh, yes sir Mister James. Back in Virginia I took care of a bunch of horses, all different kinds of horses." The memory of the animals made him smile again. "Horses, they don't care if you be black or white or anything. They just knows when someone loves them. They don't ask for much, horses don't."

A plan was beginning to form in James' mind. He would have to speak to Abigail about it later. He would need her help in the morning to make it work.

They pulled the wagon over to the west side of the paddock and out of the way. After it was secure, they started to explore the area around the barn. There were a few small cabins there as well, probably the slave quarters James assumed. He noticed that although they were small and modest, they were clean and looked comfortable. The largest of them had smoke curling from the chimney and a wonderful aroma coming from the open window at the back that lured them.

As they approached the house, an older black woman appeared at the window. "Who you two be?" she asked. She was looking them over carefully. "You supposed to be here abouts?"

They both took off their caps and came closer. "Yes, ma'am," James said. "We just brought up some cargo for Mister Key from the house in the city." He craned his neck to try and see in the window. "Something sure smells mighty good in there, ma'am."

"You hungry too, boy?" she asked, looking at Luke suspiciously.

Luke was looking down at the dirt, still holding his hat in his hand. "Yes'm, I surely is. Didn't know how much until I smelt it." He looked up and smiled nervously.

"I don't likes havin' no hungry men around here," she said sternly. Then her face brightened up. "No, sir, don't want no hungry men around here... so why don't you two boys come on in and let me feed you." Her smile dominated her face. "Go on now. Door's around the front there."

They walked around to the front as fast as they could without running and stopped on the porch. The door was wide open and they peeked inside. It wasn't an individual house after all but had several tables in the front room and a kitchen in the back. The whole place smelled wonderful.

The woman appeared in the doorway to the kitchen. "My name is Molly and I does most of the cookin' round here for the help. Theys out working now but will be back before long. You boys take a seat and I'll bring you in some food."

"May I help in any way?" James asked.

Molly's head snapped back a bit. "Ain't you the fancy one? No sir, Molly don't need no help feeding folks." She started back towards the kitchen, then turned. "But thank you kindly for askin'. What's you boys names?"

"My name is James, and this boy here is my nephew Luke. We live in Georgetown."

"Well, I knowed that you wasn't no country man with that fancy talk. Don't know 'bout him, though, he don't say much does he? Now sit yourselves down and let me get you your supper."

She reappeared moments later with two large steaming plates and set them on the table. "When's the last time you boys had a hot meal, anyways?" she asked. "Never mind. The water barrel is over in the corner there. You go on and helps yourselves."

As they were mopping up the last bit on their plates, Abigail came in and looked around. "Well, I see you two found the cookin' house and Molly all right." She came over and stood by their table. "That woman is a legend around these parts, I'll have you know."

"Any woman who can cook like this deserves to be a legend anywhere she chooses," James said, trying without luck to mop up more sauce. "That was unbelievable." He looked at her sheepishly. "Don't suppose there's any more, is there?"

"Don't rightly know… let's ask. Momma, these boys say they still be hungry."

Molly appeared in the door again, her smile as bright as the noon day sun. "Oh, Abigail, my own Abigail." The two women hugged each other warmly. "I didn't know you was back already."

She pushed her daughter away, feigning anger. "Now what you been doin' that you couldn't tell your poor old Momma you was back home?"

"Miss Polly had me up to the house, Momma. She was showing me some new things in the kitchen, asking after Mister Key and telling me all about what the children been up to. I came down as soon as I could, honest Momma."

"Well, sit yourself down and have your supper before the rest of them are back from the fields." She looked at the two men. "And I suppose you want some more, too."

"Yes, ma'am," they said in unison and laughed.

Molly looked down at Luke. She knew more about him in just a few minutes than James had been able to learn in months. "You know child, you have a very nice smile. You ought to use it a little more often."

The other hands began drifting in as they were finishing the meal. There were some curious looks from some of them. They all seemed glad to see Abigail back in the fold. She went around and spoke with all of them in turn, telling them about the trip up and who James and Luke were.

It was a beautiful late spring evening with just a slight chill that was kept at bay by a small bonfire. The sky was clear and stars filled the sky. Abigail was showing James and Luke around, introducing them as the meals were finished and everyone started to gather outside around the fire. It wasn't long before a harmonica appeared in the hands of a young man who started to put it to good use.

Luke seemed to know the songs as they came and joined in the clapping and singing as the workers sought to put the day's toiling behind them and have some fun. Most of the men came by and spoke to Luke, smiling and patting his back. James noticed they only nodded at him, not in an unfriendly way at all, but not the same way they treated Luke. It was almost like they were being deferential to him in a way that they weren't with Luke.

James sat back and watched for a while before it dawned on

him. These were Luke's people. They were slaves just as he was, they shared the knowledge and the burden of bondage, something he had never known. It was almost like a secret society that he was not a part of. He knew that he was welcome here, that he was among friends, but he also knew he was not a member of this family. He had known bigotry, hatred and mistrust Lord knew, but he had never had to face being actually owned and controlled by another. He smiled as he watched Luke enjoying himself and was happy for him.

Abigail saw James watching Luke and came and sat beside him. "I've never seen him so comfortable around other people before," James said. "It's like he's with family."

"Why Mister James, he is with family," she said, mocking him just a bit. She looked out over the group and said, "These people know him better than you do. They could tell you his life story down to the last detail."

"Abigail, we have to talk tonight before everyone retires. It's about Luke." He looked around, but no one was listening to them. "It's not safe for him to go back to Georgetown with me. There was some trouble there before we left. Bad trouble."

"Is he in danger?"

"I believe he will be if he goes back, but I have an idea." He thought for a moment. "I don't know why I didn't see it before, it's so obvious." He leaned in a little closer. "I'm going to need your help. Can I count on you?"

"Let's us go for a walk, James," Abigail said. "I have my room up in the big house. They need me around at all hours to help with the children and such. You can walk me up."

It was chilly away from the fire. No one seemed to notice them leaving as they walked out to the drive up to the house. When they were sure there was no one around, she turned to him. "What kind of trouble is that boy in, James?"

"He killed a man, a white man." He went on and explained what had happened at the stables that morning and how he had told Luke to leave before the law came. "So, basically, they think I did it."

"Who were those men?"

"They were slavers. They were trying to kidnap both of us and sell us south." He took a deep breath and let it out slowly. "That's what happened to my younger brother Jonathan about four years ago, right after I left the farm for the city. I told you about him." He was looking straight ahead, trying to control his emotions. "He was freeborn same as me, but that didn't matter to them. I don't know where he is or even if he's still alive."

Abigail put her hand on his arm and stopped him. It was very dark except for the light of the nearly full moon. She tried to see his face, but he had turned away from her. She reached up and gently turned his face to hers. "I'm so sorry, James, so very sorry." She now felt she knew why he had taken such an interest in this boy, this runaway.

Now she took a deep breath and let it out slowly, never taking her eyes off his. "How can I help?" she asked quietly.

"My father's farm is not far across the border in Pennsylvania. He lives alone after Jonathan was kidnapped and then mother died. He is doing poorly and last I saw him he didn't have much life left in him."

"I thought you said your family was from Massachusetts."

"My mother and father were born there. My father fought in the revolution with an all colored regiment from Connecticut, the Fourth. He was in the fighting all over those parts. He was even in the trenches during the fighting at Yorktown and was there when the British surrendered."

They had started to walk slowly up the drive again. "After the war, my father decided he didn't want to be anywhere near that kind of thing again ever, around all that anger and killing. He took his bonus money and what little he and mother could scrape together, and he bought some farmland out west. I believe it's not all that far from here. He just wanted to go live in peace and work his land, and he found a place far from any kind of trouble." He smiled at the memory of growing up there, he and his brother free as birds.

"It sounds like heaven, it truly does. And you want to take Luke there?"

"I was an idiot not to think of it sooner. My father needs someone to look after and to help him live again, and Luke needs a quiet place where no one knows him or where he's from. The farm is perfect. It is the one place I know of where trouble will never come, ever. There is a small town nearby with a tavern and inn and a blacksmith." He shrugged. "I just can't imagine anything intruding on the peace of that place."

"How are you going to get him there? How far away is it? You know they expect you'll be going south in the morning with a load on the wagon."

"They way I figure it has to be no more than a day's ride from here. It must be. I can take him up and come right back the next day. I just need you to explain to them about me being gone."

"What do I say?"

"You can tell the truth. Just tell them I left at dawn to visit my ailing father, but you can't tell them where I went. Just say I told you he lives somewhere west of here, and I'll be back as soon as possible."

"I don't know, James. Miss Polly might get suspicious."

"Suspicious of what? I am going to visit my ailing father, that part is true. I'd just rather no one know which way I went in case anyone comes looking for Luke later. Doesn't Miss Polly trust you?"

"I believe she does, yes," she said. "I'll do what you ask, James. I don't want to see no harm come to that boy."

"Neither do I, Abigail, neither do I. I have to do whatever I can for him. Maybe then…"

She put her hand on his arm again and stopped him just as they came up to the porch. "You need to be gone when the hands start out to the fields, and that's mighty early."

"We'll be a mile from here when the sun comes up, I promise."

She smiled at him. "What is the name of this peaceful little town of yours? This place that will never know war and killing? I just might like to go there myself someday."

71

"It's called Gettysburg. Now go on in and I'll see you in two days time."

James was true to his word. They had the team hitched to the wagon and were about an hour away when the first rays of the sun broke over the eastern horizon. There were storm clouds ahead to the west, however, along with a stiff breeze that promised more to come.

James had explained the plan to Luke when he came back from walking Abigail up to the main house. Luke was clearly nervous about the thought of being out on the road again after the encounter on the way up.

"Maybe this weather will help us out, keep people off the road for a bit," James said. "Not much of a day for anyone to be out hunting."

Luke was silent, remembering the fear he felt when the men had stopped them the day before. "I ain't never goin' back," he said quietly, looking straight ahead. "Never. I'd rather be dead in the ground before I be a slave again."

James started to say he understood, but he realized he really didn't. "Don't worry, boy, I won't let that happen. You can count on me."

"Mister James, what if them slavers or some others comes to your father's farm some time? What then?"

James chuckled at that. "I pity any fool slaver that comes on my father's land. I can promise you that man would be dead long before he even hit the ground. My father was a soldier and a damn good one. He isn't shy about protecting what's his, and that's a fact."

"I sure hope you're right," Luke said quietly as they drove on into the approaching storm.

Later that morning the clouds opened up and the rain came down in sheets, blown into their faces by a strong west wind. The rain was turning the road to mud and spooking the horses as well, so they looked for any place where they could shelter. The rain cut the visibility to a few hundred feet, but James thought he saw a dilapidated barn or house off to their left in a small open field.

"Let's go see if we can ride this out over there," he said, turning the horses off the road. There was no lane of any kind, but the ground was still firm enough so they didn't leave any obvious tracks.

When they got closer they could see it was an abandoned barn with the burned remains of a small house a short distance away. There was only one door on the front, and Luke jumped down to open it as James drove the wagon inside. He set the brake and went to help Luke close the door behind them.

Trying to see out to the road again was a waste of time as the rain was coming even harder now. "I hope this doesn't last too long," James said. "We have to keep moving."

James went back to the horses and did his best to calm them. He was grateful there had been no thunder, just rain and wind. "Settle down now, Annie girl," he said quietly to his mare. "We'll just rest here a bit, let the storm pass." He stroked the forehead of the other animal, and they seemed to feel his calmness. He went to the wagon and put some oats in feedbags and strapped them on.

Looking around at the barn, James saw there was a hay loft with a number of missing floor boards. "Why don't we go up there and wait it out. Maybe we can keep an eye on the road as well if it lets up any."

They found a nice dry spot that also had a view to the east and settled in. The rain had a hypnotic effect after a while and James began to nod off. Suddenly Luke was shaking him. "Look there, Mister James," he said, pointing towards the road.

James was disoriented for a second. He had no idea how long he might have been dozing off. He wiped his eyes and followed Luke's hand. There was a lone figure on horseback, riding slowly under a piece of canvas. The horse he was riding looked very much like one that one of the slavers had been riding the day before.

They saw him stop and look towards the barn. The rain started to slack off as suddenly as it had begun, and the entire world was strangely quiet now. They could see the man shake off his rain gear, then he started to look down at the side of the road.

"He's looking for tracks," James whispered, even though the man was a good fifty yards away. "I don't believe he'll find any after all that rain."

Sure enough, the rider gave their hiding place one more hard look, then started to ride off again slowly, heading back the way they had come from. They watched him go in silence until he was out of sight. James noticed that Luke's hands were shaking.

"It's all right now. He's gone. We'll give him a few more minutes, then we better be on our way," James said. Luke nodded agreement.

They picked up the pace when they got back on the road, trying to put as much distance as they could between them and the lone rider. The rain had stopped, but they could see more clouds not too far off to the west.

They came to a small rise in the terrain and could see the village of Emmitsburg ahead, smoke rising from some of the chimneys but otherwise no activity. Luke was worried. "Can't we go around somehow, Mister James?"

"I don't see how. The road turns pretty sharp to the north down there and we can be across the border into Pennsylvania soon after. We'll be safer there."

Luke swallowed hard and nodded. They let the horses set the pace down the road into town, and as they neared the rain started again. There were only a few small buildings on the road and no one outside in the wet weather. They were through and gone in a few minutes. James was certain no one had even noticed their passing, and he breathed a sigh of relief.

The rain fell steadily but not as hard as it did in the morning. They wrapped up in some canvas and blankets to no avail. It was cold and bitter, but they both knew the rain was on their side.

The road continued north over softly rolling hills, one after another like gentle waves. As they crested one of the larger ones, the sky opened and the sun managed to peek through the scattering clouds.

James stopped to rest the horses and survey the scene. The visibility behind the storm was improving, and off in the distance he could just make out a familiar round knob and smiled. "I know where we are now, exactly where we are," he said and clapped Luke on the back. "Jonathan and I used to hunt at the base of that little mountain over there," he said, pointing to the round knob. "We're in Pennsylvania, boy!"

The sky and their mood both lightened considerably as they went on. They had lost some time in the weather and the sun was just starting to head west. After another hour, James turned off the road onto a small, rutted lane that went due west as well.

"See that place yonder there?" James said, pointing to a small but very neat little house and barn set well back off the lane. There were cleared fields all around, a small fence separating the land from the lane. "That's Mister McGregor's place, and that one just over there, that's the Owen place."

Luke had never really seen farms like these. The one he ran away from was much larger and it was surrounded by a motley collection of ramshackle little farms where poor white's tried to eke out a living. These places were well tended to, the land clear and level. He liked what he was seeing.

"Most folks around here are Scots and Irish, good hardworking people, decent people. They don't hold with slavery and don't much care for folks that do."

"Where's your daddy's place?"

"Just another mile or so up ahead," James said. "We have a creek to cross and one more little rise, and we'll be home."

Luke looked over at him. He had never once in his short life considered the concept of home. He was born a slave at another man's home. He had run away from there and lived wherever and however he could. The idea of anyplace actually being home was something new to him, and he let the idea sink in slowly. "Home," he said softly.

When they got to the top of the next rise, James stopped again and pointed to a line of trees off to their right. "See that smoke there? That's home, boy, home."

Luke could see an opening in the fence up ahead, and James turned the team there. The path from the lane to the house had obviously not been used much lately and was a little overgrown. They could see the house up ahead, but no sign of life other than the thin wisp of smoke coming up from the chimney.

James stopped the wagon, handing Luke the reins. He jumped down from the seat and bounded up on to the little porch. He was calling out to his father as he opened the door and went inside.

His eyes took a moment to adjust to the darkness. The place was in disarray, with cooking and eating things piled up on a counter and a pile of clothes on the bed. The fire was starting to die down, and he went and threw a few more small pieces of wood into the stove.

He came back out to the porch and looked over at the small barn. A man was just coming out, blinking in the sunlight. He froze for just a moment, then he started to cross the little yard, his arms coming up from his side. "Oh, Lord, is that my boy? Is that my son?" he called, hurrying towards him with arms outstretched. "Oh, Lord."

They embraced there in the yard, tears pouring down from them both. "It's me, father, it's really me." James could feel his father sobbing softly, and just held him for all he was worth.

When the horses were tended to they all went inside. James and Luke were still soaked, but they didn't feel any chill. They pulled some chairs closer to the little stove so they could dry off and talk.

James had introduced Luke to his father while they were tending to the animals but had not had time to tell him Luke's story. Mister Woodman was watching Luke closely in an inquisitive way.

As soon as they settled in their chairs, James' father said, "Luke's a runaway, isn't he?"

"Yes, sir, he is," James said, "but there's more to it than that. Much more."

They proceeded to tell the older man about the slavers coming to kidnap them. The father looked especially pained and angry at this. When they got to the killings, he smiled. "I've done my share of killing, I am not proud to say. It was war and I was defending my country. I took no pleasure in it, but I am glad those monsters are dead, and I hope they rot in hell forever."

"Well, my friend Daniel and I told Luke to get away and stay away and told the constable that just the two of us were there. Daniel is a white man, and I think that helped sway him, but he strongly suspects that maybe Luke was there just the same."

The father looked Luke up and down. "Then it's not safe for him to go back, is it?" James shook his head. "Well then, he'll just have to stay here with me is all. That all right with you, son?" he said, looking at Luke.

No man had ever called Luke son before, not once, and he was confused for a moment, thinking the older man was speaking to James. The father put his hand on the boy's knee. "I said, is that all right with you, son?"

"I..I..yes sir," Luke said quietly. Then he stood up. "I won't be no trouble to you, sir. I'm a hard worker. I'm good with horses and I can do field work and I can fix most anything..."

"It's fine, son, fine." He looked him up and down again and turned to James. "I still have Jonathan's things in a trunk. I think they should fit him pretty close." He walked over to the bed and pulled a small trunk from underneath.

"Come on over here and let's see how these things fit you." He held a shirt up to Luke, then a light jacket. "Yes, these should do him just fine."

There was still some daylight, so they went outside to look around the property a bit. James could see that his father had not done much in the way of upkeep lately. The barn was missing a few boards, two of the fence rails in the paddock were down and the fields had not been worked at all to get ready for the growing season.

The father could read his son's mind. "I know what you're thinking, James, but it just hasn't been the same since…." his voice trailed off. "After you left for the city Jonathan and I kept the place up. We had good crops every year. We raised a few cows for milk and meat, ran a few horse too. I don't know, son. After he was taken and your mother died, I guess my heart just wasn't in it anymore."

"You don't have to say anything. I'm sorry I've been so far away, trying to make a life for myself in town."

"You never really did like farm living, did you?"

"I liked it fine when we were children here. Jonathan and I could not have asked for a better life than the one you and mother gave us. But I guess I just wanted to go see the world some is all."

His father looked at him and smiled. "I understand, son. You may find this hard to believe, but I was a young man myself once. Was a long time ago, but I can still remember what it felt like."

They were watching Luke as he looked around the farm. He had an odd look on his face, almost like he was trying to really understand it all.

"What do you think, son? You want to live here with me and work this place? It's nothing but hard work but you'll be safe here, maybe even save some money for yourself."

It was clear Luke had not even considered the thought of money. "You don't have to pay me nothin' Mister Woodman. I'm just happy to be here on this beautiful farm with you."

"I didn't say anything about payment, son. We'll be partners, you and I. We'll work together and share whatever we earn. Does that sound fair?"

"I..I I don't rightly know what to say, sir."

"Then say yes and shake my hand. Partner."

Tears were streaming down Luke's face as he took the father's hand. He could not find any words.

James smiled at the two of them. "I think he likes the idea, father, yes, I do believe he likes it just fine." He also noticed his father looked years younger than he did even an hour ago.

The older man was not used to cooking for more than one, but he managed to put together a nice dinner for them all. Luke had never seen a man prepare a meal before and he was pleasantly surprised how tasty it was. "Mister Woodman, sir, can you teach me to cook like this?" Luke asked. "I never learned nothin' about cookin'."

"You'll learn a lot more than cooking working on this farm with me, son, a lot more. You said you knew about horses. Know anything about cows or growing things?"

"Ain't been around cows much, but I've done my share of field work."

James met his fathers eyes. "I imagine you've done much more than your share, son, much more. You'll work plenty hard here, don't fool yourself. But at the end of the day, you will have something to show for it besides sore muscles, I can promise you that."

"You won't be sorry, Mister Woodman…. And I can promise you that."

They talked over arrangements as they ate, then went outside before the evening became too chilly. The sun was well down by now and the sounds of the country were like music. James' father came out on the porch with a bottle of Madeira wine.

"Been saving this for a while, waiting for a good reason to bring it out. This looks like a good enough excuse to me, gentlemen."

After he poured them all a glass, with the smallest going to Luke, he raised his glass. "I would like to drink a toast, a toast to this fine young man who providence has seen fit to bring to me here. And I would like to drink to this farm. I've been here many years now, but I feel it's best days are still ahead. I know it will, like the Phoenix, rise from the ashes and be an oasis for many years to come."

They stood on the porch in silence for a moment, just soaking in the beauty of the Pennsylvania night and the good feelings about the future. "Well, I guess we better turn in. James, you have an early departure if you're to get back to the Key place, and Luke, you have a full day ahead of you as well."

James was a little more than an hour down the road before the sun started to peek over the horizon. The day was dawning bright and clear, with no sign of the rain they rode through on the way up. He wasn't too worried about anybody interfering with him. After all, he had Key's letter and he was on the way to Terra Rubra, not going away.

It was still early morning when he passed through Emmitsburg again and took the road east. He passed the old barn they had sheltered in. Still no signs of life there. He was curious about the people who had lived there as he passed by. Who were they? Where did they go when the house burned? He would probably never know.

It was the middle of the afternoon when he turned off the road and into the lane up to Terra Rubra. Once again the yard was full of children playing, both black and white. As he came up to the house, the children all came running over to see who was visiting. The commotion brought Abigail out on to the porch, wiping her hands on her apron.

She smiled when she saw him and waved. "Welcome back, James. How was your trip?" She came down from the porch and looked up at him. "Is Luke all right?" she asked quietly.

James nodded as he set the brake and climbed down from the wagon. "Except for the rain it was an easy drive," he said loud enough for anyone listening to hear. Then he added quietly, "Luke's fine, he's safe."

They heard the door of the house open and Miss Polly came out to see what was happening. "Children, you go on back and play and leave James alone now. I'm sure he's tired after all the driving he's been doing."

"Good afternoon, Miss Polly. I hope I haven't inconvenienced you with my extra journey. I don't get a chance to see my father very much anymore."

"That's quite all right James, really. How is your father, may I ask?"

"Well ma'am, he's getting on now and is starting to show it some. He's trying his best to keep the farm going but it's getting harder for him."

She looked around the yard. "Where's that helper of yours? Didn't he go there with you?"

"Yes, ma'am, he did." He hesitated just a second. "Truthfully, ma'am, I left Luke there on my father's farm. Like I said, he's getting on a bit and the place needs a young man's work to keep it up."

"Won't he be missed back home? Won't his folks there worry about him at all?"

"Luke doesn't have any family, ma'am. He stays in my stables sometimes and I give him work when I can," James said, shrugging.

"I see," Miss Polly said curtly. "Yes, I think I see. Abigail, come inside the house. We have pies in the oven." She turned and went back inside.

Abigail shot him a worried glance and headed for the porch. "Yes'm Miss Polly."

James unhitched the horses and led them back down the lane to the paddock, leaving the wagon in front of the house to be loaded. After they were properly tended to, he started walking back towards the house. Abigail met him halfway up.

She was flustered. "Miss Polly wants to see you right now, James."

"I was just coming up. Is anything wrong?"

"She asked me was Luke a runaway slave. I said not that I knew, I only just met him on the trip up here from the city."

"Well, you told her the truth then. I'll go talk to her and start getting the wagon loaded." He touched her on the arm. "Don't worry, Abigail, everything will be fine. You didn't tell anyone where the farm is, did you?"

"I just said I didn't know exactly. You had told me it was west of here somewhere, but I didn't know where."

James waited on the porch while Abigail went inside. Miss Polly came out a minute later, her face tense. James stood there with his hat in his hand, waiting.

"Is that boy Luke a runaway slave, James? Is that why you brought him here, to help him run away from his master?"

James decided it was time for his uneducated act. "Oh, no Miss

Polly. Luke, he ain't no runaway. He's just a boy with no home to go to is all."

"Where is his family?"

"I don't rightly know, Miss Polly. I ain't never heard of anyone that's met them. He's just living where he can."

"You know very well how Mister Key and I feel about all this. We don't brook any runaways or abolitionists at all. If that boy turns out to be a runaway Mister Key will be more than angry with you."

"Yes'm I believe he would be, but he ain't no runaway,"

"We don't hold with any kidnappers either. You know my husband has helped several black folks fight for their rights and keep their freedom. But the law is the law. We didn't make the law, but we all have to live with it. For now, anyway."

"Yes, ma'am, I understand that."

She gave him another hard look. "Well, come inside then, let me show you what you need to take to town with you."

They went inside and she showed him a collection of small crates. "These are all china, James, so I'll need you to take extra care with them. Over there are some more of Mister Key's law books and such," she said, pointing into the next room. "There's also a small table and two large chairs."

James was looking at everything, mentally loading the wagon. "Is that all, Miss Polly? I should be able to fit all this and some more if you needs me to."

She thought for a moment. "No, that should be all. I'll let you know this evening if I think of anything else." She started to walk away, then turned. "I do hope your friend is safe, and James, I prefer it when you speak proper English."

James loaded the larger items in the wagon along with the books. He would load the more fragile things just before he left in the morning. The sun was just about down to the horizon as he covered the wagon with the tarpaulin. He realized he was suddenly hungry and looked down towards the cooking house below. He was glad to see the smoke coming out of the chimney and knew Molly would be working her magic.

He went around to the back of the big house and knocked at the kitchen. Abigail answered, still wearing a flour smattered apron and wiping her hands. She smiled when she saw him standing there.

"Would you tell Miss Polly I'm done for now? I'll load the rest in the morning and wait to hear if she wants to add anything else."

Miss Polly suddenly appeared behind Abigail, wiping her hands on her apron as well. "That's fine, James. I only have one more small box for you to deliver. I'll set it by the china crates."

"Thank you, Miss Polly. If there's nothing else then, I thought I might go down and see what Molly is working on."

"Why don't you go with him, Abigail. I'm sure your mother could use some help, and I can finish up in here. You go on along."

They strolled down the lane towards the collection of little houses below. It was growing darker now and the air was getting brisk. Abigail had a wrap which she pulled around her shoulders. "It's a beautiful evening, isn't it, James?"

James was lost in thought. Life was so different out here in the country side. The air smelled sweet and the sky seemed larger somehow. He took a deep breath. "It certainly is that," he said. "Have you lived here all of your life?"

"Pretty much. The Key family bought me and my mother when I was just a baby. They were decent enough to keep us together."

James thought about that perspective for a while. This slave girl was grateful for what should have been a normal thing for any decent person to do. He knew, of course, that breaking up families was a regular occurrence when you were just someone else's property. He shook his head. "It's beautiful country around here."

They were out of sight of the house now, and Abigail put her hand on his arm and stopped him. "You're a good man, James. You care about others and are willing to take risks for them." She reached up and kissed him lightly on the cheek. "I'm proud to know you," she said and started to walk slowly down the lane again.

James didn't know what to say or do just then. He put his hand to his cheek where she had kissed him, then hurried after her. He took her arm in his and together they walked on.

The cookhouse had a wonderful aroma issuing from inside. Molly was in the kitchen and some of the hands were already back from the fields and gathering around the front porch.

Abigail stuck her head in the doorway to the kitchen. "You need any help in there, Momma? I'm done up to the house already."

"Well girl, you can start layin' out the things for the table and help me serve." She looked out the doorway and saw James. "Where's that boy of yours? Where's that Luke at?"

"I left him at my father's place out west of here."

Molly cocked her head to the side and looked at him. "You mean that you took him from the city and then left him at your daddy's place?"

"Yes, ma'am. My father is getting old and I thought maybe he could use a little help is all. Luke doesn't have any family to speak of."

She knew that he was only telling half the truth, that the boy was a runaway after all, just as she and the others had suspected. James had gotten him out of the city and further away from the clutches of the slavers. She came out and gave him a big hug, gently humming a slow spiritual tune as she did. She looked over at her daughter. "I love this man," she said.

"I know, Momma. I think maybe I do, too."

It had been a hard trip back to Georgetown. The sky was spitting rain as he pulled into his own stables again. Annie seemed to pick up her pace as they got closer and he had to slow her down a bit. When he unhitched the team out in the paddock, she started for her own stall in the rear of the big barn.

It was approaching nightfall. He had taken a bit of a chance pushing on to try and get home while it was still legal for a black man to be on the streets, and he had made it with not much time to spare. He left the covered wagon in the paddock and went inside to his small quarters and sat on the bed.

It had been hard for him to leave Terra Rubra. He tried to be as quiet as possible so as not to disturb any of the occupants of the big house, but as he was finishing he noticed through the window a single lit candle making it's way to the front door.

When the door opened, Abigail was standing there looking sad. "I wonder if I'll ever see you again, James."

"If it's in my power to make it happen, you will," he said, stepping back up on the porch, keeping his voice down. "You know I have to get back now. Mister Key is expecting me, and the feeling is the British will be attacking soon. My duty now is with my militia unit."

Abigail nodded, her head hanging down. When she looked up there were tears in her eyes. "I understand," she said quietly.

He reached out to take her hands, but she threw her arms around his neck and held him tightly. "I can't stand the thought I might not see you again." Before he could respond, she kissed him on the lips. Stepping back inside the house she whispered, "Please come back to me James," and closed the door softly.

He had spent a good deal of time on the drive back thinking about that kiss and they way she felt in his arms, the smell of her hair. He lay back on the bed and closed his eyes now that he was home, thinking.

It was no use. Everything was a jumble in his mind. He got up and went out to inspect everything and make sure the boarded animals had been cared for properly. After a while he was satisfied that they had been well tended to. His morning was going to come very early and he was bone tired. He went back to his bed and this time fell fast asleep.

He awoke while it was still dark outside and was momentarily disoriented. He had been dreaming of being back on the farm with his younger brother. They had been out fishing for their dinner, but when they went back to the house there was no one there, no sign of anyone at all.

He sat up on the edge of the bed, wiping the sleep from his eyes and trying to figure out the dream. It had all seemed so real.

"No sense sitting here, I guess," he said to himself and stood up and stretched, then went out through the stables to the big doors.

The doors faced slightly north of east. It was his favorite place to watch the sunrise. He busied himself with chores for a bit, then came back to watch the sky change. He never got tired of the miracle that was sunrise, and today it was especially colorful.

He went back and greeted his big mare. "Good morning my beauty. Are you ready to greet the day yet?"

Annie stomped her hoofs and backed out of her stall. She nuzzled him with her nose then made for the front door. James roused all the others and soon the paddock was full of drowsy horses. He pulled a bale of hay outside and was breaking it up and putting it in feeding troughs when a cheerful voice broke the silence.

"Did you enjoy your sojourn out to the countryside?" It was Daniel, leaning against the gatepost with a big smile on his face. "Must have been something very interesting to keep you away for an extra day."

James dropped the last of the hay and went to open the gate. "Well, good morning to you also," he said, "and yes. You could say it was an interesting trip."

"I came by a few times to check on things for you. The boys seemed to be doing a good job, but I didn't ever see Luke around. Is he still hiding out somewhere?"

James had not had time to tell Daniel he was taking Luke with him before he left, so he filled him in on the trip to Terra Rubra and to his father's farm.

Daniel nodded slowly, taking it in. He smiled when James told him about how his father had offered to shelter him even before he asked. "Sounds like maybe they both might find what they need."

"I saw my father standing straighter and more happy than I have in a good while. He told Luke they were going to be partners on the farm, that he would share in whatever profits they could make working the place."

"That was a brilliant idea you had there, my friend, brilliant.

Are you curious at all about what's been going on here while you were out touring the countryside?"

"I'm certainly curious about what you have in that knapsack you've been trying to hide behind you there," James said, arching his eyebrows and looking behind Daniel. "Must be something of great value."

Daniel reached inside and pulled out a small tin and shook it. "Tea, James. We are going to have tea this morning despite the best efforts of our British friends to deprive us."

James was excited. He had not had a cup of tea in months, and the last one was made with leftover leaves and very weak. "How in the world did you come by that?"

"I am not at liberty to disclose my sources," he whispered, looking around very conspiratorially. "Suffice it to say that I have acquired enough for one large pot."

"Well then, why don't you go on in and start the fire and I'll finish watering these horses and join you momentarily."

It wasn't long before the aroma of tea was filling his small quarters. He took in a deep breath through his nose, letting it out slowly. "Oh, how I have missed that."

Daniel sat with a hot mug in his hands, inhaling deeply as well. "It certainly is uncivilized of our British cousins to keep us from our tea." They both knew that sugar was out of the question. The blockade was still seeing to that. "Another reason to look forward to a speedy end to this damn war."

James waited for him to go on, sipping his tea. "There has been some activity while you were gone. There are reports that the British troops that General Smith spoke of from the fighting in France are already in Bermuda and will be heading in this direction soon. They may already be on their way."

This was not welcome news. He had spent a good part of the trip back not only thinking of Abigail but wondering if there would be any reports on the enemy's movements. "So how much time does that give us to prepare for them?"

"Funny you should ask. Our unit will try to have a meeting

soon to inform everyone what we can expect in the next few weeks. Maybe tomorrow or the next day."

"Well," James said, reluctant to finish his tea, "I'll go ahead and deliver these things to Mister Key and get back here. There's work to be done if I'm going to be absent again soon. Care to give me a hand with the wagon?"

After they had hitched up the team, James drove through the busy streets to the Key house. When he pulled in the drive, he noticed there was much less activity than when he had been there before. He pulled up in front of the house and set the brake. Jeffery came out on the porch at his approach.

"Good morning, Mister James," he said in his deep baritone.

"Good morning to you, Jeffery. Is Mister Key at home this morning?"

In answer to his question, Key appeared at the front door. "Good morning, James, good morning. What news is there from Terra Rubra?"

James gave him several letters from his wife, and he and Jeffery began to unload the wagon. After they were done and all the crates were open, the lawyer came out of his office holding one of the letters and asked James to come inside.

Key closed the door behind him and looked again at the letter in his hand. "My wife mentions a young lad who accompanied you on the trip up. She goes on to say that you took him on to your father's farm."

James' face was impassive as he waited for him to go on. When the lawyer didn't, James said," Yes, sir."

Key cleared his throat. "You have done my family and me a great service this week, James, and I am truly grateful. It would pain me deeply to think that you had used my home to shelter a runaway slave, to break the law I am sworn to uphold."

James shrugged slightly. "I just took a boy with no home to a place where he is needed, where he can earn his keep and grow up properly. That's all there is to it, really."

The lawyer looked at him for a moment, then seemed to have

made a decision. He folded the letter and dropped it on his desk. "Then we need not speak about this any further."

"Is there anything else I can do for you, Mister Key? I have a few hours before I need to be at the stable."

"No, James, you've done quite enough. Thank you for the letters especially. I miss my dear family and hope they'll be joining me soon."

"I heard there will be a militia meeting very soon. Will you be attending?"

"I'll be there but I am no longer a Lieutenant as I mentioned before. I have been asked to serve as an aide to the adjutant general during the coming emergency."

James nodded and turned towards the door to leave. "Then I'll say good-bye until then."

The word had gone around that any man from any unit who was available should meet in the park in front of the new Capitol building in the city. The impressive building was still under construction, but it was obviously going to be grand in stature.

By the time James and Daniel arrived around two hundred men were waiting to hear any news about the British. After another hour, several of the senior officers arrived and made their way to the small rise directly in front of the Capitol. The men had all left their wagons and horses tied up and made their way to where the officers stood.

There was a good deal of talking in the crowd, so a major waved his hand and called for quiet. When the murmuring died down, he cleared his throat. "I want to thank all of you for coming this afternoon. I understand most of you had to leave your work or farms to be here, but we have some important developments to share with you. Nothing you hear today is secret or confidential, and we encourage you to share it, especially with any other men in your units who could not be here."

He looked over at the colonel, who motioned him to continue. "If you recall at our last encampment a few weeks past, it was mentioned that the war with France is over and several thousand battle hardened British troops would now be available for service here."

The murmuring started again and the major raised his hand. "Gentlemen, please. We now have it on very good authority that several ships full of these troops have arrived in Bermuda and may even now be proceeding towards our eastern coast. It is estimated that there are around four thousand regulars aboard."

He stopped and looked out over the crowd of men. "We can expect to face these troops sometime in the next few weeks, and in any event in less than two months from now. It is imperative that all units be prepared to respond to a muster call on very short notice. We do not know when, and we do not know where, but we must be ready to defend our homes against invasion from this moment on."

This started the men talking again, and the major let it go on for a bit before once more raising his hand. He went on again more forcefully. "These are going to be very trying times, I'm afraid, and we must not fail. We cannot fail. The British seek to break up this union of states of ours. They seek to crush our democracy and make us their subjects again. If they win here, that may very well happen." He looked out at all the anxious faces. "Our forefathers would have fought, suffered and died in vain, and we must not allow that to happen. We owe those brave men our very best efforts at the very least."

On the way back towards the stables James and Daniel were quiet, turning over everything they had been told. The officers had gone on to remind the men to make sure all their weapons were in fighting condition, and that they have adequate rations for at least several days ready to grab in a hurry when they heard the signal guns fired. There would be very short notice when the time came.

"I wish it was more certain where they will strike first," James said. "It could be anywhere from New York down to Charleston."

"They are all good targets, I suppose, but I think I am starting to agree with cousin Matthew. I believe that they may very well strike at us here in Washington. They are an arrogant bunch, the British, and it would soothe their bruised egos to burn our capital to the ground."

James was thoughtful for a moment. "I should think that Baltimore would be a priority. Most of the blockade runners and privateers are based out of that harbor, and they have been running their navy in circles. But I think maybe you and cousin Matthew are right. They are an arrogant bunch. Newspapers up and down the coast have been full of threats from their Admiral Cockburn about avenging York."

They rode on in silence for a while, each lost in his own thoughts. James turned to Daniel, hesitating. "Do you think we're ready for them? I mean, do you think we will be disciplined enough to face them on an open field and not run like rabbits?"

"That is the question, I suppose. I have never had to face anything like that before, most of us haven't, really. Some of the militias have fought brief skirmishes in some of the shore towns up and down the Chesapeake, but for the most part we are green. Very green."

They parted with Daniel going to his home and James to the stables. He led Annie into the paddock and freed her from the saddle and tack. The other horses started filing out as the big doors were opened. "Come on out, ladies, sir. We still have a few hours of daylight, so come out and enjoy it."

He went back into the building and stood looking around, hands on his hips. He saw there was plenty of hay to last for a while. There were only a few things he needed to work on to make the place ready for him to be away. He felt that at least some of the horses he boarded would be called for by their owners. There was no doubt that those who could leave the city would if the British got close.

He turned back to the doors and was surprised to see the figure of Constable O'Malley in the doorway. "Good afternoon, James. Have you been away?"

James nodded. "Constable," he said. "Yes, I was hired to move some things for lawyer Key this past week."

"I thought maybe it was something of the sort. I stopped by a few times in the last few days to see if anyone knew the whereabouts of this Luke fellow. The one old Jenkins mentioned that day of the trouble here."

"Well, Mister O'Malley, I can truthfully say that I have not seen Luke here at the stables or anywhere else in the neighborhood since then," he said, shrugging.

"Yes. Funny, it's almost like he's vanished into thin air. He was here and now he's gone," he said, snapping his fingers. "Just like that. You don't find that odd?"

James walked past him out into the paddock. "No, not really I guess. I have no idea where the boy lives. He would just stop by from time to time and ask if there were any jobs for him. Have you asked Mister Jenkins or anyone else?"

"Oh, yes, I've asked around. Old Jenkins said he was fairly sure that Luke was here when those three arrived, but he couldn't be absolutely certain. At least that's what he said."

"Do you have any reason to doubt him?"

"No, no I suppose not. It all seems a little strange to me still. Well, I'll let you get back to your animals. I hear we may be having visitors before long."

"You have heard correctly, I'm afraid. All the militias have been put on readiness to muster on very short notice."

"Well, like I said, I won't keep you any longer. Maybe we can talk again after this campaign is over. Good day to you."

James watched him walk out the gate and close it behind him. "Good day to you, constable."

It was hard for him to tell if the man was suspicious of him or not. He went into the stables and dragged out a bale of hay for his charges and broke it up into the feeding troughs. He was sure of one thing, though, and that was that Luke was beyond the reach of anyone in Washington and therefore safe.

The summer had been extraordinarily hot considering how cool the spring had been. The crushing humidity reminded every citizen that the entire city had been built on a swamp. Clouds of mosquitoes plagued anyone who ventured out near the river, and a general malaise had settled on the usually bustling town.

The morning of August 21 dawned as the day before had ended, hot and sticky without a breath of breeze to bring any relief. James and young William Jenkins, the shopkeepers nephew, were up early to make sure the horses were tended to and kept from the miserable conditions as much as possible. James had every door and window in the building open at all times and had since mid July. Even the big main doors were kept open at all hours in the vain hope of a breeze cooling off the stifling interior. They made sure that plenty of water was always available for the animals.

William was a reliable and hard working young man. James enjoyed his company and it seemed to be mutual. The conversation during their frequent breaks to avoid overheating in the thick summer air was always about the British, and when they might be coming.

"I wish I would be allowed to join the militia," William said during an afternoon break. "I want to help defend my home. It's not right that I have to stay behind when there will be fighting to be done."

"I understand how you feel, William, but you are only fourteen, and barely that. The battlefield is no place for you."

"My uncle was in the militia when he was thirteen. He was a drummer in the Maryland militia in the revolution and saw plenty of fighting."

"He saw plenty of dying as well, don't forget. I'm certain he would be the first to agree that it's no place for someone of your age."

They were interrupted by the booming sound of a single cannon not far away. They stopped and looked at each other. A second round immediately would mean an emergency at hand. If it came a few minutes later, it was the signal to muster and wait for further news.

Sure enough, after three or four minutes a second booming report was heard. "You know what to do, William. Look after the horses as best you can. If any owners come for their animal, let them take it. I'll be back as soon as I can."

He went back and saddled Annie up and led her out, went back in and grabbed his rifle and knapsack then mounted up. "I'm counting on you now, William. Those who stay behind also have important work to do, and don't forget it."

The men were assembling in the hundreds back at the field in front of the Capitol. The rumors were flying as thick as geese in the winter. The Georgetown Light Artillery always met in the northeast corner of the field, and he made his way there as quickly as he could through the growing throng. Men were assembling by unit across the field in good order.

He found his unit and left Annie with the other horses near the edge of the field, then made his way towards the unit's flag, hanging limp from it's staff in the still, hot air. He found Daniel and fell in with the others.

"What news is there? Has anyone heard anything?" he asked around.

"I heard that the British are bombarding Philadelphia," one private offered. "My cousin heard it from a fellow he knows from there.

"Well, I've been told it's Charleston that's the target," another said.

"They could be anywhere," a sergeant said quietly. "It would be best to just wait until we hear something definite."

They didn't have long to wait. A group of riders came to the rise at the eastern end of the field. Orders were barked up and down the formations to come to attention. A deathly silence ensued as they all came to attention, their eyes fixed on the riders.

"That's President Madison," Daniel whispered. "I'm sure of it."

"Quiet in the line there," a sergeant barked. "Stand at attention you lot."

A colonel stepped forward and looked out over the crowd. "I'll be brief, gentlemen. The British have landed several thousand troops in Benedict, a good days march from here. This is not a rumor, but a fact. The president and the secretary of war have both been down there to verify this news. There is no doubt that they will be moving north very soon. However, their target is still in doubt."

This started the men talking and whispering in the formation. "Silence, please, silence. Since we cannot be sure if they will go to Baltimore or advance on Washington, it is vitally important now that we be ready to deploy for both eventualities and be ready on very short notice. Make all preparations to be away from your homes for an extended period if you have not done so already. Reinspect all your weapons as well. You will be using them soon, I can assure you. This threat is real. The invasion we have been awaiting is happening now, at this very moment."

A slight breeze came up out of nowhere and the unit flags started to wave weakly in the late afternoon sun. "Remain in your unit area for now. Several officers will be coming through to brief your captains about where each unit will be called upon to go. Remember this. We outnumber our enemy in both men and artillery. We are defending our homes and families. We will prevail if we follow orders quickly and stand together."

The men stood at ease awaiting further briefing. James looked around the group of men he had been drilling with for well over a year now. Some looked fearful while others were excited. "Let them come," one of the younger privates said, "Just let them come. We'll be ready for them and give them a licking."

"It won't be as easy as that, boy," an older sergeant said. "I was with Colonel Campbell up in Canada in the early days. Believe me when I say that the British know how to fight."

"As do we now," the youngster went on. "They need to learn that."

"And you're just the lad to teach them," the sergeant said and mussed up his hair, eliciting laughs from the group.

The captain appeared and called the men to order. "This is Major Shelby, gentlemen. Please give him your attention."

A very tall, thin man stood before them. "The need for your artillery to be where we need it when we need it will be crucial when the fighting starts. I cannot emphasize that enough. Artillery rules the battlefield in modern warfare, and we intend to rule on the day. Your captains have been briefed, and if there are no changes you are to muster on the Old Long Fields northeast of the city and be prepared to move, probably to the Bladensburg river crossings. It's also possible that you may be needed to meet any advance on Baltimore, but I personally think not. If the British wish to visit Washington, they will have to cross the river at Bladensburg, and we will be there to prevent that happening. Good luck, gentlemen, and may God be with you."

The major moved on to the next unit, a regiment of rifles from Alexandria. The men all faced their captain and waited. "You heard what the man said. The next signal gun you hear will be a call to arms, you may be sure of that. Make all your preparations. We will need to again inspect our field guns and prepare them to move," he said, nodding at the gun crews, "and each individual will make sure that their personal weapons are ready. Gun crews will meet right away to prepare our pieces." He looked at the men. "We can do this, boys. Let's give them a warm welcome and send them to hell."

William was sitting atop the paddock fence waiting for James to return. He had about given up hope when he spied him coming from the direction of the city. He jumped down and ran out to meet him.

"What news is there James? Did you find out anything?"

James climbed down from Annie and walked along with the boy. "There is news, but I'm afraid it's not good news. The British have landed troops in Maryland, down at he southern end of the bay. We can expect to meet them soon."

William went and opened the paddock gate, and James led his mare inside and started to remove her saddle. William helped, waiting for more. "The call could come at any moment now, William. I will need to know that I can count on you to look after things here for me. Do you understand? Will you do that?"

"You know I will, James," the boy said, a little hurt. "I won't let you down."

"I know you won't, William. You know I trust you absolutely."

James put away his rifle and knapsack and put Annie back in her stall. After looking around to see all was well he found William back sitting on the paddock fence.

"I wish I was going too, James."

"I know you do, I know. But it's like I said, the work that has to be done at home is as important as the work on the battlefield. A soldier who is worrying about his home is not much use in the fight."

The boy nodded and James went on. "I'm going up to Jones' Tavern before it gets too dark and tell them up there what I learned. You go on home now, and I'll see you in the morning."

The alarm gun boomed just after dawn the next morning. James had slept fitfully at best, and not just because of the stifling heat. His mind had been racing since the militia briefing at the Capitol building. His doubts about the readiness of his unit, and his own personal readiness, had weighed heavily making sleep almost impossible.

His stop in at the tavern had served to calm some and excite many others. At news that the British had landed, many expressed the opinion that it was time to move their families out of the city. Others had expressed a grim resolve to repel the invaders by any means.

At the sound of the alarm he jumped out of his bed and reached for his boots. Before he could pull them on, a second report rang out and shortly after a third. He knew then that the time was at hand, that there would be no more wondering what came next or how he might react. The storm was approaching, and he would go to meet it.

As he was saddling Annie, William ran in through the big doors.

"Saddle up the big black there and hurry." They had made a plan the day before for James to ride Annie out to Old Long Fields, their appointed mustering area a couple of miles northeast of the city, and William would bring her back to the stables.

They urged the horses on through the city streets. Many people came out of their houses at the sound of the alarm gun and waved as they passed. There was no cheering, but many wished them Godspeed and good luck. Everyone seemed very restrained, almost like no one could believe this was happening.

As they neared Old Long Fields they were joined by the caissons hauling the units six pounder guns. The gun crews were directly behind and the small infantry contingent to which he belonged followed them. Altogether they numbered just over one hundred.

James dismounted and handed the reins to William. Annie was stomping her hoofs at all the noise and hustle of the men. He rubbed her nose and untied his rifle and knapsack. "Go on back now and keep an eye out for any trouble or looters. I'll be back as soon as I can." He was also thinking that he may not be back at all but kept that thought to himself. "Go on now, I'm counting on you."

The boy turned around and headed back to town they way they had come. James fell in with the infantry, his mouth dry and his heart pounding. He wondered if the others felt that way, then he wondered if the British soldiers did, too.

Major Peter and two captains were at the head of the field, watching as the sergeants whipped everyone into line. It was about an hour before the entire company was assembled, and the day was already blazingly hot. They had been standing at ease while they were assembling then were called to attention.

There was no pomp or ceremony, only a single drummer on each side of the column beating a cadence rhythm for the march. Major Peter waved his hat over his head and started the march in the direction of Marlborough. The day was clear and still, the sun blazing in the morning sky. The men and horses ahead were stirring up clouds of dust that swirled and choked those following behind, including James and his fellow riflemen.

"Close it up there, boys, close it up. You there, keep in step," a sergeant was barking as he marched alongside the column. James squinted up at the sun. The heat and the dust were already making him thirsty and they had only gone a mile or so. It was hard to tell exactly as they plodded along how far they had marched.

There was so much dust from the dry roadway that James could not see anywhere near the front of the column. He heard a shouted order ahead that was repeated down the line. "All right, men, quick march. Keep together now, keep together."

They began to shuffle in step which only made the dust more insufferable. They kept that pace for what seemed an eternity, then a halt was ordered. It wasn't long before it was followed by the order to form up in battle lines, with the guns and crews moving to the center rear.

"You men there form a line from here to the creek," a mounted captain yelled out to a group of riflemen. "You fellows form up to the edge of the forest. Gunners, prepare to fire."

They could see nothing ahead of them, just some open ground. James moved off to his right with his detachment on the double. They turned then and faced downhill towards a fence line about fifty yards distant with a small copse of woods beyond. He still did not see any sign of the enemy.

Then they heard a distant drum from ahead, and in a moment the first of the British troops emerged from the forest. They were formed in a line and advancing slowly. It was obvious they did not expect to see any Americans in their front. James was struck by how disciplined they were as they continued to advance.

"Steady men, steady," the captain called, his voice calm. "Let them move in a little closer."

After what seemed an eternity, the command was given and the field guns all fired together. The British line halted, but only for a second. The front of their line had taken a few casualties and the rest picked their way around their fallen comrades.

"Ready on the left, ready on the right." James shouldered his rifle and waited. He was responding automatically, waiting for the order. "Fire!"

An incredible sound erupted from both sides of the line. This time the British line stopped dead in its tracks. "Reload." James was again impressed with the discipline the enemy showed in the face of their withering fire. They changed their formation and began to advance again, then stopped and raised their rifles.

"Christ," James muttered as he shouldered his rifle once more. "Fire," the captain yelled again, and more British soldiers dropped. Then suddenly they returned fire. There was no sound at first, just a huge cloud of white smoke. Then the sharp crack of the British rifles washed over them, along with what sounded to James like giant bees. The man next to him dropped, crying out.

"Reload, boys, reload," a sergeant just behind them yelled out. "Steady boys, steady." Some of the men were having trouble reloading. One or two dropped their rifles and turned to the rear. "Back in the line, damn you," the sergeant cursed at them. "Get back in there."

Most of the men had reloaded and shouldered their rifles yet again. The field guns opened up and the British took several direct hits with canister. They were starting to lose their disciplined line. "Fire!" the captain yelled, and they fired right into the wavering enemy.

"Fire at will, boys, let them have it," the captain yelled from his mount. Sporadic gunfire ensued after that from both sides, punctuated by the deep roar of the cannons. The captain was waving his hat and shouting. "We have them now, boys."

James felt a slight tug on his sleeve and looked down. There was a hole where none had been before. He looked up just as the captain's horse reared up and fell dead, throwing his rider off. "Christ," James muttered again as he reloaded. He aimed at the center of the line and fired again. This time he saw a man drop his rifle as he clutched his chest and crumpled to the ground. "Christ."

The British had had enough, for now they began to fall back in disarray seeking shelter in the woods behind them. The captain was back on his feet, limping up and down in front of the men. "Cease fire, boys, cease fire." A few scattered shots rang out, then an eerie silence.

His heart was pounding and his hands shaking as James knelt down to tend to the wounded man beside him. He had been hit in the shoulder, the ball tearing the joint apart. He was covered in blood, the muscles of his upper arm exposed. He looked at James and then passed out. James stood and looked out across the field at all the red figures lying on the ground.

Stretcher bearers appeared among the fallen British. The men watched silently, each with his own thoughts. James wondered if he had killed the man he saw fall, or had he been hit by someone else. A stretcher bearer appeared and together they lifted the man who had fallen. James watched as he was taken away. He could not remember his name.

"Close up the line there. That's it, close it up," a sergeant ordered. As they reformed their line they were told to stand at ease and wait. The merciless sun was beating down on them as well as their enemy, and the air was filled with a strange buzzing sound.

They stayed where they were for several hours, the men holding a casual line and talking amongst themselves. There was little celebration, but a lot of relief.

"Did you see how they marched?" a man near James was asking aloud. "They just kept coming on, even when the cannons fired."

James nodded. "That's their strength. They have the discipline and the training to keep advancing." He looked around the men. "Some of ours skedaddled right after the first shots were fired."

A sergeant was standing nearby. He was passing among the men and offering words of encouragement where he could. "Aye, I saw two men go myself. Can't win a battle with men like that at your side. We're probably better off without them, truth be told. You lads stood your ground though, didn't you? We can beat them if we follow orders."

"They didn't have any cannon, did they?" a young gunner said. "Why do you suppose that is, sergeant?"

"They were probably just an advance unit from Ross' army, out looking for trouble. And they found it, didn't they boys," he said, trying to cheer them up. "They sure found it here."

The order to fall in and prepare to move out was called, and the men fell in, looking out across the field again. The fallen British had all been removed and there was no sign of the enemy. The captain had found another mount and walked out in front of them, pointing down the hill.

"We gave them a taste of American lead today, men, but this was just a taste. I'm proud of you all. Sergeants, proceed."

"Left face, forward march," was repeated up and down the line and the men started to move out. After several hours they were back at Old Long Fields, where several large cauldrons were tended to by cooks and a few slaves that had been loaned to the army. The men were dismissed and fell out.

The mood was still subdued, the men exhausted from the long marches in the hot sun. The adrenalin was wearing off after the heat of combat and many just lay down and slept where they were.

James found Daniel nearby, a tin plate of stew in hand. "I might have known you'd be looking for a free meal, Daniel." They sat together eating, trying to get a handle on what had happened.

Daniel had been on the left flank while James had been on the right. "Did you have any casualties on your end?" James asked.

"One killed and two wounded. How about the right? Anyone hurt there?"

"The man next to me was hit in the shoulder," James said, shaking his head. "It was a terrible wound. I've never seen anything like that."

"No," Daniel said quietly, "I haven't either, and I hope to God I never do again. That poor boy who was killed was hit several times, I think. He probably never knew what happened."

They ate in silence until a sergeant passed by. "Why did we retreat, Sergeant?" a boy nearby asked.

"There was no retreat soldier. We held the ground at the end of the day and that's all that matters. We pulled back here because if the British did come back at night our cannons would be of no help to us at all and they could have hurt us. That's how old Winder himself was captured in Canada you know, a surprise night attack. Don't think he wanted to have that experience again."

"What happens next?"

"These stripes make me a sergeant, son, not a general, but if I were you lot I would get a full belly and as much sleep as you can. We could be on the move again at any time."

The sergeant had been correct. The call to assemble came rudely before the sun was up and the men made their way into formation, many only half awake. It wasn't long before they began to move out. It became obvious as the sun started to rise that they were not going back to Marlborough but moving more to the north.

It was about four hours later that they arrived just outside Bladensburg. There were already a large number of troops there, both regulars and militia. James could see artillery placed above the town east of the river.

The order came to halt, and once again the sergeants passed among the men. "We'll wait here for further orders, boys, so stand easy. Shouldn't be long now I would think," their noncom said.

The men fell out gratefully, trying their best to find some shade. This morning was no different from the last few weeks, plenty of sun and not a breath of wind to be had. James and Daniel found a large tree and lay down beneath its branches and promptly fell asleep.

The call to fall in again came soon after, and the men struggled back to their feet. After they were in formation, they marched across the bridge that spanned the East Branch into the town of Bladensburg itself. The town was largely deserted, and except for the troops deploying, eerily quiet.

As soon as they were settled into their new positions, another call to assemble came and they were marched back across the river to the top of the hill opposite the bridge. Some of the men began to grumble, openly wondering if anyone had any idea of what was going on.

A sergeant passed and was asked about being moved about so often. "Not for me to say, private, and certainly not for you." His voice betrayed his unease. "Someone higher up must think it's the right thing, that's all the likes of you and I need to know."

This time, though, James noticed that they were near the guns they were supposed to support. The position commanded the bridge as well as this side of the town. As they stood in the blistering sun other units of militia came out of the town and deployed across the hill, most of them moving off to the left flank.

"Well, they will have the devil of a time if they try to cross here," Daniel said. The men were all aware that if the British hoped to get to Washington, they would have to cross the Eastern Branch here or to their left. They were all that stood between the capital and the enemy.

Just after noon, a large unit in unusual uniforms marched on to the field. One of the companies was mostly made up of black men. They had several large cannon with them as well. A cheer started to come up as they were recognized.

"By God," Daniel said. "It's Commodore Barney and the Marines!"

Commodore Joshua Barney had assembled a fleet of mostly oar powered gunboats that had been harassing the British navy on the Chesapeake Bay. While they had only limited success, they were a major irritant to the British who had to divert a great many resources to deal with them. Barney's flotilla had finally been trapped in the Rappahannock River and they had burned their craft before the enemy could capture them or their guns. Their exploits had been the topic of much conversation the past year.

There were about seven hundred men in the unit, and they marched in and took their position with great discipline just left of the center of the line. "That's just what we needed," James said. He was only a few yards to the right of them and they gave him great confidence. "That's just what we needed."

The sun was blazing down and directly overhead now. Their long march and several other moves after had taken a toll on the men who were feeling the effects. That didn't last long, however.

Off in the distance came the sound of many drummers, beating a march cadence. Not long after, the leading elements of the British army came into view, causing a stir in the American lines.

Captain Burch was just in front of the line near James and Daniel. "Here they come boys. We've got them outmanned and out gunned." He looked up and down the line, a grim look on his face. "We hold the high ground. They have to pass here if they want to visit Washington. Are we going to let them pass?"

A resounding "No!" swept down the line, then a cheer as Captain Burch rode down the line towards the Marines' position. James was concerned that the men to the left of Barney seemed to be falling back a few yards but turned his attention back to the approaching British as he noticed a group of them separating from the main body and setting up some type of equipment he didn't recognize.

In a few minutes it became apparent what that equipment was as several rockets flew over their heads and burst with a great explosion. Some of the men on the far left began to waiver. This was something none of them had seen or experienced before. Several more volleys of these rockets were fired as the main body approached the bridge.

"Steady men, steady. Those rockets make a lot of noise but that's all." A couple of them burst right over their heads, and a few men dropped their rifles and fled. The first of the enemy troops were starting to cross the bridge now. "Ready on the left. Ready on the right." The men shouldered their rifles and waited.

The cannons beside them roared just as the order to fire came, and the first line of British troops were cut down, the survivors retreating back across the river and in among the brick buildings in the town. The gunners kept up a steady fire at anyone who came near the bridge.

Another push to ford the river was developing off to the left in front of the Marines. It was also cut to pieces and the British fell back. During all the fighting, the rockets kept coming over, each explosion causing more men to drop their weapons and flee.

The enemy in front of James made another attempt to secure the bridge but were beaten back, but after several more tries were able to get some men across providing cover for even more to cross. They were paying dearly for it, but that didn't seem to stop them.

While reloading James glanced back at the guns nearest to him just as two of the gunners were hit and fell. He pointed at them and called to Daniel, "I'm going to the guns."

He turned with his rifle in hand and started for the cannons. A red faced sergeant screamed at him. "Get back in the line, damn you, or I will shoot you myself." James pointed to the cannons. "They need me there, Sergeant," he shouted above the growing din.

The man let him pass and James made his way over. He had trained as a matross along with lawyer Key when he first joined the militia and knew what needed to be done. He grabbed the ram and shoved it home, feeling the shot in place. He stepped to the side and the gunner fired. He picked up a bag of powder and pushed it into the mouth of the gun and another man stepped up and loaded a solid shot. James was thinking that canister would be more useful as he shoved the ram in again and stepped to the side.

All the cannons were firing as fast as they could now, all six still in action. It seemed to be having an effect as the fire from the British in front of them was decreasing somewhat. The action to their left in front of the Marines was getting much hotter. He watched as the British there fell back a dozen yards, regrouped and charged again. The Marines did not give an inch and kept up their murderous fire. He could see Commodore Barney on his mount, shouting out orders.

It was then that James saw a great many militia heading to the rear, at first in good order and then in a panic. He looked beyond them and was alarmed to see the British approaching up the hill from the far left. Behind him he could see several riders not in uniform. One of them was Key and another was James Monroe, the Secretary of War. They were looking down at the bridge in front of them and had not noticed that the British were turning their left flank.

James climbed atop a caisson and waved his hat wildly, trying to attract the riders' attention. Key saw him at last, and James gestured towards the advancing British. The militia on that end of the line were now in full retreat, exposing the rest of the line, the Marines and all the cannon. So many had fled the field that Barney's Marines were now the far end of the line. They turned as one and faced the redcoats, slowing their advance.

James helped turn their cannon to face the threat and started to reload. Several of the gunners were lying on the ground, either wounded or dead, and more had fled in panic. Captain Burch was moving among the fleeing men, yelling "Stand with Barney, men. Stand with the Fifth."

The panic was contagious and spreading faster than a flame now, with whole units throwing down their weapons and fleeing the field. The only Americans that James could see standing their ground were the Maryland Fifth Regiment, Barney's Marines and the few men left with him. The noise was deafening as they continued to fire on the British. The enemy was close enough now that he could see their faces and still he continued to load and fire.

They were completely exposed now, and Captain Burch rode up and ordered them to fall back to the top of the hill about two hundred yards behind them. James helped limber the guns and grabbed his rifle. He took one last look at the Marines just as the Commodore was shot off his horse. The Marines were also falling back now in good order. Several of them stayed with Barney as the British overran their position and surrendered.

James felt that if they could regroup at the top of the distant hill they could still hold the British at bay, but as he drew closer he saw that every man in sight was now running as fast as they could back towards Washington, many dropping their rifles as they went.

Cursing them aloud, he realized it was hopeless for him to do otherwise and he joined in the mass retreat.

James got back to his stables just before dusk. He had heard that an officer was trying to regroup some of the men at the foot of the Capitol to make a stand, but when he got there he was alone. As he made his way back, he saw that the citizens of the town were in complete panic. The noise of the battle was obviously heard by all, and many had decided to flee before the advancing British.

Others were taking advantage of the situation to loot and rob. There was nothing he could do to stop any of them as much as he wanted to. It was bad enough that the militia had fled the battle, now the people they were supposed to be defending were robbing their own neighbors. He was filled with disgust towards his fellow citizens.

When he got to the stables, everything there was relatively quiet. He opened the big doors carefully, calling out to William as he did so. "Thank goodness it's you, James. What's happened?"

James looked around the stables. Everything seemed to be in order. "Have you had any trouble here?" he asked the boy.

"I think someone was trying to get in and steal a horse. I shouted out that I had a rifle and they left," William said, his voice unsteady. "Please, James, tell me what's happened."

"The worst possible thing. The militia scattered and ran from the British," he said, turning away and rubbing his eyes. "They ran as fast as they could and left some of us on the field." He turned back to the boy and shouted, "We could have held them, dammit. We had the high ground, the men, the cannon. Damn them all to hell, we could have held them."

William stared at him wide eyed. He had never seen James angry, never seen him this close to weeping. "What's going to happen now?" he asked quietly.

James tried to regain his composure. "The British will be in the city in hours if they aren't here already. We can only hope that they will be satisfied with burning the government buildings and not everything."

At that moment, a large explosion shook the ground and they went outside. There were huge flames above the Navy Yard to the south, and then a series of smaller explosions.

"Is it the British?" William asked.

"No, I don't think so. They are probably firing it to keep the stores out of British hands." They walked a few yards towards town to get a better look. Crowds of people were passing them on horseback, in carriages piled high and even on foot. James hated all of them.

They turned to go back and saw several men entering the stables. James had his rifle in hand and ran to the large doors. One man was trying to pull a large black mare out of it's stall, another was trying to do the same with Annie. He struck the first man hard with the butt of his weapon and advanced on the other, his heart filled with hate.

"Don't shoot. My God, please don't shoot," the man cried out.

James shouldered the rifle. "You have three seconds to leave my property," he said calmly. "One, two…."

The would be thief ran for his life and out the doors. "Close the doors, William. We'll be safer in here out of the panic." He went over and helped the boy close the big doors and secured them. "If anyone else tries to get in they will regret it."

The sound of the panicked river of people passing the building grew louder. Several tried the doors but finding them secured moved on after some encouragement from James' threats. After another hour, the noise began to subside.

Suddenly there was a knock at the doors. "James. James Woodman. Are you there?"

James and William looked at each other. "I think I know that voice. Besides, most thieves aren't polite enough to knock."

James went to the door cautiously, still holding the loaded rifle at the ready. "Who's there?"

"It's me, John Graham. You helped me move some of our office to the new library last month. Do you remember."

James did indeed remember. He had spent two days helping to move important documents and archives into the new Library of Congress in the Capitol building along with several other draymen.

He opened the door and after the man stepped in secured it again. "How can I help you, Mister Graham?" James asked.

The young man was nearly out of breath. "I have been scouring the town looking for a wagon. I remembered you and came here as soon as I could. It's a mob scene out there."

He stopped for breath. "You are my last hope, James, our last hope. The British are almost in the city. They will certainly burn all the government buildings. We must move our papers now, before they get here."

"The same papers we moved last month?" James asked.

"And many more," Graham went on. "The Constitution is there, the original Declaration is there as well. We must get them away. We must!"

James did not hesitate. "William, fetch the big black and Annie. You, help me get the wagon ready."

"Thank God you were here, James. There isn't another wagon to be had. I'll give you a receipt and you'll be paid when this thing is over, I swear to you."

They were pulling the wagon out into the paddock as William led the horses out. "Let's worry about that later. There are more important things to worry about right now."

The clerk Graham climbed up onto the bench seat. "William, bolt the door again and do not let anyone in that you don't know. Understand?"

The boy nodded and went back inside. James climbed aboard after opening the paddock gate and the two men drove out into the street and turned towards the city. It took them a half hour to make their way to the Library, going against a steady stream of fleeing people. A group of men had tried to stop them and steal the wagon, but James' rifle convinced them to reconsider.

When they got to their destination the place was in disarray, with windows smashed and papers all over the floor. Two armed men were standing before a large wooden door, keeping anyone from entering. They were visibly relieved to see Graham and James.

There were several crates beside the guarded door. "Quickly, you men. Load these into the wagon. Open the door, Mister Pleasanton."

The men started to load the crates as James and Graham went into the secured room behind the door. The room was empty except for two more crates. "Is that them?" James asked. "Do they hold the Declaration and the Constitution?"

Graham nodded and went to pick one up. "Grab the other, James. Quickly now, we must be off."

When all the crates were safely aboard, Graham also climbed aboard. Two armed men climbed up and sat in the rear with the crates. "Hurry James. We must leave." Gunshots rang out somewhere near the Capitol building, followed by a large volley of rifle fire.

James climbed up and cried out to the horses and they turned towards Georgetown again. They had only traveled a few blocks when one of the men in the back called out. "My God, the Capitol is in flames!"

James looked back over his shoulder and could see the flames rising above the stately building. He slapped the horses with the reins to spur them on, worried that the British might gain the road ahead of them. Sure enough, as they rushed by the President's House, they could see redcoated figures entering the grounds.

They made good time now that the streets were mostly deserted. They turned on to the road that would take them across the river and on into Virginia, about a half mile from the stables. James reined in the horses and set the brake.

"You go on ahead. You shouldn't have any trouble from here on. I'm going back to my stables and see to their safety." He climbed down from the seat.

Graham looked down at him. "Bless you, James. You have done your country a great service tonight. I won't forget."

"I hope you won't forget that it was a black man that helped you to save these documents, even though I don't exactly enjoy the rights and privileges they describe." His voice was even, without any bitterness. "Now go… and bring my wagon and horses back when you can."

The clerk slapped the reins on the horses back and they started to move off. The two guards on the back waved, then one of them stood and saluted him.

James passed by the new Key house on his way back to the stables. He was surprised to see the lawyer and his wife out in the front garden, looking towards Washington. There was an eerie stillness after the rushing crowd of fleeing people had gone.

James stopped on the street outside the fence and looked back towards Washington as well. The light from many fires was causing the clouds to glow and could easily be seen from their vantage point.

The lawyer had his arm around his wife's shoulder, and she was weeping softly. "That's a terrible sight," James said. He felt no anger, only shame at that moment.

Key turned and saw James standing there and went to speak to him. "I'm very glad you made it back safely, James. Very glad."

"I have never been more ashamed in my life, Mister Key. We behaved very poorly today at Bladensburg."

"I saw you there, James. You have nothing at all to be ashamed of. On the contrary. You put yourself at great risk when you signaled to the secretary and me. We were watching the right side of the line and did not see that the British were turning our flank."

"It was a disaster all the same. I don't see how it could have been any worse," he said, looking back towards the city. He couldn't help but feel that perhaps the people somehow deserved what was happening to them now.

"What happened is not your fault in any way. You provided a

great service to your country on the field today, James, a great service indeed."

James laughed without any humor at that and told the lawyer about the clerk coming to him and then going to rescue many of the archives, including the most important. Key was wide eyed during the telling. He turned and called his wife over.

"Are you saying that the Declaration and the Constitution have both been saved? It's a miracle! Polly, did you hear that? At last, some good news today."

James tipped his hat. "Good evening, Miss Polly. I'm sorry that you have to be a witness to this."

"Hello James. I'm sorry, I didn't hear what you told my husband."

"Polly, James and the clerks have saved our most precious archives. They kept them from British hands."

"As a matter of fact, they are at this moment in the back of my wagon on their way to safety in Virginia. They are under the care of clerks Graham and King and several armed men." He did not point out the irony he had expressed earlier when he parted from the clerks.

"That is good news indeed. You're a very brave man, James."

"Well, James, it seems you have performed two very valuable services to the country on this terrible day. I hope a way can be found to repay you."

"All I want now is to get back to my stables and keep them secure. I saw a number of looters in the city. It was revolting to see them breaking into their neighbors houses like that, taking advantage to help themselves while others are fighting and dying. You should not leave your house unattended tonight."

"We have Jeffery with us at the moment, and a few more servants will be here tomorrow."

James winced at that description of their slaves but said nothing. "Then I'll take my leave now and wish you good night, if indeed a good night is possible."

"What do you plan to do next?" Key asked.

James had already thought long and hard on that. "I'm going to find my friend from our unit, Daniel Lawrence, and then we are going to go fight the British at Baltimore. I want another crack at them…" His voice trailed off. "I'm not going to let what happened today be the end of it," he said with determination. "No, sir, that will not be the end of it."

He did not see another soul on the way back. He turned and watched the glow from the fires and hoped that the British had not turned to burning private property in revenge for what had occurred in York. So far at least, there was no sign of them in Georgetown.

As he approached the paddock he called out to William, and the boy opened the large front doors, his eyes wide.

"Did you get there in time? What news is there? All I can see is that awful red sky," William said. "Is the whole city burning?"

James stepped inside and they bolted the door behind them. "We were just in time. They fired the Capitol building minutes after we left. I saw some of their troops at the President's House as well. I suspect it is also burning now. What has been happening here? Were you molested by anyone?"

"There were a few tries to open the doors. I chased them off, though," William said, grinning. "I think they wanted to steal the horses."

James went to the stalls and looked over the horses. They were skittish and snorting. They probably smell smoke from the fires he thought to himself.

"Mister Calvert came for his horse just a few moments after you all left. All the rest are still here."

James mussed up the lad's hair and smiled. "You did well, William. I'm proud of you. You were a much better soldier than most at the battle today, and that is a fact."

They went up to the loft to get a better view towards Washington. The wind was starting to blow, and the clouds were much lower that just a few minutes before. The glow from the fires was reflecting even brighter now that the clouds were so low.

Then, as they watched unbelieving, the storm broke. The wind was now howling and blowing debris all around the street in front of them. Rain fell harder than either had ever seen before, driven in sheets before the gale. They closed the small loft door and went down to the horses. That's why the horses were so nervous, James was thinking. It wasn't the smoke. They had sensed the approaching tempest.

The next morning dawned grey and overcast, with the humid August air clinging like a blanket. The storm that had broken the night before had damaged several of the houses nearby, and the street was littered with debris. It was utterly silent when James and William went out to survey the damage. The wind had been louder and more violent than either of them could ever remember all night, making the silence now even more intense.

Most of his neighbors had fled the night before in the panic, and several doors to the houses nearby were standing open. At the far end of the street they saw a figure leaving one of the houses, looking around warily. When the man spotted James and William, he lit out towards the city.

"Another damn looter," James said. "There will be plenty more of that, I'm afraid. We will just have to be on guard for a while." James shook his head. "I have not seen much lately that gives me any pride in my fellow citizens."

They went from door to door and secured a few of the houses. When they got to Mister Jenkins shop, they could see it had been heavily looted and ransacked. "How could anybody do this?" William wondered, holding back tears. "My uncle is a kind man. He has always been a friend to everyone. How could they do this to him?"

They straightened up the shop as best they could and secured the door, all the while looking back at the stables to make sure no one was looting there. They went back to the shelter of the big barn just as a fine rain started to fall.

"What are you going to do now?" James asked.

"I don't know. I guess I'll just wait for my uncle to return and help him get things back in order. What are you going to do?"

"I have to go find someone, a friend of mine. I haven't seen him since the battle. Do you mind waiting for your uncle here and keeping an eye on things?"

The rain began to taper off as James walked back into the city. He had thought about riding but was afraid someone might try to steal any horse they could find. He went past the Key house, but all was quiet. He continued on down Pennsylvania Avenue towards the President's House and the Capitol. There were quite a few people out looking at the damage from the fires the British had set. Most of the damage was to the government buildings, but several private homes had also been torched. It was also obvious that the damage would have been a lot worse if not for the terrific storm that had struck so unexpectedly. He felt a little sympathy for the British soldiers since they had had nothing more than tents to shelter them.

As he came up to the park in front of the Capitol, a young British officer rode past, then stopped. "Good morning, sir. Are you a resident of this town?"

James looked around to see who he was speaking to, then realized it was him. "Yes, sir. I live over in Georgetown."

"It looks as if your President Madison has no stomach for a fight, wouldn't you say."

"I think he has the stomach, but I agree he doesn't seem to have much talent for it."

The officer laughed at that. "Very well put, sir, very well put. Have you heard about the little fight yesterday?"

James took a step towards the man and looked up at him. "I was there, sir."

"Were you now? When did you start to run?"

James kept his voice even. "I was standing with Commodore Barney and his Marines. We left the field only after you turned our left flank."

The officer changed his attitude. "With Barney, you say? He's a very courageous man. Made our lives rather difficult for a while."

"Do you have any news of him, sir? I saw him wounded and fall from his horse."

"Yes, he has a serious wound to his thigh, I'm afraid. I understand that the bone was broken. I also know for a fact that General Ross met with him and made sure he was properly tended to."

"That's very kind of the general. Maybe we can repay the favor sometime."

The officer laughed again. "I do like your spirit, sir, I must say. Repay the favor, that's very good. Why don't you join us? We'll be leaving here in the next hour or two. You could join us and be a free man, beyond the reach of your master. Hundreds of negroes have already joined us, you know."

James' voice was now full of steel. "I am a free man, thank you sir. I am a free born American citizen and proud to be such. I know no master of any kind."

The officer was still amused. "I haven't met a free negro before today. I thought all the blacks were slaves. Are there many of you in the city?"

"Several thousand at last count."

"Interesting. Well, my free friend, I must be off. Duty calls, you know. I wish you good luck, sir."

James watched the officer ride off leisurely towards a group of tents beside the Capitol building. He could see a great deal of activity among the men there. There weren't very many militia aged men about. The onlookers were mostly older men and women. The scene was depressing, with the most prominent public buildings damaged to varying degrees.

James walked over to the Capitol and the Library of Congress where they had rescued those important documents just the evening before. It already seemed like something that had happened long ago and to someone else.

He started back to the stables, hoping that Daniel had come by there. He was increasingly concerned about his friend. As he passed the President's House again, he saw with dismay that it had suffered badly. There were still redcoats coming and going from the building, some of them carrying off artifacts of one kind or another.

He arrived back at the stables in the early afternoon. Some of the neighbors were tending to their damaged properties and greeted him as he went by. He cautioned all of them to be on watch for looters, telling one woman, "I have never seen anything as low in my life. They were right here on this very street, helping themselves to whatever they wanted."

William had good news for him this time. Daniel had indeed come by, but he had a bit of a limp. He explained that he had been hit by shrapnel in his leg, and that a British doctor had tended to him there on the battlefield.

"He said he would be back in the afternoon," William told him. "He said to tell you that he is going to Baltimore and stand with the citizens there. That's what he said to tell you, that he was going to find his cousin and stand with him."

James had had a pretty good idea that's what Daniel would do, and he fully intended to go along. "Did he seem badly hurt to you?" he asked the boy.

"His leg did seem very stiff if you ask me. He rode here but I don't think he can walk very far, at least not for a few more days."

He took a quick look around the stables, counting noses. "No one else has come for their horses I see. Why don't you go and see if your uncle is back. I can watch things here for a while. You go on ahead."

He watched the boy cross the street just as his uncle turned the corner. William met him before he got to his shop. James imagined he was probably trying to ease the blow about what he would find when he got there.

James went back and started doing the usual chores. He found great relief in the mundane tasks that it took keep the place in shape and orderly. He longed for normalcy in a world that in just a day or two had turned upside down, leaving everyone gasping for breath.

Daniel came back just before dusk. He had a hard time climbing down from his mount but made it with a little help. They went into the stables and sat down in James' room in the back.

Daniel told him about getting wounded. It happened after James had gone to take the place of the fallen gunner before the British had appeared on their left flank. "One of those damned rockets exploded nearby. Most of them flew harmlessly overhead, but several of them dropped just behind the line. In any event, they surely did put the fear of God in the men."

"I didn't have much time to look around, but I did see several men drop their rifles and run after a rocket would go by."

Daniel went on. "It felt more like a good hard punch here," he said, pointing to the back of his thigh. "I loaded and fired two more times before I looked down and saw the blood. It was right after that when the flank was turned. I was standing next to Barney's Marines, but it was hopeless. Those who stayed were forced to surrender." His voice was bitter.

"I met a British officer in the city this morning who told me that the Commodore was being well looked after."

"I can vouch for that. We were taken to the same hospital. I was tended to by a young British doctor, and I saw the Commodore being tended to by several senior doctors."

"Well, now what will we do? I don't think I can let what happened out there be the end of it for me," James said. "When do we leave for Baltimore?"

Daniel smiled. "I was hoping you would feel that way. I can't let that be the end of it for me either." He looked at the dressing on his leg." I just need a few days for this to feel better, then we can go. We will go to Matthew's house, and if he's already in the field they should know where he is and we can join his unit."

It had been just over a week since the fight at Bladensburg and the burning of the city. The British had pulled out the next day just as the young officer had said. Rumor had it that they were afraid of the Americans regrouping and counter attacking. James laughed the first time he heard that.

"If you had seen the militia running from the battlefield, you would know that the British have nothing to fear from us. Nothing whatsoever." He was taking a break from his chores and passing the time with Mister Jenkins. "Don't get me wrong. I'm glad they left in such a hurry but worrying about anybody regrouping is pre-posterous. It's hard to regroup when you are running away as fast as you can."

"Well, I'm glad they were worried. Anything that would get them out. Have you heard about what's happened in Alexandria? They threatened to burn the city to the ground if the warehouses weren't thrown open to them. They stole private property, they did."

Later that morning after seeing to the rest of his stable duties, James took a ride into the city to see what efforts had been made to return to normal. Many of the residents had returned shortly after the invaders left and were trying their best to restore order in town.

As he passed the Key house, he noticed a wagon in front and people going in and out of the house. He stopped in front as the lawyer appeared on the porch. "Hello, James. Where are you off to."

"Thought I'd ride into Washington and see what progress folks are making, maybe see if anyone needs a wagon for moving."

"As you can see, Mister Swenson has made the repairs to his wagon. He brought down another load of cargo just this morning."

As they were talking, Abigail came out of the house carrying an empty crate. She set it down beside the wagon, then looked up and noticed James on Annie. She smiled and waved at him.

"Good morning, Miss Abigail. How was the journey?"

"Very fine, Mister James, very fine indeed," she said as she came over to the fence. "How are you? How are the stables?"

Key answered for him. "The British never got out this far from the city. The most danger out here came from people's own friends and neighbors. It's disgusting how much looting there was."

Abigail looked back towards the house as Miss Polly called her. "I best be getting back to work. It's very nice to see you again, Mister James."

He tipped his hat as she walked away. "Are you still planning to go to Baltimore?" Key asked him.

"Yes sir, just as soon as Daniel's leg wound heals up some more. Shouldn't be more than another day or so."

"I wish I were going along with you fellows. It leaves a bad taste when I think of Bladensburg."

James rode down Bridge Street to Pennsylvania Avenue, the same route he had followed on his last trip. Most of the damaged houses already had men working on them. The government buildings too were beehives of activity, with great piles of waste in front and workmen crawling all over. It was good to see all the commotion and building going on.

He rode down to the Capitol building itself to see the work being done there. It was obvious that a large fire had been set inside. The interior walls were badly scorched and the big windows in the chamber shattered, but the damage would have been much worse if not for the providential storm that had appeared.

The sun was now directly overhead, and the heat was building. He started back to Georgetown slowly. There was plenty of evidence that the city had suffered terribly, but the air was full of men shouting and construction going on. It gave him some hope for the future.

As he passed the Key house again he slowed even more, hoping to get another glimpse of Abigail. There were two men coming out the front door with Key. They all shook hands and the two men climbed in a carriage and left, leaving a worried looking Key alone.

"Is everything all right, Mister Key?"

Key looked up, distracted. "Oh, it's you James." Then he had a thought. "When did you say you were going to Baltimore?"

"Any day now, I should think."

"Well, James, you may yet have another chance to perform a valuable service for me as well as your country if you have a mind to."

James climbed down off of Annie and came to the fence. "I suppose one more won't hurt. How can I be of service?"

"Those men who just left brought me some disturbing news, I'm afraid. A family friend, Doctor Beanes, was arrested by the British on their way back down the peninsula to Benedict."

"On what charge?"

"Well, as I understand it, he and several other men of the town arrested some British stragglers for theft from private homes. They were holding them in a local jail awaiting any British officers to collect them, but instead they have taken away the good doctor and thrown him in irons."

"I don't see how I could be of much help."

"Those gentlemen who just left have collected many letters from British soldiers and officers who were wounded, attesting to the good care they received from Doctor Beanes. I have been asked to deliver them to the British and try to secure the release of the doctor. I need someone to ride out with me. There are still stragglers and highwaymen about, and we must get through."

James was thoughtful for a moment. "I suppose Daniel and I could accompany you to meet with them, but then we are going to go and fight with the militia in the city."

"That would be most appreciated, I assure you, but we can't leave before I meet with someone from the president's office. It shouldn't be more than another day or two I should think."

James mounted his horse. "I'll find out what Daniel's condition is and let you know as soon as possible. He should be able to travel by then."

As he started to turn, Key looked back to the house and then back to James. "I'll let Abigail know you were asking about her," he said.

When he got back to the stables, James was glad to see Daniel's horse in the paddock with all the rest. Daniel was limping around the paddock as well, pouring water into the troughs against the fence.

"You look pretty good for a wounded soldier," James said as he dismounted. He walked Annie into the paddock and removed her saddle. "About ready for a ride?"

"Never better, my friend, never better. I'm as ready as you are to rejoin the fight. When do we leave?"

James filled him in on the situation with Doctor Beanes and Key's mission to free him. "As soon as he meets with someone from the president's office, we'll be on our way. We'll ride with him until Baltimore harbor and then we go and find Matthew. Are you sure you're ready?"

Daniel was serious. "I'm sure. You won't have to worry about me."

James smiled. "Well, if I don't worry about you, just who will?"

Two nights later, a message from Key was brought to James at the stables saying that his meeting had been accomplished and that they should depart early the next morning if at all possible.

He couldn't be out on the street at that hour because of the Black Codes even with the recent events, so he sent the messenger on to Daniel with instructions to meet at the stables in the morning, then he turned in for a fitful night trying to sleep. The summer heat was still stifling, even now in September.

Daniel arrived early, then they rode the few blocks to the Key house. There was already a horse saddled and waiting in front. As they approached the front door, Jeffery opened it.

"Good morning gentlemen. Mister Key is expecting you. Please come in."

They followed Jeffery through the house to the kitchen at the rear. Abigail was taking something that smelled very good out of the oven and James noticed that some food had been packed for the trip.

"Ah James, there you are. Come in, please. Are you hungry? Abigail makes the best pastry anywhere."

Abigail smiled at him as she put the cooking sheet down on a counter. "Good morning, Mister James. How are you this morning?"

"I'm fine, Miss Abigail," he said and then introduced Daniel to everyone. "I don't know what you're cooking, but I hope it tastes as good as it smells."

"Oh, it does that I can assure you," Key said. "Abigail has been good enough to pack us some to take along."

"We are ready to leave whenever you care to go," James said. "Thank you for your kindness, Miss Abigail," he added.

They started out heading to the north, away from the area of the city that had been burned. There was no sign out that way that anything had happened at all. James found that very strange.

"What are you supposed to do when we arrive at the harbor?" James asked.

"I'm supposed to meet a Colonel John Skinner at a hotel near the harbor. He's the British Prisoner Exchange Agent appointed by the president. I will present these letters to him," he said, patting the saddle bag behind him, "then we board a flag of truce vessel and go looking for the British."

"They shouldn't be very hard to find, I should think, what with them having all those big ships and all," Daniel said.

Key laughed at that. "I must admit to having a certain amount of trepidation about this mission, but I understand that Colonel Skinner has met with the British several times in the past year. He has always reported that he was received most graciously."

The ride went smoothly except for an encounter with a very unpleasant pair of men they encountered near Brookville. They gave the impression that they were very interested in Key's saddle bag, and probably his wallet as well. The sight of James and Daniel's rifles held at the ready served to dissuade them from any attempts at theft and they left them unmolested.

It was evening by the time they reached the harbor and found the hotel where Key and Skinner were supposed to meet and plan their mission. Daniel could see that James was nervous about being out late.

"Don't worry, James. No one will bother you here. Baltimore doesn't have any such strict Black Codes. Besides, most people have something else on their minds at the moment."

There were armed men everywhere they went, wearing every kind of uniform or in their usual work clothes. There was an air of grim determination over the whole city that they had not felt marching out to Bladensburg. It gave James some confidence.

They went to let Key know that they were off to find Matthew and join the militia, but Key asked James if he could have a word with him in private. They found a corner where they could sit without being disturbed. James waited for Key to speak.

"James, once again I find myself in your debt. I don't know if I would have made it here unmolested without the able assistance of Daniel and yourself. I was very fortunate to have you along."

"Well, sir, I think that since you have said you will represent me in the matter of the killings at the stables that our accounts are square."

"I'm sorry James, I don't know where my mind has been. I spoke with Constable O'Malley a few days after the British left Washington. I told him about your valuable service at Bladensburg. He told me then that he has no interest in pursuing any action."

"You mean it's all over?"

"As far as the law is concerned it is. As the good constable said, the world is better off without those men in it, then he asked God to forgive him for saying something like that."

"Well, that is really very good news. I thank you for speaking with him on my behalf."

"That was a trifle, James, nothing more. So, back to our, as you said, accounts. You may have saved me from capture or worse in the battle, you helped the country by helping preserve our most sacred heritage and now I find myself on a mission for the president that may not have happened if not for you."

James was slightly embarrassed. "I just did what I thought needed doing at the time, Mister Key sir. I'm not a hero. If anything, I'm just a free American citizen with a sense of duty."

"Well, in my opinion that makes you a hero. You put yourself at risk to help me, and you stood your ground on the field of battle when others fled in blind panic. No, our accounts are not square, and I want to offer you anything in my power to try and square them."

"I..I don't know what to say, Mister Key."

"Then say nothing now. Think about it and we'll speak of it further when this affair is over and you are back in Washington."

The next morning they were able to inquire about the location of Matthew's company at the headquarters of General Stricker and volunteer to join. The place was buzzing with activity, with men rushing about and orders being given.

The brigade consisted of three rifle companies, including Matthew's, positioned out in front of the vast earthworks that had been built on the eastern edge of the city. When they got to the area, they were very impressed, both by the size of the earthworks and the number of cannon. James almost felt bad for anyone who would have to attack it from the front.

As they passed through the American lines they were directed down Long Log Lane. They hadn't gone far when they encountered a group of militia riflemen. They found Matthew and his company of rifles who had been tasked with scouting and keeping an eye out for any sign of the British. There had been plenty of accurate information coming in about the progress of their navy towards the city.

Matthew was surprised and glad to see them. He had been out scouting all morning and was off duty for a while. "Haven't seen any sign of them anywhere, but I expect they'll be along before too much longer. Have they left Washington completely?"

James and Daniel brought him up to date on what had happened, starting with the staggering defeat at Bladensburg and the burning of the city. "That's why we had to come here, you see.

Neither of us can think of not joining the fight again after that humiliation. Besides," Daniel said, rubbing his leg, "I have something of theirs that I want to return to them."

Matthew introduced them to his sergeant and the company commander, Major Heath, who assigned them to Matthew's company as they had hoped. The major asked if they had been at Bladensburg.

"Yes sir, Major. Daniel here was wounded and I stood with Commodore Barney until our left flank was turned. I'm not proud to report that most of the militia fled as soon as those damned rockets started firing. We could have held them if we had stood our ground."

"Yes, so I've heard. Well boys, you will both have a chance to even the score very soon, that I can promise you. In the meantime, Private Lawrence will get you settled in the company. Get some rest and a bite to eat if you can. We shan't be here long."

The major was true to his word. Just before midday, the major ordered his company to form up quickly. When they had assembled, he stood before them. "Men, the enemy is only two or three miles ahead. We have just learned that they have stopped their advance to eat. Although it will be very rude of us to do so, we are going to interrupt their lunch and try to draw them on towards us."

The men moved out at quick march. Once again James felt electricity in the air as they hurried to meet the invaders. It wasn't long before the order to halt was given and the riflemen were deployed on both sides of the road and along a wooden fence. James could see that the deployment was perfect, with each group covering the other as well as the only available road. He was confident that these officers knew their jobs, unlike most of the others at Bladensburg.

One small group continued on towards the British camp and was soon exchanging fire with the enemy's pickets. The militia men withdrew in good order, and the British began to advance again in pursuit, just as Major Heath hoped they would.

The first line of redcoats appeared at the bend in the road about one hundred yards distant and kept coming on. James was surprised to see what he took to be a general officer on horseback ahead of his own lines. The man was urging his men forward and leading the way. Some firing on both sides broke out as the British advanced, but the mounted officer did not seek shelter. That proved to be a mistake as he was soon shot off his horse, which turned and charged back through the British lines in panic.

The redcoats stopped cold in their tracks, then slowly started to withdraw in a ragged line. Whoever that officer was, James thought, his injury had unsettled his men completely for a moment. It didn't take long for the British to regroup and the order came for the militia also to begin a withdrawal back towards the city's fortifications. It was a fighting withdrawal and done in good order. After opening some distance between them and the redcoats, some of the men were assigned to cut down trees to block the road as well as dig ditches to slow any artillery the British may have.

It wasn't long before the enemy started to press their advance again. Scouts on the left flank soon reported movement across Bear Creek. Major Heath realized that they were trying to turn the flank on that side. The militia withdrew another few hundred yards, and the command to form again soon came.

Once again it was obvious that the officers knew their job. The riflemen sheltered in the woods just off the single road, providing cover for each other. The one small cannon they had with them was positioned to cover the road.

They let the British close to just a few yards, the woods giving them cover. It seemed to James that the redcoats must have expected to find them formed up on the road, because when they opened fire on them, the British line wavered and disintegrated. In the center, the little four pounder opened with canister and made a mess out of the British advance there.

It was a short, sharp fight and the enemy seemed to have had enough for now. The order to fall back came and the militia started back towards the city once again. They arrived at the first

American lines as the sun was starting to sink in the west and gratefully passed through.

They hadn't been there long when the skies opened up and a cold drenching rain began to fall in torrents. The Americans were able to seek shelter, but the British had not bothered to bring along any tents at all according to information from spies. They had apparently been under the impression that Baltimore would be taken as easily as Washington had been. They all knew that the rain would have a negative affect on the British weapons as well as making their soldiers lives miserable, so no one complained about the weather.

They were all awakened early the next morning by the sound of a tremendous bombardment. Their first thought was that the British to their front had opened up on them, but soon realized that the sound was coming from the south and the harbor.

"Are those their guns or ours?" James wondered. The sound kept washing over them without any let up.

An hour later it became obvious. The British were shelling Fort McHenry out in the harbor. Everyone knew that the enemy ships could not pass the fort without destroying it first, and from the sound of the bombardment it was clear that was their intention.

One of the lookouts spotted some redcoats out in front of their position, watching them through glasses. They were too far away to create any mischief. One of the men put a glass on them and laughed.

"They do not look happy," he said. "They seem to be surprised at the works here."

The men all around stood and waved their hats at the British observers, yelling taunts and daring them to come on. In a few more minutes they were gone, and the men settled down again.

"Poor bastards," Daniel said. "First they come out on the short end yesterday, then they spend the night in the rain. Now, in the morning they get a look at this fortification and take abuse from us." He looked around at the others. "Poor dumb bastards," he said again and smiled, rubbing his leg.

The bombardment of Fort McHenry continued without let up all through the day and into the evening. As it grew dark, the men could see the glow from the many guns, and the trails of the Congreve rockets, the same ones that had unnerved the militia at Bladensburg. The enemy in their front made no attempt to advance. The thinking was that they were awaiting the destruction of the harbor bastion before advancing.

The men passed a fitful night, trying to find any news of the fort and its garrison. It was difficult to imagine that any fortress anywhere could survive such a prolonged bombardment as the one they were witness to.

James awoke around four in the morning. Most of the men around him, except for the watch, were still asleep. He made his way to the high ground just behind the earthworks to await the dawn. When he arrived there were several others also hoping to get a glimpse of the fort. One of them had a glass with him.

The crunch of the cannon and the siege mortars was almost continuous. In the dark, they could see that the gunners in the fort were firing back and that gave them some hope. As the sun started to rise a great cloud of smoke covered the entire harbor, punctuated only by muzzle blasts.

As daylight spread, the man with the glass was surveying the scene. "Too much smoke still to see anything," he reported to the others. He kept searching. The noise of the battle had subsided noticeably.

"Well I'll be damned," the man with the glass said softly, then shouted as loud as he could. "I'll be damned!"

None of the men on the high ground needed a glass to see what was happening now. A huge garrison flag, the largest flag any of them had ever seen, was being raised over the fort, it's broad stripes gleaming in the new day's sun.

The firing from the British had stopped completely now, and the silence was deafening. Then, softly and from far away, they could hear the faint strains of "Yankee Doodle" coming from the harbor somewhere.

James ran back to his company's position to break the news to the others, but there was no need. They were all on their feet, cheering like mad men. He found Daniel and Matthew. "The fort is still there," he shouted. "We've done it. We've beaten them!"

It wasn't long before the news was confirmed by some of the officers. Attention now turned to the enemy in front of them. Without support from their navy they had no chance to advance on the city. It would be suicide. Just before noon, the news came that the British were withdrawing back to North Point on land and the navy was preparing to sail back down the bay. The British attempt to subdue Baltimore in the same way they did in Washington was being abandoned completely.

Life returned to its normal patterns not long after. When it became clear that the British had indeed left the Chesapeake, the militias were disbanded and the men went home with the thanks of a grateful city.

James was working in the stables one morning when William brought him a broadsheet paper. "James, take a look at this. It's amazing."

James took the paper and started to read it. After the first few lines he broke out in a broad grin. "That's what it looked like from where I was, that's for sure."

"Well I'll be," he said softly when he got to the end. "This was written by Mister Key. Where did you get this?"

"They're all over the city. Everyone has read it and is talking about it."

"It describes the sight we all saw in the morning all right, and the title says it all. 'The Defense of Fort McHenry' is an apt title. Not sure what to think of the rest of it to be honest."

"Did you see any of the bombardment when you were in Baltimore?"

"As a matter of fact I did. Everyone in the city could hear it, of course. Several of us went up to some high ground in the morning to try and get a view. It was a beautiful sight to see that grand flag as the dawn broke. It also meant that the redcoats would have to withdraw and the fighting for us was over."

"I wish I could have been there, could have seen that flag myself," William said sadly.

"That wasn't all that happened, William. We had a serious fight with the British before they started on the fort. Several of our men were killed and many more wounded." He shook his head, then looked William right in the eye. "War is a very terrible thing, my young friend. There is nothing noble or romantic about it at all. There is only fear and blood and death."

"Were you afraid, James?"

James laughed softly. "I was terrified, don't fool yourself. It's a terrible thing to stand and let someone shoot at you." He thought for a moment. "It's a much more terrible thing to aim your rifle at another man and see him go down when you fire," he said slowly, "and I can easily go the rest of my life without doing either ever again."

Later that afternoon James rode by the Key house and was not surprised to see that it was a beehive of activity. There were several carriages and horses out front and people coming and going. Key came out to bid some of his guests farewell and saw James sitting astride Annie outside the fence.

After his guests drove away in their carriages, he walked over to the fence. "Why hello James. How are you? Are things starting to return to normal at the stables?"

"Yes sir, it's fairly busy now. Folks are hiring my wagon and team to move a lot of building supplies and such. I saw your poem this morning. A young friend brought it to me."

"Well, tell me, what did you think?"

"I thought you truly captured the scene as the sun rose. I was up on the high ground behind the earthworks myself that morning and saw the flag being raised. It was indeed quite a sight."

"It was quite a sight from my vantage point as well. After we parted in Baltimore that evening, Colonel Skinner and I made our way down the harbor to the British ships where we were received politely. After we secured the release of the good doctor, however, we were told we could not go back until after the battle as we had too much foreknowledge of their plans."

"They held you on one of their gun ships?"

"No, we went back to our little schooner, under guard of course. We could see everything that happened and were up on deck at dawn. I hated this war. We should never have declared it in the first place, but I can tell you truly that my heart swelled with pride when I caught sight of that huge flag floating above the ramparts of the fort."

"It was a very great relief to us in the east of the city as well. We knew right away that the British could never take our position without their navy. By the way, did you by any chance meet their General Ross?"

"As a matter of fact I did. We dined together along with several other officers that first night we went aboard. He was killed the next day, I understand," he added sadly. "He was a true gentleman. Why do you ask?"

"It's a strange irony that. I saw him shot off his horse, but I didn't know who he was until I read about it later."

"Why do you say it's ironic?"

James told him about his conversation with the British officer the day after Washington was burned, how he had been told that Commodore Barney had been wounded and personally been attended to by General Ross. Key still didn't understand.

"I thanked the officer for that news and said I hoped we could repay the favor some day. I never thought that the general would be killed."

There was a moment of silence after that as they each reflected on the vagaries of fate, then James said, "I've been giving your offer some thought if it still stands, Mister Key."

Key thought for a moment, then remembered the conversation. "Of course it still stands, James. I am truly in your debt. What is it I can do for you to repay you for your efforts for me and for the country?"

James had been rehearsing this bit for a few days now but was still very nervous. He climbed down off of Annie and came to the fence so he could look this man in the eye.

"I want to buy Abigail's freedom, sir."

"You want to buy Abigail?" Key said, surprised.

Now there was steel in James' voice. "No sir, I do not. I want to buy her freedom from you. I don't believe any man who calls himself a Christian could own another human being. I mean no offense. I realize we do not agree on this, sir, and probably never will. I just want her to be free to do as she decides."

"I see. And have you spoken to Abigail about any of this?"

"No sir, I have not. The idea came to me on the ride home after we disbanded." James hesitated, collecting his thoughts. "I was proud to be able to take up arms in the defense of my country. I tried to serve to the best of my ability."

"Well, you certainly did that and more."

"That may be, and I thank you for saying so. But I also want to live in a place where I won't have to do that again, where I won't have to kill another man I have no hatred for."

Key nodded. "I can certainly understand that James. I too have had my fill of fighting."

"Well, that's the service you can do for me. I will pay whatever you ask. I don't want you to suffer any loss if you do."

"How can you afford to do that? Running the stables is a good business I'll wager, but have you been able to save very much?"

"After I made my decision to leave Washington, Mister Keller, who owns the land the stable is on, offered to not only buy my lease but also the business in total. I should think that between that and what I have saved, I should be able to pay you."

"And you say you haven't spoken to Abigail about any of this? How do you know she will want to go with you wherever you are going?"

"I haven't seen Abigail, but I did tell her about my father's farm when I was at Terra Rubra before. She doesn't know I have decided to move back there and help my father."

"Is that where Luke is?" Key asked, arching one eye.

James hesitated, but then decided that if he couldn't trust this man by now, then he probably couldn't trust anyone. "Yes sir. You see, my younger brother Jonathan was kidnapped by slavers a few years ago and sold south. We've had no word since and don't even know if he lives still. My father can't work the farm alone and Luke needed a place to live, to have a home where he'd be safe."

"And if Abigail doesn't want to go with you?"

"I want her to be a free woman, free to make up her own mind about how and where she lives. If she wants to come it would make me very happy, I confess. But if she doesn't, then it will be her decision, not another's."

"Where is this farm of yours? It must be in a very quiet place."

James smiled remembering. "It's about as quiet a place as you can find, miles from any town of any size. The only thing in the town is an old tavern and inn, and a blacksmith. The farms are scattered about the rolling hills beyond."

"What's the name of this new Eden of yours?"

"It's called Gettysburg."

The early signs of autumn were everywhere on the road to Terra Rubra. The wagon was rolling along at a comfortable pace as he enjoyed all the color on the trees and the crisp feel of the air. He had everything he owned in the wagon and his Annie hitched alone had no trouble with the load.

He turned into the drive up to the main house, and again the yard was full of playing children. As he passed the smaller houses below he was greeted by many waves and smiles from the people the Key's referred to as servants. Once again he pondered the man he knew as a slaveholder and a fighter for freedom, a man who would turn in a fugitive but defend the free man as hard as he could, a man who prided himself on his Christianity but owned human beings.

Key had been reluctant to free Abigail. As he explained to James, she and Polly were very close as were all the many Key children. James reminded him that Abigail would be free to stay if she chose to, or she would be free to accompany him if she wished. The main thing was that it would be her decision alone.

After a few days he relented. "I gave you my word James, and I shall keep it. It is a small thing compared to what you have done, so I'm glad to do it."

They had completed all the necessary legal requirements soon after, and James was ready to leave the city for good. He paused in his departure from his stables, thinking back on all the hard work and the pride it had brought him, as well as the many friends he had made. He also thought of the slavers and the killings but decided those would not be the memories he took away with him.

He closed the big doors for the last time and stopped, his hand on the latch, then he climbed up on to the wagon seat. He slapped the reins gently on the big mare's back. "Come on, Annie girl, let's go home." He drove away and did not look back.

Abigail had been told of James' wish that she be freed and was expecting him to visit on his way to his father's farm. The word had obviously spread throughout the slave families as well as several of them followed him up the drive at a respectful distance.

Abigail came out on the porch as he drew to a stop. "Miss Abigail," he said, tipping his hat.

She smiled but did not say a word. She went and looked up at him sitting in the seat, tears in her eyes. When he climbed down from the wagon, she embraced him gently, and he felt her body shake slightly as she cried. "You came back to me," she whispered at last.

A few days later James passed through Emmitsburg again heading for the farm. The weather was much better this time than the pouring rain he experienced on his last visit. He turned north on the road to Gettysburg and urged Annie on. He was getting close and the feeling was overwhelming him. He had been saddened by the run down appearance of the farm when he last saw it and was anxious to see if Luke being there had made any impact. He had had no word from either in the interim and was hopeful that it would look more like it did in his youth.

He passed the McGregor farm on his left and knew the turn to the farm, and home, was just ahead on the right.

As the wagon turned in, two figures appeared in the yard from the barn and turned to see who was coming. They stopped in their tracks when they saw the wagon.

"You're going to love it here, Abigail, I promise you."

She looked around, a slight smile on her lips. "I already do, James."

They climbed down and Luke ran over to them. He no longer had the look of a beaten dog and was grinning from ear to ear. James shook his hand. "It's good to see you again, Luke. I do believe that farming agrees with you."

The older man stood off to the side, curious. James led Abigail over to him. "Father, I've come home to stay this time and I've brought someone I very much want you to meet." He was holding her hand and smiling. "This is my wife, Abigail."

The older man felt unsteady on his feet for the first time in his life as he came to them. He took both of her hands in his, looking down on her his eyes filling with tears. As the first tear fell, he said, "Welcome child. Welcome home."

PART 2
THE ROAD

New Year's Day 1830 dawned cold and hard but also with a real sense of hope, much like the land below eagerly accepting the dawn. James was standing on the little porch watching the sunrise. He too felt like this was the start of a good year for him and the farm and the growing number of people living on it.

Jonathan, his first child, was sleeping soundly in his bed by the fire. He would turn fifteen in the spring. Jonathan had been given the name of his stolen little brother. Francis, named after James' father, would turn twelve and Little Abbie, his precious little girl, would soon be eight.

Luke had found a local girl from the church to marry and they both lived on the farm as well in a house next to theirs. It made James smile to think of Luke, how he had grown so much over the last few years. No longer the shy and withdrawn child that he had known in Georgetown, he was stronger, more confident but still soft spoken and kind. He and Anna were also expecting in the spring. He chuckled to himself. He knew the farm was a good place to grow corn and wheat and rye. He hadn't thought at the time they started that it would also raise a bumper crop of kids.

Last year's harvest had been very rewarding as had the three before that. He and Luke had agreed to expand the farm whenever a good opportunity presented itself and that had resulted in another 20 acres being added. There had also been a good and growing trade in beef and horses as well.

James felt very comfortable in Gettysburg. There was a small but thriving community of free blacks in town with active churches and small schools. Several owned businesses or land that was worked. There was very little of the open racism he had seen back in Washington. The Quaker influence was very strong here and their beliefs permeated the atmosphere everywhere in the valley. He could not imagine a more quiet, peaceful place.

His reverie was broken when Luke came out of his house to also watch the sunrise. After a minute of silent prayer, he noticed James and came to stand by him.

"Well, partner. It's the first day of our fifteenth year working this farm. Doesn't seem real somehow."

Luke looked out over the fields and around the yard. "No, James, it really does not." He didn't call him 'Mister James' anymore and hadn't for quite a while. They were truly partners. "It sometimes feels like I got here yesterday, other times it feels like I been here all my life and that other life happened to someone else. The truth is I *have* spent half of my life here".

In all the years James had known him, Luke had never really spoken of his past life. Technically he was still a runaway slave and in danger, but he had lived here so long now that most folks thought he was from these parts and no one had ever asked.

James thought that he would like to know, to truly understand, what the boy had been through that made him the man he was today, but he could not. "Well, Luke, for what it's worth that life is over, and you have a home now and a baby on the way."

He looked down at the ground shyly then back up at James. His face was alight, a grin from ear to ear. "I still cannot get used to that thought, James. I'm going to be a father."

"And you will be a fine father I'm sure. Now we're wasting daylight here. I'll meet you in the barn as soon as I finish dressing and we can start on the fences in the north field."

By the time the sun was fully up they were working on the

fences. It was bright and clear with an inch or two of snow left over from last week's storm. Since this was their pasture for raising their few cattle they always had a steady stream of repair jobs throughout the year. Cows are hard on fences.

They took a break at noon and dove into the basket Abigail had packed for them. "You want ham or ham?"

Luke set the water jug down on the wagon floor. "I was hopin' there'd be some ham today." Since they had slaughtered the last hog a month or so ago, ham had been a staple of the diet.

James shook his head. "I don't know, Luke. I have to admit I never thought I would get tired of eatin' it."

They were packing up lunch and getting ready to get back to work when James first noticed them. Two riders were in the dirt lane that ran just outside the farm property, just sitting and watching them. Then Luke noticed them as well and a chill ran through him to his very core.

"Slavers," he whispered to James.

James just nodded very slightly as he met the watchful gaze of the riders. "Then they have no business here."

One of the men touched the brim of his hat and they began to move on, looking over their shoulder often as they went.

James and Luke went back to work on the fences, but after a half hour James put down the axe he had been using. He looked over at Luke. "I just have a feeling….. I don't know why but I think we should go back. I'm not comfortable with a pregnant woman and a sick woman being alone right now with all the children."

They headed back with a nagging sense of urgency. When they came in sight of the yard, they were both relieved to see Anna out in the yard, with Little Abbie playing in the snow.

"I think maybe today we should find something useful to do around the yard here," James said as he slowed the horse. "Yes, I think we can sure find enough here to keep us busy for a while."

For the next week the men stuck close to the houses and the barn-yard. There is always plenty to do on a farm so there was no short-age of things to keep them busy. If someone needed to go to a more distant area of the farm they went alone and armed while the other stayed close to home.

When Sunday rolled around there had been no sign of any other strangers. The farm sat back off the road and was shielded from view by a small stand of trees, so seeing any strangers was a rare and sometimes unsettling event.

They loaded up the wagon with some potatoes and squash they had put away as well as several jars of apple butter that Abigail loved to make and sell to raise a little extra money. When everyone was settled down and Little Abbie up on the bench seat between the men, James started the horses on their way.

Wesleyan Methodist was the largest black church in the county. It was a big affair on Sundays when everyone could see old friends and scattered family members, make peace with God and sing. Afterwards there was always food, and someone would inevitably produce a fiddle and the sound of it would fill the air along with the sound of laughing children.

The preacher on this Sunday was well known and respected in the community, a serious and sober thinker and inspiring speaker. As he came to the front to begin his sermon, he was looking down and James could see his lips moving slightly, like he was sounding something out, trying the words on for fit.

The crowd started to get a little restless and he looked up from his thoughts. "I'm sorry, brothers and sisters, but I have had some hard news from the pastor down in Petersburg. He relays to me that a number of men crossed over from Maryland in the past few weeks." He paused for a moment. "There is every reason to believe that these men are slavers and they are hunting our brothers and sisters, hunting us, for rewards."

The room erupted in sound then. Shouts of "No" and "I'm freeborn" competed with the wailing of the older women, many of whom knew the foul taste of slavery themselves.

The pastor raised his hands to try and quiet the crowd. It took a while, but the sound of voices slowly subsided. "I know that many of you here have come from those awful fields and now have your legal freedom. But I also know that men such as these care not about what is 'legal' but only about subjugation and hatred."

He looked out over the now silent crowd. "God is on our side, brothers, sisters. He is on our side and we will live in freedom. I don't know why he's taking so very long to make it so, but I sure do wish he would hurry it up a little."

With that the crowd laughed some, a little nervously. "Until that time as the Lord sees fit, we will just have to help ourselves. I'm sure I need not remind anyone in this room about who it is that the Lord helps, do I?" He looked around the room again. "I believe this would be a very appropriate time to recall the flight of the slaves from Egypt." With that, he opened his bible and began his sermon.

Afterwards the mood was subdued, with small groups of men meeting and talking. The women were organizing food on the tables and the children were happy and blissful as only children can be, running outside until they were cold then back inside to warm up. The world was still full of beauty and wonder to them. James saw Mister Anders, who owned the property just north of his, and walked over.

"James, how are you?" As they shook hands he stepped a little closer conspiratorially and lowered his voice. "Luke just told me about the riders on the lane between us. Did you get a good look at them?"

"Good enough, I suppose. They were young white men dressed like they had been traveling for a while."

"Did they say anything or do anything?"

"No. They just sat and stared at us for a few minutes, then the taller of the two touched the brim of his hat and they rode away."

"I don't know. Could be nothin' I suppose, but I don't like the sound of it... or the feel of it either. I have noticed a slight change in the air in the last week or so."

"How so? What kind of change?" James asked.

"Hard to put a finger on until the sermon just now. I been hearin' about small groups of white men riding through some other towns. They never seem to have much to say is what I hear. Just lookin' around at folks. You know my cousin in Petersburg, Thomas? He's told me he's seen plenty of them down there ridin' north. One of them looked at him as they rode by his place and smiled the devil's smile at him. Made his blood run cold, it did."

"Those were the only white strangers I've seen around here in some time. They kind of made my blood run cold also." James said. "Yes, I think I can understand how Thomas felt."

They went back to the table and the others, laughing through the windows at a group of boys trying to see who could climb the giant elm tree on the grounds the highest. The girls were inside among the women, helping set out the indoor picnic, everybody contributing what they could. The mood varied as the conversations went from one group to another.

The group started to break up earlier than usual. Everyone seemed anxious to be home and secure, or at least as secure as any black person could be in these frightening times. James and Luke loaded the wagon and gathered everyone up. Abigail wanted to stop at the mercantile store at the crossroads and drop off the jars of apple butter and vegetables.

The way back to the farm ran through the little town itself. James had a hard time calling this muddy crossroads a town at all. It was nothing like the city of Washington, D.C. in size or population. It now consisted of an inn and tavern, the mercantile, a post office, and a blacksmith. A smattering of houses were starting to go up nearby as more and more folks moved in.

James stopped at the mercantile and, handing the reins to Abigail, jumped down with Luke and the jars of apple butter. James noticed an odd feeling that he hadn't been aware of until now. He felt like he was back in the fighting with the British, but this time it was his supposed countrymen. He was suddenly very aware of his surroundings and the people around him. Everything was as it should be, but he could not shake the heightened sense of awareness he was feeling. He had had the same feeling in 1814.

As he entered the shop, Mister McDonald looked up from his figures. "Good afternoon, James. I see you have some more of Abigail's nectar from heaven with you."

"Yes sir, she sent me in to deliver these. She may have some more in the next week or two if you still want some in the store."

"Of course I do, James, of course I do. Folks around here really appreciate it, especially this time of year. Not everyone owns a farm, you know."

James was certainly aware of that. In the years he had been here, the little town was beginning to boast a robust and active black population. Most were day workers or farm hands. Many women were in paid domestic service unlike their sisters a little to the south. The Matthews family had a nice large farm near Yellow Hill. Then there was Anders to his north and the Stone family on the other side of Little Round Top from his place.

As truly kind and anti-slavery as most of the white population was, there was very little integration in town. White and black churches were separate. The new schools that were talked about being built were for white students, but he was heartened by the beginning construction of a black school right in the town itself. He had always felt safe here, or at least he had until very lately.

McDonald went to his office to get James the money from the previous sales of apple butter as Luke went back to the wagon. James was waiting as he came back out into the store. "Mister McDonald, have you noticed any strangers passing through Gettysburg lately? Any groups of men you haven't seen before?"

McDonald stroked his chin and thought a minute. "Now you mention it, two young men came by a day or two ago for some provisions. Never saw them go, may even still be hereabouts I suppose. Why do you ask?"

James lowered his voice even though the only patron was on the other side of the room. "It's just that Luke and I were out working last week, and we saw two riders watching us. Then today

Pastor Williams reported that several groups of riders have been passing through Petersburg heading north."

McDonald didn't need it spelled out for him. He was a Quaker like so many of the older folks around, and their hatred of slavery was well known to all. He started to get angry. "It's slave hunters again then, isn't it?

"Looks like that to me and most others. I have had all the association with those jackals I care to have. They even attacked me in my own home and business back in the capital."

"Well, I've seen you fight and shoot at the county fairs. Since you are here and they are not I have to assume it did not go well for them."

"No, sir, it did not, but I'd certainly rather avoid that sort of thing in the future."

"I understand my friend, I truly do. You know our group's stance on violence, but what I cannot and will not understand is how any man thinks he has the right to own another. This just cannot be what God wants."

As they walked together to the door, McDonald suddenly put his hand on James' shoulder. "That's them, that's the riders I told you about that came in here."

James followed his eyes down the street. Sure enough two riders were coming slowly up the street towards the wagon. They were obviously maneuvering their horses to put one on each side. Luke was watching their approach as calmly as possible. James saw him lean over and whisper to Abigail as he stepped on the plank walk in front.

"May I help you gentlemen?" James asked in a polite voice.

The taller of the two, the one who had smiled and touched the brim of his hat, came up on the side where Abigail was holding the reins. "Good morning, ma'am. Is this here your wagon or your masters?" he said, ignoring James completely.

"Excuse me, sir, but may I be of help to you?" James said firmly.

The riders both turned to face James, ice in their eyes. "Did you hear that? This here sure is one fancy talkin' nigger. Where'd you learn to talk like that, boy?"

"I'll just take it that I cannot be of any service then, so my family and I will be on our way."

"I don't recall anyone here tellin' you to speak, boy, so why don't you just try shuttin' the hell up."

Abigail sat stone upright holding the reins, barely breathing. Luke just stood beside the wagon. James put a small sack in the back with some sugar and flour he had bought, along with some hard candy for his three children who were hunkered down in the back, terrified.

When he saw the look on the boys' faces he started to lose his patience, but he knew nothing good could come of that even in a town like this. Luke climbed in back with the children and James started to climb up beside his wife.

"Where do you think you're going, boy? Ain't nobody said you could leave yet."

James turned to face them as they dismounted and approached on his side, putting a gap between them. James could see they each had a pistol under their outer coat but no other visible weapons. He said nothing, just watching.

"I asked you a question, boy. Where the hell do you think you're goin'?"

After a full minute of silence, James rolled his eyes and shrugged, turning back to the wagon. As he expected, the shorter one tried to pull him away. James stepped out of his reach, took his outstretched arm and pulled it behind his back. As he started to resist James shoved him face first into the side of the wagon and let him fall in the street.

The taller man stepped back and reached in his coat. "Why you lousy stinkin'…"

"I ain't thinkin' that's a very good idea," Luke said as he pointed the rifle he always had ready at the man's forehead. The muzzle was only a yard or two away from his face. "I ain't that good a shot, mister, but I never miss from this range."

The man looked around at the few people on the street. "You people can't let them niggers do this to a white man." He was getting a little frantic.

James reached into the coat of the semi-conscious man on the ground and extracted his pistol then stepped towards the other. "Give me your pistol," he said firmly.

"Go to hell, nigger."

He barely had the words out before James connected a strong right jab to the man's nose. He collapsed to his knees and covered his face, blood starting to pour from between his fingers. James reached in and took his pistol as well.

"In this part of the country, it is considered impolite as well as illegal to assault anyone, especially on the street. I have no idea what sort of people you live among that this sort of behavior is tolerated, but it certainly is not here. I suggest you go back where you came from."

The man looked up, his face full of rage and hate. "I'll kill you, you black bastard. I swear I will."

"Your language is also not acceptable when there are women and children around, so I will be on my way now. Oh, and by the way, using a double negative like 'ain't nobody' just shows your ignorance to anyone within earshot." James turned back to the wagon with the pistols in hand.

"Where do you think you're going with my property?"

"You mean these? Well, since you assaulted me with them I thought I would keep them as a souvenir. Maybe I'll need to use them at our next meeting."

The other man was getting to his feet and unsteadily moving away from the wagon. Luke motioned with his rifle for him to go join his companion.

"We want our weapons back, damn you."

James thought for a moment and nodded. "You are quite correct, gentlemen. I would be nothing more than a common thief if I take them, so I will be very happy to return them."

He went into the store and brought out a ten-pound sledge. He smartly tapped the end of the barrel to remove the charges from both of them, then dropped them in the street in front of the wagon. Taking the sledge he demolished them with four or five quick swings. He picked up the pieces as best he could.

"There you go, gentlemen. Good as new," he said, dropping the pieces in front of them. His face was blank.

"You bloody bastard…"

James made a motion like he was setting up for another quick jab, which ended the need for further conversation from either man.

"Good day, gentlemen, and good day to you, too, Mister McDonald." James climbed back in the wagon, took the reins from Abigail and smiled at his children in the back. "Let's go home."

Abigail was still very tense as they left the little town and could not relax. James was very contrite and started to say so. He understood that she had grown up a slave and she was not used to seeing a black man stand up for himself. Since she had never in her short life seen anything good come of something like that, she could not get comfortable with it.

"Did you have to take them on like that, James? Did you have to? Our children are in the back, you know. What if something had happened, what if they shot you in front of them? Did you ever think of that?"

James was calm and looking straight ahead as he held the reins. The horses were taking a slow pace and it was getting on towards dusk and very still. He thought a minute before replying.

Without turning his head he said, "I was thinking of the boys, Abigail. Not just our two boys but my father's two boys. My father grew up free but understood that 'free' means different things depending on your skin, so he taught us boys how to defend ourselves. I have had to before this and I am sure I will have to again, and I will teach my boys what my father taught his. Not only how to use your fists and fight, but also that we are free men, damn it, and we will fight to remain free. I cannot and will not let my boys see me back down to a white man or any other."

They drove on in silence for a while, then Abigail visibly relaxed and reached her hand over to hold his, the only break in the silence was Luke softly humming an old gospel song.

Anna's baby arrived just as winter was leaving, and of course it came in the middle of the night. That dawn had seen a beautiful new baby girl resting asleep in her exhausted mother's arms. Luke sat sleeping in a nearby chair breathing softly.

The baby stirred, as babies do, and Luke sat up and came quietly to the bed so as not to disturb his family. He just stood there watching his beautiful wife with their precious new baby in her arms. Under his breath he whispered very quietly, "My family….. my own family," as tears started to silently fall. This was something that had never occurred to him as even the most remote of possibilities until Anna started to show her pregnancy. Even then it was still a distant dream, really, but here they were…. right here with him, in their own home.

Anna opened her eyes and looked at her baby. Luke realized at that moment, a moment he knew would be frozen in his memory until his last breath, just how beautiful Anna was. He moved to wipe a tear from his eye when she noticed he was there.

"Good mornin' father. I didn't see you there. Have you been there all night?"

Luke was still so overcome it was difficult to speak. He was always soft spoken and reserved and now he found he could not speak at all. Finally, he cleared his throat. "Good mornin' to you, little mother and to you…what are we going to call this child."

"In my family, we usually named boys for the husband's father and girls for the mother." She hesitated for a moment. Luke had rarely if ever talked about the farm In Virginia he had escaped from or the family, if any, he had left behind. "Do you remember your mother's name, Luke?"

Luke nodded. He could not take his eyes off his child. "Constance," he said softly. "Her name was Constance."

Anna tried that on for size. "Constance… Constance," she said quietly, letting it grow in her heart. Then she nodded. "Then Constance it is and will be. Now, why don't you pick her up and greet her properly."

Luke was terrified at the prospect of holding something so

fragile in his rough hands. "Go on, Luke. She won't break I promise. Just be sure to support her little head. That's it, get one arm under her body and the other under her head. That's right, just like that. See, you are a natural father."

Luke felt his heart stop beating as he gazed down at her. "Good morning, Constance, and welcome to the family."

Spring is always a spectacular time in the Cumberland Valley, and this year was no exception. By the beginning of May the corn and rye crops were growing very well, the chicken population had exploded and the garden by the house was already producing a few early tomatoes.

The partners had learned well from James' father. He taught them to diversify their crops, never put all their hopes on only one crop no matter how the markets were last season and to love and care for the land that supported them and their growing families.

As spring drifted into summer James became fascinated by the change in Luke, how he became more outgoing, more engaging. He was always a very gentle and quiet boy before Constance came along, and now he was really blossoming as a fine young man.

He had known Luke ever since the runaway appeared under his loading platform in Georgetown, but he had no idea what his age was. Neither did Luke, for that matter. While some planters kept very accurate records of slave births others did not. They were valuable property after all, but his master did not keep good records except for the purchase or sale of other human beings.

James figured he was around thirteen or fourteen when they left Georgetown to come here so he must be nearing twenty-nine by now. It was impossible for James to understand how his childhood must have been, especially when he tried to compare it to his own carefree youth. Luke had never smiled, never raised his voice, always tried to be invisible.

After Constance he had a smile every moment he was awake.

He carried on so around his young wife and daughter that it made James and Abigail smile, too. And the baby was a character, trying to crawl around the little house with that same smile on her face as well. Like the farm itself, mother and daughter were flourishing.

"Wake up, Poppa, wake up."

James stirred in his bed, slow to wake. "Is it time, son?"

"Yes sir, it's time to go now, Poppa. We don't want to be late."

James smiled at that, at the eagerness of his oldest son. "I know, boy, I know. Remember who you're talking to now." His son was new to The Road and was extremely excited to be part of it. James was enormously proud of him but a little worried too. The Road would only be able to take passengers if strict precautions were the norm. It was a deadly serious business they were engaged in.

"Sorry, Poppa. I know. I just want to help the people get…."

"Get free, boy, that's what this is all about. Freedom. Don't ever forget that."

"I won't Poppa, don't worry none about that." James was up and dressed and as they left he grabbed his rifle from its place near the door.

James stopped and looked up at the stars. "Should be the same as last time. It's a beautiful night."

"Yes sir," Jonathan agreed. "Still a little cool, though."

"Well, I guess we oughta pick up the pace a bit." They started an easy trot toward their goal, the hills on the west side of the valley. James had learned in the militia that running a hundred paces then walking a hundred will get you where you're going in a hurry.

They arrived at the usual place with the usual caution. James entered the clearing first and looked around. The moon was almost full, the night cloudless and calm. He sat on a large stone and waited. Hearing nothing for a few minutes, he motioned Jonathan to follow him in.

They sat on the rock and watched the stars turn in the sky above them. It truly was a beautiful evening which masked the deadly serious nature of their activity.

After a few more minutes, James pointed to a particular piece of the sky. "There she is, Jonathan, just where she should be. The Drinking Gourd." He said this loud enough for anyone close by to overhear. Sure enough a figure appeared from the far side of the clearing and approached them.

"Good evening, brother James," the man said as they shook hands. "I sure am mighty glad to see you." He glanced at the young man still sitting on the rock. "Who you got there, brother James?"

"Good evening, Pastor. That's my oldest boy, Jonathan. Son, come on over here and meet the conductor on this part of the line."

The man did not introduce himself, nor did his father mention a name. "Pleased to meet you, sir," Jonathan said quietly as they shook hands.

"I'm glad to meet you, boy, mighty glad. We need all the new blood and help we can muster. Has your daddy told you how serious this is? That vigilance must be constant, that people's lives are in danger every moment?"

"Yessir, he has done that… several times."

"Well, you listen to your daddy, you hear. It was brave men like him that got the line running through these parts at last."

With that, the man turned to the opposite side of the clearing from which he had emerged a few minutes ago. He raised his cupped hands to his lips and made the call of an owl. "It's all right now. You can come out."

Four figures emerged from the trees, looking warily around them, moving slowly. They came over to where James and their conductor were standing. James could see them clearly now, four young men he guessed to be between sixteen and the late twenties, all fit and strong young men who only wanted to breathe free air for once in their lives, free air sometime before they died.

"This here is brother James, y'all. He'll be your conductor on this next part of the line. You just follow him, and he will guide you to where you need to go next." He motioned for James to follow him and they walked a few feet away. "We had some trouble startin' out tonight. We was trailed by some slavers, but we managed to shake them off. Never seen 'em in that area before."

"I've been hearing that more are being seen passing through our town, mostly heading north. I guess they want to block routes into Canada."

They shook hands again and the man turned to leave. "I know it ain't very Christian of me, but there be only one place for a slaver and that's a hole in the ground." He turned and disappeared into the forest.

James certainly agreed with that sentiment. His brother had been kidnapped and he had had his own run in with slavers back in Washington that ended in extreme violence. No, they were not to be trifled with and were best avoided.

He turned to his new charges who were watching him with a mixture of fear and hope that James had trouble with. "All right, I know you men are tired, that it's been a long night already, but we have just another few miles to go before we shelter for the day." The four men all looked at each other and nodded to James. "I wouldn't be the least surprised to find something very good to eat as well."

The oldest of the men stepped forward. "Yassir, it has been a long journey and this night one of the hardest." He looked at the others again, who nodded in agreement. "Don't you worry none about us. We can walk as long as it takes to get free." Once again he looked at his companions. "Knowin' there will be somethin' good to eat don't hurt none, either." He was smiling at James. "We'll go on as long as it takes. No need to worry about that."

James smiled back at this stranger who was also very familiar. "Then we should be on our way. There aren't many people out this way, but we best be as quiet as possible. If we keep the Drinking Gourd off our left shoulders we should be at the next station soon."

He turned and led them out of the clearing and back towards the farm, all in single file with Jonathan bringing up the rear. He walked with his rifle cradled in his arms, listening for anything abnormal in the night.

After a couple of hours of steady walking the sky started to get light in the east and James could make out some of the surrounding terrain. He motioned for the group to stop so he could verify their position. The older man approached James again and waited.

As James' eyes wandered the scene, so did the other man's. "This here sure is some beautiful countryside. Yassir, this is some beautiful place."

James, searching the valley for any hint of trouble, stopped and saw it through this fleeing man's eyes. "I grew up here and I wouldn't live anywhere else. My brother and I ran these woods and streams like a giant playground."

"That must have been a wondrous time. What's the name of that little hill over there, the one sticks up some?"

"We call that one Little Round Top. There's another Round Top back a ways. That hill was always one of our favorite hunting grounds." James smiled at the memory of the two of them running free, oblivious to the world around them, very much in stark contrast to the lives these young men had lived. "Yes, it was indeed a wondrous time."

They walked back to the group. "The farm is only around that small rise just ahead there. We have safe places, clean beds and food. You'll be among friends there and God willing we will be on our way tomorrow evening."

They approached the farm from a line of trees to the south. James stopped at the tree line and scanned the fields. In a minute he saw Luke working a team of plow horses in the eastern field.

He turned to his companions. "That's the signal. If he's out plowing, then everything is normal, no one is waiting to ambush us. Let's go."

As they emerged from the trees the fugitives all huddled together in the morning light. They always felt much more comfortable hiding in the shadows.

"It's all right now men. That man behind the plow is a runaway like yourselves. He can be trusted as he would rather die than give someone up."

Luke had seen them and led the team to drink by the barn. The others joined him there, each former slave eyeing the other, a look of recognition obvious, even to James.

"Welcome, friends, welcome," Luke said softly.

They all surrounded Luke now, firing questions at him and patting his shoulder. James and Jonathan drifted away towards the house, knowing that the language being spoken was not one they were familiar with.

He stood in the doorway to the little house and watched his young daughter and wife at work in the kitchen. Abigail had been ailing for some time, but she still moved with the same easy grace of the young woman he had brought here all those years ago, and she was humming softly to herself as she worked.

"Um boy something sure smells good in here. What's for breakfast this fine morning, Abigail?"

Abigail turned from her work. "Why good morning, James. Did you bring in the passengers this morning?"

He moved aside to let Anna, Luke's young wife, into the kitchen. "Mornin' James. It sure enough is a beautiful morning. Are those the passengers out there with my Luke?"

"Yes, ladies, those are some very hungry passengers. Are we about ready in here?"

Abigail turned and with a show of indignation pushed her husband back out the door. "It will be ready when it's ready... and besides, you know it is definitely going to be worth waiting for. Now go get those gentlemen washed up and then we'll be ready. Go on now."

It was obvious that these fugitives had never had a meal like this very often if indeed ever. There were thick slabs of aged ham and heaps of eggs, with fresh biscuits and honey. There wasn't much conversation as the men helped themselves.

The youngest of the group was crying softly. He turned to Luke, tears rolling down his face. "I ain't ever had nobody be so kind to me before, not ever." He tried to gather his thoughts, then he turned to James. "Why, Mister James? Why do you do this? I ain't no kin to you, none of us be. Why do you do this?"

James put his fork down and thought for a moment. "Why do we do this," motioning to the others around the table. "We," he emphasized again, "we do this because you need help. We do this because it's right. We do this because someone must act, someone must stand up against this evil in our land." He picked up his fork and impaled a piece of ham. "That's why we do it. Now eat up. We have your beds ready."

Luke had his hand on the boy's shoulder. "C'mon now boy. That food is seasoned enough, it doesn't need the salt from your tears."

The boy dug in again. "I ain't never going to be able to repay you. Not ever."

The men started to stir at sundown and make ready for the night's journey. They all knew that they were still some ways and some days from freedom, but they were now closer to that ideal than they were to the southern slave fields.

There were two sites on the farm for hiding fugitives. They had done this in case of a raid by slavers. Hopefully if one group was found the other would not be. As the youngest boy and one other man came down from the loft, Luke led the other two into the barn.

They gathered together nervously, more out of instinct than fear of Luke or James. After a moment, James came in carrying a satchel. There was a small table in the corner and James started to empty the contents.

"Eat up, gentlemen, eat up. We have a long way to go tonight." On the table there were loaves of bread and some ham and cheese as well as a pitcher of fresh milk. Once again the fugitives were overcome by this kindness they had never known but dug in like they didn't know where their next meal was coming from, which of course they literally did not.

They started out just as the last light was fading from the western sky. It was a chilly clear evening so navigating would be easy enough. They left the yard and cut across the north side of the farm fields.

James stopped and pointed at the sky. "You men see the Drinking Gourd there? All night we will keep it just ahead of our left shoulders and keep moving. If we get separated, remember that. Just ahead of your shoulder. Understand?"

The oldest of the group spoke for the others once more. "Yassuh we understand. We been following them stars for some time now. We'll keep on a watchin' her."

The leg to Yellow Hill wasn't the longest they had done, but it was through more populated areas than they were used to. James knew that the majority of his neighbors hated slavery as much as anyone, but with slavers out hunting down men and women like animals and offering hefty rewards, it was best to avoid any contact except with fellow conductors and passengers.

They kept moving through the night, stopping every hour or so to rest and listen. In the third hour James raised his hand and motioned for them all to get down. He had heard a noise up ahead and went to investigate.

He came back to them motioning they should stay down. "There are some men gathering their tools from that field ahead," he said quietly. "They must have been at it pretty late. I think they'll be gone soon, and we can be back on our way."

Sure enough, after twenty minutes they could hear the noise start to fade away. In a few more minutes James went to investigate. This time he walked in and motioned for them to come out. "They're all gone now. Let's get a move on."

They continued without incident and came to a stop at the top of a small rise. Off in the near distance the lights of a very small town were just visible. "That's Biglerville, right where she should be." He scanned the sky to the northwest. "We'll change our course just to the west and we should be at the next station before long."

The men all nodded silently and followed James across the next field. As the night deepened, the lights from farms and small towns all started to blink out. The increasing darkness seemed to increase the anxiety level, but James knew it was a help in more ways than one. It not only cloaked them, it would make any light showing just that much brighter. James knew the church would indeed have a light at the door to guide them.

After another hour James again motioned for them to get down. He had seen the light on the church ahead. "I'm going down there to look around. Wait here and don't move."

He didn't wait for a response but was off. He approached slowly and listened closely. He could see an occasional silhouette against one of the windows. He approached the front door and, picking up the lantern he entered.

An older white man greeted him. "Brother James, at last. We were getting a little concerned about you."

The two men shook hands. James knew this man and many of his Quaker friends. The Road would not be able to operate around here without their help.

"Brother Joshua, it is a pleasure to see you again. We had a slight delay and detour, but otherwise a good first leg for tonight. If everything is right here, I'll go collect my passengers and bring them in."

When they were all gathered in the small church the fugitives once again huddled together, especially since there were several white people in the room, something that usually did not bode well for them in their experience. The youngest of them nervously approached James.

"Mister James, who are these people?"

"They're called Quakers, son." He could see the anxiety virtually dripping off the boy like sweat. He put his hand on the boy's shoulder. "They are your friends, son, I give you my word. Quakers hate slavery deeply. They are here to help you to get free, so don't forget that."

159

The boy looked over at the small group of Quakers, both men and women. They certainly did not seem threatening to him. "I don't know, Mister James. You see, for us nothin' much good has come to any of us from meetin' with white folks before now."

James certainly understood that aspect. Even though he was free born he had had to kowtow to too many white people who had hate in their hearts. He referred to folks like that as "christian wolves."

James led the boy back to the group. "I understand you bein' nervous and all about white folks bein' here, I truly do. But these folks are different. Their God forbids slavery and asks them to help the fugitive find freedom. They have committed their lives to helping people like you, trust me."

They mumbled a few quiet words among themselves, then the oldest one nodded. "Yassuh, brother James. We all feels like we can trust you all right. If they be your friends, then they are our friends as well." He nodded again. "Sure enough so," he said with conviction.

James nodded as well. "Well, we can't tarry here any longer." He motioned to a young white boy who stood nearby watching them. As he approached the fugitives were eyeing him from head to toe.

"This boy is going to take you to the next station. It will be about as far as we have been tonight already, so you'd best be off soon. Don't worry, this boy has led several dozen folks over this leg. He'll get you there, all right."

The others all looked at the youngest among them who stepped forward. He didn't offer James his hand or look him in the eye. "We all just wants to thank you, Mister James. Thank you from the bottom of our hearts."

James reached down and took the boy's hand. "Look me in the eye, son. You are not a slave anymore, you hear? You will be a free man soon and you can look any man in the eye that you meet."

He waited until his charges were safely on their way with the new conductor, then spoke with Joshua and some of the others.

"I've been thinking I would bring my oldest boy along on this leg so he can learn it."

"Is that the young man who has been learning the route to your farm?" James nodded. "Well then certainly bring him along. Looks like we may still be at this work for a few more years to come unfortunately, and we'll need all the young blood we can get."

He started walking towards home, and later as the sky began to show signs of the coming dawn he began to sing softly to himself. He never felt he had much of a voice, and the looks from friends in the church when he was a child sort of reinforced that idea. It was always his little brother Jonathan who had the singing voice, which he was always happy to demonstrate in church. He wasn't worried about anyone seeing or hearing him now, though. After all, he was well known in the area after all the years spent there. He began to sing softly at first, then as he chose another song his voice grew louder and more confident.

He remembered when he had started to sing as a child, watching his mother sing while she worked. At first he was uncomfortable with the spirituals and old songs from the south, but the closer he grew to former slaves the more he began to appreciate what the songs were about. He began to realize the true dimensions of their beauty. On one level, they were a coping mechanism against the great evil of slavery. On another, it was a way for people to communicate, to inspire or to warn. More importantly they gave the folks singing them a sense of family and community, a sense of shared suffering.

By the time he got to the last hill before the farm the sun was well and truly up. He paused for a bit to enjoy the view from there. He could see most of the property and the two neat little houses with smoke curling from the chimney of the larger, the barn off to the side. He knew his beautiful wife Abigail and Luke's young wife Anna would be preparing a meal for his arrival.

Then he looked over at the corner nearest the woods on the south side. There, among a beautiful stand of trees, his mother and father now lay. He thought about all that his father had had to endure to build this place up and keep it running so he could make a home for his family. He remembered when his younger brother was kidnapped by slavers in the woods not far from here and he felt the rage rising in him again remembering what that act had done to his parents. Even though he was a father now he could not begin to imagine the pain they felt.

Luke greeted him with a wave from behind the team he was leading in the small pasture. James waved back and made his way to his house. When he opened the door he realized he was starving to death.

"Mm mmm, what is that delightful aroma?"

Abigail turned from the stove and once again James' heart caught. In the soft morning light she looked just as she had when they first arrived here fifteen years ago. She had been a little frightened then, her sudden freedom and new life a little overwhelming. Now, she was showing the signs of her illness, an illness no one seemed able to diagnose.

"Well, good morning, husband. How was your journey?"

James made his way to the table and Abigail brought over a steaming plate. "I don't believe I have ever been this hungry in my entire life," he said as he started to dig in.

"And the passengers? Were they delivered to the next station?"

James had to finish a rather large bite before he could answer. "Your mother sure did teach you well, Abigail, she certainly did." He finished swallowing and looked up at her. "The fact that I am sitting here with you now is proof that all went well. You know I would die before surrendering any passengers to anyone."

"I know that James, it's just that we all get so worried when you are out conducting, that's all."

"I know you do sweetheart. I know all of you do, but this is probably the most important work to be done at this time so I'm going to do it. If it makes you feel any better our Jonathan will be going with me to Yellow Hill on the next journey."

James broke the news to Jonathan over the evening meal. They had been sitting quietly and eating, resting up from a hard but productive day.

"Jonathan, son, you have done very well helping me with the passengers so far. How would you like to learn another leg of the railroad?" James was still a little hesitant to ask him, but not because he thought he couldn't handle it. The truth was that James didn't mind risking his own neck, he just had a hard time asking his own son to do the same.

"Of course, poppa. Anything to help, you know that." All the children knew that their mother had been born a slave but now lived as a proud and free woman. It imbued them with a true and undying hatred for that peculiar institution. "I would do anything to help anyone trying to escape to freedom. Anything."

James smiled at that. "I know you would, son, I know."

Summer slowly became fall that year, with the nights staying warm and dry and the days unrelentingly hot. The farm continued to be productive and secure so the families could live their lives in peace and tranquility.

During the summer and fall James and Jonathan conducted another two dozen people on The Road, people who were pursued mercilessly by slave hunters, guilty only of being born black in the wrong place.

The slavers were out hunting more often now as the number of runaways from Virginia and Maryland steadily mounted. In the eyes of the slave owners these pieces of "property" had no right to exercise the rights guaranteed all men under the Declaration of Independence, had no right to think of themselves as somehow "men" deserving of anything but the whip.

Everything was done to prove to the enslaved that they was less than a human, from counting as only three fifths of a person for the census to being denied any chance to learn to read and write or to improve their lot in life.

There were many stories of kind and merciful owners, men who saw at least that there was value in treating their "property" well if for no other reason than economics. Yet even these more kindly slave owners suffered from slaves running to find freedom. The harsh reality was that for every kind master there were ten unspeakably cruel ones.

There was a peculiar belief among white society in the south that somehow slaves were happy with their situation, that they were well taken care of and cared for much as one takes care of cattle or horses. What these people could never understand was that in every black chest was a heart beating for one thing.... Freedom.

Everyone who "worked" on the underground railroad knew the risks they faced every time they went out into the night. While many in the north were sympathetic to the slave's plight, a growing number were not. Technically what they were doing was illegal. There was often a substantial reward for the return of "contrabands", more money than could be made working a farm or shop, so betrayals were common. County sheriffs and constables were placed in an awkward situation because they were required to lock up any black person brought in by any white man with no need for cause or explanation.

There was also the very real threat of being captured by slavers and taken south. No slaver ever bothered to read any papers a black man or woman may have had. It was not at all uncommon for freeborn blacks to be kidnapped and sold south, especially in the areas near the border, near the Mason-Dixon line, that invisible line on a paper that separated people from their birthright... to live free.

During late summer and into fall, the number of suspected slavers passing through Gettysburg and nearby towns increased substantially, keeping everyone on edge in the communities. James and Luke kept an eye out for the two riders who had taken them on in town, but they weren't seen again that year. James did not feel he had seen the last of them, but he was more worried about the number of slaver hunters he did see.

They developed a system so that someone who could and would shoot was always on the farm if one of the men was going to be away. The farm was such a quiet and peaceful place that it was easy to think that nothing could happen there, but the hard lesson had been learned in Georgetown and James was not going to take a risk with his family.

The very pleasant autumn gave way to a very harsh winter, with frequent blizzards helping to at least keep the slavers at bay for a while. It also kept any visits to town to a minimum as well, but the harvest had been very good, and they had plenty of time to lay in anything needed for the long winter's night they knew was coming.

Christmas presented them with another two feet of snow so even moving around the barnyard was a chore. At dinner that evening James offered a prayer for another prosperous year, then looking around at his and Luke's families gathered together in the warm glow of the fire and their love for each other, James offered another prayer for "our brethren held in bondage" not very far away.

With the new year and the new spring, stories started making the rounds once more about slavers being seen on the roads again, plying their ungodly trade. James and Luke went back to being sure someone was always with the women and children at the farm.

James and Jonathan also went back to conducting on The Road. More escapees were heading north as the weather improved and the snow disappeared and the two legs they worked had a steady flow of passengers seeking freedom. The faces were always the same each trip. Strong young black men and now more women with both fear and hope on their faces and in their hearts, willing to leave everything and everyone behind them in order to breathe free.

Their pattern was always the same, trying to get in some sleep and then rising and leaving the farm while it was still very dark. They gave themselves three hours or so to reach the clearing and rarely had to wait very long for the passenger handoff.

As they approached the clearing this night, James motioned for Jonathan to hang back. Cradling his rifle, he strained to hear any sound in the darkness. He handed the rifle to his son and told him to listen and watch closely as he entered the clearing alone.

He took his place on the large rock in the center and looked up at the sky. There was a low layer of clouds scudding by a few hundred feet above, with an occasional spit of rain. This would not be a good night to navigate by the stars and he was glad he knew this ground like the back of his hand.

After what seemed a long time, he began to grow more concerned. Movement on The Road was always fraught with danger but the reports of more and more slavers being seen around border areas made it even more so. James stood up to stretch and was just thinking of going back to the farm when a figure appeared out of the forest.

This regular conductor looked even older than usual tonight. He came to James out of breath. "Thank God you here, brother James, thank God."

He started to fall into James' arms. "What's the matter, Parson? What's happened?" James was very worried now and was looking back the way the man had come, listening. "Are you being followed?"

James led him to a seat on the rock, raising a hand to where his son was concealed. "Let me get my breath, brother James. Just let me get my breath a moment." He was panting from an exertion that he shouldn't have had.

"Just rest a minute. Try to catch your breath, Pastor, and tell me what happened."

"I just don't know how it happened... I just don't know," he said, shaking his head.

"What happened?? How what happened?"

"I had four passengers just like most times I conduct. About three hours ago, I only had three and I don't know what happened," he explained, his anger growing. "We was makin' good time and after our last bit of rest, he just vanished."

"What do you mean, he just vanished? Did he get lost, make a wrong turn in the dark or something?"

"That's just it, brother James, I just don't know. Not one of us heard a thing, not a call, not a shout or anything."

"Do you think he was taken by slavers?"

The man looked totally defeated then as he looked up at James. "I just can't be sure of anything. Them slavers are out thick as flies and just as unwelcome. We had to hide out for an hour our first night out they was so many."

James looked around the clearing again, straining to hear any sound at all, but there was nothing, not even a breath of wind.

"Where are your passengers?"

The man stood slowly and brought his cupped hands to his mouth. He took a deep breath and blew into his hands, producing the call of an owl perfectly. A few seconds later, three men emerged from the forest, nervously looking around the clearing. James was struck once again by the pathetic scene of young men being hunted who had never committed a crime. Why did they always have to be so damn young, he wondered.

He could see that this group was even more skittish than most. The two conductors went to the fugitives and James was introduced.

"We only have a short distance left tonight then you'll be in a safe place with friends. I don't want to alarm you, but my son is over there watching. I'm going to call him in now then we can be on our way. All right?"

The three men only nodded as James motioned for Jonathan to come in. He emerged from the woods with the rifle still cradled in his arms. "Did you see or hear anything out there?" James asked.

"Not a thing, Poppa, not a thing. I believe we are alone, for now anyways."

James shook hands with the other conductor. "I never lost a passenger before, James, not a one. I don't know what I did wrong, but that boy is sure enough lost now."

"You didn't do anything wrong, Parson. You have saved so many, you can't let this loss stop you."

The man looked back down the path he had come up. "I know the work is important. I know that we are saving lives every time we go out on The Road. But I also know I'll never forget that boy's face ever. I'll keep an eye out goin' back. At least I can do that much, I reckon. Good luck, brother James, and God be with you."

James watched him walk away with his head down, eventually fading into the night as he began his long journey back, eluding the slavers and returning to the slave fields for more passengers. He turned to the group of refugees who were watching him very closely. "Anybody know the lost boy?"

The tallest in the group, a boy about sixteen stepped forward. "Yassir, I know that boy. He's my cousin. We runnin' from the same place he and me."

"Nobody saw or heard anything? Nothing at all?"

"Naw sir, we didn't hear nothin' at all. We was just walkin' and keepin' as quiet as we could. When we stopped about three hours back for a rest, he just wasn't there no more. He was 'tween me and that boy," he said indicating one of the group, "but when we stopped, he gone."

"Tell me what you think. Did he lose his way in the dark, or was he grabbed up?"

"Neither one makes much sense to me, but he probably just lost. If he'd a seed a slaver, I know he woulda called out some."

James thought about that for a moment, then made a decision. "All right, gentlemen. As I said, we only have a short distance to go before resting up. Stay together and follow me. My son will be in the rear watching our back." He hesitated and looked at the sad group. "Are we all set, then?"

The three men nodded, and they set out back down the hillside towards the farm and shelter. The sky remained cloudy and the rain continued to spit down from time to time, a cold unpleasant rain. There was no real shelter along this part of the line, but after an hour James stopped in a dense part of the forest so they could rest and try to get dry.

The refugees huddled together while James and Jonathan went off a bit. "Did you hear anything back there, son?"

Jonathan kept looking up the path they had just come down. "I don't know if I actually heard anybody behind us, but I sure did feel like someone was there more than once."

James did not like the sound of that. He thought maybe his son was just more nervous because of the lost boy, but he also knew that he was not prone to exaggeration. He too had had a feeling about tonight, and it brought him back to his time in the Washington militia. Best to pay attention to those feelings.

"Here's what we're going to do. You lead the men here down the path we usually use. I will stay behind to see if anyone is on your trail. You're going to have to take them by yourself, Jonathan. Are you ready for that?"

Jonathan nodded. "Yes sir, Poppa, I can do it."

"I'm sure you can, son. Now get ready to move out. I'll meet you down the path where the stream crosses. You know the place? Good. Now get your passengers together, mister conductor, and be on your way."

James watched them head off until he couldn't see them anymore. He turned and looked back up the hill, then moved off to his right and secreted himself in some rocks and bushes. After about ten minutes he saw a man, or the shape of a man, on the edge of the small clearing.

James thought to himself that this man knew what he was doing. He had appeared there as silently as the darkness itself. James just kept his eye on him and waited. In his experience these 'christian wolves' never worked alone. There was always at least two of them working together, sometimes many more.

Sure enough in about five more minutes another shadow appeared at the other side of the clearing. The two men exchanged a series of hand signals, then met in the center.

James could just make out what they were saying. "They was here abouts, all right," one of them said, pointing to the grass where the men had taken their rest. "They must be about ten or fifteen minutes ahead by now."

"I'm just hopin' we can catch 'em at their next stop. Now that would get us a nice hefty reward if we could nab them traffickers."

They lowered their voices some and James could not follow what they said, but he had heard enough to know that these men presented an immediate and mortal danger to him, his family and their farm. They would have to be taken on, here in the woods, tonight.

He faded back into the forest and took a path to parallel the two slave haunters. He knew how to get ahead of them and started up a small hill to his left. It would meet the path again about a quarter mile on, so he picked up his pace as much as he could in the dark, trying to be silent in his movements.

As he crested the hill he tried to see further down the path for any sign of Jonathan and his charges, but the night was just too dark, the clouds scudding by very low now. He found the spot he was looking for and settled in to wait. He was sure the slavers had not made it this far yet.

He didn't have very long to wait, and once again James had to acknowledge his opponents' abilities. They were further along than he had anticipated and moving like ghosts. They kept about twenty yards apart, moving only a few steps at a time and listening.

James let the first slaver go by, then stepped silently into the path behind the second man. When he saw his chance, he stepped on a dried branch that was on the ground. When the slaver turned at the sound, James swung the butt of his rifle and hit him just at the bridge of his nose and he landed very heavily in the path. James stepped off the path and waited. Sure enough the other man appeared on a run and as he came upon his partner he stopped and looked around anxiously. He then made a bad mistake. He laid his rifle down as he knelt to assess his cohort.

James stepped out of the shadow and leveled his rifle at the man's head. "Good evening."

For just a moment the moon appeared through a break in the clouds and James could see clearly that this man was one of the two he had the run in with in Gettysburg. For his part, this information began to slowly dawn on the slaver as well.

He started to stand, but James stepped forward and thrust his rifle in the man's face. "Just stay where you are."

"What are you goin' to do now, nigger? You gonna shoot you a couple of white men out doin' legal work."

The break in the clouds passed and they were in darkness again. "Might just do."

James saw the man move his right hand slightly towards his prostrate friend and smiled.

"What you smilin' at, nigger?"

"At you, you dumb bastard."

When the man lunged for his friend's weapon, James connected his right boot to the man's temple. The man groaned and fell on top of his comrade, who was just showing signs of life. He tried to roll over and push the weight off him, but he was pinned. Then he looked up and saw James standing over him, the rifle in his face.

"Did you enjoy your rest?"

"What? What did you say?"

"I was merely enquiring if you enjoyed your little rest."

Then recognition dawned on him. "You're that god damn black son bitch what broke our pistols last year, ain't ya? What you doin' out here?"

"I'm out hunting…"

"What? What are you huntin' out here this time of night?"

"I might just ask you the same question, friend. What are you hunting out here this time of night?"

"Go to hell, boy. We ain't gotta explain nothin' to the likes of you."

"There you go with those double negatives again. Didn't your momma teach you anything?"

"You're mighty fierce with that rifle in your hands. Let's see what a big bad nigger you are without it, or are you too scared of a white man?"

James put his boot on the inert partner and pushed him off the other. "Sure, why not. Come on, stand up." James kept the rifle leveled at his chest. "Now, open your shirt."

"What? Why?"

"Because I'll shoot you if you don't, that's why."

The man muttered something under his breath then opened his shirt. As James had suspected he had a large knife and a pistol in his belt.

James motioned with the barrel of the rifle. "Just toss them over there, that's a good lad."

When James was satisfied the man was unarmed he set his rifle down nearby. He stretched his arms and shoulders a bit and looked at his opponent. "Well?"

The man dropped his right shoulder and began to circle. James held his stance and waited for his moment. He didn't have to wait long. "You ain't so bad now, are you nigger? You shoulda never put that rifle down."

As he swung into a huge right hook, James stepped aside and landed a fast combination on the side of the man's face. The man turned, enraged, and rushed at James. Again, James deflected his attack and pushed him by. He landed on the ground on his face. He pushed himself up on his shoulders and shook his head, then got up the rest of the way.

James noticed he was a little unsteady as he got to his feet. "Hoo boy. You sure are one tricky son of a bitch, ain't ya?" He licked some of the blood off his lip then approached James much more cautiously.

James took the first punch to his midsection, but before the man could move away or get his hands up James landed another hard combination to the man's nose. When he staggered back James stayed with him and landed two more punches to his face before the man finally went down and stayed down.

James went over and picked up the two rifles and the man's knife and pistol. He used his foot to turn over the still inert partner and quickly checked him for weapons. He took the two pistols and the two knives and put them in the small knapsack he had with him. Then he went to the two prostrate men and removed their boots and threw them down into a dark ravine, then did the same with their trousers.

His fight opponent started to groan and rolled over on his back. "What the hell you think you doin', boy? Where's my boots?"

"I imagine they are right next to your friend's boots. Trousers are probably there as well I should think."

"What the..."

"You're a lucky man, do you know why? No? Well, I'll tell you why. If I had any rope with me at all, I would hang your slave hunting asses right here and now."

When the man looked James in the eye, he knew that he wasn't kidding about that at all. He wisely laid his head back down in the dirt. "What happens now?"

"I don't know about you, but I'm going to my home and get something to eat. I can tell you this, however. Stay away from these parts, you hear me? Next time I see you I will most definitely kill you without warning. Do you understand? I'll shoot you down in the middle of the street if that's where we meet again."

Again the man wisely chose not to speak and crawled over to check on his partner. James turned and took the trail that led down to the creek where the group should be waiting. In a few minutes he was at the crossing with no sign of the others.

He waited just for a moment or two in case they had fallen behind, but when they didn't show up, he headed back to the farm by the usual route. In another few minutes he caught up with the group just as the eastern sky started to show some sign of the coming dawn.

Jonathan was obviously relieved to see him. "What happened back there, Poppa? What took you so long?"

"I thought I told you to wait by the creek for me. Why didn't you do that?"

"I'm sorry, Poppa, but when you didn't come after a while I began to worry about the dawn. You always said we need the cover of night."

James let his anger go. The boy was right, of course. "No, Jonathan, I'm sorry. You made the right decision at that." He gave his son a slap on the shoulder. "Let's go home."

The rest of the spring was wet and windy, but summer moved in and changed all that. The nights were getting longer, and the days began early. Life on the farm continued as life on farms always has and always will. Little Constance was getting very good at walking on her own and Luke loved nothing more than watching her grow.

Some of the crops were almost ready to be harvested as September began. They had worked the land hard all spring and summer, and now the fruits of their labors were plainly visible with field after field green and full. Several fat cattle were also in the north field near the house.

The first Sunday in September the families climbed into the wagon for the ride to church as usual. As they drove up the road to town, James could see that all his neighbors' farm fields were also filled to bursting with healthy crops.

He looked over at his wife who seemed to be lost in thought. "What are you thinking about so hard, Abigail?"

She turned towards him and smiled weakly. Her illness was beginning to show more and more. "I was just thinking how happy I am. I was thinking that this sure is a beautiful day that the Lord has granted us. I was thinking how lucky I am to have such fine young children who will always be free. That's all, Mister James, nothing much really."

"I think I'm the lucky one, Miss Abigail." He took her hand in his and kissed it. "I'm the lucky one."

James noticed yet another new house being built as they approached the town from the south. The amount of new construction was heartening to the people who lived in the area. Two new schools were being built as well since the state legislature enacted the school law that said every town must build schools for all the children and they must be free to attend.

Mister McDonald's store was no longer alone on the street as it was when they first came to the valley. It had grown larger and now also served as the town's post office with several new businesses growing up around him as well.

As they passed by McDonald waved to him. "James. James. I have a letter for you. Came last week." He came over to hand up the envelope.

"Good morning, Miss Abigail, Miss Anna, good morning children. Off to church, are we?"

Luke was in the back with Constance on his lap. "Yessir. Lookin' forward more than usual today. We're going to baptize my little girl."

"Is that right? Well, congratulations. She's a beautiful child, she is." Turning to James he asked, "Not bad news I hope, James"

James read the letter one more time, then looked at Abigail. "It's from Mister Key."

Abigail was surprised at that. "Mister Key? What does he say?"

"Well, it seems he is coming to Gettysburg in a few weeks. He says that he has some business to conduct and he would be very pleased if we could meet him at the courthouse when he comes."

"What kind of business?"

"He doesn't say. He just said that he would be very pleased if we could meet him. That's all really."

They bade McDonald good day and started off again for the church. "What sort of business would bring Mister Key to our little town?"

"Hard to say," James said. "Could be anything, I suppose. Maybe he's buying some land near here or something like that."

As they approached the church the boys in the back jumped down even before James stopped and ran towards a group of boys who were throwing a ball around. Now that the Philadelphia Olympic Club had been formed in that city, baseball was exploding across the valley like wildfire.

As the women and girls prepared the several tables under the big elm, James went over to a group of men standing off to the

175

side. He noticed his friend Joseph Sherfy in the group that was becoming agitated.

"Good morning, Joseph. Mister Thorne, Mister Ables."

The men turned at his arrival. "Good morning, James. How is your beautiful family this fine day?"

"They are very well, sir, thank you for asking. Now what was all the excitement about? You all seemed to be talking about something of great import."

"It's another story about gangs of armed slaves roaming the mountains. You remember? They all started when they found that crazy white man up in those hills south of your place. Remember that?"

All the men nodded. "But those are just stories," James said. "I can't believe there is a gang of runaway slaves living in the rough, going around terrorizing people."

"Well, that crazy white man said he and his partner were set upon by a large number of black men who threatened to kill them. He says he was just lucky to get away. Never did say what happened to his partner."

"I heard that he was found dead, but it was from exposure, not violence," Sherfy said. "That don't sound like a gang to me. Sounds more like some crazy white boys got some bad liquor."

"Well, still sounds like a story you tell children at night to frighten them," James said. "Has anyone heard any more about slavers in the area."

"Still too many reports of groups of white men crossing over from Maryland down by Emmitsburg. My cousin says he's seen 'em down there by the score."

The men were silent, contemplating not only the danger to themselves but to their families and communities. It was well understood that being freeborn was no impediment to being kidnapped and taken south, often with the complicity of local courts.

"Seems to me we should be fighting back," James said. "There must be some action we can take. The anti-slavery feeling is holding on in this part of Pennsylvania, we all know that. Most of the time that damned Fugitive Slave Act isn't really enforced around here. Been on the books for so long now, thirty-eight years or so, seems like folks around here don't care much anymore."

"Yeah, well, I know most white folks is against it, but they's plenty still wants us in chains or in Africa. I heard one story 'bout a slaver who claimed to be a friend of the runaway, then took him back in irons. Didn't hear no one speak up for him, no sir."

"How about you, Joseph? What say you?" James asked.

The older man was thoughtful for a while. "I come here long before most folks, and I have seen some change, some good and some bad." He stopped and looked around, at the clear blue above, at the children playing and the ladies fussing. "I like it here and I ain't goin' anywhere. What are you proposing, James?"

James rubbed his chin. "I don't know exactly. I just have a feeling we must do something, we must act. No good man keeps silent in the face of evil, that's all I know for sure standing here."

Some of the men knew and most suspected that James was conducting on The Road and had been since it came through these parts for the first time. "Seems like you been doin' a lot already, James," Mister Ables said in a low voice. "You out there riskin' it all to help."

"Don't seem like it's helping much. Turner's actions down in Virginia didn't help much for us folks up here. He scared all them white folks pretty bad, and now there's laws down there that don't even let black folks go to church without a white man preachin' to them," Sherfy said.

"Well, killin' is wrong. Too many women and children were killed. I know we all sympathize with his motives, but it ain't right killin' the way he did."

"Am I interrupting you gentlemen?" The visiting pastor had started to usher everyone inside for the sermon.

James looked around and saw that all the women and children and most of the men were making their way to the church. He extended his hand. "Very sorry pastor. We were just discussing good and evil."

"Were you now?" the younger man asked. "I thought that was my job on the Sunday. My name's Matthews, J.J. Matthews. I was kindly invited to speak here today."

The men all exchanged handshakes. J.J. Matthews was a name well known in the community and everyone was looking forward to hearing him speak, Luke in particular as he would baptize his Constance.

"Why don't we continue this good versus evil debate inside, shall we?" the pastor said as he led the men to worship. "That sounds like a very important topic nowadays."

James and Abigail spent hours fussing over their children to get ready. Mister Key had sent another letter saying that today was the day he would be at the courthouse and wished for them to meet him when he conducted whatever business he had come to town to do. They still had no idea what that business was.

"Line up here, boys, and let's see how you look," James said as the boys finished dressing. "What a fine pair of young men you are. Mister Key will be very impressed I'm sure."

"Who is this man, Poppa? What is he to you and Momma?" Jonathan asked.

James had to think on that one for a bit. "Well, son. It's like this. I knew Mister Key when I lived in Georgetown many years ago. He was a neighbor and a friend. He was also an officer in our District Militia when the British invaded and served well." He hesitated a moment before he went on. "I did him a particular service and he offered anything he had to repay me. I asked him to allow me to purchase your mother's freedom."

Jonathan showed a flash of anger. "You mean that this man owned Momma, she was his slave? Why should we show any respect for a slave owner? Any slave owner?"

James took a deep breath. He had known this day would come eventually, of course, but he still was not ready. How does one explain to children, even children as grown as his boys were, the evils of slavery and the many layers of this most peculiar of institutions?

"It's like this, my sons. There were slaves in this country before there were blacks. Most called them indentured servants. When the needs of the growing country exceeded the manpower available, blacks were kidnapped from our ancestral homes in Africa and forcibly brought here in chains."

"Poppa, what gave white people the right to do that? What gave them the right to hold humans as slaves and mistreat them so?" Jonathan was getting vexed.

"That will be the question of the century, I'm sure. You see, Jonathan, there is something in men, not all men mind you, that forces them to be somehow better than others. They feel a strong need to dominate and subjugate anyone they can. It has been that way since man first walked upright, and it will be that way until civilization ends, I'm afraid."

"But why us, Poppa, why black folks?"

"Well, that part is a lot harder to explain. Something else that has been a part of human existence is a fear of folks who don't look like you, don't talk like you, don't have the same customs. In our case, we were too weak as a race to resist them. They had the weapons to make anyone do anything they wanted. The truth is they did not see us as humans at all, but as a lower animal life form. Not everyone feels this way, thank God, and change is coming slowly."

The boys looked at each other, then Francis spoke. "But they're wrong, Poppa. We are every bit as good as the white folks. We can do anything they can do and maybe even some things better. How can people with brains be so wrong about something like that?"

James paused, thinking. "Well son, I don't really understand that myself, but I can tell you this, so listen good. At one point in time every single living person on the planet believed, no, they knew in their very hearts, that the earth was flat. People were wrong then and they're wrong now."

He looked out the window to see his two Abigails hurrying across the yard from Luke's house. "Now let's get ready to go. Your Momma is hurrying here so we best look sharp now."

During the ride into town, Jonathan sat silently for the most part. James noticed that he seemed to be on the verge of asking another question, then changing his mind. He understood his dilemma since he remembered having very much the same trouble understanding racial animosity in his youth.

Finally, Jonathan turned around and asked his mother the question that had obviously been nagging at him. "Momma, why do you want to see this man again, this man who held you as a slave?"

Abigail was taken aback as she had not been a part of the earlier conversation. She looked at James for explanation, but he just faced forward driving the rig.

"Why do you ask me that question, son?"

"Poppa and I were talking about this man and what he is to us."

"Oh, I see. Well, yes son, I was born a slave and then lived at Terra Rubra where I grew up. That much is certainly true." She paused. How to go on? "I knew lots of other black folks who were slaves too. Their masters whipped them. They abused women and girls freely. They broke up families whenever it suited them. They were treated like nothing more than cattle. You've heard many of these stories your own self from the runaways you help."

"I have heard them, Momma. That's why I want to know why you want to see this man again. I don't understand."

Abigail sighed. "I truly wish we lived in a more simple world, a place where right and wrong were always obvious. But we do not. I was born a slave and was fortunate enough to have a master that treated his slaves and his workers well. He was kind to all of us. He knew all our names and our family. I never once heard of him whipping anyone and he never broke up a family, not once."

"But still…."

"I could not change my circumstances, Jonathan. I did not choose to be anyone's slave, but if that was God's plan for me at the time then I thank God I had a kind man as a master."

"Don't forget that is was Mister Key who was willing to set your mother free because I did him a service. He could just as easily have said no," James said. "Don't forget that, all right?"

When they pulled up at the frame courthouse they saw another carriage they both recognized, then Abigail became very excited. "Oh my, look there, it's Uncle Clem." She stood up in the back of the wagon and called out to him.

"Uncle Clem, Uncle Clem, it's me, Abigail."

An older lean black man was near the Key carriage and looked over at the sound of his name. When he saw Abigail his face lit up and he rushed over. "Oh my oh my. Is that you, little Abigail? Oh my lord how you has growed."

Her daughter stood up next to her. "I'm not the little Abigail anymore, Uncle Clem, this one is."

The older man had tears in his eyes now. "What a beautiful child, a beautiful child. And who are these fine lookin' boys with you?"

The boys had jumped down and were standing together, not sure what was going on as their mother climbed down beside them. "Uncle Clem, I want you to meet our sons Jonathan and Francis. Boys, I want you to shake hands with a very dear friend, Uncle Clem."

They both approached with eyes downcast, still unsure of what was going on. Since their grandpa had passed away, they had heard no mention of any family from their parents except for their kidnapped uncle. They shook hands and mumbled "Pleased to meet you."

The door to the courthouse opened and Key stepped out onto the porch in front. "James? James, is that you?" He stepped down off the porch and shook hands and saw Abigail standing by the wagon. "Why Abigail, you look as young as ever. Are these three beautiful children all yours."

Abigail felt herself blushing and grinning. "Yes sir, they truly are all mine. May I introduce you? This tall boy here is Jonathan and next to him is Francis."

Key arched his eyebrows as he shook hands with the boys. "I am very pleased to meet you, lads." Then he leaned down to Francis and spoke softly. "Francis is my name too, son. It's a very good name to have."

"Thank you, sir," the boy said shyly. "It was my grandpa's name too."

"Well, I'm sure he was a fine man and I suspect he would be very proud of both of you."

"There's someone else here to meet, Mister Key. This is our daughter Abigail."

Key bowed low from the waist. "It is my honor and pleasure to make your acquaintance, Miss Abigail."

The little girl clung to her mother and giggled softly. "Thank you very much, sir."

"How may I be of service to you today, Mister Key? What is the business that brought you to our little town?" James asked.

"It's simple really, James. I came to this fine town because first and foremost, it is not in Maryland and because it also has a county courthouse." He motioned back to the porch in front of the courthouse. "I brought along my two grandsons to witness this as well, and I very much was hoping that you and Abigail could join us."

"I'd be happy to join you, Mister Key, but I still don't understand what this is about."

"It's about Uncle Clem here, or Clem Johnson more properly. I have agreed to give him his freedom, to release him from service to me and my family and heirs."

Abigail could not believe her ears. She had known Uncle Clem since she could remember. He was known as Uncle to one and all in their community and was loved by everyone. She put her arm around his and hugged it tightly, tears running down her cheeks. "Oh, Uncle Clem," was all she could say.

James looked at Clem who appeared extremely uncomfortable at being the center of so much attention. "I would be very proud to act as a witness for such an occasion," he said. He extended his hand to Clem. "Very proud indeed, Uncle Clem."

"Well then. Let us make our way into the office and make it official, shall we? Justice of the Peace King and his friend John McClellan are both inside with all the necessary papers."

The small office was not used to such a crowd of people, but they all managed to fit in. No one wanted to miss this event. The papers were already drawn up and the signing only took a few moments. At the end of the little ceremony, Key picked up the last document and read from it.

"Whereas I, Francis Scott Key of the District of Columbia, being the owner of a certain man of color called Clem Johnson, now in Gettysburg in the State of Pennsylvania, emancipate the said Clem Johnson and having agreed with him to leave him in the State of Pennsylvania and free to continue there, or to go wherever he may please, now therefore in consideration of five dollars to me in hand paid and for other good causes and considerations, I hereby do manumit and let free said Clem Johnson aged about forty five years."

Key smiled and looked around at the assembly and noticed there was not a dry eye in the room. "Well, I guess nothing more needs to be said, does it?" He shook Clem's hand as he handed the paper back to Justice King. "What would you like to do now, Clem?"

All eyes were on him again as he thought for a minute. "I don't rightly know what to do. I only knows our Terra Rubra, Mister Key. It's the only place I can remember living at anymore. I don't rightly know what to do." He looked around the room at all the people who were so moved by this ceremony. "It's the only life I knows at all." He was clearly upset at the notion of leaving the only home he had known for such a long time.

"Well, Clem, I'll make you an offer," Key said, breaking the sad mood. "I would very much appreciate it if you would return with us to Terra Rubra and be my new overseer. You already know the land and the people working there, and they all know and respect you."

"But Mister Key, sir, you done just released me from your service. I ain't a slave no more."

"You are a free man, Clem Johnson, as free as any of us. If you choose to work for me as my overseer, it will be as a free man. You will be paid a wage and provided your own house. You will be free to come and go as you please."

Clem was overwhelmed, tears rolling down his cheek. "I'd be mighty pleased to do that, Mister Key, mighty pleased. Terra Rubra is my home and those is my people."

"Well then, it's all settled," Key said as they shook hands. "I am truly humbled that you wish to remain part of our family after being set free, Clem. I see a long and happy life for all of us there."

On the way back to the farm, James and Jonathan rode up front while the rest sat in the back. James could hear some of the conversation from there but mostly he was watching his oldest son. The boy obviously had something on his mind, but James knew better than to ask. He knew his son would speak when he was ready.

"Poppa, I'm not sure what just happened back there."

James waited a bit before trying to answer since his own feelings on the subject were in a jumble. He had known the lawyer Key for a good while and knew him to be an honest person yet also knew that he kept slaves. He knew Key as a kind man but also knew that he was an avid supporter of the ACS, the African Colonization Society, the aim of which was to remove all blacks from the United States and send them to Africa, a place no black person alive in America today had even a remote knowledge of. In short, he supported sending citizens of the United States to live in Africa based on their skin color.

"I think I know how you feel, son, I truly do, but I don't know if I have the words to explain this one to you. I don't think any man alive today has the words to do that, frankly, because there is no explaining it." He thought for another minute before going on. "You heard your own mother say that she was born into slavery because it must have been God's plan for her at the time. You also heard her thank God that if that was to be her lot in life, she was grateful to be owned by a man like Mister Key."

"Yes sir, I heard her say that. But why are our people slaves not far from here and others are free?"

James chuckled as he looked over at his boy. "There you go again, boy, asking the question of the century. Our people, as you know, were stolen away from their homes and families starting hundreds of years ago. They were forced to come here and work because there simply were not enough people to work all the land in this new country back then, and the white man had the guns. Over the years the evil became more and more obvious to some, so slavery died out in places and continued in others. And you would be wrong to think any black man or woman, anywhere in this country, is even close to being free compared to a white man in spite of the ceremony you just witnessed. Maybe someday, but not today." He was thinking back to his days in Georgetown and the Black Codes he had had no choice but to follow.

"I guess I understand that Poppa. I just don't understand the hatred that goes with it."

"There is no understanding that either, I'm afraid. The simplest way to explain it is that a lot of folks, a very great many it seems, only feel tall when they stand on the backs of others. I guess that about sums it up."

"Well, what about Clem Johnson? Why did he go back to that place?"

"Think about it for a moment. What would you do in his place? He spent almost all his adult life there, his dearest friends are there and call him Uncle Clem because they love him. Because he's a slave he never had any education at all so he probably can't read or write, and he certainly doesn't have any money to speak of. Where could he go? What could he do?"

"I don't know, Poppa. I think if it was me, I would go as far away as possible from that place."

"I understand that feeling, believe me, and I'll wager that if Uncle Clem was a younger man, he might very well do just that. Truth is, though, he is not a younger man and he feels secure there in the company of friends and yes, the Key family."

"Maybe when he saves some money he could travel a bit, you know, go out and see the world. That's what I would do."

They were turning into the lane to the farm now and they could see the smoke rising from the house of Luke and Anna. The two families always took their Sunday supper together, and as they drew closer the aroma of cooking began to reach them. "I don't think that's very likely, I'm afraid. You see, even a free black man is not allowed to travel alone in the south much."

James noticed that there were tears in his son's eyes and he was terribly moved. "I hate this world Poppa, I hate it."

James stopped the wagon in the yard as everyone climbed down. Tying the reins to the brake handle, he turned to face Jonathan. "That's no way to be, son, no way at all. You hate the world your mother lives in? You hate the world your own brother and sister live in?" He swept his arm around the farm and the fields beyond. "You hate all this too then?"

Jonathan hung his head. He hadn't meant to sound like that, and his father's harsh tone made him realize he had misspoken his feelings. "No, Poppa, I don't. I'm sorry I said it that way. Truly. I just do not want to live in a world with so much hate in it, I guess. I just can't understand it at all."

James took his son by the shoulders and faced him squarely. He was more proud of him at this moment than he could express. "Then fight, son, fight. Don't ever give up or be beaten down, you hear? You are already out there risking your life to help your brothers and sisters escape bondage with me on The Road. Those people need our help and we will help a good many others before we're through I suspect, so do not stop fighting for what's right. Not now, not ever, and do not let hatred rule your heart. If you do, it will consume you."

Jonathan wiped his sleeve across his eyes. "No sir, Poppa, I am not giving up the fight and I will never let them destroy me. I promise you that."

As the years passed peacefully, the two families watched not only the seasons change but also the very nature of the little town of Gettysburg. More and more people were moving to the valley and making it their home. White settlers were looking for more opportunity to grow and prosper as were the ever increasing number of blacks. The difference was that blacks, both as family and individuals, were often fleeing persecution on the other side of the Mason Dixon line, persecution that only grew worse in the nearby border states due to the increasing lure of freedom just a stone's throw away.

The legislature in Maryland was particularly ruthless in their actions to discourage slaves from even thinking of running away. More laws were passed reinforcing the already draconian laws affecting black lives in areas of assembly, whether in church services or otherwise, in education and any trace of freedom of movement. Before this, slaves had occasionally been able to hire out to other farms and make a little money for themselves or be able to travel to see friends or families living nearby.

The fear of southern whites had only increased with Nat Turner's actions back in the summer of 1831 and laws were again passed to make it an even more serious crime to aid escaped slaves. Southerners were also able to browbeat northern states into increasing their penalties in those states as well by threatening economic boycotts.

Gettysburg's growing black population was organizing around church and business life and doing well. More blacks owned farms every year. More black men of letters and skills were coming and making the town a lively center for trade and industry. There was one furnace for smelting and another under construction. Several mills were in regular operation and small inns and shops opened every other month it seemed. One enterprising black man, Owen Robinson, opened a small café that served oysters in the winter and ice cream in the summer that was very popular, especially in summer when the town's children would gather to watch him make ice cream and hope for a sample.

James and Jonathan continued conducting on The Road where more and more traffic was moving. They were not the only conductors in the area. There were several other routes through the Cumberland Valley which helped throw pursuers off and keep the flow of refugees moving north to freedom.

The close calls were becoming more frequent as well. In one particularly notorious encounter, slavers broke into a white family's house where two passengers were being concealed. They were safely concealed but their tiny baby would not stop crying. The wife of the sheltering family quickly grabbed the baby up and pretended to be breast feeding it. It seems even some of the "christian wolves" knew when they had gone too far because they apologized profusely after forcing entry and left. The wife exclaimed later that she was "glad they didn't take a close look at that baby" because the baby was black.

Jonathan began taking more solo trips on The Road late in the spring of 1836. James had always been reluctant to let him go alone, especially as the danger seemed to be increasing monthly. Now he didn't have much of a choice as he had managed to turn his ankle badly leading a team back from the field. After more safe trips by himself James had relaxed somewhat.

By the middle of June James was almost back to normal and was up and about, trying to get back into the rhythm of farm life. The second Sunday of June found them once again heading to church. They were all looking forward to this Sunday as the weather and James' ankle had made their attendance less than regular lately.

Jonathan and Abigail were riding up front and James and Luke were in the back with Anna and the other children. Constance was a sheer joy to all as she was becoming very vocal and loved to run around the barnyard, chasing the exasperated chickens.

James leaned his head back and watched the sky go by. It was even more blue than usual today, which he took as a good sign, with small buildups promising late afternoon showers around the valley.

"I'm mighty glad you feel like the trip today, James, mighty glad," Anna said. "I think I miss our Sunday meetings even more than the children do and that's a fact."

James sat up, breaking his reverie. "Well, I sure am glad to be here, and I am sorry that I've been the cause of missing them."

Anna was fussing with the dress Constance was wearing. The child was growing so fast she was having a hard time making clothes fit. "Stop that wiggling around, girl." She looked over at James. "No need for you to apologize, James. I don't mind telling you though that you gave Abigail quite a scare. She was afraid you broke that ankle for sure"

James looked up front and watched his oldest boy and his wife, chatting away with each other. He couldn't quite make out what they were saying but he could hear the happiness in their voices. Abigail's frame was not as erect as before her illness began, and her footsteps had slowed some. Whatever was causing her life to slip away was certainly taking its sweet time, for which he was grateful. He simply could not imagine his life without her.

"Anna, I have wanted to thank you for being in our lives and for taking such good care of Abigail. I know she loves you like a sister."

"Well, James, I think I had me a sister long ago, but our family was split up when I was only a child like this one. I'd be mighty proud to have her for my sister."

As they approached the church James could see that attendance was going to be very large. The small yard around the massive elm tree was already teeming with noisy children. As usual, the ladies and older girls were setting up tables for the after sermon gathering that was such a focus of life in their community.

James climbed down from the rear of the wagon with some

difficulty and reached back in for his cane. He looked around and saw a group of men he knew well and one of them motioned to him to join them.

"Welcome back, James. You have been missed. How's that foot of yours?" asked Joseph Sherfy.

"Well, it's certainly better than it was last Sunday, that's for sure. I'll be fine in another week or so I expect."

A man, a Mister Dunlap that James knew only slightly, looked around the assembled group. He was not a regular at the church but was thought to be involved in The Road. "That is very good news, James. There is a group of citizens from the area who want to hold a meeting next month, and we would like you to attend."

The man cleared his throat and looked around conspiratorially, although he certainly had nothing to fear from this group. "You all know James McAllister who owns the mill north of here. As you probably also know he has been very vocal in his opposition to slavery. Others hereabouts are also vigorously opposed and have decided to act."

"How can I be of help? What sort of action are you all contemplating?"

"We have already been speaking with neighbors and friends throughout the county, and we have decided to band together to form the Adams County Anti-Slavery Society. We feel it's high time we organized ourselves to aid those who are already active, people like yourself, James."

James also glanced around suspiciously since this was not something usually discussed in public places. "You can count me in, sir, me and my boy as well. When and where is this meeting taking place?"

Smiling now, Mister Dunlap said, "We all felt sure that we could count on you. We have decided that meeting on July the fourth would be a very appropriate day. It will be the sixtieth anniversary of the signing of the Declaration, and we think it's about time someone reminded folks about all men being created equal before God."

The symbolism was stark and obvious. He thought back to the day Washington had burned and how he himself had helped rescue the very document they were discussing. Even then he knew that the equality it lauded was not available to him or his kind. "I could not agree more. The date is very appropriate considering. James McAllister is a very strong ally to the cause. He's a good man."

July fourth dawned like a steam bath. The day before, Sunday, the skies had opened up early and let loose most of the day ruining any hope of going to church. Now, with the sun rising in a clear sky, a fog like steam was rising from all the fields and hillsides, limiting visibility.

James and Jonathan left just after noon to go to the meeting at McAllister's mill. James very much wanted his oldest son to be a witness to the founding. Since they had missed church services yesterday, they had no idea if anything had changed in the meeting plans. Jonathan was full of questions as usual.

"Who do you think will be there, Poppa? What do you suppose we'll do at this meeting?"

"I'm hoping that this will be another chapter opening up here of the American Anti-Slavery Society. They've been sending speakers out to most anyplace with a town hall or courthouse to speak against slavery. Some churches have let them speak there as well."

"Yes sir, I've read some of their speeches, but I've also heard of the trouble they get into sometimes for speaking against slavery. Seems not everyone is so anxious to get rid of it."

They were approaching the mill and James could see a small collection of carriages and horses nearby. "It may be a while before this scar is healed and forgotten, but in the meantime we have our work cut out for us. Let's go in and see what this is all about."

McAllister appeared at the door to the mill. He was an imposing figure at just over six feet, with the strong build of a man who knew what it was to work hard all his life. "Welcome, James, and thank you for coming. This cannot be little Jonathan, can it? Why, I remember when you didn't even reach the middle of that carriage wheel and now look at you."

Jonathan took the offered hand. "I have done a bit of growing I guess, sir. It has been a while since I was last at the mill. How is young Theodore? I trust he is well." The two boys had gone to a church school together in their early years before the other mandated schools were built in the town.

"He's just fine, son, just fine. All my boys will be here today, and you can see for yourself. He's grown to be a fine young man as well, I'm proud to say."

James did not recognize a few of the people there. Several of the others, like his neighbor Mister Anders were familiar to him, as was the attorney Thaddeus Stevens. There was an equal amount of black men and white, and he noticed that no women were present. After James greeted those he knew everyone settled in to hear what was on the agenda.

McAllister led the meeting. His reputation as a strident opponent to slavery was very well known to all those in the area. It brought him friendship from some quarters and a lot of animosity from others. Though there were many in the area who wanted to see slavery die out, there were still many others who wanted it to remain in place. These men gathered here wanted to change that. They wanted every man, woman and child in America to understand the evil that was slavery.

"Thank you all for coming out today. I won't keep you from celebrating our nation's founding today, but I felt, we felt, that this would be an auspicious day for us to once again declare as our Declaration says, that all men are created equal. That all people everywhere are God's children."

"As many of you know, the American Anti-Slavery Society was established in Philadelphia in December of 1833. Since then, the Society has been dispatching speakers and organizers to various towns and villages here in Pennsylvania as well as Ohio and throughout New England. They have set up over a dozen separate societies and helped to raise awareness of and antipathy towards slavery."

He indicated two of the white men in the front. "I want you all to meet Mister Arnold Buffum and Mister Edward Fairchild, two of the many speakers who have been at this work for some time now."

The two men took turns addressing the group. As James had hoped, they gave the purpose of the society as being to unite individuals like James and organize to help them in the work they were doing. James remembered Fairchild from a lecture he gave at the Gettysburg courthouse last December. He also remembered some in the large crowd that had gathered objected to his presence in their town and tried to make trouble for him.

That was actually the theme for most of the meeting. They not only related their own experiences but told of many others who had been subjected to abuse for speaking out against the evil. They reminded everyone of the trials William Garrison had been subjected to, how another publisher originally from Ohio named Elijah Lovejoy had been chased out of St. Louis and had his printing presses destroyed more than once. Now that the border states like Maryland and Virginia were becoming more agitated by their northern neighbors sheltering fugitives, the number of agents acting against the efforts of abolitionists everywhere was increasing, as was the violence being perpetrated towards them.

Every man in the room had a story of someone they knew being subjected to this violence. It was hard to ignore the seething hostility of the slave hunters, the "christian wolves" who sought to enslave all blacks everywhere. James had lost his own brother to these animals. Others had lost siblings, children and even parents to the hunters who did not care at all about any black person's status. They were simply chattel to be owned and nothing else in their view.

The group came up with a total of fourteen resolutions and a final note of commitment to the cause of freedom. When the meeting started to break up in the late afternoon, McAllister took a sheet of paper from one of the speakers and, addressing the group read from it.

"Gentlemen, I think after this first meeting of our Society, and with God's blessing, we will be able to weaken the grip of the evil institution on the imaginations of northern white folks, and maybe even some in the south."

There was some murmuring in the group at these words. "Let me continue, gentlemen." When the talking died down, he went on. "Be it resolved that God hath made of one blood all nations of men according to the gospel of St. Paul. Furthermore, be it resolved that if liberty is the right of all men, no human being can be rightfully held in slavery."

He let those words sink in a moment, then went on. "I know we are all anxious to rejoin our families and celebrate this great day in history, so I will finish with this final statement. I will ensure you all get a printed copy of this as soon as possible."

With that he cleared his throat and read: "It is resolved that although we may be denounced, for our efforts in the cause of human rights, by office holding and office seeking politicians, and even by men wearing clerical robes, we will not be afraid of their terror, but, disregarding their denunciations, we will continue to open our mouths for the dumb, and to plead the cause of the oppressed and of those who have none to help them, humbly believing, that, if we do unto others as we wish that they should do unto us, we shall have the approbation of Him who will render every man, according to his works, and whose approbation will be a full remuneration for the loss of this worlds favor."

McAllister's voice had risen as he read the words that would influence all their lives from this point forward. When he finished, the silence was surprising, then as one they all rose to applaud not only James McAllister but themselves as well.

The rest of the summer passed as the last one had, with both James and Jonathan busily conducting on The Road and tending to their very productive farm. Jonathan made more and more trips alone as James would sometimes pitch in on one of the other various routes through their valley that led to Canada and freedom.

The close encounters with the "christian wolves" were growing in frequency and violence and both conductors always carried a firearm on their trips. Cross border raids by these slave hunters were also becoming more frequent and violent, causing growing fear and alarm among the black population. Abigail and Anna were not immune to these fears but knew that the work of The Road must go on.

In late September, just as the leaves began to change and the night air became chilly, James was leading a group of four fugitives on a route further west in the area than he normally worked. This group was made up of young men and women, something that was becoming more frequent as the successes of The Road became better known, even in the south.

They had been together for a full night and day as they approached a long, narrow valley leading north from a small group of hills. Their next station was about a mile or so beyond this valley. James went ahead to scout the terrain, then rejoined his passengers.

"I didn't see any sign of movement ahead. There is a farm-house on the eastern side of the valley, though. I could see smoke from the chimney but no other signs of life."

The group waited patiently for him to go on. He thought for another moment and reached a decision. "I think we should stay just inside the trees on the western side as we go. I don't like the idea of trying to move in the open." He had been on this route only once before and was not completely comfortable with his knowledge of the terrain. He knew that if he kept the higher hills always to his left that they would be heading north, away from the slave fields they were fleeing.

The group nodded as one. "We be following you, Mister James, whatever you think is best is what we do," one of the women said looking around at the others.

They started down the last of the hills towards the edge of the valley when they first spotted them. Two white men on horseback emerged from the far end of the little valley slowly riding south, looking down at the tall grass as if tracking animals or men.

They were still in the shelter of the trees. "Let's just stay here for a bit and watch them go. See what they may be up to." They fell back behind two large boulders and waited.

"Maybe they lives in that farmhouse you saw, Mister James."

"Maybe, but I don't think so. They look to me more like trackers. Only question is, who or what are they tracking?"

Sure enough, one of the horsemen moved away towards the west side of the little valley, still looking down at the tall grass as he went. He stood up in his stirrups and gestured towards the woods. Another rider appeared from there and came out to join him. They were much too far away to hear their conversation, but from the gestures they made it seemed to James they were on some trail.

"I don't like the looks of this, not one bit," James said softly. He motioned for the others to follow him deeper into the forest. When they had gathered around, he went on. "I know we were hoping to make it to the next station before nightfall, but it looks like we won't. Those men are definitely hunting something, and I think they may have picked up a trail."

"Whose trail could it be, Mister James?" the young woman who seemed to speak for the group asked. "Did some other folks come this way recently?"

James shook his head. "I have no way of knowing if there was or was not. But if there was a recent passage through here, then I think that group is in danger." He paused to let that sink in. "I think we had better prepare to spend the night here and try to move on before dawn if we can. We are less than two hours from the next station. We'll be safe there, I can assure you."

The group nodded agreement. "We'll be just fine sleepin' in the woods tonight. Won't be the first time on this trip we on," the woman said. Then she turned to the others and speaking softly had them get set for the night.

James went back to the edge of the forest to keep an eye on the three riders who were now all in the middle of the valley looking around like they were trying to decide something. After a few minutes it seemed the decision was made as they all turned and rode north again. James watched them until they disappeared in the forest at the far end once more.

He was suddenly very tired, and he went back to the fugitives. He approached the young woman who spoke for the group. "I must close my eyes for a while. Do you think you can keep watch for me?"

She gave him a smile and led him to a large pile of pine needles and leaves she had prepared for herself. "You just lay yourself down here, Mister James, and let us take care of you for a while. We'll all take a turn at watchin' for you, so you just get some rest now, you hear." He had not noticed before what a pretty girl she was until she smiled up at him.

He didn't know how to respond. "That would be very nice, but don't let me sleep too long now. We have to be up and moving before the sun comes up."

"Don't you worry none, Mister James. Don't worry none at all."

James woke with a start, his rifle already in hand. "It's all right now, Mister James. Everything be fine." He was looking up into the young woman's face. "That sun will be up in about another hour, I suppose."

As he collected himself, James looked around at the sleeping fugitives as they began to stir quietly. When he was fully awake he motioned to the girl again. "I'm going to have a look at the valley, see if there's any signs of life."

"I just now come off watchin' for you, Mister James. I ain't seen nothing different from last night."

"That's good, very good," James said as he stretched. "What's your name, girl? How do they call you?"

"My name's Emma."

"Well, Emma, thank you for keeping a sharp eye out and letting me rest some. I'm not quite the young man I used to be."

"We was all happy to help you, Mister James. We know what you be doin' for us and all. Oh, and I did hear me some noise from that little farmhouse on that side of the valley, and some smoke I think. Still pretty dark when I comes to get you."

"Okay. That's very good, Emma. Let's you and me go take another look," he said, gesturing the way. "Let's just hope there's no sign of the slavers."

They went back to the safe spot to look out over the valley. The sun was just beginning to announce its presence in the eastern sky, with no sign of weather to come. They could just make out smoke curling up from the chimney of the farmhouse.

"Looks like someone's getting breakfast ready," he said without taking his gaze off the house. "But you're sure you didn't see any sign of the slavers? No fires or anything?"

"No suh, Mister James. It's like I said, it was just me and the stars is all. Just me and the stars."

He nodded and stood. "We best be getting on our way, then. Let's go get the others ready."

The other three had already gathered up their few possessions and cleaned the area to remove any sign that anyone had spent the night there. James looked around approvingly. "That's fine, just fine. No one will ever know we were here at all. Now let's get started. We'll stick to the west side of the valley, just inside the tree line, all right? Same plan as yesterday before we were interrupted."

James started off and they all fell in single file behind him, with about ten yards between them. Everyone was on high alert, looking around and listening to every sound. When the valley became clearly visible after the last small hill was passed, all eyes were on the far side and the trees there.

They proceeded as planned, staying just inside the tree line and out of sight to anyone who may enter the valley from the north or east. James raised his hand to halt the party, and they all came forward to hear what he had to say.

"There's a road up ahead a bit. We need to cross it and get back to cover on the other side. It's a clear cut road, so it must get a fair amount of traffic. Let's just hope no one is up and about this early. Now, here's what we'll do. I will go across first and get to cover. No one is to come across without a signal from me, is that clear? Good. Emma, I am going to be asking you to cross last. I need you to watch for the signals and start people off. All right?"

Emma nodded her agreement. "Yas suh, Mister James. I ain't afraid."

James smiled at that. "I know I can count on you. I'm going across now and scout it out a bit. I'll signal you in a minute or two."

With that, James bent low and hurried across the road. It was another ten or fifteen yards to the trees on the opposite side and he crossed it quickly. When he entered the tree line he started to move to parallel the road and look for any traffic that might be about. When he was satisfied, he went back and signaled for the first fugitive to cross. He waited a few minutes between each one until they were all across except Emma.

There was a gentle curve in the road just ahead of them, and from her hiding place Emma could see into it better than James could. When James signaled for her to cross, she took a quick look at the road as she had for the others and froze.

James signaled again impatiently, but Emma stayed back and motioned to James that someone was on the road. He moved ahead a few yards until he too could see up the road. The others were back a few yards and would not be aware of what was happening.

James could see a single rider in the road up ahead, but he could not tell if he was one of the three he saw yesterday scouting the valley so carefully. Could they have been searching for them, he wondered.

He looked over and was surprised to see Emma breaking cover

and coming into the road, then he saw the man behind her with the pistol pointed at her back, pushing her forward. "Go on now, girl, just keep movin'. Now, where your friends hidin' at? Can you tell me that?"

The man spotted James and appeared confused. "Hold up, now girl. Hey you, nigger, get your ass over here. Right now, damn it. Hey Lee, Leeboy, I found me a couple," he shouted up the road to the approaching rider.

James glanced up the road quickly and saw that the rider had heard his companion and had quickened his pace. There was only one thing to do now and he did it. He took one step towards the man threatening Emma, which made his rifle visible. Before the slaver could say anything, James raised the rifle to his shoulder and shot him through the head.

Emma screamed and ran towards James as he stepped into the road in full view of the charging rider. He fell back on his militia training and calmly started to reload his rifle. The rider fired at him from his pistol, but the shot went wide. He dropped his weapon and drew a sword from a scabbard at his side.

James took one more glance at him as he rammed the round home. He dropped the ramrod in the dirt and raised the rifle to his shoulder. The man was ten yards away and standing in his stirrups to make his attack. James fired and the force of the round knocked the rider out of the saddle. James picked up the ramrod and moved towards Emma who was standing in the road, sobbing.

"Emma, we have to get out of here right now. There may be more of them around. Pull yourself together now. I need your help."

The other fugitives came running at the sound of the shots, their eyes wide with terror. Like the other refugees before them, they had never seen a black man take on a white man before. They huddled together and waited for an explanation and a plan.

"Is everyone all right?" James asked as he reloaded his rifle. He looked around at the nodding heads. "Good. These may or may not be the riders we saw yesterday. If they are, that means there is at least one more around. I need you ladies to go fetch the horses. Take them back in the woods a ways and get their saddles off. You men come help me."

They took the lifeless slavers into the forest and covered them with brush. James picked up the still loaded pistol the first man had dropped and went to retrieve the one that had been fired at him. He also picked up the man's sword and looked it over. It had been issued by the US Army. He threw it back in the bushes near its owner.

They all grabbed some branches and swept the road clean of tracks and blood, then made for the safety of the forest. They had lost about an hour and that concerned James.

"We need to make up some time now. We don't have very far to go to get to the next station and they'll be concerned enough. Stay in single file and keep your eyes and ears open. Let's go."

They started out as before, with ten yards between them, moving along as quickly and quietly as possible. Everyone was straining to hear anything unusual or out of the ordinary and trying not to get separated from the rest.

The sun was climbing higher when James signaled for a stop. As usual, they all gathered around him. "I'm thinking maybe we are far enough away now. I had no choice back there. One of them was able to sneak up on Emma. When he called out to his partner, I saw no choice but to act."

"That was sure some fine shootin', Mister James," Emma said softly as the others nodded. That was the only reaction from the group.

After instructing his charges to stay out of sight and rest, James went ahead to scout the trail further. Even though he had made this trip only once before, he remembered the most prominent landmarks. Right now he was looking for a rock formation that had the appearance of a child with its hand out near a group of oaks. The stream that ran just west of there would take them to their next station, the farm of a Quaker family.

As he got closer to where he should be able to see the landmark, he noticed a small smoke ahead, like from a single campfire. He crept up as close as he dared, trying to get a view of whoever was there. He heard some clattering from ahead. Whoever was there wasn't trying to conceal themselves at all.

He was listening hard, but there was no conversation to overhear. Finally, a man stood up and leaned over the small fire. He was a white man in his early thirties, James thought, but he was not at all sure whether this man was the third rider they had seen the day before or not. If he was, why was he here so far away from his partners?

James knew he could not approach the man, of that he was sure. He might be a "free" man, but he would be hard pressed to explain his presence here so far away from his farm, especially with all the activity on The Road in the area.

The man poured what was left of his coffee on the fire and kicked the ashes around some. He put his few things in a saddle bag and went to throw it over his horse when he stopped and looked in James' direction. James froze, even though he was sure he could not be seen, and the man continued getting his horse ready to ride again.

He waited a few minutes after the man left, then came out of cover. He was getting concerned about how long he had left his charges, but he wanted to see if he could find a clue to the man's identity. The only thing he found, though, was some warm ashes and hoof prints in the dirt.

James hurried back to the fugitives as quietly as he could. They were clearly starting to get anxious. "Thank God you is back, Mister James. We was gettin' so worried," Emma said when he got them all together to brief them.

"I know and I'm sorry, but I came across another rider. Still don't know if he's with those other two, but I don't think so. He was better dressed than them, not so much like a hired hand. I had to wait for him to move on, though. He was sitting at the base of our next landmark."

James led them single file once more through the forest. They made their way due west from the pleading child and the oaks and found the stream that would lead them on. They stopped just for a minute to drink from it and fill their canteens.

"We'll just follow this stream until it turns southward. Just beyond that point is the farm of the Quaker family. We'll be safe there, I'm sure."

When they got to the last tree line before the farm, James had them stop again as he looked the scene over. He had been told to expect to see one horse and one cow in the corral if everything was safe for them to come in. Instead, he saw three horses and no cows at all.

Emma came up beside him to look for herself. "Is everything as it should be, Mister James?" she asked. "Do you see the sign you waitin' for?"

"No, Emma, I do not. Everything looks quiet enough, I suppose, and we are more than a day late. Maybe they just got on with the business of running the farm when we didn't arrive."

Emma nodded. "Just might be that I guess…" she said, trailing off. Then she looked at him directly. "How we gonna know for sure?"

He knew there was only one sure way to know what the situation was. "I'm going to have to go down there and see for myself, I guess. We can't sit up here all day and wait to see what's going on."

"Who's that?" Emma asked, pointing towards the farm. A lone rider was approaching the house from the road that ran in front.

James could see it was the same person he had come across back on the trail. "That's the man I saw near the oak trees back there." He still had no idea who or what he could be. A man appeared from out of the barn and greeted the rider as a friend and together they went into the house.

"Now that's interesting," James said under his breath. His mind was racing through the possibilities, but it would be starting to get dark in a few more hours and they needed to get to shelter. He outlined his plan to Emma.

"I'm going to go down there and approach the house from that side there," he said, indicating his line of approach. "When I find out what the situation is I'll signal you to come down."

"What if you can't signal, Mister James? What if someone grabs you up or somethin'? What would happen to us?" Emma was clearly frightened at the thought of him not leading them on.

James took a deep breath. He certainly understood her fear. "I've been thinking of that as well, Emma, but there is no other way. If something should happen to me you will have to follow this valley as far as it goes, always going north. You understand? Canada is only a few days away now."

Emma grabbed his arm. "Please don't, Mister James. I ain't never been so scared in all my life." She began to sob quietly and put her arms around him.

He waited a minute to let her cry it out, then took her hands in his. "You know I have to go, don't you? Don't you now? I'll be very careful, I promise." That was one promise he knew he would definitely keep.

Emma wiped away a tear. "I knows it, Mister James. Please, just come back to us."

James went back and explained the situation to the others who only nodded their understanding. They were all thinking the same thing… what if he doesn't come back. He picked up his rifle, checked the pistol in his belt and looked at his charges. "I'll be back so don't worry."

James left them there and followed the tree line north until he could see the side and back of the house better. He crouched and waited for a bit to see if he could learn anything, but there was only silence from the house and yard. He looked across the biggest field and saw a man leading a team of horses towards the barn. That was a good sign of normalcy, he thought.

There was nothing for it now but to try and get to the house, so he strode from the cover of the trees and trotted towards the side with a window. He took a minute to get his breath and listen, but again there was only silence from within and the sound of the approaching team from the far side of the yard.

After taking a peek in through the window and not seeing any-one, he went to take a quick look at the rear of the house. He could hear voices there but not what was being said. The tone of the conversation was friendly it seemed to him.

It was no use trying to hear what was being said, so he went to look around the front of the house. He took a quick glance up to where the others were waiting for him, then poked his head around the corner of the house.

"Can I help you find somebody?" A tall blond man was standing on the porch with a rifle pointed at his chest. "Why don't you come inside so we can get to know each other? What do you say?" He motioned with the barrel of his weapon towards the door. "Just leave your weapons right there, if you please."

From her place of concealment Emma watched James being ushered inside the house. They all had seen it and now looked at her. "Oh, Lord, oh Lord."

James felt very foolish for being taken by surprise the way he was. When he entered the front room, he was met by two stern faced white men, one the rider he had seen earlier. The older of the two men stepped up.

"What have we here, Nathaniel?"

"I saw him sneaking towards the house, Pa. After I got the horses put away I figured I'd go find out what he was about."

The older man turned to James. "Well, what are you all about, son? What's your business here on my farm?"

James had to think fast. If this really was the man's farm, then he must be a Quaker and would be sympathetic to a runaway. He slipped into speaking the way his fugitives always did.

"I'm just a tryin' to get north, mister, north to Canada and freedom. That's all I'm doin'."

"Where you from, son?"

"Oh, nowhere's near here, mister, that's a fact. I done run from a farm in Virginia."

"Nathaniel, keep an eye on our friend here. Richard and I

need to talk." He motioned to the rider and together they went towards the back of the house.

"You might's well have a seat," Nathaniel said, motioning towards a chair. "They may be a while in there."

James nodded and sat down, trying to hear the conversation in the back but once again he couldn't. "This is one beautiful farm y'all have here."

Nathaniel only grunted and looked towards the back where his father and the other man had gone. He started to say something but stopped when the two men came back in the room. The younger man, the one he had seen earlier in the forest, came forward.

"Were you up in those woods by the big rocks and the creek earlier today?"

"I don't rightly know what you mean, mister."

The man's voice softened. "What I mean is, were you in those woods by the big rocks and the creek earlier today? It's a simple question."

James looked around at the three white men, who were looking at him with an obvious curiosity. "I may have been, yassuh. I don't rightly know these here parts."

"Well, I do," the man went on. "I know them very well indeed. That's why I was sent out to locate some missing friends. I stopped and made a small fire by the rocks and the creek to see if anyone would approach. I definitely felt I was being watched. Do you know anything about our missing friends?"

James let out a huge sigh and dropped the accent. "I believe I do, actually. We got held up a couple of times and had to sleep in the forest last night. Then this morning we were set upon by slavers and when we got here the signal in the corral was wrong."

Nathaniel cast a reflexive look out the window. "Where are the hunters now?"

"Dead. I shot them both. I didn't think I had any choice."

The man Richard let out a long, slow breath. "That changes things a little, I think. How many were they?"

"There were two of them, but we had seen a group of three men the evening before. That's what kept us in the woods last night."

"I came across a team of three also, but they told me they were heading north to try and block the routes into Canada."

"I have no idea if these are the same men or not. I wasn't at all sure that you weren't one of them as well."

"No, I suppose you couldn't be sure, could you? Well, where are your passengers now?"

Emma had not taken her eyes off the house for one second, nor had any of the others. When she saw James step out on the porch and retrieve his rifle she nearly wept with joy. He looked up to where they were hiding and waved them down.

The next morning James was up before dawn gathering up his belongings. He had passed the night in the barn with the fugitives and now did not want to disturb them. They would need to rest and sleep all day to prepare for the next segment of their journey on The Road.

James slipped out the door and quietly closed it behind him. As he crossed the yard to the main house he could already see light coming from the front room and kitchen. He was also a farmer, so he wasn't surprised. A farm day starts early and ends late.

He was almost to the porch when he heard his name called softly in the still morning air. Emma ran after him. "Wasn't you gonna say good-bye, Mister James?"

"I thought it best to let you sleep as long as you can. You're going to have a hard night ahead tonight and Canada is still a few days away."

She embraced him. "You saved my life yesterday, Mister James, you truly did." She was crying softly. "If you hadn't fought for us back there, we would all be on our way back to Virginia by now, or worse. She looked up at him. "How can we, how can any of us, ever repay you for what you've done?"

He stepped away to see her better and took her hands in his. "I'll tell you how, Emma. You can repay me by getting free, getting to Canada, and breathing free for the rest of your lives. If you all want to repay me, just do that for me. Will you promise, Emma?"

The girl wiped away a tear. "Yassuh, Mister James, I promise to either get myself free, all of us free, or die tryin' to do so."

"I have to get back to my family now, Emma. I have been gone far too long, and I know they will be terribly worried if I don't get back soon. I should be able to make it by nightfall if I keep up a good pace."

"I don't want to hold you up none, Mister James. I just had to thank you is all. I just had to." She embraced him again, then headed back to the barn. "God bless you, Mister James, and your family."

He watched her walk away and went to the house. As he stepped up on the porch he was met by Nathaniel. "Are you ready to head for home, James?"

James grinned at him. "That I most definitely am, Nathaniel. I'm afraid my wife and children will be very worried. I was only intending to be gone for two days, but circumstances....", he shrugged.

"You did a fine job getting your passengers here, a very fine job. We can take care of them from here."

After saying good-bye to the father and Richard and packing some food for his journey, he started off the way he had come. The sun was just starting to peek over the horizon when he got to the rocks and the group of oaks they had passed the day before. He sat down to rest a bit and considered his next action. If he went back exactly the way they had come he would go by the bodies of the slavers, and they might have already been discovered.

He wasn't very familiar with the terrain, but he figured if he cut a little north of yesterday's path he could still find the little valley they had spent the previous night in. From there he knew the ground, and his way home, better.

After a short while he came to the road they had the run in

with the slavers on, but about a mile north. He went to the middle of the road but saw no signs of life anywhere. He crossed over into the woods on the other side and changed his course a little to the south and east, keeping him well clear of the area.

He kept up a militia marching pace for several hours. All he could think about now was how worried Abigail would be. He hated to add to her miseries. Her illness was progressing faster now so every moment with her was precious and he hated to think of her worrying about him as well.

The sun was directly overhead when he took another rest. It was a very sunny day but cool and calm. The perfect day for a long walk, he thought to himself. He pulled some dried meat from his knapsack and took in the scenery. He was near the top of a hill and could see all the way across this valley, which he figured should be the last one before the Cumberland Valley and his home ground. Off in the distance he could make out a lone rider a couple of miles away.

When he was well rested he set off again at his marching pace, covering this last valley in a couple of hours. When he crested the last hills, he could just make out Little Round Top in the distance, smoke curling up from the chimneys of his neighbors' homes. He smiled at the scene and pressed on, his anxiety about Abigail urging him to get home.

When he cleared the last tree line he could see Jonathan in the north field with a team. He figured Luke must be closer to the house as they always arranged it. He gave a loud whistle and Jonathan turned around.

Jonathan left the team and ran to his father, embracing him. "Oh, Lord Poppa. I was afraid the slavers took you, or worse. Momma has been frantic." He took a step back. "What happened, Poppa? Did you run into any slavers? Are the passengers safe?"

"Let's go fetch your team, son, and I'll tell you all about it." He put his arm around the young man's shoulder.

Luke looked up from his work in the yard and saw the two of them leading the team back to the barn, talking between themselves. "Abigail, Anna, come see," he called out. "James is home."

The two women rushed out of the house, Abigail holding on to a railing to steady herself. Anna hugged her. "I just knew he was all right, I just knew it," she said.

Abigail smiled weakly, watching her husband and son approach. "I wasn't so sure this time, Anna, I just wasn't so sure." She sank into a rocker on the porch, her eyes filling.

James saw her and, handing his rifle and knapsack to his son, ran to her on the porch. He took her hands in his and knelt by the chair. "I'm sorry if I worried you, my dear Abigail, very sorry."

"Oh, James, were you away somewhere? I hadn't noticed," she said lightly.

"Just out running some errands," James said. They both started to laugh then, the tension that had been dominating the last days gone now. He pulled her up from the rocker and held her close. "I hate every minute away from you, my beautiful wife," he whispered in her ear. "Every second."

That night over supper James recounted the story for everyone. When he got to the part about the killing of the slavers, he hesitated for a second then went on.

Abigail put her napkin to her lips and looked down at the table. "Did you have to kill them, James?"

All eyes were on him now as he considered his response. "I know how you feel about killing, Abigail. No one but an animal enjoys killing. I have thought about it ever since and I do not see how I could have done anything differently. If they had been able to get together, the slavers, they would have been too much for us to take on. I had to act then when they were still some distance apart."

Abigail was staring down at her plate as James spoke. She considered his words, nodding slowly. "Then you did the right thing, James, and I'm glad that you did. I am proud that you were able to help those poor people get free. Now we'll talk no more about killing in our home."

The winter came early and stayed late. Drifting snow brought almost all movement to a halt, especially on The Road. All of the passes through the surrounding hills were blocked for months so there were no passengers to conduct north to freedom.

When at last the thaw began, it began in earnest. The ground that had been frozen for so long was now nothing but sticky mud that could pull your boots off if you weren't careful. The men started to prepare the farm for spring, but it was difficult getting much done with the horses slipping and sliding as much as any of the men were.

When at last the weather cooperated and the ground became better suited to farm activity, an urgent message arrived from James McAllister. He had heard from his contacts in Maryland and Virginia that they were getting active and that James should be ready for movement in the next day or two.

The following month brought a steady stream of fugitives through the farm. There were more women making the hazardous journey now, and even some children as well. Jonathan would usually conduct from the south to the farm, and James would take them on the next leg to the church in Yellow Hill. Luke and Francis had to pick up any slack on the farm when they were away and keep an eye on any strangers in the area. The increase in activity also brought an increase in slave hunters as well as a growing sense of unease in the black community.

There had been very little slavery in the valley for years, and there was talk that it would be officially outlawed at the next meeting of the Assembly in Philadelphia. That did not do much to calm the fears of black citizens. If you could be grabbed up by slave hunters and sold south without any regard for legal status, without any regard for destroying families, simply because of the color of your skin, then the fear that was ever present in their lives was justified.

The story of Jude Hall and his three sons was well known to all in the valley, not just the black population. Even though Hall was a decorated hero of the American Revolution, three of his sons were kidnapped and sold south into slavery. Their status meant nothing to the kidnappers, only the color of their skin. Only one of them, William, was ever able to get free again escaping to England, but he never again returned to the United States, the country his father had fought so bravely for.

The work on the farm kept everyone busy, right down to little Constance who toddled around the house and yard feeding chickens or collecting eggs. The men stuck to their routine of making sure at least one was close by and armed at all times. Abigail seemed to rally a bit with the warmer weather and the farm coming alive again, but still had days that were hard. James was just thankful for every single day they had together.

James was up before the sun as usual. He had been notified that another group of fugitives would be arriving at the rendezvous rock late tonight and he had a lot of work to do before he could set out to conduct them on this leg.

He went to check on Jonathan who had been suffering from a fever. He looked down on his grown son, his firstborn, and saw him again as a small child. He was momentarily overwhelmed looking at him, remembering his brother and the wonderful life that their father had given them in this place.

He eased out the door so as not to disturb the others yet and went to the barn. Luke was already at work, getting a team and wagon together.

"Good morning, James. How is Jonathan this morning?"

"He looks about the same, so I let him sleep. Looks like I'll have to take his next leg on The Road after all."

They started to pile tools in the wagon for the day's work. "I'm sure he'll be fine in another day or so. He's a strong young man."

"I hope so. It pains me when any of the children are ill," James said. Luke just nodded. Now that they both knew the joys and perils of fatherhood, there was no need to say more.

They set about their tasks after the wagon was loaded and Anna had made them some breakfast. The sun was just starting to climb the sky when they turned into the north field and set to work on the fences and the gate. They always worked well together, as a real team, and the tasks proceeded smoothly.

James called a halt late in the afternoon. "I think we can finish up here for now. I'm sure we can find more to do in the yard. Maybe Francis needs some help in the barn."

They were loading up the wagon for the return trip when Luke stopped and motioned to James. Two white men were riding by on the road between the farms like the two that had caused them some problems before. They were roughly dressed and seemed to pay them little attention, but there was something in their manner that troubled James.

They drove back to the barnyard without seeing the riders again, but they both were concerned about them. It was at times like these that they felt more vulnerable living on a farm. There were no nearby neighbors to help if they were attacked in their homes by slavers. They were well armed to be sure, and James had taught Luke and his sons to shoot and defend themselves as well as he, but the unease felt by the black population at large was ever present in their lives as well.

After supper James laid down to get some sleep. He would be up very soon conducting and would need the rest. He had been dreaming about hunting with his little brother back on Little Round Top when he suddenly awoke. He sensed something was wrong and he tried to put his finger on it. He listened hard and close, but there were no sounds coming from outside, just the sounds of his family sleeping close by.

The night was clear and brisk with just a light breeze. He put on an extra shirt and made some tea from the kettle that was always at the fire and went outside to watch the sky. He didn't have to worry about any rain this night it seemed. He put his tea mug down, picked up his rifle and set out.

He made good time to the clearing. He knew this ground as well or better than anyone around, so he was able to make good time even at night. He waited just outside the clearing and listened, not moving.

When he was satisfied that he was alone for the moment, he stepped into the clearing and took a seat on the rock. The Drinking Gourd was once more in its proper place, waiting to guide people to freedom.

He heard the call of an owl, and knew his charges were nearby. Sure enough, the usual conductor who worked this leg appeared at the edge of the clearing. James greeted him and he came over.

"Good evening, James. It's certainly a nice night to be out on a stroll. Where is your boy tonight? He's well, I trust."

"Evenin' pastor. It is indeed a fine night for a stroll in the woods. My son is well, thank you, but he has a fever and I felt it best for him to stay at home tonight. Are your passengers with you?"

The pastor put his hands to his lips and made the owl call again. In a moment five figures appeared from the trees, bunched together, eyes wide.

James was once again struck by the desperation and fear on the faces of the refugees, and it made him more determined than ever to help. It also made him angry that The Road was even necessary, that people had to flee and suffer just to take a breath of free air. He shook his head at the thought.

"How long since your last rest, pastor? We have enough time to wait here a bit if they need to."

"That would be good, I think. We have been on the move for the last four hours without stopping anywhere. I want to tell you about this group. They are all one family. The father, the tall one there, refused to leave without his wife and child and the other two boys are their nephews who have no other relatives anywhere."

James looked them over again, more closely this time. A whole family of fugitives in search of basic human decency. Once again he felt the weight of what they were doing, he and the pastor and

McAllister and the many, many others who risked everything to help them, risked their lives and their own freedom.

"Don't worry about them, pastor. I'll get them to where they need to go."

The pastor motioned the father in the group over. "Jerome, this man is going to conduct you and your family to the next station. It's not far now. You can rest here some before you set out again. I have to leave now and get back home." He turned to James. "God bless you, sir, and your boy. I hope he feels better soon and can rejoin us."

They shook hands and the pastor vanished silently into the forest once more. James walked Jerome back to the group. "We'll be leaving in a few minutes. The next stop is about three hours away and you'll find shelter and plenty of food. You will be safe there, I assure you."

Jerome's wife stepped forward. "Thank you, sir. It has been a long night, but we don't need no rest. We can walk all the way to Canada tonight if we has to."

James smiled at that. He never ceased to be impressed by these people, their endurance and their patience. It was truly humbling. "What's your name, missus?"

"Lucy's my name, sir. I heared the pastor tell you about us, that we is all one family. We felt that if we couldn't all go together, then none of us would go and we would just stay and be slaves as long as we was all together. Those boys belongs to my sister, but she dead." She looked over at them, then back at James. "They be mine now."

After a short rest, they set off down the path to home. They stopped for a rest after another hour and James climbed out on a ledge to get a look ahead. It was still dark, but he wanted to see if any lights shone anywhere. The countryside right around was uninhabited, so there shouldn't be a light showing anywhere.

Just as the eastern sky started to lighten, they came to the last tree line before the farm. James had the group stay back and he went ahead to look for Luke out plowing in the field near the house, the signal that all was safe.

He wasn't there. James had made this journey dozens of times over the last years and Luke had always been there. Always. He waited until the sun was well and truly up and there was still no sign of Luke anywhere, not in the field or the barnyard.

"Oh Jesus Christ," he muttered under his breath.

It was all he could do to stay calm and not rush the house. He had to have a plan. He looked the familiar terrain over again with new eyes, the eyes of a soldier. The house had been built by his father to make sure no one could approach stealthily. It would have to be approached from straight on, something he was loathe to do. The trees had grown closer on the eastern side, so he circled around to that side, watching the house intently.

He was just getting ready to break cover and try to make it to the house when he saw Francis looking at the house from behind the fence on the north field. He came out of the trees and waved to him. When Francis saw him, he came out from behind the fence and ran to him. James tried to get him to take cover, but he kept coming.

The boy was out of breath. "Poppa, thank God you're home. Thank God."

"What happened here? Where's Luke?"

"They came early this morning, Poppa. A man came to the farm and said he was lost, could we help him find Mister Ander's farm. Miss Anna came out of her house and asked the man if he wanted some water, if he'd been riding all night."

"Hurry, boy. What happened next?"

"It wasn't a half hour after he left that he came riding back with three others. They just charged right up our road. Luke was just coming out of the barn and tried to get his rifle from over there," he said pointing to the porch, "but they got to him before he could. Then they went into the houses and started ordering everyone out."

"Where were you, son?"

"I was over in the north field doing chores. When I heard the commotion I came running but stayed out of sight and watched. Poppa, they took Luke and Miss Anna and even little Constance and Abigail away. I saw them." He stopped and looked down. "I let them, Poppa. I just watched and let them," he said quietly.

"No, son, you did not let them do anything. If you had tried to stop them, they would have killed you or taken you away as well." James started for the house, his rifle ready to use. "Let's find out what has happened to your mother and brother."

As he stepped on to the porch James heard the sound of a rifle being cocked. "Jonathan, it's your father, son. Don't shoot."

He put his head around the corner and saw his son had indeed positioned himself to shoot anyone who came through the door. He was lying on the floor with his head propped up with blankets. When he saw his father and brother he lowered the weapon. "Thank God."

James went to his side and knelt down. The side of his son's face was bruised and discolored, one eye swollen shut. His breathing was labored.

"What have they done to you, son? Where's your mother?"

Jonathan pointed to the rear of the house. Since her illness had begun taking more of a toll, James had built a wall in the room that gave her more privacy at the rear. He went to the door and, hesitating, pushed it open, afraid of what he might see inside.

Abigail was lying on her side with her back to the door. James went over and sat on the edge of the bed, gently touching her shoulder. Until she rolled over at his touch he had been unsure if she was alive or dead.

Her face was swollen and covered in tears. "I couldn't stop them, James. They took my baby and I could not stop them."

He looked down on her sadness and he knew it too. He leaned down and kissed her softly on the forehead. "I'm going to get her back. I'm going to get them all back. You just rest and take care of Jonathan."

"Oh, James, they beat the boy so. He met them at the door and fought like the devil. I believe he broke the arm of one of them." She stopped to get her breath. "They were just too many for him, too many."

James went back out to his sons. "Francis, go saddle two horses. Right now, go. Jonathan, how long ago did they leave? Did they say anything to give you any idea of where they were heading after they left?"

"Been about two hours I would guess, Poppa. Only thing I heard them to say is they had enough now, they should head back home. I would guess they're heading south."

James looked around his home. The invaders had trashed everything inside and stolen anything of any value. He went to a section of the floor that was unremarkable in every way. He took his knife and worked it between the boards and pulled two of them up. His father had built it there to hide anything he did not want found. He pulled out two small bags of powder and several dozen rounds.

Francis reappeared. "I got the horses ready, Poppa. Am I going with you?"

James handed him a rifle and a cartridge box fully loaded. "I'm afraid you are going to do a little growing up today. I have to go bring my passengers in before we can go after the slavers. Make sure we have enough water for a day or two."

He knelt down by his oldest son again. "Your mother says you gave a good account of yourself last night."

Jonathan smiled weakly up at him. "I guess I did that. One of them needed some help leaving."

"I'm taking your brother and we're going after them. I'll need you to take care of your mother and my five passengers. Do you think you can manage that?"

"I'll be better in a little while, Poppa. I just need to rest a bit more. I'll be fine."

"Why didn't they take you and your mother? Did they say anything about that?"

Jonathan barked out an angry laugh through the pain. "Well, Poppa, I think they left me for dead to be honest. They definitely tried to kill me, that's for sure."

"Did they say anything about Momma?"

"I heard one of them say 'we don't need no sick niggers. No one wants to buy a sick nigger.'"

James stood up, his jaw firmly set. He started for the door and grabbed his rifle and supplies. "Let's go boy. We have a hard day ahead of us." Jonathan watched his father and little brother go, not knowing if he would ever see them again.

They had no trouble following them for a while. The raiders had stolen a wagon and a horse with a bad shoe. Both left unmistakable tracks in the soft soil of the main road to Maryland. Stealing that particular horse had been a big mistake, and James knew that between the horse and the young children the raiders were being kept to a slower pace than they probably wanted.

As they rode further south, they came upon Reverend Jackson and his wife in a small wagon and stopped. James tried to sound calm but failed.

"Did you see a wagon and some riders go by heading south?"

"Well, good morning to you, James, and to you Francis. Why, yes, we did see a wagon go by less than an hour ago."

"It's slavers, damn it, they've kidnapped Luke and his family and my daughter Abigail. Are you sure it was an hour ago?"

"Oh my Lord, I had no idea. It was just some white men is all we saw."

James thought for a second. Was this the same wagon? Was he on a wild goose chase? "Was the back of the wagon covered? Could you see if anyone was in the back?"

The reverend thought for a moment, then looked at his wife who was shaking her head. "No, come to think of it, we could not see what was in the back. Something was, though, there were lumps in the canvas."

James was sure now that he was in pursuit of the right wagon. "Thanks for your help. I can probably catch them on this side of the border if we hurry."

"What's your plan, James? You think you can take them on alone?"

"They have my friends and my family in that wagon, and as you can see I am not alone," James said quietly.

"I have a better idea," Reverend Jackson said, again turning to his wife. "We'll go back to my cousin's place just a short ways from here, and we can get some men together to help. If they are on this road heading for Maryland, they have to cross on the Emmitsburg road or very near. We can meet you at the farm just before the river crossing, you know near the Keagy place, but you'll have to give us an hour or so to catch up to you."

James was thinking, trying to remain rational in his approach to this problem, but all he could see was Abigail's little smiling face. He also knew that there would be a better chance if he had better odds.

"All right, we can hold up there if we haven't caught up to them by then. But please hurry, hurry. Let's go, Francis."

They continued on southward as Jackson turned the wagon around. "Do you think they can catch up to us, Poppa?"

"I don't know, but we'll give them a chance and see how this all goes. We will wait if we can or act alone if we need to."

They spurred their mounts on, sure they were pursuing the kidnappers after all. They couldn't be so far ahead that they wouldn't catch them up by the time darkness fell. Yes, James thought grimly to himself, we will have them by tonight.

They rode on without resting for hours. They passed one more wagon going north who reported seeing the same covered wagon and four white men passing them heading south, one with his arm in a sling. Finally, they had to stop and rest the horses. As soon as they were cooled off and had some water, they mounted up again and rode on south, always south. Towards the slave fields and away from home.

It was still several hours before dusk when James first spotted them ahead. As he had hoped, the older horse and young children had slowed the kidnappers down enough to let them catch up. The kidnappers did not seem to be hurrying as they probably felt very safe, and in the eyes of the law they were. Any white man could have any black person arrested and held without explanation in accordance with fugitive slave laws, even in states where slavery was illegal. If they were confronted, all they would have to say is they were returning "stolen contraband" to the rightful owner and that would be the end of that. What they didn't know was James was on their trail.

James lowered his glass. "That's them all right son. It's definitely them." He looked again to see if he could see Luke or anyone else, but the canvas was covering the back. "Let's go. We should have them well before dark now."

"Are we going to wait for the others to catch up, Poppa?"

"We'll just play that one by ear. Right now I just want to keep them in sight."

It was not long after that James spotted some smoke from a small fire just ahead. They stopped in the road. "That may be their campfire. Maybe they're stopping for the night on this side of the river," James said. "Let's get off the road and I'll go have a look."

Francis stayed with the horses well back off the road as James went ahead on foot to scout out the situation. He was able to get within a hundred feet of the wagon and get in a position to see and hear what was happening. Sure enough, the canvas was pulled back and Anna and the children climbed out. Two of the kidnappers reached in the wagon and dragged the inert Luke out and dropped him on the ground. Anna tried to go to him but was restrained.

"He'll be all right, Missy, don't you worry none. Hell, a dead nigger ain't worth very much to us," James heard one of the kidnappers say. "Now, you and the little ones here stretch out some before we move on. Go on, now, go get you somethin' to eat."

James watched as two of the kidnappers sat Luke up and leaned him against one of the wagon wheels. One of them threw a cup of water in his face, rousing him. "Ah, he don't look so bad, do he Joe?"

"Still plenty of fight left in him, that's for sure," the other said, laughing as Luke struggled against his bonds. "Yessir, I do believe this here black man would do us some harm if he got free."

As James watched, two more very young men climbed out of the back of the wagon. They seemed to be wearing leg irons as their gait was awkward, but he could not be sure from his position. What he was sure of was that one of them was the son of Mister Todd from the church and was not a runaway but freeborn. They went and stood by Anna and the children. They all looked frightened and miserable. He could hear the children crying and it tore at his soul.

The white men stayed standing near Luke talking and laughing, saying something to Luke every once in a while. Luke kept his head down and wasn't responding. James could only imagine what was going through his young friend's head. He knew that Luke would die before going back to being a slave again, of that James was certain.

James hurried back to bring Francis up to date and explained the situation. "They may be in for the night or just resting. I don't know, but if I was them I'd want to be on the other side of the river before dark."

They tied the horses and crept up to where James had been hiding. They had only been there a few minutes before the kidnappers hoisted Luke back up into the wagon and gathered up their things.

"Come on now, Missy. You and the children climb on in the back, you hear. Come on, boys. Get up in there now."

When everyone was aboard they started off, but not the way James was expecting. They turned on to a smaller track that led off to the east before crossing the river a few miles further on. That was their second mistake. He would be able to cut them off and contain them in a small stretch of sunken road further on that he was familiar with.

"Listen son and listen well. I want you to ride towards the Keagy farm where we told Reverend Jackson we could rendezvous. If he's not there yet, ride towards his cousin's place until you find him.

Tell him the kidnappers are on the Old Smith Farm Road, not the main road to Emmitsburg. Have you got that?"

"Yes sir, Poppa, I got it. Smith Farm Road, yes sir. What are you going to do?"

"I'm going to stop them on this side of the river if I can. I'll probably be needing reinforcements soon after, so I need you to hurry as fast as you can."

Francis nodded grimly and went back to his mount. James heard him ride away and turned back to the raiders. They heard nothing over the noise they were making themselves getting back on the road. James watched them go for a minute and went back to his horse.

He followed along behind them for a half hour or so. It was obvious the stolen horse was slowing them down even more now. He almost ran into them from behind when they were forced to stop. He got close enough to hear them complaining about the horse's shoe.

"Damn, Bob, why the hell did you have to steal a lame horse for?" one asked as he lifted the affected leg of the animal. "You can see the shoe ain't right just by lookin' at it."

"She was in the stall next to the wagon is all I know. Shit, she seemed all right to me lookin' at her in that barn."

"Well, she ain't all right, Bob, she ain't right at all. She'll get us across the river maybe, but after that we'll need another horse from somewheres."

The sun was getting lower as they moved on again and James knew it would be starting to get dark in another couple of hours. He had no way of knowing where Francis was or even if he found Jackson or not. He just knew that he had better act before they crossed the river into slave country.

James followed a narrow creek bed that paralleled the road the wagon was on. He had no plan as yet other than to get ahead of them and stop them in the narrowest stretch of the sunken road they were traveling on.

When he figured he was a good distance ahead of them, he

turned back to meet them on the road when they came up. When he came out on the sunken road again he saw he was just shy of where he wanted to be to ambush them and rode on a little further to the east. In a few minutes he was in a position to see the road and anything on it. There was only room for the wagon in this stretch. The riders would have to go in single file ahead and behind. There would be no place to turn around. Only riders behind the wagon would have any cover at all. He smiled grimly at that.

He thought he could hear them approaching in another few minutes. He had tied his horse up far enough away so it wouldn't be seen or heard. James went behind a large boulder and laid his rifle across the top. He took off his cartridge box and put it next to the rifle and the pistol he was carrying. He also had a sword he had taken off another slaver. He looked over his arsenal again, then back down the road just as they were coming into view. James took a very deep breath and raised the rifle to his shoulder.

Looking through his sights he could see one man driving, his arm in a sling, and one leading the way. The other two must be following in single file through this narrow stretch of road. He let them get as close as he dared then fired, taking the driver of the wagon full in the chest. The horse of the leading rider reared up at the unexpected sound, causing the rider to grab both reins. He turned his head toward the wagon then turned back to where the sound of the shot had come from. James stepped out from behind the boulder and shot him off his horse. He then scrambled under the wagon, but James could see he had been hit by his shot. He stepped back into cover and immediately started to reload his weapons.

The old horse pulling the wagon was in a blind panic and now driverless. She tried to plunge ahead on the road, but the other horse was blocking the way. He could hear the other two kidnappers yelling from behind the wagon.

"Bob, god dammit Bob, what's happening up there? Johnny, you okay? What the hell is happening?"

James started to circle around to his right to try and get a view behind the wagon. He stopped when a round flew past his ear and ricocheted off the rock behind him.

"I see you up there, you damn nigger. Get down here now or I'll start killing these children. You hear me? I'll kill them."

James had no doubt that was true. To men such as these a black life had no value, didn't matter at all. They were only on earth to be enslaved by their natural masters. He had anticipated they might say something like that, but he figured these men wanted to live as well so that made it an empty threat.

"You hear me up there, boy? I am tellin' you right now, I will cut their throats one at a time if you don't come on down here and surrender right now. I'll start with the pretty little lady first."

James took a quick look down at the road but wasn't far enough behind the wagon to see anyone or anything. He assumed all the captives were still under the canvas in the rear. He looked out to the west for a sign of Francis approaching but saw nothing.

"C'mon out now, boy. You just wastin' time now and we got places to go."

James moved a few yards back towards the front of the wagon. He could see the horse was still straining at the harness, thrashing in blind panic, still trying to move forward. He raised his rifle and took aim. "Sorry old girl," he said and shot her through the head. She dropped dead still pulling on the harness.

"Damn, boy, what the hell you do that for?" All of the kidnappers were cussing and yelling now. "You think that will stop us, boy? Do you?" They sounded like they were beginning to panic.

James had reloaded the rifle and taken up his position on his right above the road again. "Only one way you will ride out of here, mister. That wagon isn't going anywhere now."

He could hear them talking it over but couldn't make out what was being said except for the men cursing their captives and telling them to keep quiet. There was a minute or two of quiet, then one of them called out to him.

"What you propose we do now, boy? I mean, do you have some

plan or other? There are still three of us and only one of you. Ain't that right, boy?"

James looked around at the terrain. He could not move any more to the rear of the wagon without exposing himself. He thought about going back to the front and trying to get behind them but figured that would also leave him exposed part of the way.

"My plan is pretty simple, really. You gentlemen get on your horses and ride on out of here to the south and I won't kill you. What do you think of it?"

There was some laughter. "Hey, nigger, I have a better plan. Why don't you come on down here and give it up, or we start killing children. What do you think of that plan?"

James leaned back trembling. It was essential that he remain calm and in control of the situation. "Don't like it much, to be honest. The only question I have, I guess, is how much do you all want to suffer before you die?"

"What are you takin' about, boy? I said I will kill these here children and by God I'll do it. What do you say to that?"

"I say that's fine. We'll all just sit here and after you kill everyone I am going to give you an opportunity to find out what your testicles taste like. What do you say to that?"

That gave them something to think about and shut them up for a minute. He could hear them talking again but was still unable to hear them clearly. "What do you say, gentlemen? Do you care to ever see your homes again or do you want to die here tonight?"

"You really think you got a chance out here agin' us, don't ya nigger? These boys I'm with are pretty unhappy with you for shootin' their brother like that. I don't think they're much in a surrenderin' mood."

James took another look to the west and saw a large cloud of dust being raised by approaching riders. He knew his son would be leading them on, frantic about his father. "You might want to take a look out to the west there about a mile or so before you make any kind of decision you might regret."

"What are you trying to pull here now, boy? What you talkin' about?"

"You can stick your head up to look if you want. I won't shoot you, I promise. You really should take a look. Might affect your decision making a bit."

Sure enough, a hat appeared above the wagon side. It waved back and forth, obviously in someone's hand.

"Told you I wouldn't shoot. Come on out and see for yourself. I think we're going to have company in another few minutes."

This time a shaggy man's head appeared and craned to see out to the west. James heard him mutter something and then duck back down. He could hear a hurried conversation along with curses for their captives.

"My friends and family will take a very dim view of you if they get here and find you threatening their loved ones, I can promise you that, and as you've seen I keep my promises."

"How you know who they are, boy? Could be a group of white folks comin' to keep you from murdering us. Did you think of that, boy? Huh, did you?"

Actually that thought had occurred to James but only fleetingly. He was sure it was Francis coming with help, and from the size of the cloud there was going to be a lot of help soon.

"Well, what do you say we just wait here a minute and find out, shall we?" James stood and fired the pistol into the air to signal his position to Francis. "Shouldn't be too long now."

Francis and two other men soon appeared in the road only a hundred yards distant. James stood again and waved his hat in the air. He pointed down to the wagon in the road and signaled to Francis to get behind the kidnappers. Francis turned to the two men and spoke to them, then they turned and disappeared.

"Well, gentlemen, what's it going to be? Do you want to ride out of here, or do you want to die here?"

"Go to the devil, you damn nigger. I don't care how many of you there are, we ain't givin' up."

"You do realize that you are surrounded by angry men who want you dead, don't you? You can either ride away and leave us alone here, or you are going to die here. It really is that simple."

"How do we even know they's anyone else here? How do we know those riders didn't just ride on by?"

Just then a single shot rang out from behind them and a round crashed into the side of the wagon wheel an inch above the kidnapper's head.

"Jesus Christ, hold your damn fire, hold your fire." The hat appeared above the side of the wagon again. "Now just hold on, damn it."

There was another flurry of conversation behind the wagon, then a man stood up. "All right, all right. We'll ride on out of here, just don't shoot."

"Tell the other two to come out right now and keep their hands where I can see them. Come on."

The man moved out onto the road and another emerged from hiding. Finally the third man stood and came out, his right shoulder a bloody mess. James could see him clearly. He was just a boy, really, probably didn't even shave most days yet he imagined. They all stood in the middle of the road behind the wagon looking very unhappy.

"Anna, you can come on out now, it's James. Abigail, come on out girl, it's your father. Bring those boys out with you. Don't be afraid." He turned to Francis. "You boys go get Luke out of there."

Slowly the captives emerged from under the canvas and took in the scene. The two boys shuffled over to the road. "Get those irons off of those children right now, damn you, right now."

He watched as the man who had been doing the talking took a key and went to the boys, kneeling down. "Why don't the rest of you come on out now and introduce yourselves," he called out.

Francis and ten more men emerged from the brush and surrounded the kidnappers, not saying a word. Then Reverend Jackson appeared, holding his rifle at the ready. James tipped his hat to him. "Mighty glad you could make it this evening."

"Wouldn't miss it for the world, James, not for the world," Jackson said as he shoved one of the kidnappers with his rifle butt then snarled at him. "Get over there with the other filth. Go on, move."

After the kidnappers had been thoroughly searched and disarmed, the one who had been doing the talking spoke up. "You said you was goin' to let us ride out of here now, didn't you? You ain't goin' to go back on your word? You promised," he added, looking nervously at the angry black faces around him. "You promised," he added once more.

"I'll keep my word, as long as no one was harmed by you scum." He turned to Francis. "Help these gentlemen get their friend and all their horses and point the way south to them."

"Yes sir, Poppa. This way, gentlemen," Francis said, bowing slightly. He and four other young men followed the kidnappers around to the front of the wagon. The riderless horse was standing some yards away and one of the young men went after it.

"Best get up there and get your friend," Francis said, indicating the dead driver of the wagon. "We're going to want our wagon back and we don't want some dead white man in it."

They lowered the body down just as the other horse was brought back. They laid it across the saddle and secured it for the journey. James brought over the other three horses and handed the reins to the spokesman. "South is that way," he said, pointing. "I suggest you get a move on." He turned and started to walk away.

The kidnappers suddenly found themselves surrounded by five very angry, well-armed black men. They tried to back away but found there was nowhere to go.

"Before you go, I have a question for you. Why us? Why did you come to our state and think you could steal any of us away? What right do you think you have?" Francis seemed genuinely curious.

"Look, boy, we just want to ride on out now, you hear? Your own father give us his word. Y'all heard him. You're not goin' against your Poppa's word now, are you?"

"No, I'm not going to go against my father's word. Unlike you three, he is a man of honor, but you will pay for the insult you paid my mother and that's a fact." He struck him across the face with the butt of his rifle. The other two were set upon by the other men as James came running up.

"That's enough, enough," he said, pulling the angry men off the kidnappers. "Now get them on their horses and out of here." James turned to the kidnappers, who looked a little worse for wear. His face was an inch from the speaker. "I suggest you get the hell out of here right now, boy, you hear me, boy? If you ever come back to Pennsylvania my sons and I will hunt you down. You understand me, boy?"

The hard work of farm routine helped the days to go by as the families tried to get back to a normal life. Jonathan recovered from his illness and his beating by the slavers. Luke, too, was recovering physically but his mood was often dark and brooding. The close brush with being returned to slavery had taken a toll on his spirit.

James also felt the darkness as he tried to keep his farm functioning well. He found himself lost in dark thoughts at times when he was working alone, thinking about what had happened to them, and worrying that it could happen again.

The word of the situation had spread to the entire town. At church meetings they found themselves the subject of much concern and worry. They also learned that the number of kidnapping incidents was on the rise as other parishioners shared stories from their own families and friends.

Recent events were causing a distinct change in the racial climate in their little town. It was subtle at first, but the changes were coming faster now, and none were for the good. Even though Governor Ritner had come out as an abolitionist and praised Pennsylvania for starting to outlaw slavery in his annual message to the State Legislature, the atmosphere was changing everywhere and not just in their town.

A Constitutional Convention was called for, and there was great relief at first in the black communities when black suffrage was not questioned. That soon changed as false charges were brought in a Bucks County election and the Convention heard speaker after speaker condemn the very notion of blacks voting. This was particularly bad news coming from Bucks County since it had the most affluent and professional black population of anyplace in the entire country and they were considered to be valued members of that community. If the right to vote was in danger there, then smaller less affluent black communities had much to fear.

Increasingly in many places, animosity both overt and covert was growing. The Nat Turner rebellion in Virginia had started a slow steady stream of fear and vitriol towards blacks on both sides of the Mason-Dixon Line. The right to vote was mostly academic in a lot of small towns across Pennsylvania and New England in reality. Angry groups of white men often barred black citizens from exercising their rights. Connecticut was the first state to actually expressly forbid black Americans the right to vote way back in 1818. New Jersey followed in 1820 and now it seemed likely that Pennsylvania would follow down this path to second class status for a good many of its citizens.

James Forten had served with distinction during the Revolution serving with Stephen Decatur yet he, too, was blocked from voting even though he was a very prominent citizen of Philadelphia with a large and well known sail making business He petitioned the State to allow him his rights under the State Constitution, with such prominent men as John Peck and John B. Vashon of Pittsburgh backing him. James and many others in Gettysburg were cautiously optimistic that the Legislature would do the right thing by him, especially with so many prominent men, both black and white, in his corner.

It was at an evening meeting of the Adams County Anti-Slavery Society that the group of men who saw the struggle for freedom up close learned their fate at the hands of blind hatred and racism. McAllister himself brought them the news directly from an express rider they had sent to the meeting. It was well known and well discussed that the Constitutional Convention was meeting and among the many topics now being covered was black suffrage. Most were hopeful the law would remain unchanged.

There was great anticipation among those gathered when James McAllister stood to read the dispatch to the group. It was obvious from his voice that the news was not good.

"This is from a reporter at the scene in Harrisburg," he said, waving the sheet of paper over his head. The room became very still. "He writes to tell us of today's events at the Convention." He looked down at the paper again and started to read.

"This morning a Mister E.T. McDowell of Bucks County began a debate on denying all black citizens their basic right to vote." A collective groan went up at the mention of Bucks County again.

McAllister held his hand up for silence, then went on. "Representative McDowell once again accused black citizens from neighboring communities of voting improperly in Bucks County, without any evidence of any kind I might add. He then continued by saying that if the people of Bucks County allowed the black man to vote, then they would take over and white's would be forced to flee their homes."

James looked around the room at these men from the community, his community. Almost all of them, black and white alike, risked their homes and their very lives to help slaves escape to freedom. Almost all were property owners like himself. Others worked as hired hands, shopkeepers and tradesmen. One or two even owned small restaurants and an inn. There was not one person of color living in the county poorhouse, and there had not been for many years. Yet now, they had no rights in the land of their birth. No right to a voice. No right to speak out. Because of the color of their skin.

"As many of you are aware," McAllister's booming voice once again brought silence to the group, "a document entitled the 'Pittsburgh Memorial' was sent to the Convention to be read aloud and entered into the proceedings by the representatives from that fair city. Other Memorials were also brought to the Convention.

They were all ignored, all but the one's submitted by white groups seeking to disenfranchise all blacks."

This brought most of them to their feet. Shouts of "No!" and "How could they!" filled the small room. This time McAllister knew it would be fruitless to call for quiet. His eyes met James' from across the room.

"In the case of James Forten that many of you have been following, there is also news. It seems that the State Legislature, in its infinite wisdom, has seen fit to just ignore Mister Forten entirely. Him and his petition both."

Again angry voices filled the meeting room. "How could they do that? Forten fought for this country. He fought bravely and hard, and this is how his country, our country, repays his service?" A man James did not know well was shouting from the back of the room. "How could this be allowed to happen? Have we no rights at all?"

McAllister looked back down at the paper in his hand. He felt shame and his voice started to crack. "It would appear that the answer to Mister Franklin's question is that no, the black citizen has no rights at all at present."

A stunned silence met him as he looked around the room at the faces of the men. They all looked like they had been kicked in the stomach, whites and blacks alike. A few had dared to hope that progress was being made, real progress, especially in their town and the surrounding valley. Relations between the communities had been mostly good for as long as anyone could remember. Those in the room who knew the bitter taste of slavery were especially down hearted at the news from the Convention and many felt that the ice cold hand of slavery would follow them always, no matter where they went or how they lived their lives.

McAllister could feel the desperation creeping into the room like a physical presence. He cleared his throat and began again. "As I said, it appears *at present* that these fellow citizens of Pennsylvania have no rights. This is not a time to quit the struggle, gentlemen, but it is a time to rededicate ourselves to it." He let that sink in a minute as he looked around at the group. "We here in this room do not need to be sold on the basic argument of human decency. We all understand the sin that is slavery, and that its eradication from this country should be our highest priority."

"What else can we do, Mister McAllister?" a voice called out from the back. "We already fightin' every single day to help our brothers and sisters. What else can we do?"

"The very first thing we must do is we must not lose heart." James found himself standing and addressing the men. He was known as a quiet man, a good neighbor in every sense, but he had never stepped forward like this. Luke was looking up at him from his bench, curious and waiting.

"These acts, these attempts to dehumanize us, to make us something less than men, must not be allowed to succeed. We must not let them achieve their evil ambitions. We must resist them at every turn."

"How do we do that, James? How do we fight back when they will not even acknowledge our very humanity? Why should we even have to?"

James started to pace, just a few steps back and forth collecting his thoughts. "That is a very fair question, brother Franklin, a very fair question. Why should we have to prove our humanity to a group of people who will hate us for no other reason than we appear to be different? Why should we?"

There was only a quiet murmur at the rhetorical question. James waited a minute, then went on in a quiet voice. "I'll tell you why. We have to do it because others question that very proposition. We have to do it because if we do not, they will win. We have to do it because we are free citizens of this country. It is our home. If we want our children and grandchildren to live in dignity, then we must fight this fight. We must!"

James saw that many in the group were nodding along with him. "If we want our future to be one of hope and dignity, then we must make today full of hope and dignity. We must try harder than a white man to prove ourselves. I know that is not fair, but it is the way of this world so we might as well just face that fact and move on." He looked around the room again, somewhat embarrassed that he had spoken out. "I guess that's all I have to say except that I am not beaten as long as I can breathe."

McAllister stood again and the group waited. "Well, James, that was quite unexpected, but quite right of course. There are loud voices calling for complete segregation, for banishing black Americans to live a second class life, to not know the simple beauty of freedom, or worse yet, to 'recolonize' by evicting people from the only home they have ever known, to send them to Africa, a land totally unknown to any black person living here today."

He reached in his coat pocket and brought out another piece of paper. "I want to read a letter to the editor of the Pittsburgh newspaper. It was written by Mister John B. Vashon, a name we all know and respect. It starts by condemning one of the 'recoloniza-tion societies' in their town. It condemns men who want to banish blacks from *their* native lands, and here I quote, 'to forsake this soil which was enriched by his labors and watered with his tears.'"

"And his very blood. This land was watered with the blood of our ancestors," Franklin shouted out. "Never forget that!"

"No, brother Franklin, you are quite right, quite correct my friend," McAllister went on quietly. "We must never forget that sad fact, never. This land we all love has indeed been watered by the blood of all of our ancestors, but some citizens are denied the basic rights enjoyed by others. James is also quite correct in saying we must not lose heart. No man can turn his back on this struggle now, when the facts are there for all to see. It says, 'All men are created equal', it does not say some are more equal than others although that is plainly the truth." He looked around the room at the rapt faces, desperate for some hope, some inspiration. "Like my friend James there said so beautifully, I am not beaten as long as I can breathe. No sir, I will *not* be beaten as long as I have one single breath in me."

The meeting broke up about an hour later after they had dis-cussed possible courses of action for the coming year. It was decided that a committee would write another Memorial for publication and submission to the State Legislature. It was also decided that Gettysburg should be regularly included in the circuit of the many abolitionist speakers who were travelling from town to town to speak out against slavery.

An ambassador of sorts was named to be liaison with the national anti-slavery groups. The group tried to get James to take the position, but he demurred. With his work on The Road and his farm, he would be hard pressed to fulfill the duties properly. The group then elected Mister Franklin to be their liaison and the meeting ended.

"You did good back there, James. You sure surprised me the way you stood and spoke your piece like that," Luke said, laughing a little. "Yes sir, that sure was something to see. Glad I was there for it." He and Jonathan had been trading off going to the meetings so one would be on the farm and one with James.

James was a little sheepish. "I don't know what came over me right then. I guess I just felt that it needed saying, that's all. It sounded to me like people were thinking of giving in and giving up."

They mounted up and started for the farm. The evening air was chilly, and the breath of the men and their mounts turned into clouds of steam under the full moon. "I don't think Mister McAllister would let anyone even think of giving up the fight. He looks to me like a believer in the cause."

James nodded. "He is that and more. He's raising his boys to join the fight as well," James said. "His oldest is conducting now. It seems funny that some people use the word of their God to justify slavery and others use it to denounce it."

"Well, I just wish God would make up his mind is all. We all been waitin' a long time for him to make his mind up."

James was quiet for a moment. "I can't believe there is a God as long as one innocent child is living and dying in slavery. I just can't believe any of that."

The two men rode on in silence after that, each lost in their own thoughts. They were passing the shuttered shops along the main street, past Mister McDonald's mercantile, past the little café that was recently opened by a black woman from South Carolina who had moved to town that spring. They kept riding south out of town towards the farm a few miles distant.

They had gone about a mile or two further on, not saying much but watching the stars overhead, when two riders came out of the trees onto the road ahead of them. James was startled by their sudden appearance. "Luke. Riders ahead."

Luke had been looking up at the Drinking Gourd lost in thought, his rifle across his lap. When he saw the riders, he slowly brought the barrel around to a more effective direction. "I see 'em."

As they got closer, James put his hand inside his bulky coat drawn up against the chill night air. He rested his hand on the grip of his pistol, ready. The two riders made no sign they even noticed them until they were very close.

James nodded to the riders as they drew abreast of them in the dark. "Good evening, gentlemen," James said, touching the brim of his hat. He did not slow down or make eye contact.

"Hey, hold on there, fellas. What's your hurry?" one of the riders asked as James and Luke passed.

James answered without turning to face them. "Just goin' home, that's all. Just goin' home."

They were now less than ten feet apart. James kept looking straight ahead, Luke kept his rifle ready. "Hey, ain't you James Woodman?"

The question startled them both and they stopped in the road, turning to face the riders. "I am he. Who is asking?"

"Why, my name is Robbins and you are the dirty nigger that killed my brother," the nearer of the two said pulling his pistol from his belt and firing.

James was just a little faster and got off a shot. Luke's rifle spoke once, and the other rider was on the ground. Luke jumped down from his mount and went to the man he shot and shoved him with his foot. He approached the other rider who was still in his saddle with the pistol he had hidden in his coat drawn and ready. He looked up at James then back to the rider.

"Get down off that damn horse, mister." Luke was looking back and forth from him to James, who was silent and leaning forward in the saddle.

"Oh, God, James! James!" He turned back to the rider. "I told you to get down off of that damn horse, mister. Now move!"

The man slowly turned to face Luke, then his eyes rolled back and he slid off his mount and landed at Luke's feet. He looked up just in time to see James start to fall as well. Catching him, Luke lowered him gently to the ground. Even in the moonlight Luke could see the stain spreading across his friend's chest.

Luke didn't know what to do. He looked around in the darkness and tried to fix their location on the road to the farm. He looked across the field and saw a light coming from the Owen's farmhouse. Luke jumped back on his horse and rode as fast as he could towards that light.

Owen was standing on his porch with his rifle at the ready as Luke rode up. Owen recognized him immediately. "Luke boy. What's going on there? What was all that shooting?"

"Two men ambushed me and James on our way home from town. They knew who he was. James is bad hurt, Mister Owen. I need your wagon to get him home."

Owen laid his rifle against the wall. "Of course, of course. I'll help you get it out and hitched," he said as he headed for the barn. "Where are the two other men, the ones who ambushed you?"

"They're dead," Luke said flatly and started pushing the wagon out into the yard. "The hell with them," he added softly. "To hell with them all."

Jacob Owen wanted to race the wagon to the farm as fast as he could, but he had to keep his speed down to avoid jostling James any more than necessary. Luke was in the back with him, keeping pressure on the wound as he had been taught by James himself back when he taught him to shoot.

At last they reached the road to the farm and Owen eased the horses into the turn. All the while James had not uttered a single word or sound. Before the wagon stopped Luke was out and running towards the big house.

"Jonathan, Abigail, come quick. James has been shot." He burst in the front door as Jonathan was opening it. "Oh, please, come quick, Abigail. I don't know what else to do for him." Anna came out of her house at the commotion. She had just put Constance to bed.

Jonathan ran to the wagon. "Poppa, Poppa," he called out. When he got to the side of the wagon his heart stopped beating. His father, the strongest and bravest man he ever knew, was lying in the back of the wagon in a crumpled heap with bloody rags on his chest. Abigail was trying to get in the wagon but was too weak to make it on her own, so Luke had to help her up. Jonathan noticed the hard steely look of determination on his mother's face.

"Jonathan," she said calmly, "go get some water boiling on the stove. Bring me back some of the clean towels from the closet. Go on now, boy, go. Anna, can you help him please?" She turned to her wounded husband and fought back the temptation to scream as loud as humanly possible, to scream until the world and all time ended. Instead, she leaned over James and ripped his shirt down the front. The bloody mess frightened her. It looked very bad to her as she set about cleaning the wound.

Jonathan came running up with Francis and little Abigail. The girl looked inside the wagon and began to wail. "Hush now, girl, hush. Your Poppa doesn't need to hear that noise. Jonathan, hand me those towels and get up in here with me right now."

With her son by her side and a candle held by Francis, she began to feel some confidence after the shock of seeing the wound initially. The blood loss was slowing, and his breathing was weak but regular. When she cleaned right at the wound, James moaned and moved his head.

Abigail smiled down at him. "You go right ahead and complain, my love, just you go on ahead. You are not dead yet, James Woodman, do you hear me? You still have much too much to do."

Luke ran up with a large pot of steaming water. "Here's the first one, Abigail. We put another on already case you need it."

In a few minutes Abigail stood and wiped her hands down her dress. "Luke, Jonathan, we need to move him inside now. You boys grab his feet and shoulders but be gentle, be very gentle. Francis, go inside and straighten up your father's bed for me son."

He seemed as light as a feather to Jonathan. They got him to his bed and laid him down. Once more he groaned with the movement and Abigail's heart soared at the sound.

"Jonathan, ride into town and get Doctor Findlay and bring him here quick as you can even if you have to carry him across your shoulder. Go on, son, quick as you can now."

Jonathan turned towards the door but stopped and looked back at his father lying in bed, silent. He went over to him and kissed him lightly on the forehead. He was terrified at the thought he may die before he got back. Then he bolted out the door and rode off into the night like the devil was after him.

Abigail sat down next to James on the bed they shared. "Luke, would you bring me some more towels and hot water, please," she said with impossible calm. "Francis, get another bucket of water from the well, please son."

Francis seemed not to have heard her speak. He was across the room and staring at the sight of his father possibly bleeding to death. Little Abbie was clinging to his leg.

"Francis, honey, I need you to snap out of it and help me. Do you hear me son? Good. Now go get some more water from the well and more clean towels, please, and bring them to me."

Francis did snap out of it quickly. "Yes ma'am, Momma. Come help me Abbie." He took his little sister's hand and left quietly.

Luke was standing close by, just watching. He had never realized how much he truly loved this man who had given him his life back. His mind was racing with possibilities, but Abigail's remarkable calmness helped ease his mind some.

She sat on the edge of the bed, gently cleaning his chest and humming softly. She really wasn't aware of Luke's presence as she worked and was startled when he spoke.

"Is there anything else I can do, Abigail? It's hard to just stand here and watch like this."

She turned to him and saw him in his pain. He was also very disheveled from the night. "Oh, Lord Luke. Are you hurt? There's blood on your shirt." She came to him and started to feel his shoulder. "Were you hit too?"

"It all happened so fast, Abigail, so damn fast. One minute we were ridin' home, just lookin' up at the stars. Next minute, two men are lying dead in the road and James is hurt bad." He shook his head. "I don't even remember the other man getting a shot off. It was just so fast."

She led him to a chair at the table and went to get some water and towels. "Sit down here, Luke, and let me have a look at you. Unbutton your shirt so I won't have to tear it." Anna followed, too frightened to speak.

Sure enough, there was a nasty running gash on his left shoulder. There was a sharp gasp from Anna. "Looks like you were hit after all, Luke. It's a nasty flesh wound. Another inch to the right and you would not be so lucky. Might have destroyed your shoulder."

Luke looked over at James in his bed as Abigail tended to his wound. "I don't feel too lucky right now to be honest, Abigail."

Abigail followed his gaze towards her husband. "Don't you worry none about James. I refuse to let him die." She finished wrapping a clean bandage around Luke's arm and walked back over to the bed. "You hear me, James Woodman? I do not give you my permission to die just yet."

She sat down and started to clean the blood that was still oozing out of his chest. "You better go get a clean shirt, Luke. I'm sure Anna can fix that one."

Anna helped her husband to stand as Luke was starting to feel dizzy. "Come on, Luke. Let's get you home and you can lie down and rest. We can take care of James 'til the doctor comes, but we need to take care of you too. Come on now, my love, let's go home."

After they left, Abigail took a moment for herself, letting all the fear she felt in her heart voice itself to her. As the tears started down her cheek, she started to sing "Swing Low, Sweet Chariot" very softly as she worked on James. As a former slave, she knew the code behind the song. It was that the singers were pleading for abolitionists to "swing low" or come to the southern slave states, and "carry them home" to freedom. It was the song everyone working The Road knew by heart, black or white. Her pride in her husband and her son was boundless for helping to carry people home.

The first rays of dawn found Abigail still sitting by the bedside, with Anna sitting quietly nearby. Luke had been put to bed and was resting as comfortably as could be expected. Anna stood and came over to the bed.

"Why don't you rest a minute, Abigail? I can look after James for a while. You need to rest now, big sister."

Abigail nodded slowly and stood. She was clearly spent. "I will not allow him to die, Anna, I will not." She shuffled slowly over to Jonathan's bed and fell into it sound asleep.

Jonathan returned with the doctor about an hour later. Anna met them out on the porch, motioning them to be as quiet as they could. "How is my father, Miss Anna? Is he still…."

Anna smiled and put her hand on his arm. "Yes, Jonathan, your father is still alive. Your mother refuses to allow him to die, so he wouldn't dare."

Jonathan smiled a little at that. He knew his Momma well and was certain that she would go argue with God himself to get her husband back. He nodded, relieved. "This way, doctor. He's in here."

"Jonathan, your Momma is sleeping. She was completely exhausted and needed some rest. I have been looking after your Poppa for her. Please try not to disturb her if you can." She turned to Doctor Findlay, who had looked after her when she was pregnant with her baby. "Good morning, doctor. Thank you very much for coming."

The two men entered the house quietly, and Anna went to her

kitchen to start making breakfast for everyone. No matter the circumstances, folks had to eat.

Doctor Findlay went to the bed and leaned over his first patient, inspecting the wound. He sat down on the bed and pulled back some of the towels that blocked his view as Jonathan watched anxiously nearby.

The doctor was making approving noises as he went. "Uh hmm. Okay. Uh hmm. Not bad, not too bad at all. Who cleaned the wound?"

"My Momma was working on him when I left to get you, so I assume it was mostly her and Anna."

"Well, they did an excellent job of it. Really excellent." He fished around in his bag for a flask of liquid. "Ah, here it is. Jonathan, do you have any clean towels left? Yes? Bring one, please."

He tipped the flask and wetted a part of the towel, then started dabbing at the wound itself which caused James to moan loudly and move his head back and forth. "Thought that might happen. Hoped it would, actually. Jonathan, I need you to help me."

The sound of James' moaning awakened Abigail who came over to the bed. "What do you see, doctor? How bad is it?"

"Well, Abigail, it could have been much worse. The ball missed anything truly vital in his chest, but it has torn some muscles and may have broken his clavicle. Did you clean him up yourself?"

"No sir," she said sheepishly. "I had some help."

"Well, you did an excellent job, my dear, excellent. You probably saved his life. We have a ways to go yet. The ball is still in there and must come out right away. I will need you two to hold him down as this is going to hurt like hell, and even in his present condition he will thrash around some. You'll need all your strength, both of you."

"Don't worry, doctor, if you need him still then he'll be still. Jonathan, take your father's shoulders and I'll hold his legs down."

The doctor rooted around in his bag again and brought out a set of instruments in a little wooden case. "Just let me clean these up some and we'll get started. Is there some hot water?"

Jonathan brought him a small pot full of the hot water from the stove. The doctor took it and stood at the little table cleaning his tools, talking softly to himself. Finished, he came back to the bedside.

"Are you both ready? All right then, take a hold now and we'll begin." He began to probe for the ball and found it almost immediately. The intense pain caused James to struggle against their grip. He dropped his first instrument in the pot of hot water and took a second larger one out.

"This will be the worst part now, so hold on tight." He inserted the instrument into the wound and felt around. "Ah, there it is. Hold him now, hold him."

James was struggling with all the strength he had left, but they did not let him move. "That's it. That's it. Wait. Wait. There it is," he announced at last as he held the ball aloft for them to see. Then he dropped it in the pot of water. "Well, that ball shouldn't cause him any more problems."

James stopped struggling and they relaxed their grip on him. They all three stood by the bed, looking down on James who finally seemed at peace. "He's got a little bit of a road to go yet before we can be sure if…"

"I'm quite sure he won't be dying anytime soon, Doctor Findlay," Abigail said firmly. "I simply will not allow that to happen. No sir. It is simply out of the question."

"Well, then, I will leave him in your good care." He gave her two small bottles of ointments. "Use these as needed and keep the area around the wound moist and cleaned. After I finish bandaging him up I'll be on my way."

"Not just yet, doctor. Would you please look at Luke over in the other house? He has a nasty gash on his arm, but the ball did not penetrate. After that, I'm sure Anna will be very happy to serve you breakfast."

Doctor Findlay picked up his bag and the flask of liquid and started for the door. When he opened it, the smell of cooking bacon reached him from Anna's kitchen. He inhaled deeply.

"Mmm mmm. That would be most delightful." He tipped his hat and went out.

The ball had indeed torn a gash in Luke's arm as it passed, but otherwise did him no harm. Doctor Findlay cleaned it up using some of the same liquid from the big flask he had used on James. Luke had to fight hard not to cry out when the wet towel was applied. Tears welled up in his eyes as the doctor finished treating him, then he lay back in the bed.

Doctor Findlay stood and surveyed the scene. "Well, it looks like these two will be down for a while. Luke will be fine with a little rest." He looked at Anna sternly. "He is not to use that arm for several weeks, is that clear? The muscle was torn and needs to heal properly and trying to use it will only cause it to take longer to get better."

"Don't you worry none, Doctor, I'll keep both eyes on my Luke. I will tie his arm to his body if I have to. I certainly will."

The doctor chuckled at that. "Must be something in the water out here on your farm. I have never met two more determined women in my life, truly. I'm sure that neither of these patients would have the nerve to get worse."

"We'll take good care of our men," Anna said as the doctor gathered up his things. "They still both have too much to do in this life."

When he had all his things together, the doctor cleared his throat. "Miss Abigail mentioned that there might be a chance for a little breakfast before I ride back to town…"

Anna laughed, a sound that worked like magic on Luke, who struggled to sit up. Anna rushed over and held him back, fluffing up pillows behind his back so he could see everyone. "Certainly Doctor, I wouldn't dream of sending you away hungry. I'll go ask Jonathan to join us if you don't mind."

Anna took some food over to the other house and set it on the table. Abigail was in a chair by James' bed. "I brought over something for you and the little ones. If you don't need Jonathan I'll feed him his at our house."

Anna went to the barn to find Jonathan and found him tending to his horse. "Jonathan, if you're not busy, please come and have some breakfast with me and the doctor."

"Thank you, Miss Anna. I'm not feeling hungry at the moment," he said, brushing his horse. "Maybe later."

Anna stepped inside so she would not be overheard. "Please come now, Jonathan. There is still an important matter to discuss and I think we will both want to hear what the doctor has to say."

"What matter? What else is there but that my father may die…."

Again Anna took another step towards him. "Jonathan, there are two white men lying dead in the road back there. There will have to be some kind of accounting for that. Some folks are going to be upset about it and will want answers."

As Jonathan started to protest, she cut him off. "Now's not the time to talk about the rightness or wrongness of this thing. This is the time to take a deep breath and prepare for what will come next is all. I'm not sure but with the changing feelings towards runaways and abolitionists we can all see in our valley, I'm not sure that right and wrong still matters much anymore."

When the sheriff rode up, Abigail and Jonathan were surprised to see he had some extra company with him. The sheriff had sent word to the farm that he would be out to take statements from everyone involved in the fatal shooting of the two white men, but they had not expected him to come with so many others.

Doctor Findlay was there as expected, and Jacob Owen was also there to give his testimony. The others did not seem to belong at such a gathering. There was Caleb Buhler, a well-known supporter of fugitive slave laws, and another man they didn't know well but did know him to be a recent arrival compared to most in the valley. He had bought up a few struggling farms and was very active in trade to the south with Maryland and Virginia.

Abigail and Jonathan were in the yard to meet them, the others on the porch watching nervously. The farm had been a very quiet oasis in their lives. It had never witnessed such a scene with so many riders arriving.

The sheriff stopped and tipped his hat. "Miss Abigail, good afternoon." Turning to the others he said, "Good afternoon, Miss Anna, Abigail, gentlemen."

There were a few murmurs from those on the porch who were still watching warily. Luke, with his arm in a sling, was especially nervous. He knew in his heart that nothing good could come of so many white people taking an interest in them or their farm.

After an uncomfortable silence, the sheriff spoke again. "This sun sure does feel good on an old man's skin, Miss Abigail, but I wonder if there might be someplace indoors where we can do this."

Abigail was unmoved by the courtesy being shown. "Where we can do what, sheriff? What is it that you want to do here today? Is it just to get to the bottom of this matter?"

The sheriff sighed. "Miss Abigail, I am sure that you can understand why the community has some questions about the events that led to the death of two men not far from here. I think you would agree that they have a right to the facts of the matter."

"That's enough of that, sheriff," Caleb Buhler said. "I think we should just lock these damn niggers up until we can get some reliable witnesses and get to the bottom of this."

The sheriff sighed again, loudly. He also noticed that both Luke and Jonathan were suddenly standing much closer to their firearms than they had been just a second ago. "Caleb, I'll remind you for the very last time that you are here at my invitation and I am here at the gracious invitation of Miss Abigail. You are here to observe, not to talk."

"Miss Abigail, I sincerely apologize for Mister Buhler's behavior. May we dismount now and set about the job of getting your statements?"

"Don't you apologize to no nigger for my 'behavior' you damn fool," Buhler muttered. "I owe her nothing."

The sheriff seemed to be getting older by the minute. As he began to dismount the others followed suit. "Don't be in a hurry to get down, Caleb. I would not ask a lady like Miss Abigail to sully her house any by allowing you inside. So, you just wait out here or go on back to town. It's your choice."

While Jonathan and Luke glared at Buhler as he regained his saddle, edging closer to their weapons, Abigail spoke to the sheriff. "Where are my manners? Of course we can go in and talk. May I get you or the other gentlemen something cool to drink?"

As she led them into her home she continued. "My husband James, who is the victim here let's not forget, is still bedridden. He is able to sit up and speak some, but I will not allow you, any of you, to upset him or rile him in any way."

Doctor Findlay broke away from the others to examine his patient up close for the first time in the week that had passed since the shooting. As he sat gently on the side of the bed, James opened his eyes and tried to smile.

"I am very happy to see you today, James. Very happy indeed."

"Well, doctor, I am just happy to be able to see anybody today and that's a fact," James replied with a small, painful laugh.

"Well, my friend, you have your own good wife to thank for that. I just came along after the main show was over."

James looked over at Abigail who was still holding court over her visitors and making them welcome. The light from the early afternoon sun was streaming in the window behind her, giving her a soft halo of light about her head and shoulders. She had never looked more beautiful to him.

After Abigail had seen to the needs of her guests, the sheriff started the proceedings. "Miss Abigail, I would like to thank you for your hospitality today as we look into the matter of the killings that took place near here around one week ago."

He looked around at the group. "Now, who here has firsthand knowledge of what occurred that night? Who here was actually at the scene when this all happened?"

"That would be me, sheriff, me and Luke," James said weakly

from his bed. "We were the only people there except for the slavers."

The sheriff stood and came over to the bed. "Are you saying that these men were hunting runaways, James?"

"No sir. I'm saying that those men were out hunting people. They were also apparently hunting me as well."

"Why do you say that James?"

Luke came in the door just then and heard the question. "They called him by his name, sheriff. They asked him if he was James Woodman, just like that."

"Well, Luke, why don't you tell us what happened so we can all be clear," the sheriff said, taking his seat again.

"Yes sir, I can do that all right. I ain't never goin' to be able to forget it anyhow. James and me were coming back from a meeting in town…"

"What kind of meeting was that?" The man known to them only as the rich new arrival said. "Was it another one of those damned abolitionist meetings?"

"Mister Cummings, need I remind you, sir, that we are all here at this lady's invitation to conduct a proper investigation. If you insist on interrupting again, I'm going to have to ask you to go keep Buhler company outside." He looked around the room. "Am I clear on this subject?" He nodded to Luke. "Go ahead, son."

"Well, like I was sayin', James and me were heading home after a meeting in the town. It was a clear night with stars all over the sky." Luke hesitated at the memory.

"Go on, Luke. What happened next?"

"We were just sorta slow walking, just talkin' some and lookin' at the stars. It was such a beautiful, clear night, you know?' He hesitated again before he went on. "All of a sudden like, there was two riders in the road ahead of us."

"What were they doing in the road, Luke? Were they riding somewhere, coming from somewhere?"

"No sir, they were just sittin' there in the shadows. Like they was waitin' for us or something."

"Go on."

"They must a just ridden out from the trees. They are mighty thick along there. Anyhow, when we saw them there, we were surprised at first. We always travel with our weapons after what happened with those other slavers, so we were ready for the worst."

"Did they threaten you directly, Luke? What exactly did they say to you?"

"Well sir, the first one, the closest one, he says to James, 'Are you James Woodman?' and James asks who wants to know or something like that."

Cummings stirred in his seat and muttered under his breath. The sheriff shot him a dirty look, then said, "Who fired first, Luke?"

"I did," said James weakly from his bed. "I was a little faster than he was."

"That's what I thought," thundered Cummings, jumping up from his seat. "They murdered those two white boys for no reason."

This brought a swift reaction from Abigail, who stood toe to toe with the much taller man. "How dare you enter my home and call my husband a murderer? Who do you think you are, Mister Cummings? My husband, like all men everywhere, has the right to defend himself. Even against slavers, even against them."

"Sit down, Cummings, or leave the room," the sheriff said slowly, glaring at him. "Which is it going to be?"

As Cummings took his seat, he went on. "Why did you shoot first, James? Was there a threat against you?"

"Yes sir. After I asked him who wanted to know who I was, he said something like 'you're the nigger that killed my brother' and started to raise his pistol. I had my hand on my pistol inside my coat, so I just pulled the trigger when his intention was made clear."

The sheriff nodded, visualizing the scene. "Did you hear him say that Luke? About James having killed this man's brother?"

"Yes sir, I surely did."

"And what did you do then?"

"I shot the other man when he raised his rifle. Next, I jumped down and pulled my pistol and told that man who fired at James to get off his horse. He just sorta looked at me funny like, then slid off his horse and landed in the road."

"And the man you fired at?"

"He was already dead layin' in the road. When the other man started to fall off his horse, that's when I noticed that James was hurt. I caught him and helped him down."

"Is this where you came in, Jacob?"

"Yes sir, sheriff. I heard the shooting and not long after Luke here came running up asking for help. We hitched a team and got James home as fast as we could. He was hurt bad."

"Doctor, do you have anything to add? When did you arrive?"

Doctor Findlay thought for a moment. "Jonathan came riding up to my place while it was still dark as I recall. We got back here just at sunup and I took to treating both of the men."

The sheriff took his seat again and wrote a few notes in a ledger. He closed the book, set it on the table in front of him and crossed his hands over it.

"It seems pretty clear to me from the evidence heard here and the knowledge that I have of these two men, that there is no reason to doubt their account of that night. They were ambushed by two men who laid in wait for them to arrive. When attacked, they defended themselves as the law allows any man to do."

He looked around the table from face to face. Only Cummings was shaking his head. "Therefore, I find that these killings were justified and will consider this matter closed."

Cummings shoved his chair back and stood up. "The hell with this. The hell with you all. We just can't let these damn niggers go around shooting white folks at will. Someone has to pay for those two boys."

Abigail went rigid and walked to the door, holding it open. "You will leave my home, sir. I do not allow language like that in my home or around my family. Good day to you."

Cummings looked at the other men at the table. "So that's your answer then, is it? You are just going to allow these.... these people, to just shoot anyone they want? Well, I am not sitting by and let this happen. No sir!"

As he stormed through the door, Cummings almost collided with Jonathan who stood there impassively watching him. When he refused to move out of his way, Cummings started to raise his voice again.

"What do you think you're doing there, boy? Move out of my way right now."

Jonathan just watched him, his eyes half closed. "Looks to me like there's plenty of room for you to pass on either side. Sir."

Cummings brushed by him and went to his horse. He mounted and looked around at the tidy farm yard. "Why don't you people just go back to where you came from?"

Jonathan stepped to the edge of the porch. "How do you mean? Sir."

"None of your type belongs here, that's what I mean. Just go on back to where you came from and leave the rest of us alone."

"Well, Mister Cummings," Jonathan said with a small bow, "Sir. This is how I see it. This land you're on belonged to my granddaddy. You see, he fought for this country in the Revolution. He was born in this country a free man. His father was born in this country a free man."

Jonathan had to pause to let the anger die down before he went on. He took a deep breath while his younger brother and sister and Luke watched him closely. "Do you even know who your granddaddy was? Do you? Do you know where he was born? I will bet your granddaddy fought against mine, didn't he? He was a damn British soldier, wasn't he?"

"I think that I am back where I came from…. sir. I suggest that it is perhaps you that should think about going back to where you belong."

"Are you threatening me, young man?"

"Not at all, Mister Cummings, not at all. But you really should be on your way now, don't you think…..sir."

Abigail passed away gently one night as winter was approaching. She had spent all her strength, all that was left in her, nursing her husband and in fact her whole family back to health. She died with all that was precious to her in the world gathered around, a sweet smile on her lips. When James leaned down to hear her final words, she whispered "Thank you, Mister James" as his tears fell on her blanket.

His recovery had been slow but steady, with Abigail watching him closely, keeping him from trying too hard to get his strength back and hurting himself. She had always been his rock, his anchor, and the weeks after her death left him bereft and unable to think clearly. He considered selling Luke his share of the farm and moving back to Georgetown or going to live in his father's hometown back east.

Luke and Jonathan just let him talk. They knew him well enough to know that nothing would ever get him off this land, especially now that both his parents and his wife, the mother of his children, were there to stay. All that summer and fall, with Abigail in close attendance, the men had worked the farm as usual and the results of their hard work were obvious to anyone.

They had grown even closer as a family that year. They had helped dozens find their way north to freedom and had fought the slavers themselves up close when attacked. With all that, they also kept the farm prosperous and growing, sharing in the beauty and the bounty of their world.

But as the days had grown shorter, so too did Abigail's steps and stamina. She knew she had traded a part of her life span for her family's sake, and she was very happy with that trade. She could never imagine any higher calling than caring for the people she loved so dearly.

So, in late November when she took to her bed it was not a total surprise to the family. It was now their turn to care for her, and they did so with the love and tenderness she had always shown each of them. When the time came for her to leave, she motioned for James to put his ear near her lips, whispered something softly and closed her eyes, smiling at something only she could see.

When the spring finally rolled around, Luke took stock of the farm and its prospects for the growing season. The winter had been long and harsh, but the plentiful snowfall insured there would be plenty of groundwater for this year's crops. The days were growing longer and warmer, and the farmer in him was itching to go, to make the land productive again.

Luke was far more concerned about his partner and friend. James had taken the loss of Abigail very hard, as they all had. She had kept them together as a family after the brutal events of the past year, tending to all their wounds including the ones only she could see, the ones in their souls.

It was now time to get back to work, the very hard work of running a farm. Luke hoped that the job at hand might bring James back from the place he had retreated to. His children needed him, the farm needed him and hell, he needed him too.

By midsummer, Luke was cautiously optimistic that James was coming back. He and Jonathan went back to their conducting roles on The Road, and Luke could see that James was different after every group of passengers went through their station. He was at times energized by the courage and bravery of the refugees. Other times he came back clearly depressed at what he saw as a never ending stream of people who had committed no crime yet were having to flee imprisonment and worse.

The farm, on the other hand, proved to be a tonic. Luke could clearly see the fire come back in James' eyes when they worked together. He was more relaxed and talked more, but it was also clear that James was slowing down as well, that his boundless energy and enthusiasm had at last found their borders.

At his father's urging, Jonathan was taking on more and more responsibility on the farm. Luke had of course known him all his life, so there was no discernable change in their plans for their future. They both saw the farm as the center of their universe, a place where Jonathan would soon be building a house and starting a family of his own.

At the church meetings in late July, stories of people having to sell their farms began to circulate among the parishioners. It began as folks reporting that offers had been made on their property, and gradually became stories of darker tactics being used to gain title to the land.

By late August it was clear to the community what was happening. A number of the more successful farms were doing very well trading with the nearby slave states of Virginia and Maryland, and they did not want any abolitionist talk to ruin that business. The slave states had been threatening the economy of the northern states all along if they didn't pass, and strictly enforce, ever stronger fugitive slave laws.

Now, a group of white farmers and businessmen were actively trying to reduce black land ownership and participation in the economy. Any land they could acquire, legally or otherwise, would go into production to increase the trade with the slave states. If they could also get a black family to move out of the valley, then so much the better.

This effort became the main topic of conversation at the next meeting of the Anti-Slavery Society at McAllister's Mill in September. When McAllister asked for a show of hands of those who had been approached to sell, around a third of those present raised their hands, both black and white.

James had raised his hand as well. He had been approached by Cummings and another man he didn't know one afternoon in town. The conversation had been pleasant enough, James reported to the meeting, but he had made it clear that he would never sell any portion of the farm to them or anyone else.

"And have you had any problems on your place since then, James?" asked another farmer. "We been hearing that some may turn to sabotage, like poisoning wells and the like."

"No, sir, we haven't seen anything like that at our place, have we Luke? You can be sure we will be watching the place more closely, but like I said it was mostly a polite conversation. Short, but polite."

"Well, my cousin down to Fairfield says one of his neighbors barns burned down one night. Wasn't no reason for it, but all the same it still happened."

This started a lot of conversation in the packed room. People started to recall other seemingly innocent conversations and incidents in a different, more sinister light. It had been clear for a while that the pressure from southern states to stop runaway slaves from escaping their bondage and fleeing north would continue. The threat of withholding business from the farms and factories in the north had been enough to lead some to actively campaign against what had been a rising tide of sympathy and compassion for those fleeing to freedom.

It was becoming apparent that this effort in their valley was being led by both Cummings and Caleb Buhler, both well known for their virulent anti-abolitionist stance. It was also obvious to everyone that these efforts were more than economic. They were known to be hostile to any rights at all for any black person, including the right to vote or own property.

"How long ago did that …." James started to ask about the barn burning when they were all distracted by some commotion outside. McAllister went to the door to see what was happening when a volley of stones crashed through the windows, sending broken glass scattering through the room. When McAllister opened the door, there was a dead and mutilated cat on the landing outside. He also caught sight of two men riding away at a gallop.

Some of the others gathered around him at the door. "Who were they?" someone asked.

"Did anyone get a look at them? Anybody see anything?" James asked hopelessly. The only person who had seen anything was McAllister himself, and he replied.

"I just got a look at their backs. They looked like a couple of white men, maybe thirty or so. Hard to tell. Couldn't see their faces. One had a dirty grey hat."

He then looked down at the unfortunate cat that had been left as a warning. "It's my little girl Martha's pet. She never harmed anyone," he said, his voice filling with anger. "Why did they have to do that?"

The black men in the room knew the answer to that question. Hate is a powerful motivator, they understood. Hate will twist any man's heart until he wants to crush and destroy those he hates. That hate manifested itself virtually every day in their lives in one way or the other, from being kept away from the ballot box to everyday slights and insults that white folks never had to deal with.

James knelt down by the destroyed animal and covered it. "I'll take care of her for you, Mister McCallister."

It was like a cold bucket of ice water had been thrown on them. No one spoke as they filed back into the mill and took their seats once more. McAllister came to the front of the group.

"Well, brothers, we have just seen another example of the changing attitudes in our little valley, not that we really needed it. It has been building slowly, maybe many never even saw it coming, I don't know. But it's here now, and you just saw the ugly side of it."

He stopped and looked around the room at the faces of men he had known for years now, good hard working men who meant no harm to anyone. Men who just wanted to raise a family and live in peace. "I think it would be wise for everyone leaving here today to ride together as far as you can."

The harvest that fall was again plentiful, as was the fresh crop of freedom seekers heading north with the help of James and Jonathan. James was still alternating between admiration for the courage of those seeking their freedom and frustration at the steady stream of refugees that seemed to have no end.

The dangers the enterprise faced were also steadily increasing. When The Road had started, there weren't a lot of people out hunting the escapees. When the trickle turned to a flood, however, when the slave owners saw so much of their valuable "property" fleeing into the night, the business of slave hunting became busy as well as lucrative. It also attracted the lowest form of humanity to it.

Encounters with the slavers were becoming more and more frequent and almost always ended in violence. Local people who had no affiliation with The Road also became incensed at some of the extreme actions of the slave hunters, sometimes attacking them and freeing their captives.

Jonathan had been very fortunate to not have any actual encounters with the 'christian wolves' when he conducted his charges, although he did have to occasionally make a detour or a delay to avoid any contact. His portion was almost all woods and fields and away from any villages, but no place was completely safe.

James on the other hand was regularly challenged with avoiding the slavers. His name was known now, that much was obvious, and he felt sure that now he was being hunted as well. There had already been some high profile abductions of conductors who were taken south and sold into slavery.

The pressure to sell smaller farms was also increasing. One or two of the older black families, families who had been in the valley for a decade or more, were bought out and moved away. Most who left went to the cities, either Pittsburgh or Philadelphia, where they felt more accepted.

James had again been approached to sell, this time by a man he did not know. The man claimed to speak for Cummings and a 'group' of prominent farmers.

He related the encounter to the others at dinner that night. "He made what could be considered a fair offer for the place," James said to no one in particular.

"Don't much care to sell," Luke said. He looked around at the others. "This isn't just a farm to me. This is my home, the only home I have ever known. No sir," he added quietly. "A man doesn't just up and sell his home."

Jonathan laughed. "Why don't they give up on us? They have to know how we feel about this place."

"Well, I think our little place here is right in the middle of what they want to take over. Seems we may be in the way."

Francis had been listening in. At just twenty years of age, he didn't feel confident enough to voice his opinion often around the adults. "They would have to kill me to get me off," he said firmly. "I'm with Luke. My mother is buried here. I am not going anywhere."

Little Abigail put her hand on her brother's arm. "That goes for me as well," she said softly. "I am home."

"Why are you telling us this for, James? You know you are not ever gonna sell this place. Not ever," Anna said.

James leaned back in his chair and looked at his family and friends. "No, I'm not ever going to sell. I just wanted everyone here, everyone who has a stake in this land, to know what's going on." He got serious, leaning forward on the table. "I also want everyone to know that this is not the valley that my father settled in. It's getting harder and harder for black folks here. The resentment is building because of the pressure from the slave states."

"We all know that Poppa, but this is Woodman land and it's going to stay Woodman land. Now, is that apple pie I smell from the oven there?" Jonathan asked, arching his eyebrows.

"Poppa, wake up. It's time to go," Jonathan said, softly shaking his father's shoulder.

James rolled over at his touch and saw his face in the candlelight. Jonathan had a man's work to do tonight, but James was struck by how much he looked like just a boy sometimes.

"All right, son, I'm awake. Did you check the time?"

"Yes sir, and I have my passengers up and ready to go. Just wanted to wake you before we set out for the church."

This was a rare back to back night for James. Normally he would bring a group of passengers to the farm and Jonathan would take them on the next night. Tonight Jonathan was taking the group he had brought in last night onward while James went back for more.

James watched his son lead his charges out through the field north of the house and went back inside. After a quick bite to eat, he picked up his rifle, slid his pistol into his belt and slipped out the door quietly.

He felt if he left a little early, he could be in a better position for the arrival of the pastor and the passengers at the clearing, and he checked the night sky one more time. There was no moon up yet, and a layer of broken clouds moved by high overhead. It was a beautiful Indian Summer night, but the darkness did slow him down a bit.

As he started up the last hill before the clearing on the east facing side, he had a premonition of sorts. With the increased activity of the slavers in the last year, he had found it wise to change his routine in small ways from time to time. He had started to do that after the dead slaver had called him by name during the ambush that night.

He stopped and thought for a moment, then took a side path that led off to the north. He knew these woods well enough to know that it would bring him into the clearing from the northwest, the side opposite of where he would normally approach from.

When he was about thirty yards away from the large boulder he usually sat on to await his charges, he heard a sound that did not belong in the woods at night. He froze instantly and lowered himself to the ground behind a fallen tree.

He cautiously raised his eyes above the tree, but there wasn't anything to see except the dark night. He couldn't even be sure of what he had heard, but he knew it was not right. He listened intensely, straining to hear any sounds at all.

After what seemed an eternity, James heard the soft call of an owl and knew the pastor was approaching from the southwest, his usual direction. Then, James heard the unnatural sound again, and this time he could tell where it was coming from. There was a horse on the east side of the clearing, and if there was a horse then there was a rider.

James had to warn the pastor, but how? He started to move off to his right, to try and intercept him before the clearing. He didn't have much hope that he would get there in time, but he had to try. A quarter moon had risen during the night, and as a break in the clouds went by, James could see a figure hiding behind a large stone just outside the clearing.

He picked up a small pebble and threw it at the back of the figure. The pastor felt the stone and turned to see where it had come from. When he saw James his heart started beating again.

"When you didn't answer the owl, I just knew somethin' was wrong, James. What's the matter? What's goin' on?"

James explained his early arrival and the circumstances that led to him using a different path than usual. "I heard a sound in the woods there," James whispered. "After your call, I heard it again. There is at least one rider in those woods the other side of the clearing. At least one."

"What do you propose, brother James?"

"Are you armed, Parson?"

The moon appeared again for a brief moment. "I'm a man of God, son, not a fool," he whispered as he brandished a pistol. "I ain't afraid to use it."

"Where are your passengers?"

"They be down the path a couple hundred yards. They won't move none until I get back." The pastor looked around at the forest. "What are we gonna do, brother James?"

James wanted to know how many riders were in the woods with them but moving around to scout them out was just too dangerous. He looked back down the path to where the refugees were concealed. What are we going to do, he thought to himself. It was still at least two hours until dawn. They would just have to sit tight and see what happened next.

They did not have very long to wait. A rider came into the clearing from the south, yelling as loud as he could. "I got 'em, boys I got 'em."

Two more riders came into the clearing. "What the hell are you yellin' about, Frank? You want to scare off anybody hidin' in these woods?"

"They ain't no one else around. I'm telling you we got 'em. We got four runaways down the path. Johnny's down there watchin' em right now."

"Oh, Lord," the pastor said, his eyes wide with fear. "They got my passengers down there."

There was no time to plan. "Let's go," James whispered and took off down the path where the pastor had indicated the refugees to be hiding. He disappeared into the darkness, the pastor hot on his heels.

As they approached the area, another break in the clouds revealed a rider mounted on a large grey horse pointing a rifle down towards the hillside. They could hear him talking but couldn't make out everything that was being said.

"There's a small cave there in that hillside. I told them to wait until I got back. Wait in there. He's got them cornered now."

It was only another minute before the other three riders rode down from the clearing. "Whatcha got there, Johnny? Smells like a nest of polecats."

"Nah, just four dumb niggers thought they could get away from us is all. Don't see anyone else with 'em."

The oldest of the group stood up in his stirrups and looked around the area. "They have to be around here somewhere. These runaways didn't get here by their own selves."

"That's for darn sure, Jeff. Just look at 'em. They're scared of their own shadows," one of the other riders said. "You want us to go out looking for the guides?"

Jeff sat back down in his saddle. "Nah. I think we'll let them come to us. Should be light in another hour or two. I think they may turn up then." He climbed down off his horse and tied the animal to a branch. "Might as well get comfortable and wait."

"You people come on out here now. Let's see what we have caught up here," the man with the rifle said. "C'mon now. I won't bite ya."

Four terrified black figures emerged from their hiding place and huddled together before the white men with guns. The group was made up of three young men and a young woman, all clearly afraid for their lives.

"Well, lookee here. Looks like we caught us a pretty young girl. How about that, boys?" the man with the rifle said. "C'mon over here and let's get a look at you, sweetheart."

The girl nervously took two steps away from the men, looking back and forth and down at the ground, not meeting the eyes of the leering white men.

"Now that, gentlemen, is some fine Virginia blackstrap, that's what that there is. What's your name, girl?"

James leaned down to the pastor. "I'm going to take out the man with the rifle and the one over there," he said softly, indicating with a nod of his head which of the men he meant. "I'll need you to keep an eye on the other two."

The pastor nodded. "I can do that. Don't you worry none."

"There's going to be killing."

"I know."

The older man, Jeff, looked the girl over. "She's a pretty one, all right, but I'd rather have that bastard Woodman here right about now."

Without any warning at all, James strode into the area by the cave and shot the man holding the rifle in the head. The nearest man started to turn in shock at the sudden sound when James caught him across the chin with the butt of his rifle. He hit the ground with a resounding thud.

James pulled his pistol from his belt and pointed it at the man Jeff, who already had his weapon out but not at the ready. "Why don't you just put that thing down, mister?" James said. "Just put it down and relax."

There were two men on the ground and two men standing. "Who the hell are you?" Jeff asked. "We're here on lawful business."

"That's funny, I thought you were waiting for me. That is what you said a few moments ago, anyway."

"You're Woodman," Jeff said flatly, not asking.

James nodded. "That's right. Now then, what did you want to talk to me about so badly that you came up into these dark mountains to find me?"

The four runaways were now pressed into the side of the hill, trying to figure out what exactly what was going to happen next. Like all the fugitives before them, they had no experience with a black man getting the better of a white man.

"These contrabands belong to a prominent planter down in Virginia, and he has authorized us to find them and return his property to him. There ain't nothing you can do about it. It's the law and you know it."

The sky was just starting to show the first hint of dawn in the east. James looked around at the scene. "I don't see any contraband around here. All I see is people."

Jeff and the other man were slowly putting a little distance between them as he talked. "Ain't for me to say, Woodman, nor you either for that matter. The law is the law, and the law says these here folks belong to a man in Virginia."

The other man suddenly made a move towards the saddlebags on his horse as Jeff moved to his left. James shot the other man as he came up with a pistol from his saddlebag and he fell dead next to his horse.

Jeff flung himself at James with an angry growl. "You goddam nigger," he snarled. Before James could get set Jeff was on him and knocked him to the ground. He kicked James once and sat on his back, choking him from behind. "What are you going to do now, nigger? I'm going to kill you with my bare hands."

"Not today you're not," the pastor said as he stepped from cover. He pointed the pistol square in the man's face. "Not today you're not," he said again and fired.

The mood at the church meeting the following week was electric. The word had spread about the three dead white men, and another one badly injured with a broken jaw and concussion, found up on the mountain trail to Maryland.

"Seems like white boys like to go up that mountain and die to me," chuckled Ables. "Didn't we hear something like this a while back? Somethin' about two white boys found half naked wanderin' the woods."

"Well, last year the rumor was that a large gang of black men was roaming the mountains and attacking white folks. Wonder what the rumor will be this time round," said Sherfy.

Everywhere it was the same, small groups of people speaking in a very animated way about this latest killing of slavers. There was no official word about the men of course, but these folks knew they must have been slave hunting to be in those particular mountains at night.

"I hope that God can forgive 'em, because I sure can't," said Luke. "No sir, I be glad they're dead and that's a fact." He and Jonathan alone in the group knew what had happened up on that trail. James had filled them in completely when he returned to the farm that night with his terrified passengers.

After the fight, they had all dragged the bodies of the dead white men off the trail. James had thought the other man, the one he clubbed with his rifle butt, was dead as well. When they went to drag him off the trail with the others, he moaned and tried to roll away from them.

For a brief moment, James considered finishing him off but relented under the watchful eye of the pastor and the passengers. He had had to kill the others in self-defense but killing this one would be cold blooded murder. He had no doubt that if the situation were reversed the slaver would do him in, but he still could not bring himself to do it.

The preacher came up behind Luke and put his hand on his shoulder. "That is not a very christian attitude, son. Don't forget Jesus himself said that we should love our enemies."

"I'm sorry, preacher. Jesus was a far better man than me, I guess. I could not love anyone who steals another man's freedom from him. I've known me too many like that."

"I think I understand, Luke, but we must at least try to follow His teachings when we can." He of course had no idea how deeply

Luke felt. No one outside the farm family knew that he was a run-away all those years ago.

"I'll try, preacher, that's all I can promise," Luke said.

"That's all the Lord asks of us, son, that we try." He gestured towards the door and spoke more loudly. "And now, ladies and gentlemen, it's time for the sermon. Let us all go inside now."

After the sermon as usual on these remaining nice days, the group assembled around the giant elm tree and socialized. The children did what children do, running and chasing around, the older girls helping with the food and tables.

Mister Anders, who owned the farm adjoining theirs, came over to talk to James and Luke. Jonathan joined them when he saw him walk over.

"James, Luke, Jonathan, a beautiful day today."

"That it is" James said. "We won't be having our social outdoors for much longer. You can feel it's comin' on."

Anders looked around the gathering and lowered his voice conspiratorially. "Have you been getting any more pressure to sell your place? You had any unusual problems?"

James looked from Luke to Jonathan. "No sir. We haven't talked to anyone about that for a while now." He stopped to think. "Seems like maybe about two or three months back Cummings approached me in town one day and made an offer for the place. I thanked him and went on my way. A little later another man I didn't know made an offer, and again I said no thank you."

"And nothing since then from anybody? Was Cummings alone that time?"

"No, he had someone with him. Didn't get his name. That was the end of it, I guess. It was polite and all. No threats or pressure either time."

Anders looked the group over again and motioned to another farmer to come over. "You all know Sampson here. He owns the place with the big apple orchard on the north road. Go on, brother Sampson, tell 'em what you told me."

Even though he knew everyone there, Sampson spoke in a low

voice. "Last week, I saw some lights in my orchard close to the road. Didn't think nothin' of it then, but next day I goes out there and most of my trees have been banded."

"What does 'banded' mean?" Jonathan asked.

"It means someone cut a piece of bark off the tree all the way around the trunk, in a circle like, you understand? That will kill the tree sure as the sun comin' up."

"Tell 'em the rest."

"Well, week or so before, two white men came to the door and offered to buy my place. I said no, thank you very much, but I was not interested in sellin'."

"Do you know who these white men were? Had you seen them before?"

"No, brother James, I ain't never seen them before then." He shuddered. "I hope I never sees them again ever."

"Why do you say that? Did they threaten you?"

"That's just the thing. They never actually said anything that was a threat, but I sure felt like they wanted me off the land and would do whatever they needed to make that happen."

"That's not all, James. I spoke with Adams and Jones too. They had something like this happen to them as well. First an offer, then some kinda trouble."

On the way back to the farm that afternoon, James and Jonathan rode up front and Luke, Anna and the other children all rode in the back. Everyone, it seemed, was still back at the church. The children were smiling and laughing, remembering the games they had played while the adults were thinking about what appeared to be a growing threat from these men who were trying to buy up the land.

James and Jonathan were each lost in their own thoughts as the wagon entered the town. As they passed by McDonald's store the sheriff greeted them.

"Afternoon James, Jonathan. Mind if we chat for a minute?"

James brought the wagon to a halt. "Not at all, sheriff. What can we help you with on this fine day?"

"Well, James, it's about those killings up on the mountain last week or so. You have heard about them, I trust?"

"Matter of fact it was quite the topic of conversation at church today."

"Is that a fact? Well then, maybe you can help me out. You wouldn't happen to have any information about any of that, would you?"

"Well sir, what kind of information are you looking for?"

"Maybe how they wound up dead for a starter. That would certainly be helpful. Another thing I would like to know is what they were doing up there on that mountain at night like that. You have any intuition about that?"

Jonathan spoke up. "Folks at the church figured they were slavers out hunting runaways."

The sheriff nodded. "Yes, that would make sense, I suppose. No other reason to be there at that time that I can think of. I just thought since that unpleasant business last year that you may know something about this unpleasant business as well."

"Wish I could help you, sheriff. Is there anything else I can do for you?"

The sheriff took of his hat and scratched his head, looking around at the street. "No James, nothing really. I just thought you might know something about this. You know, like maybe you heard something."

"If that's all then, we'll be on our way. The children are getting a little chilly and we have a ways to go."

The sheriff glanced at the back of the wagon. "Good afternoon, Miss Anna, children. I won't keep you any longer then. By the way, did you hear that one man was left alive? Makes you wonder how that came to be. Why didn't whoever did this just finish him off? It wouldn't have taken much. He was pretty bad off when they found him. Makes you wonder though. What kind of man would fight someone to the death, then not finish him off?"

"Hard to say sheriff, hard to say. There's all kinds in this world."

"That is very true, James, very true. This survivor will have a story to tell when he can talk again. Well, good day to you."

James slapped the reins on the horse's back, and they moved off down the street towards home. James had been having the exact same thoughts about the man he left alive. He must have heard the man Jeff say his name. He must have known they were out hunting someone named Woodman as well as any runaways. He had wrestled with the right and wrong of leaving him alive. It would have been a lot more expedient to have just finished him then and there. Even at that moment, James knew his decision would come back to haunt him someday. He also knew in his heart that Abigail would not have understood nor forgiven him if he had killed the man, and that was reason enough for him.

"What about that, Poppa? You think that man will have anything useful to say to the law?"

James was quiet for a moment, turning it over again. "I don't know, son. I guess we'll just have to wait and see."

They didn't have very long to wait. The sheriff rode into the farm yard five days later in the company of two others. He knew that everyone would be around the house for their lunch. As he rode in, he could see that he was correct. James and Jonathan came out on the porch to greet them.

"Good afternoon, sheriff. What brings you to the farm this afternoon?"

The sheriff sniffed the air. "Well, James, if I didn't have business I would have come for some of whatever that is that smells so good. Am I interruptin' your lunch?"

"That's quite all right. Always glad to see our law enforcement at work."

There was an uncomfortable moment of silence. "James, you know Mister Cummings here. That's Mister Bradley over there. We, that is, I wanted to talk to you about those killings up on the mountain again."

"Don't know what else I can tell you really. Haven't heard anything new on that. Just been here on the farm since we talked on Sunday."

"I realize that, James. But, on the other hand, I have heard some news."

269

"The hell with this polite chit chat, sheriff. Arrest this damn nigger right now and let's get on with it," Cummings exploded. "Why are you pussy footing around here?"

The sheriff sighed deeply. "Once again I have to remind you Cummings. You are here as my guest, and I am here as a guest of these folks. You may observe, but that is all. Now, James, the man who survived the attack up there has made a statement that may implicate you."

"How would it do that exactly, sheriff?"

"He said that the man who was in charge, name of Jeff Mason, told the other three that they were out hunting a, excuse me please, these are his words, not mine, a damnable nigger named Woodman."

"Must be a lot of black men named Woodman in this part of the country. Why are you thinking he was talking about me?"

"Well, again according to this fellow, this Woodman person has a reputation as quite the conductor on the Underground Railroad. Says this Woodman character has helped dozens of slaves escape, maybe more."

"God damn it, sheriff. That is all the evidence we need to arrest this murderin' nigger. I insist you do so immediately." This time it was Bradley chiming in.

Jonathan opened the front door and reached inside for his rifle. It was always loaded and ready near the door. He picked it up and sat down on one of the porch chairs.

"Do you see that constable? Do you see? That boy got his gun to try and intimidate us. Well, it ain't goin' to work, boy. You hear? It ain't going to work."

"What's this all about really, sheriff? Why are these two gentlemen here? What is their interest in this matter anyway?" James asked.

"That man I mentioned that was killed, that Jeff Mason? Well, he was Mister Cummings' sister's boy."

"That's right, you murderin' son of a bitch. You killed my nephew and I will see that you hang for it if it is the last thing I do on this earth. Sheriff, why aren't you arresting him?"

The sheriff sighed again. He was thinking that he was getting a little too old to put up with this for much longer. "As you are well aware, sir, the only witness to this attack cannot name the person who attacked them. He never saw the man. There was a shot, then he was lying on the ground unconscious."

"That's all the evidence I need, damn you. We have had enough around here of these uppity dirty niggers thinking they can come into our country and demand to be treated as equal. Now they're banding together to disrupt legitimate, lawful business by assisting runaways. That is against the law and you know it as well as I do."

The sheriff did indeed know it was against the law to help runaways, but like a sizable portion of the local population he was sympathetic to their plight and did not interfere. "I know that as well as you, Mister Bradley. Have you ever seen James here leading runaways through the woods? No? Do you know anybody who has actually seen him do that?"

"You know I haven't, damn you."

"Well then there isn't anything I can do today." He cast a hard look at James. "But if you should find such a witness, or see something yourself, then we can talk. Otherwise, I think we'll be on our way."

"The hell with this, Bradley. Let's get back to town," Cummings said as he yanked on the reins angrily. "We're not getting anywhere here. Good day to you, sheriff."

James, Jonathan and the sheriff watched them gallop down the road. "Well, that was certainly a nice visit. We must do that again sometime," James said. He turned to go back inside. "Would you care to join us for lunch as long as you're here?"

After a long lunch, the sheriff and James went for a walk around the property. He had something he wanted to say to James and wanted to be alone with him when he did.

"You know, James, I don't know if you were involved up there or not. Tell you the truth, I really don't care. I've known you for a while and know what kind of man you are."

"What kind of man is that sheriff?"

"I know that you are not a murderer for one thing. Oh, I'm not saying you didn't do this, but I am saying I do not think it's murder to rid the world of slave hunters."

"Yeah, well, I can certainly agree with that."

"Thought you might. But there's more now. These men, Cummings and his friends, are talking about making real trouble around here for anyone who supports abolition, especially those who directly aid the runaways. You don't know anything about that either, I suppose? Didn't think so. Anyway, now that his nephew has been killed Cummings is going to be a very formidable enemy."

"What do you think he might do?"

"I think that they will take the law into their own hands if they can. I think they're going to go after anyone they suspect of working for the Underground Railroad in any way and causing them very real harm one way or the other."

They had now walked back towards the house and their guest's horse. "What are you telling me, sheriff?"

The man untied his horse and climbed up into the saddle. "Well, I guess what I'm saying is that if I, or anyone I knew, was in the business of helping runaways, I would advise them to be very, very careful from now on, and trust no one you don't know personally."

Anna and the two girls came out onto the porch. The sheriff sat up straight and tipped his hat. "Miss Anna, ladies, thank you very much for a most delightful afternoon. I must be on my way sadly."

He looked down at James and extended his hand to him. "Remember what I said, James. These are becoming very dangerous times."

The onset of another fiercely cold winter slowed the stream of runaways to a slow trickle before drying up completely. People were still fleeing slavery in search of freedom, but the traffic went on the less mountainous routes that were easier to navigate this time of year.

James took the words of the sheriff to heart. He and Jonathan had a very long talk about the risks. James would have preferred that his son stop conducting, at least until things were less dangerous.

"And when do you think that might be, Poppa? When do you think it will be safe to help folks by breaking the law? Will it ever become so dangerous that helping people flee to freedom is not worth the risk?"

James had a feeling then that his son would not be frightened off so easily, and he was immensely proud of him for that. Very worried, but very proud as well. They continued their work on The Road, but with the slowdown in numbers they had the time to go out together for safety instead of each taking a leg alone.

That proved to be a good idea as the activity of the hunters did not decrease. The bounties being paid by rich southerners for the return of their "property" were increasing as more and more of the enslaved sought to be free at any cost or hardship. Bands of these slavers had been known to kidnap free blacks and take them south into slavery for the bounty. They had to regularly detour or delay to avoid the hunters who seemed to be focusing their efforts for the most part in the valley and not in the hills to the west because of the season.

They barely escaped with their passengers when they were fired on by a group of white men just before dawn as they were leaving the shelter of the woods while on the leg to the church in Yellow Hill early one morning. The hunters faded away after James and Jonathan fired back with accuracy, but James was concerned that they might suspect the farm of being a station on The Road since it was the closest place. That had led them to curtail activity until the weather improved.

The increase in the activity of the hunters coincided with a decrease in sympathy for the fugitives that passed through the valley heading north. Meetings of the two active abolitionist groups in the valley were regularly harassed and interrupted by angry crowds. Meetings of the Anti-Slavery Society that James was active in had to move their meetings every month in an attempt to avoid any trouble. That tactic was not always successful as the word would somehow leak out about the location of the next meeting.

James and some of the others in the Society were becoming suspicious that one of the members was not on their side, that he sided with the anti-abolitionists and fed them information about the group. James was sure that Luke and Jonathan were safe, and certainly McCallister and his boys were safe, but he couldn't say definitively how some of the others stood. He had considered that no black man would do such a thing, to help the hunters in their vicious business, but the amounts of money being offered for captives was becoming too large for anyone to ignore.

An incident had recently occurred that forced James to change his mind on that score. A young runaway, a boy still in his teens, was tricked into leaving his secure sanctuary by another black man who claimed to know his family. It turned out he was far from a friend when he turned the boy over to slave hunters for money.

That story not only made him sick to his stomach, it also instilled a new caution in James. He did not like the thought that he couldn't trust his neighbors, but one loose word in the wrong ear could cost him his farm, his family and even his life.

Even at the church meetings there was a general feeling of unease in the air as rumors swirled around about the abolitionist movement. Some felt it would weather this storm, others felt that it was being severely crippled by the changing attitudes of the population, not to mention the ever present slave hunters.

One afternoon in early March, James and Luke went into town for supplies. As they pulled up at McDonald's store, they were met by McAllister and two of his sons who were just leaving.

After exchanging pleasantries, McAllister motioned for all of them to move away from the store front and any prying ears. "James, I am very glad to run into you. It saves me a trip out to your place."

"What can I do for you, Mister McAllister?"

He looked from James to Luke, then at his sons. "I know I can trust everyone here. I am getting suspicious that we have a spy in our midst, someone who is working against us and our cause."

"To be honest, I have felt that way for some weeks now," James said. "Someone is leaking the location of our meetings, that much is sure."

"I'm afraid there may be more to it than simply disrupting our meetings. They also know who all is attending and what was said as well."

"Do you have any feeling for who it might be?"

McAllister ran his hand through his hair. "No, damn it, and it pains me tremendously that someone in the room, a man I have known for at least a short while, is doing this terrible thing. It is unconscionable."

"I think I have an idea," James started slowly, still playing it over in his mind. "There must be a core of good people in our group, people who can be trusted to not betray us."

"Do you think we have more than one enemy in the group?"

"I don't know," James said, "but I have a plan that might just tell us who this person is." They walked over to McCallister's wagon that was loaded with their supplies.

"The next meeting is in a few days. Here's what we should do. Tell everyone at that meeting the location of the next one. We will have to choose a place with some cover nearby, but not too close. Jonathan and I and your two oldest boys will get to the location very early and wait to see who shows up to disrupt us. They have been showing up closer to the start of every meeting, so I feel they are probably hiding somewhere nearby even as we arrive."

"You're probably right about that," McAllister said. "Go on with your plan."

"Well, I hope that if we can get there even more early and hide in any nearby cover, we can be in a position to see whoever it is that shows up."

"How will that help us identify our Judas?"

"First, we will disrupt the disrupters. Whoever is left standing after that will probably be happy to tell us who hired them and who is giving them information….. with a little persuasion, of course. Even if they do not know who the spy is, we can get to the bottom of who is hiring them and deal with that person next."

McAllister took off his hat and brushed away some imaginary dust from his trousers. "You think the four of you can handle something like that? What if they start shooting?"

"Who else can we trust? As much as I would like to I just cannot trust every man in the room anymore. As far as shooting, I hope we can do this without bloodshed, but if they start shooting we'll respond."

McAllister looked at his two oldest sons. "What do you think boys? You think this will work?"

"Might just do that, Father," Theodore replied. "Besides, we have to do something, or our work will come for nothing and we won't be able to help anymore. I say we should do it. We have nothing to lose."

"Where should the meeting be then, James? You will want some cover nearby as you said. Any ideas on that score?"

The next meeting was set to be held in a recently completed house that one of the members of the Society built but had not moved into yet. Being in town did not stop the harassment and probably would not this time either.

"Why not back at the mill? There is only the one road that goes by there, and the woods come down fairly close behind and on the west side. Shouldn't be difficult to find a spot to watch from while we wait for our guests."

"All right, James, the mill it is. I'll make sure everyone knows at the meeting coming up and we'll get ready to set our trap."

James and Luke arrived in town for the Society's meeting a little early. They left the wagon a short distance away and walked up to the house, looking for hidden threats. None were detected and they went inside. There were several lanterns burning, along with a small fire in the fireplace. It gave the room a warm, cozy feeling that belied the ugly purpose of their work.

As McAllister called the meeting to order, James was casually looking around the room at all the faces that were at once so familiar and yet now so suspicious. It could be any one of them, he decided finally and hated the thought.

It was beginning to look like they may get all the way through the meeting without any harassment. The order of business was about different legislation then under consideration in Harrisburg that directly affected black citizens, from the right to vote to owning property in some towns with restrictions on black ownership.

When the actions of the group in relation to the issues were decided, McAllister started to end the meeting. "As you are well aware, we have been targeted by a very ugly element. They will do whatever it takes to end our work, short of killing any of us, at least so far. I fear that day may not be too far off. So, the next meeting will be back at the mill in three weeks. I hope to have some news from the capital by then, hopefully some good news. So then, three weeks from tonight at the same time as usual."

As the members left, they were suddenly pelted by stones and rotten eggs. "Get out of our town, your filthy nigger lovers. And take them dirty niggers with you. We don't want them around here," several of the attackers were yelling.

James and the others protected themselves as well as they could. Luke was knocked to his knees but quickly stood up again. He and James ducked between two other houses and into a small stand of trees. "You hurt, Luke?"

Luke put his hand on the back of his head and found blood. "I'll be all right, James. I been hurt worse than this."

James had no doubt about that. "Let me take a look," James said, but it was so dark in their hiding place he couldn't see much. He too came away with blood on his hands. "Here," he said, handing Luke his handkerchief. "Hold that there until we can get a better look somewhere else."

He went to the edge of the trees to scout the situation. The angry crowd was nowhere to be seen. They and the Society members had simply melted into the night, so he went back for Luke. "There isn't anyone around anymore. Let's go find the wagon and get you to the doctor's."

They left the cover of the trees and stayed close to the shadows. They found the wagon where they had left it unmolested and climbed in. A few minutes later they were at Doctor Findlay's home.

"Doesn't look too bad, Luke, but you'll need a stitch or two I'm afraid. By the way, how is Miss Anna and little Constance?"

The mention of his family helped to ease his pain and relax him a little, just as the doctor had intended. Luke broke out in a big smile even as he winced when the doctor cleaned the wound. "They're just fine, doctor, thank you for asking. You'll probably be seeing my Anna again in a few weeks."

"Oh, why's that?"

Luke looked down at the floor, embarrassed. "She thinks she's gonna have another baby is why," he said sheepishly. He looked up into two beaming faces.

"Luke, why the hell didn't you tell me," James said as he slapped his back. "That's great news, just great. Looks like we'll have to add another room onto your house soon."

"Anna only told me this afternoon right before we left for the meeting. I was plannin' on telling you on the way home after."

On the ride home afterwards they chatted about their kids and the prospect of another joining the family soon. Then Luke turned to him. "Why didn't you want me to go with you for the plan, James?"

"Well, two reasons actually. First, don't forget that you are still technically a runaway. I think the further away you stay from these people, the better."

"And the second?"

"Because you're a young man with a young family. My wife is gone, and my boys are grown. Little Abbie is getting to be quite a young lady as well. If something happens to me, they will be just fine. But your family still needs you, Luke. You have a new baby coming, don't forget. If you were gone for any reason they would have great difficulty."

Luke thought about that for a minute, nodding his head slightly. "All right, James. I can accept that." The talk on the rest of the ride home went back to the family.

The next three weeks passed in a blur of farm work. The weather had been quite mild of late, allowing them ample opportunity to get all their crops planted and a million other things that make up a farm life done.

The entire farm family was thrilled to hear that Anna was going to have another baby, especially little Abigail. She already thought of Constance as a little sister, and now another baby was on the way. She was not shy about expressing her wish that another girl would join the family soon.

When the appointed day of the meeting arrived, James and Jonathan rolled the wagon out and hitched one of the horses. Jonathan had only been to the meeting that founded the Society and one or two others because James thought that he and Luke represented the farm well enough. James was also concerned about the rising tide of violence that was building in response to those meetings and he wanted to protect his son as much as possible from that ugliness. He already faced enough of it working on The Road.

Francis looked unhappy as they prepared to go. "Why can't I go too, Poppa?"

James put his arm around his youngest son's shoulder. "I'll feel a whole lot better knowing that you're here protecting the farm. Luke is leaving for the meeting in a few hours, then you will be the only man on the place. Do you understand, son?"

"Yes sir, Poppa, I guess so. I just want to help more is all."

"It will be a great help to me if I don't have to worry about any of you here while we are away. A very great help."

As they drove away, Jonathan looked over his shoulder. The entire family was out in the barn yard to see them off. He hoped there would be no violence tonight so they could return safely home to them.

The ride into town was uneventful. There was a slight chill in the air, but the sun was still shining so it was a very pleasant ride. The amount of traffic increased as they drew closer to Gettysburg. James once again wondered at the evolution of what had been nothing more than a muddy crossroads when he lived here as a child. McDonald's store was not only the biggest mercantile store, it was also something of a social center for the growing town.

James slowed as they passed by, greeting some of the people coming and going along the street. Along with the store, there were the two small cafes, the blacksmith which had grown considerably, and a number of houses that were in various stages of construction.

The people and traffic thinned out as they turned onto the road to McAllister's Mill, about two miles out of town.

"How many people do you think there were throwing stones last time?" Jonathan asked as they drove along.

"Well, it was very hard to tell. It all happened so fast and it was a very dark night. If I had to guess, I would say probably a dozen or so. Why do you ask?"

"What if a dozen or more show up this time? How are we going to handle them?"

"Believe me, I have had the same thought. I don't think there will be that many tonight. A lot of those people last time only had to take a few steps out the door to harass us. We will be a couple of miles away from town this time. No, I think we'll have three, maybe four show up."

They pulled into the mill yard and greeted McAllister, who helped them unhitch the wagon and move it into the barn. His two sons Jimmy and Theodore came over to join them.

"Is everyone clear on our purpose tonight?" James asked the group. "I know this plan has some holes in it, so if anyone has any suggestions, better give them now."

The older son thought he knew the best place to hide and suggested that they split into two groups so they could cover each other if it came to that. James agreed and they all went in to an early supper before setting the trap.

They hiked a half mile or so back up the road afterwards. There would not be any place to hide a wagon along the road without it being spotted, so putting it in the barn was a good idea. Theodore pointed out possible ambush sites along the way until they came to what seemed the perfect spot.

The boy had chosen well, James could see that right away. There was a slight bend in the road before a short hill with cover on both sides. James took another look around and decided.

"This is excellent, Theodore, really excellent. You're going to make a fine officer someday with an eye like yours." James knew the boy dreamed of a career in the Army.

"Thank you, sir. I am hopin' to someday. Where do you want me and my brother?"

"Here's what we'll do. You boys go on back up the road a bit more and find a secure place where you can also see the road and anyone on it. You know a spot you can do that? Good. When any riders that you're suspicious of approach, let them pass, but let us know that they're coming. Can you do that?"

"Yes sir. What kind of signal?"

"I don't want you to be more than an arm's throw away, so why don't you heave a small stone back out here in the road where we'll hear it. That should work. After they pass I want you to follow along behind them at a safe distance out of sight. I will be in the middle of the road with Jonathan covering me from over there. I want you boys to be a surprise coming up from behind them. Any questions?"

They went to their respective places and got ready for whatever was to come. If James was correct, the troublemakers would come out before any of the Society members so they could find a place to hide and wait to strike. They would never suspect that he was going to beat them at their own game. At least he hoped they wouldn't.

It was getting on towards dusk when James heard a stone land in the brush by the side of the road. "That's the signal, Jonathan. You ready, son?"

Jonathan was excited but he had enough experience on The Road to know he could handle himself. "I'm ready, Poppa. Let's catch us a spy."

James smiled and stepped out of cover to the middle of the road. He had a rifle at hand, a pistol in his belt and a sword in a scabbard. He felt he was ready. As long as there were not too many to handle they would do fine.

In another moment he heard voices and then horses approaching. He was glad to see it was only three riders coming towards him. "Good evening, gentlemen."

"What the hell you doin' there, boy? Move out the road and let us pass." The man in the center was obviously a little older and was probably in charge.

"May I ask you your business this evening?" James asked politely.

"Get the hell out of the way, boy, or we'll just go over you. Go on, git."

James brought his rifle to bear on the man he perceived to be in charge. "I'm going to have to ask you gentlemen to dismount if you don't mind."

"The hell we will, and don't you threaten me you damnable nigger."

The man on the left was reaching in his belt, so James pointed the rifle at his face. Suddenly, the man groaned, slumped forward and fell off his horse into the road. Young Jimmy McAllister stepped out from behind the horses, hefting a large stone in his hand. There was another one lying in the road by the fallen rider.

"Hello there. This here isn't a friend of yours is he?"

Theodore stepped around the horses from the other side, rifle at the ready. Jonathan then made his presence known.

"What the hell is this? What's goin' on here, God damn it?" the rider who had spoken before yelled at them.

"This is what's going on," James replied coolly. "You're going to get off that God damn horse right now, mister. You can climb down, or I can shoot you out of the saddle, but you are dismounting."

The two riders still up looked at each other, then slowly started to dismount under very watchful eyes. The man on the ground moaned and rolled on his back.

"Boys, take their horses. You two, drop your weapons in the road right there, then go help your friend. I think he has a bit of a headache," James said.

They set off back to the mill with their three captives leading the way, James and Jonathan keeping guard and the McAllister boys bringing up the rear with the three horses.

McAllister was out in front of the mill as they walked up, and he came to meet them. "Looks like you bagged yourself a motley crew there, James."

"They surrendered pretty easy for a bunch of hired trouble-makers. Too bad. I was kind of hoping I could shoot at least one," James said as he met the eyes of each of the men.

McAllister took the rifle from his younger son and started to direct the captives towards the barn. "Oh, don't feel too badly, James. The day is not over yet. You may still get a chance. All right, you three, move."

"Any of them look familiar to you?" James asked.

"No, not really," McAllister said, then looking at the backs of the men, he noticed one was a little taller and wore a dirty grey hat. "Hold on there, you three. Theodore, which is this man's horse."

"This one here, sir."

McAllister took a hard look as the three men fidgeted nervously. "You mind tellin' us what the hell is goin' on?" the taller man said. "You ain't got no right to keep us here like this."

"Just turn around, mister and face the barn," McAllister said, then he nodded. "That's the one who killed my daughter Martha's cat a few meetings ago, the one he left at the door."

"You sure?" James asked.

"I'm sure. I only saw him as he ran away, but I got a good look at his back and his horse. That's him."

"What's your name, mister?" James asked the man.

"Go to hell, nigger." He said, his back to James. "I ain't tellin' you nothin'."

James took the butt end of his rifle and slammed it into the back of the man's head, not enough to hurt him much, but enough to send him sprawling. He went and stood over him, the barrel a few inches above the man's face.

"I asked you a polite question, mister, and you call me names," James said, shaking his head. "And what is it with you ignorant slavers, anyway? None of you seems able to speak English very well. Using double negatives makes you look pretty ignorant, you know. Now, what is your name, mister?"

"Miller, damn you. My name is Miller."

"Now see, that wasn't so hard, was it?" He turned the barrel of his rifle towards the other two men. "Names" he barked at them. "Now."

The two were clearly terrified. "I'm Taylor, this here's Johnson. We ain't from around here. We rode up from Virginia. What's going to happen to us?"

"Well, now. Maybe there is a smart one in this group. Since you asked politely, here is what's going to happen. You're going to tell me, tell us that is, who sent you here, who is paying you to harass us like this and what their plans are."

"And if we don't?"

"Well, in that case we're going to go into the barn there for a few hours, then you're going to spend eternity in the bottom of that abandoned well over there," James said, indicating an old well on the edge of the yard.

The two men tried to edge away, even more terrified than before. "Just stop right there you two," James said, again aiming his rifle at them. "Miller, get your sorry butt up out of the dirt and come over here. That's a good boy. Now, put your hands out in front of you."

James moved around behind the men and put the barrel of the rifle against the back of Miller's head. "Jonathan, tie this man's hands first. Miller, if you fidget, I will blow your head off and throw what's left in the well. Go ahead, Jonathan."

After following that procedure on the other two, the three were led into the barn and seated on hay bales. "You can't keep us here like this, damn you. You can't just take a man and tie his hands and hold him prisoner."

"Is that so? Isn't that what you do every time you take a black man south into slavery? Isn't that what happens every day down there in Ol' Virginny?"

"That's different and you know it, damn it."

"How exactly is it different, Mister Miller?"

"Because they're just damned nig......" his voice trailed off.

"Yes, Mister Miller, because they're just..."

Miller looked down at the floor. "It's just different, is all." He wisely decided not to go on.

"Well, now that we have that settled, here's the program for tonight. I am going to take the three of you into the tack room there and ask you a few direct questions. If I get three different answers, I will shoot the two I think are lying and let the other go free. See how it works? Good. I'll start with you, Miller. Stand up."

"Go to hell, you son of a bitch."

James struck him with the rifle hard enough to knock him off the bale. He nudged him with his boot and saw he was out this time. He turned to the other two. "I guess I'll have to speak with him last, so I'll start with you, Taylor. Get up."

Taylor sprang to his feet. "Please don't hurt me, mister. I don't know nothin' about all this, honest. We was just..."

"Go on, Taylor. Tack room is over there towards the back. You boys all right with these two out here?"

James asked Taylor the questions about who was paying them and more, then repeated the questions to Johnson. So far, the answers were vague but similar. They named the man paying them, but they had no idea who the spy in their midst could be.

People had started to arrive for the meeting as James dragged Miller to the side and asked him the same questions. It was clear the fight had gone out of him, and he confirmed what the other two said. James was suspicious, however, that he knew who the spy was.

He left the men guarded and went over to the mill. The Society members were still greeting each other, and the meeting had not yet started. He pulled McAllister aside and they went out front.

"Well, we now know who the paymaster for these men is, but no one seems to know who our spy is. I think Miller's lying. I think he knows perfectly well."

"Who's the paymaster?"

"It's Cummings and that friend of his Bradley."

McAllister clenched his jaws in anger. "I had a feeling it might be him. I met him when he first arrived in the valley. He seemed a very decent sort then," he said, shaking his head in disbelief that he could be so wrong about a man. McCallister's intense hatred for slavery and those who support it was well known. "Well, now what?"

"Go ahead and start the meeting. Go ahead and tell the men that there is a suspicion of a spy and let that sink in. I'll be right outside the door. As soon as I hear that you have done that, I'll march Miller in, and we'll try and see who is the most unhappy to see him here."

McAllister stroked his chin. "Yes, yes. That's perfect. I'll tell of the suspicions and maybe hint that we may have someone who knows who it is."

"That's even better. You go ahead then but give me a minute to get Miller up and over here."

James headed over to the barn as McAllister went back to the mill house. Miller was still sitting on a hay bale under the watchful eyes of Jonathan and young Theodore.

"Get up, please, Mister Miller."

Miller rose slowly, his face a mixture of fear and hate. "Where we goin'? Where you takin' me?" he asked sullenly.

"Mister McAllister has invited you to join our meeting tonight if you don't have any pressing engagements. No? Good, then let's go."

They stopped just outside the door as McCallister's booming voice was calling the meeting to order. He could hear him start to talk about the suspicions of a spy and the possibility that they may be able to name him soon.

At that point James opened the door and shoved Miller inside. He and McAllister were scanning the reactions of the men in the room. While all were surprised by the sudden entrance, only one started to stand then quickly sat back down. It was fairly obvious he was frightened. That was enough for them.

"Well, what should we do with these three then, James?" McAllister asked after the meeting had broken up. Think we ought to just throw them in the well anyway?"

They were sitting with the three captives in the mill house. The traitor in their midst had been exposed and confessed, and surely realized his days in the valley were numbered. It was all McAllister and James could do to keep the members from tearing him limb from limb. Others suggested lynching as an appropriate punishment.

"What do you think, Mister Miller? You prefer the well or the rope?"

Taylor and Johnson both began to make unpleasant sounds trying to control their fear. "Honest, mister, me and Johnson just rode in the other day. Some men asked us if we wanted to make some easy money. Said all we have to do is scare some folks, just scare 'em is all. We didn't mean no harm, I swear it."

"So you didn't come up here to our valley to hunt runaways? To tie a man up and take his freedom away?"

"No, sir. Ain't no way we would do anything like that. Hell, I was just a poor dirt farmer myself, but I lost my place over the winter. We both just come up here lookin' for honest work, and that's the God's truth of it."

"What about you, Miller?" McAllister asked. "Did you come here to my valley to hunt down men?"

Miller hung his head, but he was beyond lying. "Yes sir, that was my line of work." He stopped and looked around the room into several very angry faces. "Tell you the truth, the attraction has sorta gone out of it for me."

James laughed. "I wouldn't be surprised. So, what caused this tremendous change of heart if I may ask."

Miller was clearly finished. "Look, mister, I don't want no more trouble. Let me go and I swear I'll skedaddle. I'll head back for Maryland tonight if that's what you want."

James and McAllister looked at each other, then McAllister asked the room at large. "What say you, gentlemen? Do you believe Mister Miller here is sincere?"

There was some grumbling from the others, the only clearly heard words were 'well' and 'lynching', which only served to increase the anxiety level of the three slavers.

"All right, Mister Miller, stand up please," James said.

Miller was terrified. "Why? What are you going to do to me? Please...."

James' voice was more firm. "Stand up, Miller. Now."

Miller stood slowly, his bound hands still out in front of him. "Please, mister..."

James took a step closer until the two men's faces were only inches apart. "Listen to me closely, Mister Miller," James began in a soft voice. "I've been forced to kill a few men in my time. It is not something that brought me any pleasure, but I'll do it again gladly in my defense or that of my family and friends. If we should happen to meet up again, I will kill you without warning."

He leaned in a little closer. "Have I made myself perfectly clear?" He stepped back and looked at Taylor and Johnson. "This goes for you two as well. If you are truly in this area to look for honest work, then you are welcome. I strongly suggest, however, that you keep riding north in search of employment. Folks hereabouts may have some ill will towards you after tonight."

The three just stood there, unsure of what the next move would be. They had no experience at all dealing with a black man who controlled what was happening, who had their fate in his hands.

"Gentlemen, I hope you have gained some understanding of what it's like to have no freedom, to live every minute under threat, to have no control at all over your own life, your very existence. And I hope you'll take that understanding with you throughout your life."

He turned to Jonathan. "Cut them loose, son. Empty their weapons and return them to their rightful owners. Theodore, would you please bring our guest's horses around front?"

Miller, Taylor and Johnson were stunned. "You mean you're just going to let us go?" Taylor asked.

"Like I said, I am not a violent man unless forced to be. As I also said before, if ever I see any of you again I will consider it a direct threat to me and my family, and I will remove that threat immediately. I'll ask you again, is that clear?"

Johnson spoke up. "Yes sir, clear as glass. Me and Taylor here were headin' for Pittsburgh before all this business anyways. We'll be on our way tonight, I swear."

"See that you do. Miller, I recommend heading back to Maryland tonight as well."

Taylor and Johnson were already heading for the door. "You ain't got to worry none about us, mister," Taylor said. "Come on, Bobby, let's get the hell out of this place."

Miller was rubbing his wrists, sore from the rope. "You know you're fightin' an uphill battle, don't you Mister Woodman? Even people who don't hate your kind do not want our two races to live together. Some feel it just ain't right."

James was not surprised that Miller was familiar with his name. The slavers up on the mountain he had dealt with before knew it, too, so it was safe to assume he was also a wanted man. "Yes, sir, Mister Miller, I do understand it is going to be a long struggle, maybe even a very, very long struggle. I am confident, however, in final victory for this cause of freedom. I am confident that this nation, which claims to have been founded on solid Christian values, will find the path to righteousness in time."

Miller shook his head. "It ain't nothin' personal with me, Woodman. I just growed up thinkin' what everyone else did, that one race was over the other. I never owned a slave. Hell, I don't have any land. To me, it was just a livin', nothin' more and nothin' less.

"Just remember that these people you hunt are human beings who want the same things from life that you do, nothin' more and nothin' less, as you said." James indicated the door by tipping his head. "Go on now please, Mister Miller. Leave us."

Miller seemed like he wanted to say something else but could not find the words. He met James' eyes and nodded, then went out the door.

"Well, James," McAllister said. "Think we'll see any of them around here again?"

James thought for a moment. "Not Taylor or Johnson. I believed them when they said they were just hired to harass us." He thought for another moment. "Miller, I'm not so sure about, to be honest."

It didn't take long for the word of what had happened at the Anti-Slavery Society's meeting at the mill to spread through the valley. A large part of the community saw justice in it, but a very loud and vocal minority found it to be very threatening. Most who held that view were not longtime residents but were more newly arrived farmers and businessmen who cared about profits and not much else. They saw the work of the abolitionists as directly threatening their way of life. They felt nothing for the human tragedy playing out not only in the valley but the country at large.

James started to receive word that Cummings and Bradley, along with a few others, were determined to break the back of the abolitionist movement by whatever means necessary, including bloodshed.

When he got the word from McAllister himself on a shopping trip one day in town, James had a simple reply.

"Well, Mister McAllister, it seems we are scaring the hell out of them," he said. "I'm glad they see us as a threat because we are and always will be."

"Trust me, James. You know that my commitment to the struggle, to our fight, is total and complete. I understand your motivations. Mine are rooted in God's word. We're going to win this fight, of that I am sure, but victory is going to come at a terrible cost, one I feel we cannot even imagine today."

"Maybe that's what's needed. Maybe if it takes an ocean of blood to cleanse this evil from our country then so be it. I am staying in the fight. I'm ready for it."

They parted company after some discussion about the next meeting of the Society, and McAllister left James with a reminder. "Remember, they know your name, James. You will have to be extra vigilant in the days ahead." James was well aware of that fact.

After loading two kegs of nails and a repaired plow blade in the back of the wagon, James set off for home. Along the way he thought about his chat with McAllister. He already knew that the slavers knew his name. Not even McAllister knew he was the one who had killed two of the three slave hunters up on the mountain.

He also knew that no one who worked on The Road or helped fleeing slaves was safe from their depredations. The stories in the valley were rife with examples of white people being terrorized as well as blacks. James had to admire folks who could have just as easily turned away, turned a blind eye to the evil everywhere since it didn't directly affect them. It was their sense of moral outrage that kept them fighting, a strong belief in right and wrong, as well as the promises of the Constitution and the Declaration.

He also realized that he probably shouldn't be out this close to dark and he hurried along. Once again he felt unease, that he may have been followed or watched. He had never been wrong about that, and he trusted his instinct. He was relieved when he pulled the wagon into the yard and saw that all was well.

Jonathan and Luke came out to meet him and unload the wagon. "Anything unusual happen? Any strangers around?" James asked.

"Nothing at all, Poppa. Just another busy day on a workin' farm is all," Jonathan said, then stopped.

The others followed his gaze down the lane. A lone rider was approaching, riding slowly. James thought there was something familiar about him, then was stunned to see it was Miller. Jonathan and Luke walked nonchalantly to the front porch and picked up their rifles that were always at the ready.

Miller rode into the yard and stopped a few feet away. "Good evening, Mister Miller. What brings you to our little farm?"

Miller looked around at the farm and surrounding fields and took off his hat. "Good evening, Mister Woodman. This here truly is a beautiful spot you've picked out for yourself."

"Well, it was my Daddy who picked the spot a very long time ago. He was a soldier in the Revolution. He said that all he wanted after that experience was peace and quiet, so he came to Gettysburg to raise his family."

"Well, I can see why he chose here, yes sir." Miller hesitated, not meeting James' eye. It was obvious something was on his mind, so James just waited for him to go on.

Finally, Miller looked at James, looked him hard in the eye. "I've been giving what happened the other day, and what you said, a great deal of thought, Mister Woodman."

James took a step back and motioned towards his house. "Would you like to come inside and talk? Are you thirsty? My daughter makes a wonderful cup of coffee and we grow our own rye if you like something stronger." Luke and Jonathan exchanged wary glances.

"You see, Mister Woodman, I just don't understand that, don't understand you. I came to this valley to hunt you like the others. I meant you harm, you know that, and now you invite me into your own home, offer me refreshment. I don't understand that, I'm afraid."

James came to stand directly next to Miller's horse and looked up at him. "Mister Miller, my fight is not with you. My fight is with the cruel and evil men who manipulate you and millions of others. They manipulate you by teaching you to fear and hate a whole people that you do not even know, a people who just want to live in peace and raise a family. Isn't that what you want as well?"

Miller looked out at the fields again and smiled. "Yes sir, that's exactly what I want. After our unfortunate experience the other day and thinking about what you said, I decided maybe I would head out west, maybe even all the way to California."

"Well, I've read that there is a whole new county to be had there. It sounds like a beautiful spot to raise a family."

"I'm hopin' to find out for myself soon, but I felt that before I go, I owe you a debt and I came to repay it. I went to Cummings to get my pay and quit. After the other day, I do not want any part of this dirty business. That's another reason I'm going west. You need to know. Cummings and Bradley are coming for you soon. They want this land, but they want you even more."

Luke and Jonathan took a few steps closer to hear. Miller had all their attention now. "How soon," James asked, "and how many?"

"Soon, very soon I heard them say. Maybe as many as ten men, maybe more. I didn't hear that part well, but they are coming."

"Well, I guess in a way I knew that this would happen sooner rather than later," James said looking at Jonathan and Luke. "We've all been expecting it in the back of our minds. I appreciate your coming here, Mister Miller, I truly do. Would you like some supper before your journey begins?"

Miller shook his head slightly. "No, thank you Mister Woodman. Thanks to you, my journey has already begun I suppose, so I'll just wish you good luck and be on my way. I mean it," he finished and reached his hand down.

As the three of them stood and watched Miller ride slowly back down the lane, the others came out into the yard.

"Who was that man, James? What did he want here?" Anna asked. She clutched little Constance close. Anna's fear of the white man was still very real.

"I believe that he is a traveler on the road to Damascus," James said quietly. He turned and looked at his family, his reason for living, and smiled. "Let's go get some supper."

The next few days passed nervously at the farm as they waited for the next shoe to drop. James was opposed to confronting Cummings and his cohorts directly on the flimsy evidence he had. One thing he did know for sure, trouble was definitely coming their way. He had seen the look in Cummings' eyes when he was last at the farm.

They developed a system for a lookout to be in a position to see anyone approaching. His father had picked the site because it was so hard to see from the road, and that made it hard for them to see outward. All hands were needed to work as once again the fields were producing a bounty. Danger or not, the work of running a farm had to go on.

James had also taken an inventory of weapons at hand. He and Jonathan counted a total of five rifles, three pistols and a sword. "They're going to have to get in pretty close for the sword to be useful," James said to Jonathan as they were cleaning and inspecting the firearms.

"You think we can hold them off, Poppa? Even if they come on strong like that man Miller said?"

James had tried to move Anna and Constance into town to stay with friends, but Anna would have none of it.

"No sir, James. No sir. This here is my home and I will stay and fight for it," Anna had said very firmly. She was definitely showing her pregnancy now but was ready for the fight to come. "It would not do for me to run away when I'm needed here. No sir, I am stayin' put."

"We have one more firearm here, one I've never brought out

before," James said as they were finalizing the checks. "It's out in the barn. Let's go get it."

Jonathan watched as his father went to a large trunk in the back of the barn and opened it. He had seen the old trunk back there but had never paid it any mind. It was usually under a pile of something like harnesses or hay rakes.

He could hear his father muttering to himself as he searched, moving things around and digging deep. "Ah, there you are," James said after a minute of searching. "I always felt you might come in handy someday."

He unwrapped an oil cloth from what Jonathan thought was almost a small cannon. "Son, I want you to meet Brown Bess, a most fearsome weapon. My father carried this with him every day fighting the British. Come over here and say hello."

Jonathan took the weapon from his father and was impressed with its heft. He looked it over carefully, including the bore. "I never saw a bore like this, Poppa. Do we have any balls it can shoot?"

James dove back into the trunk and came up with a small tin box and shook it. "I thought there might be some left." He opened the box and counted a dozen balls inside. "We probably ought to cast a few more."

Jonathan had also noted the barrel was not rifled like their more modern weapons. "How far out is this going to be accurate with that smooth bore?"

"I asked my father that same question when he first showed her to me. He said he had no idea because they were always closing on the British when he used it. He belonged to a very aggressive battalion, and the British feared them very much. He taught me what they called a buck and ball loading."

"A what?"

"Buck and ball is what the soldiers who used this called it. You load it like any other, then after the wadding you drop three or four smaller shot down the barrel. Anyone within twenty yards will be cut in half."

Jonathan tried to picture the gentle, kindly old man he knew as his grandfather as a young man, a fierce warrior, fighting for his life and his country and using such a fearsome weapon. He let out a slow whistle.

After firing it twice to confirm that it still worked, they added it to the arsenal. They had each taken a turn, and Jonathan was again impressed with his grandfather. The weapon did indeed kick like a small cannon.

They kept to the routine on the farm by day, but it was the nights that worried James the most. They developed a watch system through the night that changed eyes every three hours, but the anxiety level kept creeping up with every passing day. They all clearly understood that it was not a matter of if trouble was coming, but when.

A few days later Francis came running in breathless as they were finishing supper. "Poppa, there's riders coming across the north field. They were trying to stay out of sight along the tree line, but I spotted three, maybe four of them from the hay loft."

They all looked at James. He was proud to see not fear, but a steely determination to fight. He pushed himself away from the table. "All right. We all know what to do. Anna, take the girls to your house, please, and take one of the pistols. Luke, boys, let's go."

Jonathan was posted to keep an eye out in the other direction, down the regular approach lane that led out to the county road in case this was only a diversion. James posted Francis by the gate and he and Luke moved out into the field.

They let the first two riders get close, then James stood to challenge them. "That's far enough. State your business or get the hell off my land."

The first rider still had his rifle slung over his shoulder, a bad mistake that James took note of. "One more time. What's your business?"

"Well, what have we here Jesse? Looks like a darky with a rifle pointin' at us," the first rider said to the other. "What do you mean your land, nigger? You mean your master's land, don't you boy?"

James just stared at the man, watching them both closely and not moving the rifle muzzle off his chest. "What's the matter boy, cat got your tongue. I been told you are one fancy talkin' nigger, but that don't seem very true to me."

The man pulled the right reins to move the animal's head to the right and cover any movement of the other, but not before James saw him pull a pistol from his belt. He fired and caught the first rider full in the chest and dropped the rifle to pull his own pistol out, but the other was faster. He was turning to fire around the horse's head when Luke stood and shot him out of the saddle.

In the gathering dusk, they could see two more riders charging across the field at them. Luke had used his pistol on the second rider and now leveled his rifle at the new threat. He fired and dropped the leading man as James calmly finished reloading his rifle. The fourth rider pulled up short, took a quick look around and retreated as fast as he could.

"Guess he had a change of heart," James said as he finished the reloading. "Quickly now, let's get back."

They were met by Jonathan. "There are riders in the road, Poppa. Looked like four."

James looked around quickly. It was getting darker but there was still enough light to see around the yard clearly. "Francis, up in the hayloft. Hurry now, son. Jonathan, behind the corner of the house. I don't think we'll see anybody else coming from the north tonight."

James and Luke trotted down the lane until they came to the first trees, where they took cover and waited. In another minute, Cummings and another man approached on the lane. James waited until they were almost on top of them, then stepped out.

"State your business here," he barked.

"Now hold on there, Woodman, we just rode out here to discuss a business deal is all," Cummings said with a sneer. "Heard some shootin' over there just now. You boys out hunting at night now?"

Again, James just stared at the man who started to fidget. "Aren't you going to ask me what business it is that I want to discuss?"

"I already had that discussion with four of your friends a minute ago. I told them no thank you."

"Now you just hold on a damn minute here..." Cummings started to say. A shot rang out and a ball smashed into the tree just above James' head. It was answered by another shot from the yard somewhere.

James stepped back into cover and looked over at Luke, who was holding up two fingers. Jonathan had reported four riders and only two were in the lane. A man suddenly appeared on foot from behind a tree well off the lane with a clear shot at James.

"James. Down," Luke cried out and fired. The other man fell where he was. Cummings and the other rider were suddenly nowhere to be seen.

"Let's fall back," James said quietly. They began to move slowly out of cover and back down the lane to the yard. Two riders suddenly appeared and charged towards them as they approached the yard. James had his pistol out and used it to bring one down. Luke raised his rifle, but it misfired. The other rider was bearing down on him with a blood curdling yell, brandishing a cavalry saber.

Luke stepped back, but the man was on him. Another shot rang out from the hayloft and knocked him off his horse, then they made a run for the yard.

"Any one hurt? Jonathan, Francis?"

"No sir, Poppa," they both replied. Francis stayed in the hayloft and Jonathan came to join them. "I heard someone moving over there," he said, indicating the right side of the lane towards the back of the barn.

"Luke, go around that other corner and get ready. Jonathan get into hiding and cover him. I'm going out to the left, so be sure who you're shooting at. Go on now."

A torch came flying out of the gathering dark and landed on the roof of the barn. Jonathan dropped the man who threw it. Another stepped out and fired at Jonathan, hitting him in the upper arm and spinning him around before Luke drove him off.

Suddenly, four or five shots rang out almost as one and

shattered the top fence rail James was covering behind. It would take time for them to reload, so he ran into the trees and made his way to the left. He moved quickly and silently away from the houses before starting to circle back, hoping to approach the raiders from behind.

Almost immediately, he came up behind a man crouching behind a fallen tree. James crept up behind him, readied his rifle and used the butt end on the back of his head. He moved off looking for more. He glanced back to the barn and saw the fire was taking hold on the roof.

In a few more yards, he could hear voices but could not quite make out what was being said exactly. He looked out from behind a tree, and against the glow of the fire he could see Cummings, giving orders and indicating different attack lines.

James raised his rifle to fire but heard a sound behind him. "Give it up, Woodman," someone said.

He did not hesitate. He dropped to a knee as he turned and fired. The man had a look of astonishment on his face, then fell forward. Cummings and the others started to run over, crying out.

There was nothing for it now but to retreat to the houses. James faded back and started making his way there as fast as he could. He heard two more shots from somewhere behind the barn and kept moving. One more shot hit the fence beside his head as he gained the yard, and he turned with his pistol out but there were no targets.

He dared not call out to the others, so he was glad to see Francis give a quick wave from the loft and duck back in. He went to the near corner of the barn as Luke and Jonathan came back around to the front.

"Anyone hurt?" James asked, then noticed Jonathan's bloody arm. "How bad is it, son?"

"It's not bad, Poppa. I can still fight."

"Good boy. Now get over there on the corner of Luke's house and watch the fence there. I heard a few of them over that way. Luke, get over by the water trough so you can cover him. They may try to work around behind the barn."

"Where you going, Poppa?"

"I'll be around. I'm going to find Cummings and end this now. Go on, you two."

As they ran to their new positions, James went to his porch, picked up his father's Brown Bess and disappeared into the night. Jonathan watched his father go and issued a silent prayer.

The respite was short lived. Three men rushed the fence at once. Jonathan dropped one but the other two gained cover and took aim at him, balls hitting the house near his head. He could hear Constance crying inside and he became enraged. The fire was casting a dancing light on the yard, making shadows everywhere. The two behind the fence fired again with no result, and he stepped out and shot one through the head then stepped back. That left only one on the front.

He looked over at Luke just as he aimed and fired at someone coming around the barn. The scream that followed attested to his accuracy. He laid his rifle down and drew his pistol firing again, then ran towards Jonathan. The last man behind the fence stood to fire at him, but Francis was first and forced him back into cover.

Luke slid in beside Jonathan. "How many you figure are out there?"

"Too damn many," Luke said. "Too damn many."

Luke was getting nervous about their situation, Jonathan could see that. Luke was looking over the yard, trying to see it through James' soldier eyes but could not. Just then, there was a tremendous blast from the tree line behind the barn, then quiet. The only sound was the barn fire burning.

A voice called out of the darkness. "Madison, Matthews, all you men. Let's go. Let's get out of here. They got Cummings. Ain't nothin' here for us anymore. Let's go."

Fearing a trick, no one moved out of cover. Even Francis was bravely hanging on in the burning barn, which was very much ablaze now and throwing out an even fiercer light.

They heard Francis call out from the loft. "Look. Look you guys! It's Poppa comin' up the lane."

Sure enough, they looked around the corner and James was just coming into the yard. He looked up and saw Francis waving down at him from the loft. "Don't you think you should come down from there, son? Must be getting hot up there."

The others all rushed out into the yard now, running to James who was bleeding from his scalp and stopped short.

"Is it over, James?" Luke asked.

"Well, it is for now. I think we better get the animals out of the barn before they hurt themselves, don't you?" The could hear the horses kicking their stalls in panic now.

They got the horses and Francis from the barn, but there was not much else they could do after everything was out. The wagon and most of the tools were saved, along with the big trunk of his father's things when James said, "That's all we can do. Everybody out now."

They retreated to the houses and watched their big, beautiful barn burn down to the ground. There wasn't enough water in the trough to make any difference, but it did help to keep burning embers from setting the houses alight.

In the dancing light and shadows Jonathan turned to his father. "What happened out there, Poppa? Did you find Cummings?"

James did not take his eyes off the fire. "My daddy was right," James said. "That old Brown Bess really will cut a man in half."

They were out working in the yard the next afternoon just after lunch time when the sheriff rode up along with a younger man. He stopped at the gate and surveyed the scene of destruction. One or two hot spots from the barn were still sending up smoke, and the smell of gunpowder and ashes hung in the still, humid air.

James was expecting his arrival sometime, so he was not at all surprised to see him. "Good afternoon, sheriff. Who's your young friend riding with you today?"

The sheriff glanced at the other rider then back at the yard.

"Good afternoon, James. This here is my new deputy, Frank Sanger. I told 'em I was getting to be too old for this job, so they gave me a deputy. Frank, say hello to Mister Woodman."

After the pleasantries were exchanged, the sheriff went on. "A rider came by my house very late last night. Didn't catch his name, but he was not from around here with that accent. Anyway, he said that he had heard a bunch of shooting and commotion out here, so I figured I'd ride out and see for myself." He shifted in his saddle and seemed to be waiting for something.

James glanced around at the others who were watching from the front porch. "Well, that must have been a hot and dusty ride out here on a day like this. Would you care to come inside to talk, maybe have a little lunch?"

"Why, thank you very kindly, James. It was indeed a hot and dusty ride as you say. Climb down, Frank, you are in for a treat. Miss Anna there is the best cook in the county, hands down."

Anna brought a large jug of fresh lemonade to the table as the men settled in. The sheriff got right to the point. "Passed a few bodies riding in, James, and I couldn't help but notice your barn seems to have burned down. What went on out here last night?"

"Well, Mister Cummings said he came out to talk business with me, but he seemed very unhappy with my answer."

"And, uh, how many business partners came along for the discussion?"

"Not really sure to tell the truth, sheriff. Seemed like quite a few at the time. Anyway, there are three in the north field behind the house and probably five or six more along the lane there. You'll find Cummings out behind the barn with a couple more of his associates."

The sheriff leaned back in his chair, nodding his head in thought. "Miss Anna, this is the best stew I've ever had in my long life. Didn't I tell you she was something, Frank?"

"That's very kind of you to say, sheriff. Would you like some more?" Anna said standing near the woodstove. She seemed to be very tense, her motions jerky.

The sheriff looked around the room. The children, normally very engaging, were in a corner and would not meet his eyes. Jonathan had a bandage on his arm and his hand shook sitting at the table. Luke was outside, watching.

"That is a very tempting offer, Miss Anna, but I think I'll have to pass. James, why don't we go talk out on the porch." He did not want to add any more anxiety to an already obviously traumatized family.

"All right, James, tell me what happened as best you can," he said when they settled in the porch chairs.

James and Jonathan went over the previous evening's action, filling in gaps in each other's knowledge. Luke came over and joined them. The sheriff listened closely, nodding and asking very few questions.

When they finished, he leaned back in his chair and nodded one last time. "I see. Yes, I can see that there was one hell of a scrap. You hurt bad there, Jonathan?"

"No sir, not too bad. Smarts some now, though."

"I imagine so, son, I imagine so. Well, James, let's you and me go see who these fine examples of businessmen were."

The three by the fence were unknown to them. They moved the bodies together to be in a better position when a wagon came for them. There was another by the tree that Luke had dropped, but he was not known to them either.

"There may be one over there behind that fallen tree. I used the rifle butt on him. Don't know if he was finished or not. He may have got up and left."

They found him where James had left him, the back of his head a bloody mess. James took the toe of his boot and turned the body over. "Damn," he muttered.

"You know this one?"

"Yes sir. His name's Taylor. He said he was from Virginia. He was one of the three that tried to break up our meeting a while back."

"Cummings told me about that. Wanted me to ride out here

and arrest you the next day for kidnapping or some such. You said there were three that day. You figure the others are here as well?"

James was still staring down at the dead man. "Damn," he said again. "How could I have been so wrong about him? He gave me his word he'd leave the valley after the incident at the mill."

The sheriff was surprised by James' reaction. "Isn't like you to take the word of slavers, James. I wouldn't feel too badly about it if I was you. You say Cummings is behind the barn there? Any chance he may have survived?"

"I shouldn't think so, no sir. You see, I had my father's old Brown Bess with me."

The sheriff grimaced at the thought of it. "Well, then, I expect he's still there. Let's go finish the roll call."

There were three others with Cummings. James was saddened again when he turned Johnson's body over. They looked down at Cummings who was nearly unrecognizable from the fatal injury. Sanger turned away and vomited in the brush.

They started to walk back to the house, but the sheriff put a hand on James' shoulder. "You know how strong the anti-abolition folks are getting around here, James. I do not need to tell you of all people, Lord knows. When word gets out about this, I'm afraid there's going to be hell to pay and the word is already spreading I expect."

James sighed and nodded. "I suspect you're right about that. Believe me, it has been on my mind since I woke this morning. What do you suggest I do?"

"I think it might be a good idea if you left the area for a while, until this thing settles down a bit. There are already some who want to string you up just for the meetings and all. This will incite them all the more, I'm afraid."

"Can't you do something, sheriff?" Jonathan asked, his voice rising. "It was us who were attacked. We were just finishing our supper. We had to defend ourselves."

"I know that, and you know that, son, but I am only one man here. Scuse me, Frank. We are only two men here against Lord knows how many. You already know they have no respect for the law. No, there's no other way that I can see I'm afraid."

"It's not right, damn it," Jonathan said. "My father didn't do anything wrong."

James was taken aback. He had never heard either of his boys use strong language before. "He's right, son. This is not about the right and wrong of the thing. It's just the reality of it. Nothing more to say, I guess."

As they walked slowly back to the house, the sheriff asked James, "Where will you go?"

"I really don't know. Haven't had any time to give it much thought. I only know this farm and Washington, and I don't think going back there would be a very good idea."

"No, I suppose not. Not from the reports I get from there, anyway." He stopped and faced James directly with a knowing look. "You know, my friend, if I had the acquaintance of someone, anyone, who worked on the Underground Railroad I think I would let them know I needed passage. Yes sir, that's most likely what I think I would do. That is, if I did just happen to know someone engaged in that enterprise."

James turned it over in his mind for the next few days after the sheriff's visit. The man had looked right through him when he mentioned The Road the way he did. He had been the sheriff for a good bit of the time since James had moved back to the farm, and he trusted and liked him.

Luke and Francis had ridden in to town with the wagon to pick up some supplies, and when they returned they reported a definite change in the atmosphere of their little town. Very few people had spoken to them, and some treated them like they had small pox. No matter which side of the slavery question you stood on, no one it seemed wanted this kind of attention brought to their valley.

His two boys argued against him leaving, and Abigail sank into depression, crying almost constantly. She said she would feel like an orphan if he left and would not talk about it.

After another visit from the sheriff, it became clear that staying was just not an option anymore. The mood in town was such that he was concerned the farm was not safe for any of them at this point, although he reckoned it would die down if James left for a while and the other's kept to themselves as much as possible. The station that was the farm on The Road would have to shut down for now.

After a very somber supper soon after, James announced he had decided. "I just don't see any way around it anymore. I am open to suggestions if anyone has one."

"You should stay and fight, damn it," Jonathan said, again surprising James with his intensity. "There's enough of us here to protect you. They won't come for you out here again."

James was nodding as his oldest son spoke, but when he was finished said, "They came once, they will come again. And again and again." He looked around the table into the sad eyes of the people he loved most on this earth. "You all know how I feel about our home here. I don't need to say it. If it's going to continue to be our home, then we all have to do what we can to keep it and make it a safe refuge, not only for all of us here now but those that come after. Even if it means that I have to leave you for a while."

A few nights later, James, Jonathan and Francis gathered up rifles and provisions and prepared to set out across the north field to the church in Yellow Hill. James had sent word through McAllister that he would be seeking passage to Canada, that he also was now in danger of losing his freedom.

James had wanted to say his good-byes at the house, to all of them at once, but his sons had prevailed. They insisted on walking with him at least on the first stretch of his journey as a passenger on The Road.

He had spent most of the day talking with Abigail. He was deeply concerned about the effect his leaving would have on his youngest child, and he made her promise that she would be brave, that she would continue to be a good big sister to little Constance and a help to her brothers and Luke in running the farm.

He also promised them all that he would write often and regularly, and insisted they promise him the same as soon as he had an address. He had decided his target would be to reach Fort Malden in Amherstburg, Ontario, just across Lake Ontario from the northern United States border, so that he could continue his work helping escapees fleeing from slavery.

After another long and painful farewell to Luke, Anna and Abigail he set off across the fields of his own property to escape what slavers would call justice. He was very proud of his daughter for having such a brave face for their last embrace.

"I'll think about you every day, Poppa, every day until you are safely returned to us. Don't be worried about us here. We will stay strong and await your return to our home again," she had said with great conviction. "We'll be right here, waiting for you," she said again.

Her words echoed in his mind as they cleared the last hill on the property, and James turned for one last look homeward. There was a fire in the yard, and he could see them all out there, just watching.

He took one last deep breath, then blew it out. He wanted to remember the feel and the taste of the air on his land. He turned to the north, checked the position of the Drinking Gourd, and started. "Let's go boys," he said quietly to his sons. "It's time."

Made in the USA
Columbia, SC
17 May 2021